Gate in the Fence of Time

A Journey to the Birth of America

David Robert Berry

David Robert Berry

Gate in the Fence of Time
A Journey to the Birth of America

BISAC Historical Fiction, Time Travel, American Revolution

© 2016 Fairhaven Lantern Media, (@ Registration TX 8-25-729)

info@fairhavenlantern.com

Order Gate in the Fence of Time at your favorite bookstore using ISBN 978-0-9858680-2-4

or online at: https://www.createspace.com/4027994

Acknowledgments

Thank you to the many friends who made useful comments and edits:

Trudy Gold,	Sharon Franquemont,	Bill Sanda,
Linda Winrow,	Lama Sonam Gyatso,	Betsy Stang,
Connie Neil,	Alice Olsen Williams,	Don Stauffer,
Murray Liebman,	Myra Jackson,	Mariama Thera,
Elizabeth Berry,	Pamela Jayson,	Sandy Wiggins,
Sarah Berry,	Mary LaBarbera,	Anna Woods,
Jeremy Berman,	Cheryl Little,	Matt Wright.
Tracy Bowen,	Lark Lovering,	Peter Boag,
Sue Conklin,	Michael Mitchell,	Rev. Drew Christiansen S.J.,
Perri K. McCary	Marion Neiman,	Elissa Courtney Bellassai Strati
Rosalie Fedoruk,	Rabiah al Nur,	

Thank you to the Colonial Williamsburg Foundation for making journeys to the birth of America possible for millions of travelers and for confirming that this book does not infringe upon the Foundation's intellectual property.

Photo Credits

Declaration of Independence on Cover from National Archives
http//www.archives.gov/exhibits/charters/

All other photos: David Robert Berry

Contents

Day 1-1:   On the Road to Williamsburg

To the people of the Virginia Colony in 1775, the forests and fields flanking Interstate 95 might look familiar. The smooth highway from the Potomac to the Tidewater would seem a marvel. The cars hurtling through a misting rain early this Friday morning in May would be beyond their wildest imagining.

Peter Sinclair, a sandy-haired college senior, steered the Ford through a curve on the only interstate connecting all of what were once the thirteen original colonies.

In the back seat, his eighteen year-old sister Megan fussed with her curly hair. "Isn't there an outlet mall down there? Let's hit that."

"If we hit a store at this speed, we'd crash right through it—definitely no time for shopping," Peter teased.

"No morbid thoughts! Peter, slow down." Susan Sinclair sat next to her daughter, biting her lower lip. She brushed long auburn hair away from her face and focused her blue eyes at the road ahead.

Megan rolled her eyes and sighed. "Why did we leave so early?"

Her mother replied, "Once again, Megan, we want a full day in Williamsburg. Peter is home on a break and we're doing this together before you leave for college next year. You can do your own exploring."

John, reclined in the passenger seat, muscular arms folded on his chest. His jaw tightened under short dark hair flecked with gray. "Slow down, Peter. Megan, quit griping. You have a paper to write—you'll get ideas in Williamsburg." He did not open his eyes but Peter and Megan were immediately quiet.

1

Along the median, a double row of blossoming trees flashed past as the car sped by. Peter moved left behind a white van passing an eighteen-wheeler to the right.

Up ahead, the driver of a red Hyundai had overshot his exit and used the service drive "for authorized vehicles only" to make a U-turn. His vision blocked by the treed median, he pulled out in front of the white van, which at sixty miles per hour was seconds away.

Suddenly, brake lights lit ahead and the van left black skid marks then hit a wet patch. Peter jammed the brake pedal; his tires skidded over the wet stretch of pavement, the Ford gaining on the van. The big truck on the right seemed to leap ahead and Peter swerved into the opening. The left front of the Sinclairs' Ford narrowly missed the van's tail light as the car went into a slow rotation on the wet road. Peter struggled to steer out of the skid without success.

Within the slowly spinning car, John entered the space of a timeless moment for the first time since his days in combat. Back then, senses alert, he scanned for the tip of a weapon protruding from behind a rock or a place to dive behind a natural shelter. Back then, as shots were fired from a hidden location, the interval between heartbeats seemed an eternity. Now, without hesitation, he called out in a commanding voice, "Hold on!" as his right hand braced against the dashboard and his left shielded his face in case of flying glass.

The sense of time decelerated. Each second seemed a long time... sliding at forty, thirty, twenty miles per hour, the occupants waited... let go...

As the van bore down on him, the driver of the Hyundai swerved into the lane where the truck had been and went into a spin—right in the path of the Sinclairs. The Hyundai spiraled at twenty, ten, five miles per hour as the Ford slid closer…

Peter stared through the windshield. The landscape became streaks of color blending into each other as in the forgotten experience of newborn babies before they begin to distinguish among objects.

Susan experienced a faint luminescence and a familiar sense of a long-ago loss. "Lord, help my family," were the only words arising from the silence within her as her arm went out to protect her daughter.

Megan watched the kaleidoscopic patterns of branches streaming past the window. As the car slowed, she exhaled. For once she was speechless, her irritation dispersed, leaving stillness.

The cars came to rest on the asphalt shoulder facing in opposite directions—seven inches apart—no room to open doors on the passenger side of either car. In both vehicles the people breathed deeply, adrenaline subsiding.

Peter stared at the blossoming tress on the median. The colors seemed more vivid. John looked into the wide-open eyes of two Asian-American children in the back seat of the Hyundai. Susan felt a wave of gratitude that her family was unhurt. No one moved.

The white van was pulled over on the shoulder ahead. A man in painters' coveralls walked back to the two cars. "Are you OK?" The sound of his voice broke the trance-like silence.

"Yes. I think so, thank God." Susan relaxed her grip on the armrest.

Megan watched a dragonfly glide past the trees.

"That was close!" The van driver shook his head. "You folks wait 'til the next cars go by and then straighten out. I'll wave you out when the way is clear."

Once the cars were safely onto the gravel, the Sinclairs and the Asian family in the Hyundai got out. The air held the scent of grass and blossoms.

The driver of the red Hyundai apologized.

"No harm done," offered Peter. "I'm sorry I was too close to the van for a wet road. We're all lucky to be alive."

"We're always lucky to be alive." John exhaled slowly.

"I was afraid we were crashing. It feels like we shared a miracle," whispered Susan, touching her husband's tanned arm, wishing he would pat her hand.

The contractor scratched his chin. "There's no damage and no one is hurt, so this wasn't an accident. We can go on our way." Wishing each other well, everyone got back into their vehicles and, being very sure the road was clear, pulled back onto the highway.

Peter drove just below the speed limit. "You could have left more room between you and the van..." his father told him. Peter drew a breath. "...but you showed good reflexes and instincts." Peter relaxed and turned the radio to classical music for the first time anyone could remember. After an hour without speaking, he asked, "Where do we go from here?"

Susan looked at her phone. "Exit 238 won't be long now. Follow the signs to the Colonial Williamsburg Visitor Center."

Day 1-2:   Peter Sees a Woman in the Garden

Outside the Visitor Center, Susan stopped by a bronze model of Williamsburg. "I feel strange, as if I'm in an altered state looking down on the town from somewhere else."

"What do you know about altered states, Mom?"

Susan ignored Megan's question and they entered the Visitor Center where beams of light streamed from windows high above as they walked past shops, flags, and historical images to the ticket counters. John picked up passes and keys to their colonial-era quarters. In the bookstore, Susan bought a guidebook and John got colonial currency.

The Sinclairs climbed into a shuttle to the Historic District. The bus rolled past woods and pastures enclosed by white picket, split rail, and worm fences. "Capitol Bus Stop!" called out a recorded voice.

Peter took the lead as they walked with a crunch on crushed oyster shells on the way to their rooms. They stepped through the gate in a white picket fence. An iron ball hanging in the middle of a chain pulled the gate closed behind them. Inside, the rooms were quaint and comfortable with eighteenth century décor.

Megan shrieked, "Eeew! There's a wasp on the window!"

"Calm down!" Peter grabbed a towel from the bathroom and seized the wasp in it. He opened the door and with a flick of the towel, the wasp flew away. Peter was impatient. "Let's go."

"Do we have to stay together? I want to look around by myself."

"Is being with your parents so embarrassing, Megan?" Susan asked. "We'll start together then you can go off to find something to write."

They walked down the street to benches shaded by a tree. Susan opened a map. "OK, that brick building is the Capitol. Where do we begin?"

"We began on the bus. This sure has been fun so far."

"Peter!" exclaimed Megan, nudging her brother.

"Good day! Would you care to join the Powell's in the parlor to see family life in 1775?" A maid in a blue-and-white-striped cotton dress, apron, and mobcap stood on the porch of a tiny building behind them.

"No waiting in line?" asked Peter.

"No, Sir. You may join these other guests and come right in."

Peter made a sweeping bow, "After you." Passing through the building, they entered a courtyard among buildings with brick foundations and white siding.

"You entered through the office," the maid explained. "These buildings are the kitchen, laundry, smokehouse, sheds, milk house, and outdoor oven. You may look around after you join the family in the parlor."

As they climbed the steps to the porch, movement caught Peter's eye. A tall African woman gracefully crossed a garden, a basket on her arm, wearing a white bonnet and blouse that contrasted with her deep brown skin. The hem of her full print skirt floated as she glided by. Beyond a fence a pair of draft horses white as fresh laundry, grazed in a perfect postcard image. Peter was enthralled until a thought hit him. That beautiful woman is a slave! Why does she have such a peaceful look? I would be furious. I wouldn't stand for…

"Please join us in the parlor for children's games in 1775." The maid pointed to a door.

"Oh, excuse me; I was looking at the garden."

Peter followed his family into the centuries-old house over a plank floor buffed by millions of visitors' footsteps and the feet of inhabitants long ago. A prim reenactor in the role of Annabel Powell wore a long blue linen dress and rocked in a chair by a fireplace next to two girls sitting on the floor. The hearth was empty but for the andirons. "Welcome. Please choose a seat." Mrs. Powell gestured to a circle of chairs. Peter sat in an oak spindle-back chair next to his father. The room was sparsely decorated with prints on white walls.

"My husband undertakes construction projects and employs men in the trades." To her guests Mrs. Powell looked dressed for a formal occasion yet for a middle-sorts woman in the Virginia Colony, this was everyday attire. She chatted and embroidered a fine-chain floral border for curtains.

"Mister Powell erected the steeple of Bruton Parish Church. Have you seen it?" A few visitors indicated they had. "His largest undertaking was the first Public Hospital in all the colonies for poor souls so troubled of mind that their families cannot care for them. We started our life humbly but through his work, Benjamin has provided well for us and improved the prospects for our daughters to marry into better-sorts families."

Yeah, thought Peter, bitterly, prosperity built on the labor of slaves!

The Powell children played a game of Bilbo Catcher—a wooden ball attached by a string to a wooden peg with a shallow cup at one end. The children held the peg and tossed the ball to land in the cup. The guests discovered how tricky it was when young Hannah Powell coaxed them to try and the ball missed or bounced out every time.

Peter fumed. Don't the people of this house see how beautiful that woman is? This family has a slave in the backyard, people! They play happily in the living room as if slavery is normal! What a graceful walk. What a perfect face. She must descend from African royalty…

Peter's thoughts were interrupted. "Would you like to try, Sir?"

"Huh?" Peter's mind replayed the question he missed. "Oh, OK." He took the peg Hannah offered and tossed the ball. It made a circle the length of the string, orbiting the peg. "Hold on. Let me try again." A challenge, particularly in front of an audience, usually got his attention.

"Toss it straight up and catch it as it falls," Hannah encouraged. Peter waved the peg and the ball flew up and jerked back from the end of the string. Peter had the cup under the ball but it bounced off as far as the string allowed, causing Susan to duck and Peter to blush.

"Good reflexes," Missus Powell complimented Peter. "With practice you shall have it. These games teach children to be quick of eye and hand to prepare them for their work as adults in a craft or running a home."

"Is there talk of war around here these days?" John asked.

"More than talk I'm afraid," she replied. British troops occupy Boston. Colonies have committees of correspondence to work in concert."

"Are any people here still loyal to the King?" asked Susan.

"Heavens, yes! Our Burgesses resist acts by Parliament that violate our rights as Englishmen; but we are loyal to our Mother Country and King."

I want to slip out to the garden, Peter thought. Why did I sit far from the door?

"The servants are preparing dinner in the kitchen out back. Have a look around our home and then you can go to the kitchen to see how the cooking is done." It was a cue that this was the end of the visit.

The visitors crossed the hall to a bedroom. To dally until the others left, Peter pretended to study candlesticks that had dripped wax on the mantle. Looking out the window, he was disappointed — no one was in the garden. He followed an elderly couple onto the porch. They started down the steps, and Peter suddenly found himself one pace from the slave woman. She was tying a knot in a thread. He was speechless.

The couple left and Peter found his voice. "What are you sewing?"

The woman looked up at him surprised that he was interested in what she was doing. "It be a doll for little Hannah, Sir, one of the Powell girls."

"I saw Hannah inside. Do you have children?"

"Yes, I got two boys. The older one is helping in the kitchen."

Peter hesitated then spontaneously decided to get into character as the reenactors did. "I live north of here. I'm on my way home from buying uh, rum in the West Indies. I came to Williamsburg … to add tobacco to the shipment. Where I come from," he lowered his voice, "we don't mind paying a good day's wage for a good day's work."

The woman continued sewing. A couple and their young daughter wandered onto the porch. Peter leaned his left shoulder against the wall to make room for them to pass. The little girl hurried ahead of her parents to the woman and asked, "Hello, what are you sewing?"

"Good day, Miss. I'm sewin' a rag doll for Hannah."

"Is she your little girl?"

"Hannah is one of the Powell girls. They like to play wit' dolls I make."

The mother caught up with her daughter. "OK, Honey, let's keep moving."

"Is she a slave, Mom?"

The mother looked embarrassed and turned to Peter, "I'm sorry. Jenny has a vivid imagination." They walked toward the kitchen.

Peter watched them go. "The mother acted as if you weren't even there. Are you a slave?"

"Yes, I'se one of three slaves in this house. I do laundry."

"Do you wash laundry by hand?" Peter did his best to make conversation.

"Yes. We get spots off fine cloth by rubbin' wit' bran or powdered sheep bones to absorb grease like Massa's blotter do ink. Some call it 'dry cleanin'.'"

"Where do you find powdered sheep bones?"

"We save bones after boilin' them for soup stock. We bake them and grind them wit' a mortar and pestle." The woman had a scent Peter took a moment to recognize. It was plain unperfumed soap. He had not smelled that since his great grandmother died.

When no one else was near, Peter asked the woman, "Do you know the stars called the drinking gourd or big dipper?"

"No, what do you mean, Sir?"

"There is a constellation of stars that looks like a water dipper. The two stars on the pouring side are the called the Pointer Stars. If you imagine a line from the star at the bottom to the one at the lip and follow that line out five times the depth of the dipper, you will see a bright star called Polaris or the North Star."

The woman held up the doll to examine the line of stitches.

"That bright North Star is directly north of us. If you follow it each night, you will reach the far northern colonies where slaves can be free."

She stopped sewing. "How do you know this 'bout the stars?"

"My grandfather taught me. He learned from his father. I've heard churches and good-hearted people can help along the way."

"You talkin' 'bout the Church of England where vestrymen own slaves?"

"I'm not sure if that's the only church. I don't really know."

She looked into Peter's face. "Sir, the kindness of Missus Powell might stop if she angers at me runnin'. She gave me an old white dress her girls wore to sew into shirts for my boys. I dried them in the sun so you cain't see the spots. When my boys wear those shirts to church they feel handsome and they knows I love them. How'd they feel if they saw their Mama get a whippin'? What do they do if I get sold away?" She looked furtively toward the kitchen. "I heard 'bout folks runnin'. Most was brought back and whipped or sold. Some we never hear from again and we don't know if they is alive or dead. When I was a girl, people ran to Spanish East or West Florida but some was caught in raids from the Carolinas. Now the Floridas is British so they ain't no place to run."

The woman sighed. "I heard life is a gift flowin' through us like a stream. We should help others wit' that gift. You tryin' to help but I need somethin' to run to, not just to run from."

Peter was about to ask where she heard those ideas when a woman in a long green dress walked through the gate and asked the slave, "Is lunch ready for the prisoners?"

"It should be done, Ma'am. They will have it in the kitchen." The slave woman stood to enter the house and nodded to Peter as she turned.

Peter left the porch and walked the short path to the kitchen. He squeezed into the group gathered across from the open hearth. He realized he had not even asked her name.

Day 1-3:   Bearing Arms — John Encounters the Militia

The Sinclairs walked along the oyster-shell path leading to the Capitol. Peter stopped suddenly and behind him, Megan, looking to the side, accidently stepped on his heel.

"Hey, watch where I'm going!" she taunted.

"Good move, Megan. Always alert." Peter was unprovoked.

They sat on benches along the low brick wall where people waited to enter the building. "It will be less than twenty minutes before you enter the Capitol," a man in a tricorn hat trimmed in gold braid called out.

A woman squinting in the light and pursing her thin lips walked slowly past the seated visitors, her hair tucked under the hood of a brown broadcloth cloak too heavy for the season. A white apron covered a faded gray dress. She greeted an elderly couple, "A good morrow unto thee. I confess I am fearful about the savagery up North. War cannot be the answer to the problems we face."

John's attention drifted to soldiers camped across the grounds. He had lived in tents or in the open for a year in the jungles of Nicaragua and months in the dry mountain valleys of Central Asia. War had assaulted his eyes and ears and crept into his nostrils. War had punctured and torn him and he had dealt out the same. He rarely brought these experiences to mind. He was forbidden to talk about them. Other than the First Gulf War, he fought in secret operations in which America was not officially a combatant. A thin coil of smoke wafted in a light westerly breeze. Too easy for an enemy to spot, John knew. "I'd like to visit that camp if you don't mind holding my place."

Susan was curious about the strangely familiar woman coming down the line. "You boys go ahead. Come back when we're close to getting in."

"Good. Should we make reservations for lunch?" John suggested.

"The Guide Book says Christiana Campbell's is open for dinner. Shields Tavern has lunch."

Megan saw an opportunity for liberation. "I'll go make reservations and meet you there!" She jumped up from the bench.

"Am I being abandoned completely?" Susan asked.

"Peter and I will visit the Capitol with you," John assured her. "Megan, reserve dinner at Christina Campbell's and lunch at twelve-thirty at Shields Tavern." Megan was instantly off.

John and Peter crossed to the camp. A soldier stood with one boot on a stack of firewood putting a flint into his musket as he spoke to visitors.

"How often do you have to change flints like that?" asked a boy.

9

"A flint is a piece of stone. It could take fifty rounds to wear down, but could shatter any time we pull the trigger. We need fast volleys in battle, so soldiers must change a flint fast."

"How many shots can you fire from that rifle?" Peter asked.

"This is not a rifle. It is a Brown Bess musket. It takes twenty seconds to prime, load, and fire one round. Not accurate beyond fifty yards, it misfires often. I'll show you how it works."

The militiaman took a paper powder cartridge from a leather box on his belt, and bit it in two at the mid-point where it was twisted thin like an hourglass. He poured a bit of black powder into the priming pan in the base of the barrel from the half cartridge in his hand. He poured the rest of the powder down the barrel, spat in a musket ball from the paper in his mouth, and wadded the damp paper behind it. Taking the ramrod from hoops below the barrel, he gently tamped the paper, musket ball, and powder down. "Somebody give the order to fire."

Various voices shouted, "Fire!" and he fired into a target on straw bales.

"That was a quarter-charge of powder and a papier maché ball. A musket barrel is smooth so a ball flies out with no spin. At fifty yards, I'd often miss" He picked up a flintlock. This barrel is rifled inside with spiral grooves to spin the ball for greater distance and accuracy."

The reenactor continued, "A strange vagary of war proved fortuitous for the American Colonies. A British officer named Patrick Ferguson developed a rifle that did not need a ramrod. The soldier dropped a ball into the breech and sealed powder behind it. With a cock of the hammer, it was ready. He demonstrated it in 1776, hitting a target six times a minute at 200 yards, four times the range of a musket. He then fired while walking forward, hitting the target almost every time on a rainy day, in conditions when muskets often misfire. The British ordered a hundred breech-loading rifles to test in action. They gave Ferguson command of a regiment that sailed for America in 1777."

John felt they were being watched. Past Peter to his right, a gray-bearded man in a militia uniform leaned on a post. The man nodded and John returned the nod.

The reenactor continued, "At Brandywine, Pennsylvania, Ferguson saw a colonial officer riding beyond the creek beside an officer in French uniform. He ordered riflemen to shoot them, but called them back, disgusted; he explained later, that the officers were helpless victims at that distance. Later Ferguson learned he had spared General Washington and the Marquis de Lafayette. September 11, would have been remembered for centuries as the date of an American disaster. That day, the rifles held little advantage when the British attacked within range of

Americans' muskets, fired from behind stone walls. Ferguson lost his right arm and forty of his men were killed or wounded. The rifle company was disbanded and most of the rifles were somehow lost without a trace."

"Where did those breech-loading rifles go?" John asked, "Used to their capacity, they would have been devastating. Losing Washington would have changed history!"

"Where the rifles went is a mystery. Continental forces had a difficult time as it was. The British won most major battles using muskets."

"Thanks for the demonstration." John was curious about the disappearance of the rifles but he felt drawn to talk with the militiaman leaning on the post. They sauntered over to the man whom John recognized by his insignia to be a sergeant. A rugged scar began at his cheekbone and disappeared into his trimmed gray beard. "Good day, gentlemen." His eyes were confident and flashing a glint of humor.

"Good day," John returned the greeting.

Peter asked. "Can you tell us why the British wore red uniforms that were so easy to see?"

The sergeant drew a breath before replying. "There are many myths that are not true. Redcoats need not hide. They concentrate so much firepower it doesna' matter if ye are hidden. The puff of smoke from your musket gives away your location. Lad, are ye good at arithmetic?"

Peter nodded, hoping he would get the answer in front of his father.

"With three lines of infantry firing, each line able to reload, and fire a musket three times a minute, how much time is there betwixt volleys?"

Peter was quick and hoped his father noticed. "Nine volleys a minute, so about six or seven seconds."

"Right! The ranks fire in turn: ready, present, fire! The volleys sweep the field like a scythe. Now add cannon balls that cut men in half, grape shot that can take down a whole group, and cannons firing lengths of chain that shred men and the bushes that hid them. What does that add up to?"

Peter did not respond. John saw in the sergeant's bearing that he spoke from experience. He felt, without knowing why, that the sergeant saw the same in him.

"If ye made it to British lines you'd be met by this." The sergeant fixed a bayonet to the end of his musket. Redcoats win most of their battles. A militia can make a surprise attack but they best move on before the British mount a coordinated response. Wars are not glorious, they are 'gorious' if ye get my meanin'. 'Tis chaos amidst screams of the wounded, the smell of burnt powder, and parts of your friends flying about."

John did not think about "his wars." Yet this sergeant's stories resonated so strongly with his experience that he shuddered. It was strange that no one else had joined them to listen.

"Perhaps the myth that 'tis easy to shoot Redcoats from behind trees arose from the hapless campaign of General Braddock in 1755. He marched northwest into Indian country building a road as he went. Everyone for miles knew where he was. He forded a river without meeting resistance then marched into an ambush. Troops in the rear marched into retreating troops and all discipline was lost. Braddock was killed."

"Building a road does not help a surprise attack," observed John.

The sergeant studied John. "Young George Washington was there. He wrote his mother, 'I luckily escaped without a wound though I had four bullets through my coat, and two horses shot out from beneath me.' He told his brother John he was spared 'by the all-powerful dispensations of Providence'. Those who survive a battle may assume they were protected. Those killed stop assuming altogether.

"At age twenty-two, the year before Braddock's defeat, Washington led His Majesty's Virginia Regiment to the western frontier of Pennsylvania where he met superior French forces. His men hastily built Fort Necessity where the French offered him terms of surrender. His captors treated him well in spite of his surprise attack on them weeks before, killing ten."

Peter noticed Susan talking to the woman in the hooded cape. She was close to the Capitol entrance. He nudged his father; it was time to go.

"You know a lot of history," John complemented the sergeant.

"I witnessed more than I wanted to. Ye are familiar, did we meet afore?"

"I don't think so. I haven't been to Williamsburg before."

"But an old war fighter knows another by a look in the eye. I would'na be surprised if ye had a tale to tell yourself," the sergeant ventured.

"Possibly so, but we must get back to the Capitol. Good to meet you."

As they walked back, Peter asked, "Was war like that for you, Dad?"

"I hope you never have to experience what that sergeant told you," was all John replied.

Day 1-4: Susan Hears Jane's Plea for Peace

As she watched the woman in the cloak approach along the line, Susan thought about war, too. She marched for peace before the Iraq War. Why did leaders choose to send their young people to kill and to come home wounded, traumatized, or not at all, leaving families in grief and uncertainty for the rest of their lives? She was grateful her children had not been caught up in war.

"The troubles with Britain can be settled peaceably," exhorted the woman. "Why discard abundance and safety to make war? Why send our children forth to kill other people's children? Why doth Britain send soldiers against her own people? Do our leaders pray? Their choices seemeth of neither sound mind nor spirit."

"Have you seen terrible things in war?" Susan asked the woman.

"I was born in western Pennsylvania on the frontier. The French and Indian War was a mighty struggle betwixt the English and the French. Both sides armed the Native peoples and set them against settlers of the other side." Her eyes narrowed. "That was long ago."

"I'm sorry," Susan offered. "Did you lose someone in that war?"

"My father and my brothers Nathanial and Adam were killed." She crossed her arms over her breast like a troubled child hugging itself. Susan wondered why a reenactor would be so strongly into character.

"My name is Susan Sinclair."

"I am Jane."

"Jane, I married a man who fought in wars," Susan shared. "He still does not talk about it. Were your father and brothers soldiers?"

"They were peaceful farmers, my brothers but boys. The memory pains me." She looked around nervously. "Amidst the strife men do not recall the lofty notions that sent them forth. They fear for their lives or become filled with hate against the enemy. For every man who has scars on his body, more have scars of fear, rage, or regret in their souls."

"It is hard for them to find help," Susan said quietly.

Jane flashed emotion. "They were marched off under banners to the sound of drums, filled with ideas about the sins of the enemy and their leaders' assurances that God was on their side. They hoped to help their nation but rare is the man who returns at peace. No community can be whole when so many fathers, husbands, and sons are wounded in their hearts. If you have a son, keep him away from hateful hostilities." The woman's suffering seemed genuine.

"I pray for peace, Jane, but I'm not optimistic."

"It looks dark I grant thee, but if our prayers and actions cannot stop the war, perchance it might end soon or both sides might take more prisoners and treat them better. If that much can happen, the victors, the defeated, and the world shall be the better for it."

"Amen," whispered Susan. As Jane left, Susan felt again the hidden sadness that war had bequeathed her, a grief she had never shared with her children, or even fully with her husband.

Day 1-5: Rousing Debate in the Capitol

By the curved brick walls of the Capitol, the man in a tricorn described the pattern as Flemish bond. Courses of headers, bricks placed edgewise, alternated with stretchers, placed lengthwise to make the wall stronger. The ends of some headers were vitreous blue from being near the fire in the kiln. The precision and grace of the Capitol implied authority.

The Sinclairs entered the high-ceilinged House of Burgesses where a brass chandelier hung low to illuminate note taking by the clerks. Light poured through round windows onto rich hardwood panels that suggested serious matters were discussed here. Susan took John's arm as he led them to a bench. A tall Burgess addressed the assembly. "Britain sends troops to quell the turbulence because Massachusetts is in revolt."

"No! A Provincial Congress is the People's right. The philosopher John Locke wrote that when there is a long train of abuses the people 'rouse themselves to secure the ends for which Government was erected.'"

"Aye, but Locke also pointed out that after past revolutions, our King and Parliament were reestablished. God gave us a King to maintain order and prosperity. We have no need to rise up to alter what is satisfactory."

"Satisfactory? Why are the Administration of Justice Act, Boston Port Bill, Quartering Act, Massachusetts Government Act, and Quebec Act called the 'Intolerable Acts'? They violate our rights as British subjects!"

A student in the gallery shouted, "No taxation without representation!"

"Young man, you are late. Have you not heard of the repeal of the burdensome Stamp Act and Townshend Duties years ago."

Bang! The gavel startled everyone. Peyton Randolph, Speaker of the House of Burgesses, imposing as the massive chair he sat in, called out, "Order, or the Sergeant at Arms will clear the gallery!" There was an immediate hush. "Leave the unjust taxes in yesteryear where they belong. Scribes busily write rumors of events that never happened to burden our grandsons in their history studies." He looked at several raised hands. "The Speaker recognizes the gentleman from Richmond."

"At the Albany Conference of 1754, Benjamin Franklin called for a federation of colonies as the Iroquois Six Nations had done. Britain has over thirty colonies in the New World, about twenty on the mainland. Mister Speaker, I suggest we form a federation to resist injustice."

A Burgess rose, recognized by a gesture of Randolph's chubby hand. "Only twelve colonies joined the First Continental Congress. The Floridas and Georgia did not. Our fellow Colonials in Nova Scotia petitioned His Majesty to avoid fighting. They get rich supplying Royal Navy ships at Halifax. Even Quebec, defeated by Redcoats a dozen years ago, declines

15

"I did not fear Indians, I worked with them. Nevertheless, I ran without knowing where to go. That added a year to my bond. I got another when I was found in a barn in the Carolinas. By then I knew which way was south. One night at gaming cocks, I made a desperate bet with my owner and lost. I may be worn out before I am free."

"You can be bought and sold like that?" Megan asked incredulously.

"Just like African people, but they are owned as property their whole lives while our bond just seems eternal. Now Simon has run. I hope he has coins. I sometimes go over in my mind how I would do it better now." He pulled on the bellows and a column of smoke puffed into the air. Mark paused to watch the draw of air pull the curved white line into the chimney. He placed the tyre on the anvil.

"It's not fair that you are not free. Do you like being a blacksmith?"

"In three years, I shall be free. That would not happen in England. This forge is the best situation I have known. I like making things and I eat every day. At home, getting food is a problem for many." Clink!

"You are like a slave and slavery is not right!"

"In Southern colonies many are in servitude. On the frontier, others struggle in bondage to clear the land. Dutch sailors brought the first Africans to Jamestown. They were indentured until they worked off the cost of their purchase. Now Africans are enslaved for life. I agree slavery is wrong. A planter should set his slaves free after their work has paid for their cost. But few people pay any mind to what is right." Clink!

Megan was stunned to realize so many were owned as property. "What will happen to Simon? Those were very bad men chasing him."

"If Pamunkey Indians find him, they will help him get to the Carolinas, maybe to the Cherokee. He may find a new life. In those hills, they do not like the rich landowners of the coast. Some escaped themselves years ago. But fighting in Boston may sweep away the life we know today." Clink!

"Mark, I'll be here for four days. May I visit you again?"

"I would enjoy that. Thank you for not giving Simon away."

Megan curtsied and stepped into the sunlight. He's cute, but uptight about something, she thought. She resolved to find out what it was.

Day 1-7:   A Colonial Lunch in Shields Tavern

Megan hurried up the steps into Shields Tavern, a white building with black shutters, and a row of gables protruding from the roof. She saw Peter and her parents being seated at a table with a hurricane lamp on it.

"You can order brunch or from our lunch menu," explained a hostess.

"Leave both menus and we'll figure it out. We're a family with a wide range of firmly held opinions… speaking of which," she waved to her approaching daughter. "Hi Megan. That's a lovely apron."

"Thanks, Mom. What did you guys see at the Capitol?"

"In a short time we learned a lot we didn't know before."

"Like if we don't order quickly I'm going to starve," Peter exclaimed.

A server stepped up. "Sorry. I didn't see you were ready to order."

"We're not. We have an impatient teenager among us."

"I'm twenty-one and look who's talking, Megan!"

"I'm not stalking!" Megan laughed.

"Kids, our waitress is busy. Let's order a Shields Sampler appetizer to share and I'll have the chicken." Susan jumped in quickly, hoping John would not lose patience with the kids. "What are the salsify and sippets?"

"Sippets are rectangles of dried bread like a cracker. Salsify is a root— whitish yellow like a parsnip. It's very good pickled."

John looked up from the menu, "I'll have cornbread-stuffed quail."

"I'll have the pecan waffle and sage sausage," decided Megan.

"If the pig were so sage, she wouldn't be sausage," Peter quipped. "I'll have the crab cake."

As the server left, Susan asked, "Are you enjoying this visit, Megan?"

"I'm learning tons of stuff. Many white people in Virginia were not free. They were indentured servants. I've decided to write my paper on that."

"We heard at the Capitol that the Revolution was maybe not for the reasons we thought. Burgesses were concerned about the Quebec Act."

John scowled, "They got it wrong. Everyone knows about 'taxation without representation.' It says that on Washington DC license plates."

"Maybe public sentiment was whipped up for a senseless war that generated profits for a few people. If people saw what motivated their leaders and what war looked like, they would not send their kids to war."

John nodded, "Always the protester, Susan."

"How come you never talk about the Army, Dad?" Megan asked.

Susan winced. John's testiness could be due to being with the soldiers.

"I went where they sent me and did what they told me to do. Peter, you heard the sergeant say it's not glorious. He was right." John was grim.

"Amen. The woman I spoke with by the Capitol was troubled by war."

"She's a reenactor, Susan. She could be upset about something or maybe she's nervous about playing her role right." John shook his head.

"I don't think so, John. Did you notice anything strange this morning? In the Capitol I smelled tobacco and candles but no one was smoking."

""Something scary happened after I left you!" Megan blurted out. "A skinny servant ran by me chased by two guys."

"They stage events like that all the time around here."

"But Dad, why would they put on a show where no one can see it? One guy pulled a knife. I got a bad feeling about him. His friend called him Dagger. They wouldn't let someone work here who didn't shower. He was scary and he stank!"

"Honey, be polite. We're in a restaurant!"

"Why were the smith and Indian relieved the servant got away, Mom?"

"What smith and Indian?"

Megan told them about the blacksmith and his servitude.

"Was he cute?" Peter teased.

"I didn't notice, and it's none of your business. Oh, another thing—in the yard behind the blacksmith shop I smelled pig manure like when we drove past those hog farms last year."

"Pig manure? Nice—what's strange about that?" John asked.

"There weren't any pigs anywhere, Dad. That's what's strange."

"Maybe the reenactors practice on that back street, Megan."

"It was real, Dad. I would have been less scared if you'd been there."

Peter thought the slave woman was not acting either but he kept silent.

"Your victuals have arrived," announced the server.

As the hungry quartet dug in, Peter asked, "At the Capitol they talked about Wilkes and the 45. Who were they, Dad?"

"I never heard of Wilkes. Let's look it up."

Day 1-8:   Peter Meets Annie by the Fence

Outside Shields Tavern, the Sinclairs agreed to meet at five. A poster invited one and all to give Peyton Randolph a sendoff to the Continental Congress in Philadelphia. "How will we find each other?" asked Susan.

"Mom, I'll say 'I'm in front of the tree' and you'll say 'I'm so pretending I'm in the past that I forgot I had a cell phone...'"

John grew irritated. "If we don't connect at five, we'll meet at six at Christiana Campbell's Tavern where Megan made reservations, OK?"

"OK, bye," Megan called out as she left on her shopping quest.

"That girl can be impatient, Susan."

"She'll grow out of it," Susan assured John. He was not often this short with the kids — something was bothering him. "Did you hear her say she'd be less scared if you had been there when the guy pulled a knife?"

John nodded. "She hasn't said anything like that to me since she was eight. I guess she was really frightened of those reenactors."

Peter followed John and Susan, glancing behind Powell House for his new acquaintance. They strolled on Nicholson Street to the gaol where they were greeted by the woman in a green dress whom Peter had seen picking up food at the Powell House. As his parents entered, Peter spoke to the woman, "I've come to turn myself in. I urged a slave to run away."

"That is a serious crime! Slaves are the gentry's most valuable possessions; more valuable than land and buildings combined. Helping a slave escape is stealing, like helping horses or silver candlesticks escape. You could hang on that gallows." Behind the jail, three stark columns were joined with beams forming a triangle at the top. The grisly form and its function unsettled Peter.

"My husband is the gaoler. A quarter of those convicted of a felony are hanged. For hideous crimes, their bodies are put in cages called gibbets hung on posts by the road into town. Buzzards and crows picking at the corpses warn others to avoid their crimes and their fate. Until dry bones remain in the gibbet, people entering Williamsburg cover their noses."

Peter asked, "How can a slave escape to freedom? Do churches help?"

"Escape to where? In 1775, slavery is legal. I know of no sanctuary since the Floridas became British in 1763. Some people help slaves improve their lives, but I never heard of churches helping slaves escape."

Peter was disheartened — there was no Underground Railroad in 1775.

The gaoler's wife continued, "A judgment by Lord Mansfield in 1772 declared slavery not within British law and slaves on British soil were freed. However, getting to England is near impossible for a slave. Some run west into the wilderness where they risk death or capture. Demand for slaves is great, and some Native tribes trade in slaves."

"But slaves are human beings! How can a slave get a better life?"

"Most people in this world are not free. In Europe, most are serfs or tenant farmers to nobles who control the lands. Many here are indentured and only one in a hundred Africans here are free. Some were rewarded with manumission because of extraordinary service to their owners or they saved money to buy freedom when their owners were desperate for money. Slave owners believe slavery is the only hope of saving themselves from ruin. There is no excuse, but it is how they see the world.

"Slaves trained in carpentry or other trades are more valuable and have better living conditions than field hands, so learning a trade helps them."

"You say 'There is no excuse.' Are you opposed to slavery?"

"You are perspicacious. My parents were servants. Pa was so worn out he could barely put food on our cracked plates. When he died, Ma did washing to get salt and meat for the soup. She taught me to pray for children in bondage, including African children. There was a school for Africans in Williamsburg, set up by the British Society for Propagation of the Gospel. After Missus Wagner, the director, died last year, it closed. Lord knows what those children shall do now.

"Don't be discouraged. There is that one chance in a hundred," suggested the gaoler's wife. "A slave with a strong desire to be free can watch for opportunities to seize the moment. He would also need God's help." They stood in silence.

"Would you like to see the cell they will lock you in if you help a slave?"

"Will they let me back out? I'm still an innocent man—so far."

"Aye, they all say they are innocent men. The gaoler will release you if you follow the law while you are in there." The woman smiled.

Peter walked up the steps into the gaoler's house. His parents stood near the hearth in the tiny front room. "They really kept mentally ill people in here?" a young visitor asked.

"Until the Public Hospital opened, insane people were locked up here if they were a risk to others. It must have been frightening for the gaoler's children to scurry past cells in the narrow hallway to their bedroom. This gaol held thieves and murderers, pirates, debtors, Loyalists, and runaway slaves. The accused could wait months for their cases to be heard."

The visitors moved out of the house into a bare yard behind high brick walls and stepped into one of four cells. It took a moment for their eyes to adjust to the shadows. Walls of hardwood planks were securely anchored by great bolts. The toilet seat was anchored by iron straps and rivets.

24

"You wouldn't want the toilet to escape," someone suggested.

"This cell must have reeked. I don't see any showers."

"The prisoners got a blanket and corn mush and occasional dried salted meat," explained the gaoler. "Prosperous families might bring a relative clothing, blankets, food, or even liquor. Most people would be unable to offer a blanket or food when they lacked these things themselves."

"Looks like the prisoners slept on the floor."

"Yes, but a cover of straw made it softer, warmer, and easier to clean. It seems rough treatment when you know this is not punishment, but just waiting for trial. Three of the four cells have no window for ventilation."

Susan pointed. "Look at those chains and leg irons!"

Peter did not notice his father shudder.

"At least there was no torture," John murmured. He rubbed his thumb, once dislocated when he was hurled into a gully by an exploding shell. He had snapped it back himself. He remembered the stab of pain, but he was ready for battle — for ten minutes until he was taken prisoner by bearded mountain herdsmen pointing rifles him. He was chained in a hut for two weeks until Special Forces parachuted out of a night sky to rescue him. He forced his focus back to the present and walked behind Susan and Peter into the sunlit yard, through a heavy door, and out to the street.

On leaving the gaol, Susan saw a woman in colonial dress approaching with a basket. She seemed distraught. "Are you all right?" Susan asked.

"Yes, praise God. The Lord has provided food to bring to my husband. He has been here two months but I pray not much longer. Forgive me Missus, but I must hurry in. It has been five days since I last found food to add to the mush and dry bread he gets here."

The woman reached the door. Susan called out, "Why is he in the gaol?"

"When called by our Lord to preach His Word, he answered the call!"

Susan found this puzzling but she caught up with her husband and son. As they strolled, she chatted but John was silent. Peter was preoccupied. If there was no Underground Railroad for years to come, was there hope?

They came to the cabinetmaker's workshop beside a gurgling stream. A young black man in a beige vest and gray knickers opened the door. John and Susan moved into a hall flanked by finely made chairs, cabinets, and a handcrafted harpsichord. Beyond was an ancient workshop where tools hung on pegs: saws, C-clamps, a large compass, and a set square. Tables were cluttered with tools and finishing rags stained many shades of brown. A bin held boards and dowels. The windows were large and the walls and ceilings painted white to reflect the light needed by the artisans.

Peter paused by the door when he noticed a black woman on the far side of a small pasture. She worked with something in her lap and a bowl in front of her. "Who is that woman sitting up there by the white fence?"

The man at the door looked surprised. "She be Annie, a free African."

"She's free?"

"Yes. A free black be rare and Annie be rarer still."

"May I talk to her?" Peter was eager but gaol and gallows came to mind.

The man hesitated. "Best to talk to her when no one around."

Puzzled, Peter approached the large woman with short-cropped curly hair. He glanced behind to be sure he was not followed. He had a feeling of stepping across a threshold. Annie diced a soft white cube into a bowl on a cloth spread with piles of wild garlic and dandelions.

"Excuse me. Are you preparing food?" A stupid question, he thought.

The woman studied his face with a kind expression. "I'm Annie."

"I'm Peter."

"Well, Mister Peter. I'se surprised you came to see me and ain't much surprises me." She gave him a long look. "I'se cuttin' pork belly for tonight. We don't always get to flavor corn mush wit' smoked salt pork."

"What's happening tonight?" Peter asked, but what he thought was, stop beating around the bush and get on to what you need to ask her.

The woman paused as if to not interrupt his thoughts. "If we speakin' out loud, nuthin happenin' tonight. Slaves ain't s'posed to gather 'cept in church. But we speakin' jus' you and me. Can you keep a secret?"

"Well, to tell you the truth, Ma'am, I just got here and I already am."

"Thank you for that. White folk don't call me Ma'am." Then she whispered, "You already am what? Keepin' secrets?"

"Yes. The man back there told me you are free. I'm curious to know how you did that."

"I was born free."

"My family is visiting the cabinet shop. Since I can keep a secret, may I help you while you tell me why you're making food?"

"You don't give up easy," Annie chuckled. "Sit by this bush so folks in the street don't see us talkin'. You can tear them leaves into pieces. I'se makin' food for a gatherin' of African folk in the woods. It called a Hush Harbor. Free blacks ain't 's'posed to help slaves come together."

"I have questions but I'm afraid to ask you."

"What you 'fraid to ax me?"

"I was talking to someone at the Powell House about running north to get free. I'm troubled to think people live with no chance of freedom. You were born free. Can you tell me of paths to freedom for slaves?"

Annie tilted her head slightly to the left and studied Peter. She smiled. You was at the Powell House? Evie is a handsome woman ain't she?"

Peter blushed. "Well, yes she is. I didn't know her name was Evie."

"You didn't know her name? Why does you want to help her get free?"

"She is there against her will. Her two sons are slaves. That's not right."

"It ain't right that's true. There be a whole lot of 'ain't right' in the world. It ain't fully against her will. If she does what she do and don't do somethin' else, there be will in that. And if she has a hint of somethin' and she don't look at it to figure it out, there be will in that."

"I don't understand."

"I gonna say it slow and you listen careful. Sometimes there be a chance for somethin' we don't see 'cause we is so sure things is the way we think they is and sure they cain't be otherwise."

"Is there a way for people to get free they are not seeing?"

"Most people don't see what is there to see. 'Most everybody who look like me is owned by somebody who look like you. Many people is sufferin'. As a girl in Africa, I was catched and brought over the sea. It was years before freedom and I found each other again." Annie sighed. "Here we sit, a white man in strange clothing, talking wit' me about helpin' a slave get free. Tell me why you interested in helping Evie."

"She could choose where to go and what to do. I have confusing feelings about her. It feels like we're family." He was startled by his own candor.

"Well that be the truth, Mister Peter. Most folk 'round here of any color ain't free. Middle-sorts planters be chained to their land and work wit' no end. Better-sorts gentry got big houses but most be hidin' a painful truth that they burdened wit' debt. Burgesses meet only a few weeks a year so they can rush home to struggle to keep they lands. They called free but they feel tied up by the strong rope of they situation just the same."

Annie sliced another cube of fat. "Living life free ain't bein' a feather floatin' in a gentle breeze. There is always somethin' each of us needs to be gettin' on about. Sometimes we choose it and sometimes it comes to us. We be free to choose what we think and what we pray for. We struggle, rejoice, and grieve as we go along."

"I think that's true—but I don't like the idea that somebody can own you and make all the choices for you. Owners can even hurt their slaves. You are free. Do you care about freedom for others?"

"Yes, I talk to folk 'round here, and a mother at the Powell House is one. If I see a way they could live a better life, I give a seed of advice. They take up the seed or not. That also be a kind of freedom. I been free for years and there is people who never once done axed me about freedom for they self.

"You ask how folk can find freedom. You could ask how to let freedom find its way into folk 'cause it always be right here. Sometimes a massa give manumission like I got, but most times the massa's children gets the slaves when he die. Sometimes slaves work all night for money at tobacco packin' time, when the massa fear bein' late would bring ruin. They work Sundays if they allowed. Once they get money, some buy and sell things to make mo' money. Some take a dangerous path and run."

Annie shook her head. "Slaves who run into the forest can die if they don't know how to get along. If a slave pay a ship captain to carry him away, the captain might sell him to a sugarcane plantation. People in the islands feel more whips and shackles than in Virginia and life is short. They ain't no ship back home to Africa and folk who jes' come over say wars and slave catchin' goin' on more than ever."

"Can you give me advice on how I could help?"

"My advice is be careful what advice you give folks. Your care for Evie be true. I see danger but my caution ain't likely to scare you off. Better not grab the first answer that comes when you ax a question. Sit patient wit' that question. Maybe ideas gonna come into you head that change the question and a deeper answer come. In time, a door may open."

"Peter!" Susan called from the porch steps. Peter was embarrassed.

"Don't be shy yo' mama be callin'. Many folk don't got a ma no mo'. Go on now. You saw me once so you bound to see me again."

Peter caught up with John and Susan. They did not ask about Annie. At the bend in the path he looked back to see that she had already gone— bowl, cloth, greens, pork belly, and all.

Day 1-9:   William the Brick Maker

As they entered the Brickyard, a tall, black man looked up. "Hello, folks. I'se happy to see you walking in here. Massa hired me out to the owner of this brickyard to do what? To make mortar and bricks that's what. I does that all day and part of the night if we is busy as we oft times am. You know why I likes mortar and bricks? Because they ain't tobacco fields in a cold rain, and they ain't a stable full of horse manure that needs cleaning out on a hot summer day, that be why. We make what this town is made of, that be mortar and bricks. You know 'burg' mean town, don't you? Williamsburg mean William's town and William's town made from William's bricks and them bricks is made here by William. That's me."

You know why they call me William? 'Cause that be my name, that's why." He grinned.

Peter wondered how a slave could enjoy himself so much. John wondered how William could keep that routine up all day.

"Let me show you how bricks and mortar is made right here. Yesterday this fire burned a pile of oyster shells taller than me. Them oyster shells was changed, which ain't no surprise. You and me would change too if we burned in a hot fire all night. Once cool, they crumble. Don't touch them 'cause what do you get when you burn shells? Quick lime, that's what Massa say to a Scottish man who was lending money. I don't know what quick lime is 'cept that's what we reduce shells to. Yes, we do."

William picked up a bucket. "We shovel burned shells into troughs and pour on water. We get what I heard is a comical reaction wit' water and shells. We push it back and forth like this to make mud and add sand and animal hair to bind it together. It becomes the mortar to lay the bricks. But you cain't be stickin' your hands into that mortar even when it cools."

"Is it an acid?" Peter asked.

"Massa told me quick lime is called basic. Maybe they call it basic 'cause basically it can burn your skin right though. Yes, it can. Besides mortar, what else do you suppose we make here in this brickyard?"

"Bricks," John called out.

"I'se happy you knows the point of a brickyard. We make bricks out of clay and you can see we been cuttin' some raw bricks just over there."

"Do you dry them in the sun?" Susan asked.

"In Spanish colonies wit' hardly no rain to soak brick walls and weaken them and no frost to crack them, people dry bricks in the sun and reinforce them wit' straw. The Spanish call sun-dried clay 'adobe.' Do you know why? 'Cause that be the name in Spanish."

John laughed, surprising Peter. He did not hear his father laugh often.

"Sun-dried bricks ain't good where winters are cold enough to freeze water in a crack and break 'em. Here we fire bricks to make them hard enough for all kinds of weather. I heard that over in Europe, there are brick buildings standing after a thousand years."

"We stack bricks in that kiln and fire it up day and night for a week. That ain't half-baked is it? We make the bricks to build Williamsburg. Did you see any bricks that look shiny blue on the end? Why might that be?"

"The ends of bricks used as blue headers were next to the fire in the kiln. The heat gave them a glaze-like finish" John had paid attention on the tour of the Capitol. "Why don't you stack some bricks sideways toward the fire so you get blue stretchers as well?"

"That's exactly right, Mister... who?"

"John."

"Mister John, you know a header from a stretcher. Stack 'em sideways to get blue stretchers? We don't because... Huh, we may have to try that someday. Thank you for comin' by the brickyard. If you want bricks, I can load up your wagon for you."

Susan asked John and Peter, "Would you guys like to look in some shops? I need a hat now that the sun is out." She hoped to talk again with the woman she met at the Capitol and felt an urge to move on.

"I think we'll visit another tradesman," John decided, to Peter's relief.

Day 1-10:   Susan Chances Upon a Tailor

Susan felt restless as she left the brickyard. In the window of the Margaret Hunter Milliner Shop, she saw a man with spectacles and bushy eyebrows, sitting cross-legged on a platform, hand sewing a hem on a bolt of brocade. His breeches were the color of pekoe tea with milk, buttoned tight below the knees. Susan nodded to him and he nodded back.

As Susan entered, the tailor looked up. "Good day, Madam."

Susan noted the fine stitching of his waistcoat and the lace edges of the loosely tied white cravat. His long hair was tied at the nape of his neck. "You are sitting in what my grandmother called the tailor position. Do tailors really sit that way?"

"I sit next to the window to get light for sewing. I spread the cloth around me on the tailor's board to keep it off the floor where it might be soiled. Customers such as I hope you might be, see me in the window and may give us their custom when they note the quality of our materials and our work. This manner of working is typical of a colonial era tailor."

"What is that beautiful fabric you're working on?"

"This fine brocade was imported from Belgium. I will make a formal gown to be worn to a ball at the Governor's Palace. Please have a look at the garments we fashion here for better-sorts people."

"Were richer people actually considered better?"

"The names better-sorts, middle-sorts, and lesser-sorts do suggest that. I have great expectations of having my own shop one day to finally attain the middle." He smiled. "I was a foundling, abandoned in a basket one winter morning in a pew at Coventry Cathedral and raised in a church school where orphans were fortunate to learn a trade. I learned tailoring and by sailing to Virginia, trebled my earnings. I wager the poor woman who left me under a blanket did not have the opportunities life gave me. I am grateful for what I have and don't complain about what I don't have."

"That's a great attitude. Tell me about that navy blue cape with the exquisite gold embroidery along the hem."

"I fashioned that mantua after a French design. It sells for eight hundred dollars. In 1775 you could have purchased one for a few pounds."

"It's tragic I'm so late. You called it a mantua?"

"Yes, it is common in fashion to use French and Italian words. The word millinery comes from the textile city Milano. Mantua is from the town in Italy by that name."

"What about those hats?"

"The brimmed straw hats with ribbons are for fashionable attire, and the mobcaps are undress caps for ordinary wear at home."

"I'd like a dressy hat." Susan tried on several hats in front of what the tailor called the looking glass and chose one trimmed with a wide blue satin ribbon. She paid the tailor in colonial currency. As he thanked her, his eyes twinkled.

Outside the store, she paused in front of the Golden Ball jewelry store. Hmmm, that was a strange urge, wasn't it, to buy a new hat? I'll resist the temptation to buy jewelry, she thought.

At the end of the street, she walked to the Secretary's Office behind the Capitol. With stone floors and brick walls, it was designed to protect public records from fire. She stepped into a bookstore. Next to books on religion, she brushed against the only other customer who asked, "Are you interested in religion in the colonial period? I am giving a sermon on that subject tonight at the Bruton Parish Church."

"Are you an interpreter?" Susan asked.

"We're all interpreters of something aren't we? I am James Walker, an Episcopal priest. Tonight I'll talk on the faiths of our forebears."

"Nice to meet you Reverend Walker, I'm Susan Sinclair. I will get tickets for my husband and me. You are an Episcopal priest? I thought only Catholics had priests."

"The Church of England kept the term priests when we broke with Rome. After the American Revolution, our clergy were called ministers in the U.S., but we are now priests again."

"See how little I know? I look forward to your talk." After the priest left, Susan got tickets for the sermon. As she put them into her bag, her restlessness subsided. She felt impelled to follow an invisible trail. A trail toward what she was not sure.

Day 1-11:   Megan Learns of Indentured Servitude

After leaving Shields Tavern, Megan walked west to the Mary Dickenson Store. She went straight to the array of colonial costumes—stacks of straw hats with colorful ribbons, aprons and pretty dresses on a rack, and hooded capes hung on pegs. She tried on a blue print dress with tiny yellow and white daisies and did not take it off. She crammed her jeans into her daypack, paid for the dress, and stepped outside.

She marched straight to the blacksmith shop. As she entered, she saw the Indian again speaking with Mark. "Am I interrupting?"

"You are welcome here."

"May I ask about indentured servants for a history paper?"

Mark frowned. "Nothing I do is worthy of being called history."

"First, I'll introduce myself to your friend. I'm Megan Sinclair." She reached out her hand.

"Megan Sinclair. I am Standing Elk. In the iron foundry, they could not pronounce my name in my language. What does Megan mean?"

"It was my great grandmother's name. I don't know what it means. You worked at an iron foundry? Do Indians do that?"

"Some have. That is where Mark and I became friends. Long ago, my ancestors attacked foundries because whole forests were cut and burned to make iron. I worked at a foundry to buy back land for my people."

"Do Indians still live around here?"

"Yes, I am a chief. My people are part of the Algonquin group, which we call the Anishinaabe. We are related to many tribes from the Micmac in the Northeast, to the Ojibwa in the upper Mississippi. Near here are the Pamunkey, the tribe of my mother and the Mattaponi, the tribe of my father. Time has passed since elk were here, but this Elk is still standing."

"I had no idea elk once lived in Virginia. Where did they go?"

"For countless generations we hunted elk and wood bison in the eastern forests as did the wolves and cougars. We were all in balance."

"There were bison here too?"

"I saw them graze west of here when I was young. Settlers cleared the forest home of the animals. They got harder to find in a hunt then they were gone. Life is out of balance." Standing Elk looked out the open door. "I remember crystal winter nights listening to wolves calling to the moon over the lake. My son and daughter have heard them only on a long hunting trip west of the hills. Their children may never hear them."

Megan responded, "We cut all the trees, eat all the fish, burn all the oil, use up soil and water, and poison everything. If we keep it up there'll be no forests or fish anywhere, like there are no more elk in Virginia."

"My father named me Standing Elk to remind me of that danger so I would live in balance. He was a medicine man who joked that the white man calls it 'history' because it is *his* story. You want to talk about indentured servitude. That is *his* story." He pointed to the blacksmith.

"Mark, you told me you signed a contract. How did you sign if you can't read and how did you know what you were agreeing to?"

"They handed me a quill and showed me where to put an X. I surprised them as I printed the letters M-A-R-K." He smiled enigmatically. Megan did not detect he had a secret. "They read the good parts to me. We learned the bad parts later."

Megan reread the reward notices for runaways. Most described the clothes they wore. Standing Elk spoke furtively to Mark, nodded, and left.

"He didn't say goodbye."

"He looked in my eyes and nodded. Words are not the only way to talk."

"Would it be rude to ask what you and your friend were talking about?"

Mark tightened. "It would not be rude to ask, Megan, but not safe to answer. Bonded laborers and the original peoples of this land suffer much. There is danger in making your concerns known. Sorry to be abrupt but I hope to protect people, including you." He returned to hammering then paused, "Thanks for coming to visit again."

Megan left more curious than when she arrived. She explored historic sites and when she met indentured servants, peppered them with questions: How long was their contract? Did they have plans for when they were finally free? Did they know former servants who prospered?

She discovered only one in three servants eventually succeeded by the humble standards of the day. Life was particularly harsh for unskilled laborers. They often took another term of servitude for the meager food and shelter it offered. Others got small land grants and wandered unprepared and ill equipped to the West. Many perished.

An educated man, brought from England to tutor a Burgess's children, explained that rising population and enclosure of common land into private ownership by wealthy families displaced rural people. Many among them grasped at a chance for a new life.

Megan's mind raced. So many people were stuck in poverty. Was it possible for them to improve their lives? It was time to meet her family.

Day 1-12:   President Randolph Leaves for Philadelphia

Leaving the brickyard, John and Peter strolled west to the Deane Shop. Working at a bench was the sergeant they had seen by the Capitol.

He looked up. "I knew we would meet again."

"Good to see you, Sergeant."

"Does it take patience to cut and sand wood day after day?" Peter asked.

"A day has twenty-four hours whether we hurry or not. When our hearts are in a craft, 'tis satisfying. A wheel made by these methods is sound for more years than a man has to live."

John and Peter saw work in progress on sawhorses and glue pots incrusted with layers of ancient resin. John had helped Peter on school projects using Grandpa's old tools so they recognized the wood planes, chisels, and brace-and-bit hand drill. Spiraled shavings were swept into leather pails. Each shaving showed the grain pattern of the board from which it came and exuded the wood's perfume.

John inhaled the scent. "I should work here. I love the smell of wood."

"Dad, it's almost five and we should get over to Market Square."

"Good timing." The wheelwright looked at the clock. "Today Peyton Randolph, the first President, sets out for the Second Continental Congress. Get close to his red house on Nicholson Street for a perfect vantage point."

"He was called President at the Capitol," John recalled. "Why is that?"

"We don't like titles such as 'Your Highness'. At the First Congress, they called Randolph 'President' because he presides over the meetings. Our second President, Henry Middleton, serves while Randolph is in Virginia. The Militia calls Randolph the Father of his Country."

"Does George Washington know about this?"

"He would say that himself. Washington was a colonel in the Virginia Militia. You had best be over there promptly to see the President off."

They walked to Randolph's house where a crowd gathered. A footman cleared the way for a coach-and-four pulled by a pair of white horses with magnificent manes, followed by a pair of handsome coal black horses. John spotted Susan. "Your Mom is working her way over to us. I don't see Megan yet but she can't get into much trouble in the Historic District."

Peter, already concerned about getting into trouble, did not respond.

Peyton Randolph, President of the Continental Congress, came out carefully, following two men down the steps. An extremely portly man,

35

his fine clothing trumpeted his wealth and station. He wore an expensive white human hair wig and carried a gold-trimmed tricorn hat under his arm. His royal blue coat, fashioned in London, hung regally to his knees. A cravat covered his triple chin. He stepped onto the running board of the coach with the help of an assistant. The sergeant of his security escort, needed because of the British warrant for Randolph's arrest and execution, called out, "Huzzah for the President!"

"Huzzah!" shouted the militiamen.

"Thank you for seeing me off to Philadelphia. For many days, these bones shall be shaken along the rutted way. To hasten the end of this tedious journey I must begin it, so my words will be brief. I can announce that the Congress is about to name John Hancock of Massachusetts as third President to show our support for our beleaguered brethren in Boston. If I clung to power, what would separate us from the corruption and mendacity of the Royal Ministries? Who in his right mind would not prefer to attend to his farm and family?

"Georgia is now represented in Congress. We expect all colonies from Newfoundland to the Floridas will join in time. Our descendants may speak of the 'Twenty Colonies' with reverence. I like the sound of that.

"We must avoid the tragedy of wider war. On this note, the *Gazette* berated my brother John Randolph, who is loyal to the Crown, as 'defective as a friend and insignificant as an enemy.' I suggested he ignore the insult. We call the Tories 'Tories' and they use that name themselves, but we do not benefit by insulting them. As when Governor Dunmore seized our powder, I urge moderation in speech and comportment. We were reimbursed for the powder without making widows though the threat of retaliation from Patrick Henry and Hugh Mercer, and the militias they gathered, accelerated payment. Henry, under my guidance, fired not a shot and Mercer stayed in Fredericksburg.

"To stop the spread of this malignant war we need good men with the ear of the King and his Ministers across this ocean of disagreement to build bridges to a peaceful resolution. Save your feathers for pillows and your tar to mend your roofs. Not long ago we shared the Tories' view. If we changed our minds, so might they. And now, I bid you all farewell."

People standing nearby heard Peyton Randolph wheeze as he stooped to enter the coach. Was that a groan as he sank into his seat? The coach pulled slowly away to a trio of huzzahs. No one knew as they waved goodbye that in three months Peyton Randolph would be dead of a stroke in Philadelphia and his return would be in an oversized coffin.

Day 1-13: Dinner at Christiana Campbell's Tavern

Megan heard Peyton Randolph's farewell from the back of the crowd. As her family moved across Market Square, she found her way to them. Her father was fretting. "I think the reenactors are improvising. I've never heard of many of the things they're saying."

Twice they moved to stay clear of oncoming horses as they walked past the Capitol to the broad front porch of Christiana Campbell's Tavern. They were shown through the crowded restaurant to a table by a window.

Susan opened her menu. "What a strange vacation! Much of what I thought about the founding of the United States seems to be wrong."

"I doubt it, Susan. I want to find a library. When I got home from Central America and… other places, I was shocked the press accounts were so different from what we witnessed." He refrained from talking more about his secret wars.

"Who knew Randolph was first President and 'Father of his Country'."

"I'm learning strange stuff too, Mom, and something is bothering me."

"What's wrong Pete? Got bubonic plague? I'll move to another table."

"Thanks for your support, Meg. I'm bothered that ordinary people saw slavery as normal. I think that if you are in a bad situation, you can find a way to change it, walk away, or wait it out. Imagine you were a slave in 1775. There is no Underground Railroad, no boat home, no way out for four generations until Lincoln's Emancipation Proclamation. It's hard to accept that people were trapped for their whole life."

"We still have millions trapped in poverty and a few very wealthy people who often put their own interests first." Susan was fired up. "More than one in a hundred of us are in prison, more than any other country. We are far behind many countries in how we take care of our elderly and our children. The Bible says 'Thou shalt not kill,' but we almost constantly make war, often killing innocent civilians."

John looked at his wife. "Susan, some of us think people should be taught to take care of themselves."

"Not easy if we underfund education and parents are underemployed."

"We don't hang a quarter of convicted felons or keep slaves," Peter countered.

Megan jumped in. "I talked to servants today. They worked until the cost of their passage was paid for. If they screwed up, more years were added to their bondage. Most got bad food, one set of clothes, and poor places to live. Our ancestors were probably poor here or serfs in Europe.

37

Why did nobody tell us? Were our grandparents ashamed about how uneducated their grandparents were?"

"I don't think they were ashamed," Susan suggested. "Surely our ancestors were proud of the first person in the family to read. There is no shame in that. We're all slowly learning."

Peter turned to his sister. "Meg, you say that some things here seem real. I've had that feeling. Mom and Dad, remember the woman I talked with behind the cabinet maker's shop?"

"I saw you walk down the hill but I didn't see you with anyone."

"Wow! She was hard to miss, Mom. She was quite... uh wide, an African-American in a colorful print dress, sitting by the fence."

"I guess we weren't paying attention, son."

"That's weird, Dad, because she seemed to be really in the past."

"That's what good actors do, Peter, they use their imagination to bring characters to life. I like going to a good play. On-stage, the transformation of an actor in character can be astonishing. What did you talk about?"

"It seemed real, Mom. She must be a great actor. We talked about uh... the food she was preparing and how a slave might escape."

Megan looked at her brother intently. "Did you guys have anything weird happen this afternoon?" she asked her parents.

"I had a sense something was calling me. It faded when I got tickets for a sermon at the Bruton Parish Church tonight. I didn't think you kids would want to go."

Savory food arrived in abundance. Part way through the meal Megan asked, "Mom, a guy asked me what my name means and I forgot."

"Megan was my grandma's name, honey. It means great or powerful."

"Did you hear that, Pete? Great and powerful!"

"I heard 'grate' like when someone gets on your nerves!"

When dinner was over and they were making their way to the door, Megan whispered to her brother, "Are you thinking about how you could actually help someone escape?"

Peter whispered "Yes," before he could catch himself.

"Me, too."

Day 1-14:   Peter Visits Evie's Family

The Sinclairs stepped through the door of Christiana Campbell's to the porch banister. The sky was deepening toward a more royal blue and the sun gilded the edges of billowing cumulus clouds—a radiant glory of pink, mauve, and gold. This porch, this town, and the whole Earth on which it stood was slowly turning eastward. And this place on the world would turn all the way around and return to about this angle to the sun late tomorrow. And the people would count the passing of another day.

A gentle zephyr rustled the leaves of giant hardwoods, deeply rooted for centuries between the tavern and the Capitol. Susan took John's hand. "It's a timeless evening. Those clouds have a magical quality."

"A billion prisms—we seldom pause to look," John marveled.

Megan, standing a few steps from her parents, murmured to Peter. "Mom is wondering what's going on. Dad mentions his time in the army. He never does that, so maybe something's happening with him too."

"It's confusing. Sometimes I'm right here and sometimes... there."

"Yeah, Pete. I'm talking to someone from a long time ago and snap—I'm on a trip with my family. Do you think we could get lost or stuck?"

"I don't think so. It changes without us doing anything."

"Right, it's just like that. Do you get a feeling there is something we could do here? Like help somebody for real?" Megan asked.

"Maybe—we can see where it leads." Peter turned to his parents. "I'm going for a walk to explore. I'll see you at the house."

Peter walked to Powell House and found it dark. He leaned on the fence, sorting out his experiences. He had never met anyone like Annie. It was strange neither of his parents had noticed her. He walked into the lane by the kitchen and heard a child laugh. Two African boys played in worn canvas pants too large for them, rolled up at the cuffs. They were close in age, one about eight and the other six. The younger, light-skinned one threw a stick into the air and caught it after it flipped end over end.

"Good catch, Dilli!" the older one called out.

On the next throw, Dilli threw the stick in a high curve. He ran to catch it with an irregular gait, his right foot swinging around to the side, scuffing a curve on the ground. The stick flew over the fence and Peter caught it.

"Good throw!" Peter He tossed the stick back in a slow arc toward the boy. "Here it comes!" The boy caught it in both hands.

"Thanks, Mister! Are you here to see Massa Powell?"

"I..." Peter broke off. The boy looked strangely familiar.

39

"Who you talking to, Dilli?" The voice came from around the corner.

"A nice gentleman be here at the gate, Mama."

Evie stepped from behind a wall, faced Peter a few yards away, and stopped. Peter's right hand moved involuntarily in a wave.

"Oh! Good evening, Sir."

Peter looked for words but those he found were meager. "Ma'am, I heard the children laughing. Evie, I hope I'm not disturbing you."

"The Powells went to sup wit' friends. How you know my name?"

"Today I spoke with Annie about free Africans. She called you Evie."

Evie's eyes widened. "You saw Annie today? You talked wit' her?"

"Behind the cabinetmakers' shop. She was preparing food…"

"…for a gathering," finished Evie. "She tol' you my name?"

"I'm Peter."

"'Scuse me, I got to sit. Boys, fetch us water. Mister Peter, please come through the gate lest a neighbor think you fixin' to steal something valuable." Evie sat on a bench patting her chest and taking deep breaths. Peter sat on the steps next to her.

"I apologize for just showing up like this. There is a lot going on here I don't understand." He heard a splash as the bucket hit water in the well.

"You called me ma'am in front of my boys, which they never heard a white man do, then you apologized to me, which nobody do. I never knew someone like you talked wit' Annie. I don't understand neither."

The boys each carefully carried a cup of water. The older boy gave one to his mother. Dilli presented a cup to Peter. "This is for you, Mister."

"Thank you, Dilli." Peter asked the older boy who stood barefoot holding his mother's skirt. "What's your name?" The boy looked at Evie.

"Go ahead and tell him your name, son. Do like you do after church."

"I'm James." He looked at her. She nodded approval.

"I'm pleased to meet you boys." Peter extended his hand. Dilli smiled and shook his hand but James held his mother tighter.

They sipped water as the sky gradually darkened to blue-black. As they talked, the first stars directly overhead were slowly joined by others, one by one, then by tens, then by hundreds until too numerous to count.

Peter exhaled slowly. "I was careless when I suggested you run," he began. "I see it would be hard with two little boys especially…"

"'Specially when one is lame?"

"That could make you easy to identify, but that's not what I meant. I learned that people who might help are not around here, at least not yet."

"Mister Peter, I thought a lot about your visit. Even thinkin' that runnin' wit' my boys be crazy, I felt I knowed you. You said bein' free would be better. Why should you care about us?" Her eyes searched Peter's face.

"It may seem strange, since you live in a time… I mean a town where there are slaves and it's normal, but I think slavery is wrong. All people deserve a chance to find their own way."

"That be what Annie think. Some say Annie knows our mind better than we do. When Annie say somethin', I think and pray about it. She is deep like the salty sea. You be blessed. She don't talk to just anybody."

"When I was thinking, she stopped speaking, as if waiting for me to finish. I heard she was free and I wondered how she got her freedom." He stopped. "I went to her because I wanted to find a way to help you."

"What we think wit' Annie matters. Why was you thinkin' 'bout me?"

"You are the first slave I ever met. I don't like it that you're not free."

"You never met a slave before? You must live in a strange place."

"How long have you worked for the Powell family?"

"'Bout fifteen years. I was the size of James when I was brought here after Mama died." James hugged her and Dilli leaned against her leg. "Boys, don't worry. My mama was old and she had no strong boys to help her. I ain't gonna die until you be old and have your own families."

Peter figured Evie was two years older than he was. "Annie will tell me how she got free. If I find a chance for a better life, would you go?"

"I am dizzy wit' you carin' about us and talkin' wit' Annie. We's lucky to have the Massa we does. I don't know a better life than what we got."

They listened to songs of birds and looked up at the stars. "Them stars over the pine tree look like a ladle. Is that what you was talkin' 'bout?"

"Wow, there it is! That's the Big Dipper. Evie, you found it!"

"Stars move across the sky. How can that bright star always be north?"

Peter thought a moment. "The stars aren't moving across the sky. The Earth turns to the East so the stars seem to be moving. The North Star is above the line around which we turn, so it's always to the north."

"I heard there be slaves in New York and Boston has war, so why go north?"

"You heard right. I made a mistake. This is not a good time to run."

"You know a star that tells which way is north. Do you know a star that tells what be a good day to run or a good day to stay put?"

"Sorry, I don't, but if you are OK with it, I'll see what I can learn about ways to get freedom. Annie knows more than she has told me, I am sure."

"I am sure she do. What is 'okay'?"

"OK means all right."

"Mister Peter, I'se afraid. When the Powell girls marry, my boys might get sold away. Tell me if you hear a way to get to a good place. Annie could help me see what to do." At the sound of feet on gravel, Evie held a finger to her lips. They sat quietly as two men passed the house. "Ain't no good reason we could say for you bein' here. I had best get the boys to bed and light lamps. The Powells comin' home soon. You is a kind man. Maybe I gonna hear more from you by and by."

"I hope so, Evie. Good night, boys. Mind your Mama and get your rest."

"Good night, Mister Peter," said Dilli, as James clung to his mother.

Peter had walked barely a block when a carriage passed him going the other way. A lantern shone from the porch of the Powell House.

Back at the house, Peter opened the unlocked door to find Megan in the living room reading by the light of a hurricane lamp and two candles.

"Hi, Pete! Did you find anything interesting?"

"I talked to a slave family at the Powell House—amazing! The reenactors have been off work for a couple of hours."

"It's strange when the weird stuff starts to happen, isn't it?"

"You can say that again!"

"OK, I will. It's strange when the weird stuff starts to happen, isn't it?"

"How did the little bundle in a pink blanket get to be such a smart-ass?"

"I studied with my brother for years. He shared everything he knew, and then I learned lots more from other sources."

"Not bad. Megan, I admit you're kinda funny. I think I'll go for a run."

"It's dark out there. There is no electricity and hardly any street lamps!"

"This is amazing. But there's a half moon so I can run on the paths."

"I'll look for brighter light to read by. Maybe I'll run into George Washington and he can explain the Revolution to me."

Megan watched her brother jog down the road and then she set off carrying two history books under her arm on a quest for reading light.

Day 1-15:   Megan Studies History by Firelight

Megan passed closed shops and taverns with dimly lit interiors. One inn to the south had brightly lit windows. She entered to see an array of lamps on the mantel over a blazing hearth. She sat in a massive wing chair, looked up topics in the index of her text, and jotted notes. There were many indentured servants in Southern colonies. More than half of early English, Scottish, and German settlers in the South served a period of indenture to pay for all or part of their passage.

A man in a well-pressed waistcoat approached. "Would you like a chocolate?"

"A chocolate? Can I order a hot chocolate?"

"All chocolate is served hot, isn't it?"

When the man returned, with a large mug of hot chocolate on a tray, Megan handed him her last twenty-dollar bill of colonial currency. "Oh my, I rarely see a note so valuable!"

He returned with four pounds and nine Spanish dollars, two half crowns, ten shillings, one with the edge obviously shaved to take off silver, and many sixpence coins and large pennies. "Keep all that money tucked away, Miss, and don't let the transitory people see it. The chocolate was four pence. We are forbidden to keep sterling so I gave you all the British money we had. I hope you don't mind."

"No, I don't mind. Can you tell me how many people in Virginia are indentured?"

"I do not know, Miss. Virginia has many indentured servants. I heard there are two hundred thousand slaves, more than twice the number in any other colony. Owners prefer the life-long bond of a slave to a contract that ends in a few years. Owning slaves is for the very rich. They say only one white family in twelve owns even a single slave."

"What happens when a servant escapes?"

"Please, we should not talk about that. Running is a bad idea. Sorry, I must get back to work." The server left hurriedly.

Megan read what she could find in her history books about indentured servants then spent an hour reading about the events leading to the Revolution. She reviewed her notes, first looking for easy connections like the edge pieces of a jigsaw puzzle, and then for other associations. She closed her notebook and drained her mug. "This might upset people when I get home."

Megan stepped outside and began to walk toward home. A man approached from the shadows ahead of her. She veered to the right to avoid him but he stepped right in front of her. "Where are you going in such a hurry?" he probed.

Megan stepped to the left but the man blocked her way. He was shabbily dressed. "Excuse me, I am going home," she insisted.

"You ain't got to be in a rush. Can you spare a coin for a new friend?"

Megan stepped backed a step.

"Maybe 'tis best if you give me all your coins and I'll have no need to hurt ye." The man moved closer. "You are a pretty one."

Megan tightened and decided to run.

"Away with you!" A strong voice came from behind her. The man ran away.

Megan looked behind and made out a tall silhouette she recognized. "Oh, Standing Elk! You came just in time."

"Miss Megan, I saw you leave the tavern and followed you at a distance so as not to startle you. You should not be out alone."

"Is this a dangerous neighborhood?"

"All neighborhoods are dangerous. Many desperate transient people take what they need when it is not theirs to take. Remember the man with the dagger? The gallows here is busy and yet hungry ones make the mistake of stealing or worse."

"Thanks for watching out for me. I'm still freaked out."

"You are safe now. I will walk you home and we can talk as we go."

"Phew! I wasn't sure I could outrun him. That was just as scary as the man with the knife."

They walked in silence for a block as Megan calmed down. "It's a coincidence you should show up to help me. I was reading about your people tonight, Standing Elk. I read about the Proclamation Line of 1763 in which King George declared... just a minute, I may be able to make out my notes in this lantern light... here it is:

"...the Nations or Tribes of Indians with whom We are connected, and who live under our Protection, should not be molested or disturbed in the Possession of such Parts of Our Dominions and Territories as, not having been ceded to or purchased by Us, are reserved to them as their Hunting Grounds"

"I have read the King's' proclamation many times."

"How did you learn to read? Do Native Americans go to school?"

"I studied at the College of William and Mary here in Williamsburg. Those who show promise or are related to native leaders are brought here to study in the hopes of cooperation and to civilize us. I am happy to say I remain quite uncivilized to this day."

"Standing Elk, is it true that the King wants to protect the tribes and nations and keep land west of the Appalachian Mountains as Indian Territory administered by Quebec?"

"England was almost bankrupt from war against the French. The King made that declaration in 1763 to ensure peace on the frontier. Last year, he gave control of the land west of the line to Quebec because French fur traders travel the West to trade with Indians and do not clear land or bring settlers."

"Is it working?"

"Not at all. Powerful people here and in England anonymously formed land companies to settle the Ohio Valley far west of here. Some of His Majesty's governors are investors. Those companies claim land the King reserved for Native people. Besides that, many land grants given by the King to the soldiers who served in the war are the lands reserved for us."

"Everything I learn about the history of your people in this country does not make a happy story. I'm sorry. Is there anything I can do to help?"

"Few care about Indians, but this is too risky for a young woman."

"I don't mean to be bold, but where I come from women assert their ability to be a part of whatever is happening. Some of us are leaders and some even go to war."

"I have seen war and I pray you never do."

"Well, if I stick around here for long, I probably will. If I can help, please let me know."

"Miigwech for your persistence and courage."

"Meg Witch? Do you think I am a witch?"

Standing Elk chuckled, "Are you? I think you are powerful, like women warriors in our legends. No, Miigwech means 'thank you' in our Anishinaabe language."

"I asked my parents the meaning of my name today. It means great or powerful."

"Your parents named you well."

"Miigwech, Standing Elk. How do you know Mark?"

"I have known him for years. We became friends working at the iron works."

"He is a good man. I'm sorry he is not free."

"We all have to work in different kinds of weather, some that is not favorable. He is now doing well in his situation. Anderson the blacksmith is not unkind to him."

"I hope it gets better for him. That's our house. Miigwech for walking me home."

"You are welcome. Today you helped Simon escape from pursuers. I have sad news."

"What happened? Did they catch him?"

"No, Megan, they shall never catch him. Simon slipped in a ravine and struck his head. Two men from my village found him alive but he died this evening. He did not suffer much and died as he lived, smiling. We shall bury him in the custom of his people. Only his friends will know what happened. Those who owned the rights to his labor and those that pursued him for a reward will think that he has escaped forever. And in truth, he has."

"Oh that's terrible! He was not a reenactor?" Megan asked mainly to herself.

"He was not a what?"

"I'm sorry. This is upsetting news. I didn't know Simon but I was hoping I helped him."

"You did, Megan. My people and his friends have already heard how you helped Simon on his last day in this world. Good night. Our paths will cross again."

"I hope so. Good night." Megan entered the house to find she was the first home. Troubled, she lay awake in bed thinking about poor Simon's smile, the man with the knife, and how Standing Elk saved her from the man blocking her way.

Day 1-16:   Peter Jogs to a Hidden Hush Harbor

Peter ran beyond the buildings through cleared land. By the light of the moon, he followed a trail into the woods, dropping into a steady rhythm. He shuddered at the memory of the car spinning on the highway and of how close they had come. It was strange they had been so calm. As he jogged, he listened to the rhythmic crunch of his feet on the path. Suddenly a shriek tore through the other forest sounds. "What the...?" He spun and ran back along the path. Who knows what might be out here?

He stopped. It had sounded like a small animal. What was he afraid of? He jogged back to where he had heard the cry. It occurred to him that a small animal might have encountered a larger predator. He pushed ahead up a rise and on the down slope, he saw flickering light through the trees ahead. He slowed to a walk as he heard voices. A group of Africans sat around a fire set in a shallow pit. High above, lashed at the corners, a piece of canvas blocked the firelight from shining into the treetops. The people gathered in this hollow did not want to be spotted from a distance.

Peter approached quietly. Two men lifted a stout spit and rotated a small feral pig a quarter turn. It had not been over the fire long. Peter concluded the squeal had been the pig's final statement. Next to the fire, two pots simmered — one full of grits and one with greens in salted water.

Old growth trees of enormous girth towered high above the clearing. He moved closer in the shadows and saw Annie sitting next to someone on a mossy patch set back from the circle. She looked across the fire directly at him and subtly signaled him to be silent and come closer. Peter sat against a tree without being noticed by anyone else.

Peter recognized the voice of William the brick-maker holding forth by the fire on catching pigs in the woods. "Spring be a good time to catch a pig, yes it is. When the acorns be gone, there ain't much for pigs to eat so they's hungry. You set a snare wit' a loop of cord and put apples from a cellar in that snare. A pig ain't smelled apples since last year's wild fruit rotted away. Best you wash yourself else he will smell you and run off snortin'. You sit quiet 'til a pig come into your snare and you'll be settin' by a fire tellin' stories 'bout how you catched a pig jest like I is tellin' it."

Peter smiled and rested his head against the tree. How does this guy have so much fun while living as a slave? Peter closed his eyes and listened to the banter as the drippings from the pig crackled on the fire. The scent whetted his appetite.

Opening his eyes, Peter was startled to see Annie listening to Evie but looking intently at him. She moved her fingers slightly to beckon him closer. He circled the group and sat a few feet behind Evie to her left. No one other than Annie reacted to his presence. He had a thought that sounded like his own voice but strangely seemed to come from Annie: "Listen to the questions of others and your own answers will come quicker."

Peter wondered what it meant.

"Hush and listen," another thought came to him.

"There is so much to think on, Annie," Evie was saying. "I cain't help Dilli not be lame. James be so shy he hardly speaks. A gentleman came today, talkin' about us bein' free. Then he came back and say he made a mistake. If they ain't no place to go, how is bein' free better than the life we livin'? The Powell's is kind, they don't beat us, and they give us old clothes, but they ain't gonna give manumission like you got."

"Why you try to carry them problems, child? Take your burdens to the Lord. When you got no idea what to do, do the best you can and learn from what happens. Evie, some things like your boys growin' up takes many years. Say you want a sorrel plant so you have sour greens. If you pull that plant instead of lettin' it grow, you gonna have a little bitty plant in your hand and no greens tomorrow. The Lord will fix them problems over time."

Evie was not convinced. "There is big things like my boys gettin' sold away or I never knowed what happened to James' pa. And little things, like ol' Rosie complain all the time. The Lord and his son Jesus watch over me and my sons even when life be hard. We gonna be in heaven but how can I make life here better for my sons? Don't the Lord want that?"

"You can do somethin' wit'out all that strain." Annie looked at Evie and tilted her head to the left. "You seen children rollin' a hoop, hittin' it wit' a peg?"

"Yes, Annie."

"Take a good look at how they play that hoop. Happenin's in your life is like a hoop rollin'. Some things in the hoop ain't just about you but about many folks, like many people is slaves or a country has peace one year and war the next. Sometimes there be a drought, and sometimes rains come in a flood and everybody got to run to higher ground. You know what I'se talkin' about?"

"Yes Annie, many troubles ain't 'bout me but about sufferin' everybody got."

"Well, child, if you stand in front of that big hoop rollin' wit' all those problems, it can roll right over you. It too heavy to lift and you cain't help by gettin' in the way, unless you want to make you-self into mashed potatoes and gravy."

Evie put her hand to her mouth to cover a laugh.

"It be funny but ain't you doing that? Standin' in front of a problem is danger. To wish it gone be a waste of your mind. If you run alongside and tap like children do, you may help the hoop roll left or right so it don't fall on you. When you is alongside you knows which way the hoop goin' so you stay out the way. Leave the weight of your burden to the Lord."

Evie closed her eyes. "Annie, I see them problems like a hoop rollin.' I gonna stay out the way. I pray the Lord gonna help me roll it right."

"Do you have patience to wait for slow things to grow and big things to change?"

"I gonna do my best, Annie."

Peter was not prepared for the shock of Evie walking past him, her skirt brushing against his knee, without her noticing his presence in the slightest. As Evie walked to the circle, two people moved toward Annie. A light-skinned man sitting close joined her and the other sat nearby to be next. Clearly, people respected Annie and left distance for others to talk in confidence. Peter wondered if he was intruding but Annie nodded at him to stay.

"Hello, 'Gustus," she greeted the light-skinned man. "Did that cut foot heal up good?"

"Yes, Miss Annie. The poultice took down the swelling. It don't hurt no mo'. I got no problem to ax about. I want to thank you for teachin' me how to heal my foot."

"You gonna remember how to crush them balm-of-gilead poplar leaves to make the poultice and how to boil white oak bark until the water is dark then mash it and gently put it on a wound to slow bleedin' and avoid festerin' and pus?"

"Yes, I will."

"How you know what be white oak?"

"The leaves has round ends, not points like other oaks. I wash my hands good in boiled water before I put a poultice on the cut. If I cuts my foot again I can do it."

"Good, 'Gustus. How else can you use a poultice besides if you cuts your foot?"

"Do you think I'se ready to make a poultice for somebody else? I could help them not swell up or poison they blood like you told me. Annie, I ain't done physic for nobody 'cept water when they was thirsty wit' fever. It will be good if I can help other folk. Would you teach me more things to do? People get into more kinds of trouble than just cuttin' they-self."

49

"I will, if you want to learn, 'Gustus. There be someone you can help right now."

"Who is that, Miss Annie?"

"Dilli is your son, and James is his brother, and Evie was your woman."

"She wasn't my woman 'zackly, Annie. We never jumped the broom. My massa had me stay in Massa Powell's kitchen back in '68 when he worked on that hospital."

"It was just before Christmas."

"Yes'm. It was cold and Massa sent me to the kitchen to sleep. I climbed into the loft and lay next to Evie to keep warm. She was learning to be a washer woman back then and wit' the cold night and one thing and another, she had herself another boy and that was Dilli."

"The boy Dilli knows you be his pa. He might like to see you."

"I never knowed my daddy 'cept I know he was a white man like Mama's daddy was so I has light skin. I thought I already done what a daddy was 'posed to do. Anyhow, Dilli is lame and I ain't got no way to fix that."

Annie grew stern. "We all be lame in some way, 'Gustus. Dilli be lame in his leg but he ain't lame in his head or his heart. He be a shinin' light of a boy. Tell Evie you be happy to see her and give her somethin' for the boys. Don't worry 'bout what to say. Ax how they is doin' then hush and listen. People feels better when someone care about them. Don't you visit me sometimes just to be heard? You learned the poultice and you can learn to listen to folks."

"That sounds good, Annie. Even if I cain't get there much, I gonna ax her tonight how she and the boys is doin'. I will bring them somethin' sometime. You right like usual, Annie."

"'Gustus, be helpful to folk. Lord knows we all need kindness!"

"Phew," breathed Peter. Annie looked up at him and suddenly an idea came to him that it was not for him to listen to the next conversation. Annie had invited him to hear about Evie and her family, but now it was time to step away. He sat in view of the fire. Peter's interest in Evie's freedom had begun with no idea of her situation, but now he had much to sort out. He looked into the luminous dance of the flames.

Day 1-17:   Evening Service at Bruton Parish Church

"The sermon begins in an hour, John. We can take our time." They strolled past the Capitol. When they reached Palace Green, it was still early, so they turned to the circle at the Governor's Palace. John looked at the regal brick mansion, and down the broad boulevard.

"Shopping for real estate?" asked Susan.

"Our house doesn't convey this kind of authority. I'm getting ideas for an extra story, a cupola, plus east and west wings to make a stronger statement in the neighborhood."

On a pond near the Palace, wild ducks fed near a grassy bank. "I wonder if their ancestors cruised on the Governor's pond," mused Susan.

"They risked a special appointment to the Governor's platter."

Along the west side of Palace Street, Susan looked into the windows of the stately homes. "They've got wild wallpaper but I like the furniture. I want to visit the houses." Susan was enjoying the evening, happy seeing John less stressed than earlier. These relaxed moments were too rare.

They arrived at Bruton Parish Church, in use since 1715. The steeple was added sixty years after the building was completed. It had three square stories with tall arched windows, two hexagonal stories, and a conical roof. For colonial parishioners — living in cabins of rough boards nailed to posts imbedded in the earth — this steeple stretched toward heaven.

Inside the church, Susan was struck by the elegant brass organ pipes and candelabras gleaming in sunlight streaming at a low angle from the windows. Plaques on pews named distinguished families, including Washington and Jefferson, who once sat there. Floral arrangements appeared poised to greet a bride at the altar. They found seats near the pulpit with its wooden canopy inlayed with a 32-point Radiant Glory.

James Walker, the Episcopal priest, mounted the pulpit steps. The rumble of conversation ebbed to a few coughs. "Good evening, friends. Welcome to Bruton Parish Church. We begin with a hymn sung here for centuries, the Doxology, known as 'The Old Hundredth.' Psalm 100 calls us to make a joyful noise unto the Lord and come into his presence with singing!" The organist played a verse as the congregation rose to sing:

"Praise God from whom all blessing flow; Praise Him all creatures here below;
Praise Him above, ye heavenly host; Praise Father, Son and Holy Ghost."

"In colonial times, that hymn was one of a few sung throughout the year. They were sung by heart, for many were illiterate. The hymnal in your hands would not help them. Religion was central in settlers' lives. Today, polls show three-quarters of Americans believe in God and half the rest believe in a Universal Spirit, higher percentages than other advanced countries. Tonight we explore the colonial roots of our faiths.

"We think early America was a haven of religious tolerance where Pilgrims and others escaped persecution. We learn Maryland was a refuge for Catholics. Compared to Protestants and Catholics burning each other at the stake in Europe, there was relative tolerance here. But tolerance is more than refraining from killing people of other beliefs." He looked around. "At least, for those of you not Episcopalian like me, I hope so."

There were a few chuckles in the congregation.

"Colonists, like many people the world over, thought their form of worship was blessed in the eyes of God and perhaps the only true way."

Susan noticed movement in the empty balcony upstairs. Jane, the woman from the Capitol, quietly took a seat.

"Colonial Virginia had no separation of church and state. The Church of England was the official religion or 'Established Church'. Everyone was obliged to pay taxes to that church and attend services once a month or pay a fine of five shillings or fifty pounds of tobacco. Those in other denominations were called 'dissenters'. Some Revolutionary leaders called for disestablishment of the Church of England. Although re-establishment of my church would be lucrative for our organization, I do not support antidisestablishmentarianism as Patrick Henry advocated for a time. And you thought you would never hear that word in a sentence!

"In Maryland, founded by the Calvert family as a colony where Catholicism was legal, Governor William Stone, a Protestant, signed the Toleration Act. Under the Act, if you insulted someone's religion you could be fined. If you defamed the Virgin Mary, you could be whipped. The penalty for not believing in the Trinity was death. How's that for tolerance?

"When Thomas, 3rd Lord Fairfax, and his second-in-command Oliver Cromwell defeated the Royalists in England, Maryland became a Puritan colony. Former Governor Stone attacked the Puritans at the Battle of the Severn in 1655. The Puritans won, captured Stone and executed four Catholic prisoners on the spot in a religious war fought an hour from our nation's capital. No wonder we prefer to forget our history."

John shifted in his seat. The thought of war at home in which religious fundamentalists executed prisoners made him uncomfortable.

"In 1691, the Church of England became the established religion of Maryland. When Maryland was returned to the Calverts in 1715, Benedict Calvert had converted to Protestantism. Catholics were forbidden to vote and masses were banned but secret masses were held in homes, celebrated sometimes by Jesuit priests who married, owned land, and secretly maintained their faith.

"On this side of the Chesapeake, the seating in this church reflects hierarchy in the Established Church. Members of the Governor's Council and Burgesses in the front pews had status clear to all. Middle-sorts then lesser-sorts people sat in more remote pews. In the back benches were servants and visitors from the hills. Slaves and free blacks sat out of sight in the empty North Gallery up there." As attention turned to the North Gallery, Jane sat still as a statue.

"Every Sunday saw readings from the Book of Common Prayer, hymns, and a sermon. Four times a year parishioners were offered Communion, taken mainly by the elderly as they faced their impending end. Peter Pelham, an organist here, was also the jailer. To some of you the practices might resemble a spiritual jail but there was benefit in repeated rituals.

"In a *Short History of the Book of Common Prayer*, William Huntington, Rector of Grace Church in New York, wrote, 'For the origin of liturgy… go a long way back; beyond synagogue worship, …to that dimly discerned groundwork we call human nature. Where two or more assemble for supplication, some form must be accepted if they are to pray in unison. When the disciples came to Jesus begging him to teach them how to pray, he gave not twelve forms… but one. 'When ye pray… say Our Father.'

"The Book of Common Prayer guided Bible readings, baptism, communion, visitation of the sick, and many aspects of life in this community. Last week, on the fifth Sunday after Easter, congregants would have heard from Deuteronomy 8:

"For the Lord thy God bringeth thee into a good land, a land of brooks of water, of fountains and depths that spring out of valleys and hills. A land wherein thou shalt eat bread without scarceness… a land whose stones are iron.

"That verse would have encouraged people who scraped sustenance from the land. At evensong service that same Sunday in 1775, they heard:

"Hear, O Israel: Thou art to pass over Jordan this day, to go in to possess nations greater and mightier than thyself, cities great and fenced up to heaven.'

"That may have given the Founders courage to rise against Parliament. This coming Sunday, the reading will be from Deuteronomy 12:

"Ye shall utterly destroy all the places, wherein nations which ye shall possess served their gods…

"What would repetitions of this passage mean for native peoples?

"For some, rote practice is unsatisfying. Have you heard of the Great Awakening? Charismatic preachers from Britain and New England were called 'enthusiastic', which in those days meant fanatic. The passionate preaching, singing, and body movement were unlike the sedate rituals of the Established Church. The Great Awakening may have arisen from the longing for direct spiritual experience that still calls people today."

Susan wanted to join Jane in the gallery. She felt after their encounter that they had experiences in common. The invisible trail she was following had led her to Jane. She waved but couldn't catch Jane's attention.

"The Bible is the main vehicle through which Christians hear the word of God. For most of the time Christianity has been practiced, most believers were illiterate. Although we now read the Bible, we differ in where we place authority to interpret it and to define beliefs and practices. I can only hint at distinctions among churches to help us understand the paths of others. The names of each denomination give clues.

"Do you remember Simon bar Jonah, the Hebrew fisherman? Jesus told him, 'You are Peter, and on this rock I will build my church.' Simon Peter traveled to Rome to found the Catholic Church. With a small 'c,' catholic means: broad-minded; liberal; universal; pertaining to the whole Christian church. With a capital 'C' Catholic pertains to a theology declaring it possesses the only, true, and universal church with unity, apostolic succession, and sanctity. Not the same meaning is it? In the Catholic Church, authority rests with the Pope, heir to the apostle Peter."

Susan hoped Jane would look down, but she was enrapt by the sermon.

"In the 1500s, the Reformation sought to reduce corruption in the Church. In England reform merged with other desires of Henry VIII who wanted to divorce Catherine, daughter of Ferdinand and Isabella of Spain, and marry Ann Boleyn in hope of producing a male heir. He separated the English Church, placing the Archbishop of Canterbury in charge. The Church *in* England became the Church *of* England, born of reform, nationalism, and a King's desire to remove limits to his power. This was the religion of over half the Founding Fathers.

"'Episcopal' means of the bishops. The Archbishop of Canterbury leads the Church but there were no bishops in the Colonies. Each Virginia county had two parishes governed by a vestry of landowners who chose their own members. Burgesses and militia commanders were usually elected from among vestrymen. So wealthy, slave-owning landowners put themselves in charge of the religion, military, and government. Most middle-sorts did not aspire to change this system. The ambitious among them sought to rise within it.

"There were four thousand people in Virginia for each established clergyman so access was limited. The gap was filled by the arrival of other sects. Presbyterian ministers came from Scotland. Authority was in the hands of a 'Presbyter' or Council of Elders. Presbyterian ministers worked in areas where the Church of England was not established. When they entered parishes, they needed a license or faced being jailed.

"German and Dutch Protestant denominations were known as German Reformed, Dutch Reformed, and Lutheran after Martin Luther the German reformer who founded that Church. German ministers preached to their communities here in their own language.

"A group originated in the Church of England, derogatorily called Puritans by others for seeking pure worship and less worldliness. They wanted to eliminate bishops and revise the Book of Common Prayer to emphasize Christ and individual holiness. Some separated from the Church or were ejected by the bishops. Later many called themselves Congregationalists placing authority in the congregation. This resonated with levelers in New England, who boldly contended that all men were created equal. The very idea threatened established hierarchies.

"Methodists originated within the Church of England through teachings of John Wesley and others. As their name suggests, they emphasized method and experience over doctrine. Methodist missionaries rode circuits from county to county, preaching in barns, taverns, and fields.

"Baptist preachers also called for experience of Spirit. If illiterate, they quoted scripture from memory. They followed solemn customs and called each other Brother and Sister. Their name shows the importance placed on baptism, immersing adults in water as did John the Baptist, to signify rebirth in the spirit. Some Baptists opposed slavery and attracted slaves and free blacks into their fold. Followers giving 'testimony' to how Christ worked in their lives, were respected no matter how humble their station.

"The Society of Friends, known as Quakers, did not emphasize the Bible but believed that in silence, an Inner Light can express itself through us. Virginia's establishment worried that a religion without hierarchy would lead to a breakdown of society. In New England, Puritans hanged Quakers for preaching, a century before the Revolution."

Susan glimpsed the back of a hood in the Gallery and Jane was gone. She whispered to John, "Something scared her. I've got to go outside."

"Scared whom? Can't you wait until the end of the sermon?"

To stand up in the front row and leave before the sermon was over would be awkward, so Susan resigned herself to wait.

"How did we move beyond such intolerance? Young Thomas Jefferson attended the Classical School of Reverend James Maury, son of a Huguenot Protestant who escaped persecution in France. Maury taught that people had a right to worship in their own way if it did not interfere with others. Five of his students signed the Declaration of Independence and three became American Presidents. Since Jefferson lived with Maury and his family, he surely was influenced in those formative years.

In June 1779, the month he was elected Governor of Virginia, Jefferson introduced a 'Bill for Establishing Religious Freedom' despite other priorities during the Revolution. By the time the bill passed in 1786, he was Minister Plenipotentiary to France. We call that Ambassador today.

"How significant was this bill to Thomas Jefferson? At his request, his epitaph lists three accomplishments: author of the Declaration of Independence, founder of the University of Virginia, and author of the Bill for Establishing Religious Freedom. These were more important to him than serving as President.

"I hope I said nothing to offend you. I did not include all faiths, just Christian denominations prevalent in the Virginia Colony. There were a few Jews in the colonies and Native Peoples and Africans had their own spirituality, which I am studying. Freedom of religion is a gift our Founders gave us. Let us close with a prayer.

"Dear Lord, we are brothers and sisters in your great family of life. Please guide us to open our hearts to all people and open our minds to your infinite gifts as we walk the paths of our lives. May our many paths lead all your children to You. Amen. Thank you for coming. God bless you and God bless America."

As the priest left, Susan jumped up. The entry to the North Gallery was chained and locked so she hurried outside.

When the aisles of the church were clear, John walked outside to find her breathless. "I ran a block in each direction but couldn't find her."

"Who?"

"That woman from the Capitol left early. I need to talk to her."

"You are bound to find her tomorrow. Why do you need to talk to her?"

"I think we have something in common. Maybe we can help each other."

John waited for Susan to explain further but she said no more about it. They walked to their colonial quarters and checked on the kids. Megan was asleep, but Peter was not home yet, so they left the door unlocked and went to bed. John dropped off to sleep immediately and Susan lay awake a few minutes, aware of the faint familiar sadness.

Day 1-18:   Many Colors in the Glass

At the sound of Annie's voice, Peter came out of his reverie. He had a clear view of her sitting on the other side of the fire. "This be a good gatherin'," she was saying, "but somethin' goin' on that ain't good. Who got a bottle of Jamaica rum?" The circle got quiet. "I need that bottle so I can 'splain somethin' to you. I'se closin' my eyes. You all do the same and don't peek. I want that bottle to git over to the earth in front of me now!"

There was a thud and gurgle as a half-empty bottle landed in the pile of soft soil dug up to make the fire pit. Annie pulled the cork from the clear bottle with her teeth and poured the contents into a bowl. "That be a pretty white shirt, William. You wear it on Sunday?"

"Yes Ma'am."

"Come on up here by me and let the people have a look at that shirt."

"It ain't my rum, Annie, I swear!"

"I know, William. We need your white shirt to show somethin' to the folk. We also need you not to talk for a bit." As William moved up next to Annie, she placed the bowl filled with rum next to a pile of dry pine needles. She then scraped the edge of a metal bowl under the broiling pig to catch liquid fat in the bowl, and she placed it next to the bowl of rum.

"William, you hold this bottle near your shirt facing the fire so folk can see behind it. You folk across the fire, move to one side so you can see his shirt behind the bottle. Do not watch me. Watch the shirt. Some of you gonna see what I'se showin' and some ain't. Which is you gonna be?

"'Gustus, sit by William and pick up handfuls of pine needles. When I says 'Now!' throw them over the fire." Augustus shuffled over, gathered up needles in both hands, and watched the fire intently as Annie took the bowl of rum in her left hand and the drippings in her right.

"Now!" shouted Annie, and Gustus threw the needles as she threw the liquids into the fire. Pine, rum, and pork fat ignited in the air above the fire in a dazzling flash. Peter watched William's shirt. For an instant, light shone through the bottle and cast bands of red, orange, yellow, green, blue, and violet light onto the white shirt. It was there and gone.

"What did you see?" Annie asked the circle of faces.

"I saw a bright light."

"They was a little bitty rainbow on William's shirt."

"Anybody else see colors?"

"Uh- huh, they was there but just for a blink."

"That's good. William, hand me that bottle. You and 'Gustus sit over there. Thank you for helpin'. Now, Robert, Claudius, and Samuel, please

57

come on up here by me." The men were not in a hurry to come forward, but after some fumbling, they sat in a row by the fire.

"Samuel, did you see the colors on William's shirt?"

"Yes, Ma'am, I did."

"Good. Now, tell me how that bruise got on yo fo' head?"

"I... I ain't gonna trouble you wit' how it got there."

"Robert, what did you see when the fire got bright?"

"I saw colors and 'den white."

"Can you tell us the truth about how Samuel got a blue spot?"

"He got that bruise while I was defendin' myself." Robert stared into the fire. "It ain't his fault. I tol' him if he did not go to church, he gonna burn in Hell. I was tryin' to help him."

"Did you share this bottle that I used to do this ceremony?"

"I don't want to make trouble for nobody."

"Claudius, Robert ain't havin' an easy time. Can you help him out?"

Claudius looked downcast. "I was at the dock last month unloadin' cases of rum. One fell and broken glass was all over and bottles rolled into the river. The overseer made me climb down into that muddy water and feel around for bottles. It was so cold my teeth was clickin' and my lips was blue. I got six bottles and the overseer called me out. They gave me a mug of hot water so I would not die on them, least not 'til the work was done."

"How did this bottle come to be wit' you, Claudius?"

"Wit' this gatherin' comin' I hoped they was a bottle in the river for pourin' libations. So I snuck into the water, which was not so cold like last month, and felt around beside the dock. Sho'nuff this bottle was stickin' up in the mud. I bet they be more down there."

"Well, that ain't stealin' but still dangerous and could get you whipped. Claudius, what did you say 'bout libations?"

"Annie, my Mama learned Yoruba Ways from her Daddy in Africa and wanted to teach me pourin' libations and such. When I got sold away, I forgot what she taught me. Spirit gave me that bottle to honor my ancestors like Mama done, but I drank some and shared some. I feel bad."

"What can do you remember of what she taught you, Claudius? You people listen."

"She say there was Spirit in everything. She say that be hard to understand, so people names Spirits in mountains and animals and trees. Spirit help us and Spirit stop us when we doin' bad. Spirit be like light shinin' inside us. People tell stories 'bout different spirits to help them slowly, slowly see somethin' that be hard to see. She told me her Daddy was a story teller and singer called a gri... a gri..." He stopped.

"A griot, Claudius, you say it like gree - oh. You done a good job tellin' us 'bout your wise Mama. You be the grandson of a griot and you can learn those ways. I can tell you more 'bout libations if you want.

"Now, Samuel, how old was you when you was catched up?"

"I was a boy, Annie. We lived in a town, big as ten Williamsburgs, with markets and many places to pray."

"How did you pray in your town?"

"Every mornin' at first light they would call us from a high place like a steeple. The first time was at dawn and they called that Fajr. And at noon we prayed again and they called that..." Samuel struggled.

"The place to pray is called a mosque, the tower called a minaret and the noon prayer is Zhuhr." Annie's voice was comforting.

Samuel looked up at Annie surprised, "Yes, Zhuhr." Tears came to his eyes. "I didn't think I would hear them words again. On the horrible ship, I prayed every day. But here, nobody knew those ways and time went by. I fell away."

"Samuel, when you was a boy what was your name?"

"My name... there are too many dead folk back there."

"Remember them wit' love, Samuel. They knew you by what name?

"I was Abdul Latif." He began to cry and put his head down.

"Abdul Latif, you raise your head up and look out at these people." Firelight reflected in the salty streams down his cheeks, his wet eyes radiant. "Did you go to school and learn to read when you was young?"

"Yes, Annie, until the war came." He wiped his nose on his sleeve and turned to her. "It wasn't supposed to be like this, Annie."

"I know. Everyone here has the pain of a life stolen. Hope comes from findin' what is left of our old path and goin' ahead on whatever road the Lord gives us now. None of us is forgotten, I promise you all."

"I read a holy book but the letters was different. I cain't read the writing here. My father sold fine cloth; silk was carried from the East. I got no kin and no holy book. Robert says I'm going to Hell." His face was full of anguish.

Robert interrupted. "Annie, I tol' you I was defendin' myself, but I hit Samuel and he was defendin' his self. He did not hit me. I is sorry, Sam."

"Thank you fo' the truth, Robert. When did you get here, Abdul Latif?"

"'Bout twelve years ago, Annie."

"When you was catched as a slave did people die?"

"A big war came and many people died. My father, my uncles, and big brother died with their... how do you call them... swords in their hands."

"On the ship with people loaded like fish in a salt box, did anyone die?"

"Maybe one in three died before we got to 'Napolis."

"Them people had names, had plans and dreams, and people they loved, and we should remember them in our prayers, shouldn't we Claudius?"

"Yes, Annie, we should." Claudius, born into slavery, was captivated by the story.

"Did you die, Abdul Latif?"

"Many times I thought dyin' was better than livin', but I did not die."

"What was you doin' all that time on the trail and in the ship?"

"I prayed to God, Annie. I prayed to the Merciful One. I spoke the three tongues I learned from my father and mother and told people if we got through this, it could be the worst we would ever see. I prayed in the dark to be with God, and prayed we would have a life again if that was God's will."

"Insh-Allah," Annie looked at Samuel. "If God wills it. And he did."

He was startled and stared at her. "Yes, Annie, Insh-Allah."

"Where are those people from the ship now?"

"I don't know. In 'Napolis we was sold off and I never saw them again."

"I want to tell you all somethin' important. Six months ago, I was at a Hush Harbor in Maryland, and folk was testifyin' how Jesus came into they life. Robert, is you listenin'?"

"Yes, ma'am, I know Jesus do miracles."

"At that Hush Harbor a woman told us she done been wit' child on the ship. It looked and smelled like Hell and people wailed like she heard they do in Hell. She was scared her baby would be born in Hell. Then she heard a young man prayin'. He prayed somethin' like 'in Shalla' and she think Shalla is Heaven. She think, a boy who pray so much cain't be in Hell.

"The baby came four days before they got to 'Napolis. They hollered up to the men who took the mama and baby and washed them. If they could get that woman to auction lookin' healthy, the baby would be worth money too and they had lost many slaves to sickness. So they gave her food and used a sheet for a dress and she felt better when they got to port.

"A Catholic planter who hid his religion, was in 'Napolis to buy field hands. When he saw the woman up there wit' a sheet to block the sun from her child, lookin' like Mary and baby Jesus, he took it as a sign. He bought them to help his wife at the house."

Abdul Latif was sitting upright. "She is alive? And the baby girl?"

"The woman cooks at a good home in Maryland. She teachin' her girl to cook. She got two secrets. She be Catholic like the family where she live. They pray to Jesus and Mary wit' beads like you used back home, Abdul Latif. Her other secret is she go to Hush Harbor meetings and tell folk Jesus sent a holy boy to save people on the ship. Her name be Esther now and she named her girl Sally after Shallah in the boy's prayer."

"Praise Jesus!" shouted Robert, "That's what I'se talkin' 'bout!"

Annie looked at him. "Robert, you was only half listenin'. That holy boy was Samuel Abdul Latif who saved the woman on the ship."

"He was? You was workin' for Jesus, Samuel?"

All eyes turned to Samuel. Tears again streamed down his face, but they were tears of joy. "Annie, I am ready to serve the Most Kind One again. I am sorry I lost my way for so long."

"Samuel, you got through Hell and came out alive wit'out a bitter heart. You jes' forgot for a while. If you want, I can show you English letters."

"Annie, I want to learn."

"Please stand and face these people." He stood up. "Listen, everyone. Samuel lost his way and tonight his way found him. Don't call him Abdul Latif because that could make trouble wit' his massa. Call him Sal and if anybody ax, say it be short for Samuel. Look here." Annie picked up a stick and traced the letters S, A, and L in the earth. "S be for Samuel, A be for Abdul, and L be for Latif. S-A-L is for little Sally saved by a miracle through you. Samuel in the Hebrew tongue means 'His name is God' and Abdul Latif in the Arab tongue means 'Servant of the Kind One'. When we call you Sal we callin' you by all your names."

"How do you know the meaning of my name?"

"I traveled wit' the Fulani to towns wit' mosques built around 1100, a long time before 1775. Later, Muslim slaves here taught me some of the hundred names of God. Sal, if I find a Koran, I will give it to you. I learned to read this book." She reached into her sack and held up the Holy Bible.

"Robert, when you be down, do Jesus and this Holy Bible lift you up?"

"Jesus helps me every day and wit'out that Holy Word I might be dead."

"Do you see how God came through Sal to help Esther and Sally? Could Claudius help folk through the spirit of his griot grandpa in his heart?"

"Yes, Ma'am."

"Do you know how to read, Robert?"

"I know some letters like R and S. Somebody showed me once."

"I believe that was the time I spelled R, O, S, and E in the sand."

"Yes, you tol' us roses looks and smells beautiful even fenced in. We can feel the sun and breeze like roses do and love one another and remember the Lord smilin' on us until someday he open the gate for us to be free."

"Good, Robert. You was listenin' that day. When Sal learns to read English, would you like to ax him to teach you to read Bible stories? That might help open your heart."

He was shy about asking. "Samuel, I mean Sal, I'se sorry. If you could teach me to read the Bible, I will be thankful my whole life."

"I will learn the letters and teach you," Sal answered. "The Bible tells about Jesus, and Mary his mother. They are also in the Koran. When I hear about Jesus and Mary here, it comforts me that they led me from Africa through Hell to Virginia. Like Annie says, I was not forgotten."

Annie smiled. "You men did well. It be late and the pig is 'bout cooked."

"Annie, what about them colors on William's shirt?" Augustus asked.

"I showed you colors on William's shirt and then Claudius, Sal, and Robert showed you the colors again. Who knows what I'se talkin' about?"

Claudius spoke first. "Spirit is like that bright light when you put pine and rum and fat on the fire. When Spirit shines on us it be like light comin' through the bottle. One white light make many colors, like sunshine make a rainbow. Each color is somebody's way home to the light of Spirit."

"That is a good way to say it, Claudius. You have the soul of a griot. Should we respect the ways of others as they go up the road?"

"Yes, we should," answered a number of voices.

"Anyone else?"

"All the colors come from the light in they own way," Robert added.

"I is happy you all listenin'."

"Claudius, some warm night carefully fetch another bottle by the dock and hide it. Next time we gather I can show you how to pour libations and give thanks for your Grandpa the griot and all who went before like Jesus, Moses who led the Hebrew Children out of slavery, Sal's Prophet Mohammed, and the Prophets in the Bible."

"Yes Annie, I will do that. I want to learn my Grandpa's way."

"Your Mama will smile down on you. Now let us celebrate all the colors. William caught us a fine pig and we is going to thankfully eat it ain't we?"

William offered a very short grace. "Thanks Lord, thanks pig." What he had witnessed touched him deeply. He placed succulent slices of pork on squares of corn bread and handed portions to everyone. Most had not eaten so well since Easter Sunday. Annie took one to Peter. It was the best sandwich he ever had.

Peter heard the twang of a banjo and rhythm of a homemade drum. People took turns leading the call and response. Some songs were spirituals, and others so bawdy that folks laughed even without rum in their bellies. On the upbeat rhythms, people danced. Songs were sung in harmony, in sweet major keys and haunting minors. When the music ended, people looked into the embers, immersed in the glow of the moment. In spite of hardships, life had glimmers of joy. They were renewed.

Annie stood by the fire. "Well, it be closer to mornin' than to last night, so until we meet again, help each other along. 'Gustus, 'fore you go, step over here, please." He came close. "'Gustus, this be Mister Peter."

Augustus looked where Annie indicated and was surprised to see Peter. "Don't know why you didn't see him before what wit' that firelight shining on his white face." Annie smiled broadly. "Please show `Mister Peter the short way to Williamsburg from your quarters. You ain't got time to take him all the way yo-self. And don't let nobody see you together."

Peter was full of questions yet speechless. Annie made a little circle with her index finger that somehow told him now was not the time for questions and that she would talk to him another time. How does she say so much with just a move of a finger?

Men took down the canvas and filled the fire pit with the pile of soft earth as people dispersed into the darkness.

"Can you run fast and far, Mister Peter?" asked Augustus. "I never seen a white gentleman run and we ain't got time to dally 'round here no mo'."

Peter winked at Annie. "Let's see if I can run fast. You lead and I'll follow."

Day 1-19:   Peter and Augustus Run Home at Dawn

Last week's heavy rain left puddles and with the mud now dry, Augustus ran barefoot, stepping on smooth patches. A hint of dawn lightened the sky above the trees. He kept a quick pace, lifting each foot high and placing it straight down like horses trotting. That way he would not trip or stub his toe badly, a lesson learned the hard way. As he felt a burn in his legs, he smiled at the memory of dancing. Recalling the drum added rhythm to his gait. Tokah Tam, Tokah Tam. That was some fun!

There was already too much light. He had to get to the quarter while everyone else was still abed. He heard Peter's footfalls behind him. Even as Augustus ran flat out, Peter kept up. Half a mile to go. That smell of wood smoke might be from the kitchen fire at the main house. Tokah Tam, comin' home, Tokah Tam, legs sore, Tokah Tam! He wiped his forehead with his sleeve. Hoo boy! He was going to make it home on time.

Augustus' world suddenly exploded in a burst in front of him. He cried out and fell flat on the road, palms down to cushion the fall. He saw the tail of the wild turkey he had tripped on disappear into the woods. The wind was knocked from him so he sat up to draw deep breaths. "Turkey!" He looked at his hands. "Ain't too bad." Peter helped him up.

Augustus panted, trying to catch his breath. "Whew! You cain't find them turkeys when you hungry." His breath finally slowed. "I ain't never seen a white man run fast as you. Keep on down this road to town. I gotta cross to the quarters quick so they don't find me gone."

"Good luck, and thanks, Augustus."

Augustus veered across the field to the slave barracks. He avoided the corn stubble that can puncture a foot and slowed to a walk. He entered the rough cabin, stepping lightly across the dirt floor to the plank he placed beside his pallet so his feet would not touch cold clay on a frosty morning. He lifted the edge of the blanket and sat on the straw mattress. With an old rag, he wiped his feet. With a sigh, he lay back.

An hour later, the overseer called outside the door. "Up you get now! Get movin'! We got ourselves a big day."

DAY 2-1:   May 1775   Surprise Breakfast by the Hearth

Susan awakened early and quietly slipped from the bedroom. In her bare feet, she stopped and stared. The bathroom was gone. Gone... the discontinuity so complete her mouth opened but no words came. Fear arose and passed, leaving calm curiosity. Where a tub and shower had been the previous night, Susan stared at an open fireplace, coals glowing.

She sat by the fire and gazed at the embers. A blackened wood-grain pattern was etched on the logs dwindling under yellow-peaked dancing blue cones of flame. What is this...? Susan wondered. Peaceful—nothing to fear. "What is this?" Phrases moved through her awareness:

The extraordinary — extra ordinary, forever underlies the apparent.
Beneath habitual, behind familiar, all form animated,
All pattern emerging, resolving, and dissolving.

Susan lingered, and then pulled on slacks, sweater, and sneakers. Out a door that was not there yesterday, was an outhouse. Convenient, she thought. In the trees, American goldfinches chirped over the rasping calls of grackles. Far away, a rooster crowed. A wooden pail with oak staves like a little barrel sat on the wall of a well. The sky was reflected in the water below. She lowered the pail by a rope tied to its handle. It struck the surface of the water, scattering the reflection of the sky into concentric blue fragments. Water sloshed over the rim as she drew it up.

She carried water to the kitchen, added wood to the fire, and put pots on the wrought iron rack at varying distances from the fire. "I'll warm one for washing and set one over the fire to hurry along a cup of coffee. If I'm dreaming, will a dream of coffee wake me up? Do I have any...?"

In the antique armoire were the snacks they brought. When the water in the first pot was warm, she washed in the oriental-design porcelain washbasin and returned to the kitchen to prepare breakfast. She arranged a platter with cheese, apples, and muffins and called out, "Breakfast in ten minutes! There's a big surprise out here!"

"Good morning, Hon." John emerged, a towel over his arm.

"No shower this morning. I've got hot water for the washing bowl."

"What the... What happened?"

"Maybe remodelers worked all night? There's an outhouse in back."

"Unbelievable! This happened as we slept?"

"I don't know but I've had a peaceful feeling since I got up. We can go to the office and change rooms; but this is authentic don't you think?"

Megan called out from her bed, "Why do we have to get up this early?"

"There's something here you should see."

Megan came into the living room rubbing her eyes. "Hey, there's the fireplace. I used the outhouse before I went to bed."

"That's not possible. The bathroom was here last night when we got back from the presentation at the church, and you were already asleep."

"I know it's not possible, Dad. It wasn't there when I was reading last night and it isn't there now. What's possible got to do with it?"

"How could someone remove the bathroom and put it back and remove it again just like that?" John asked, snapping his fingers.

"I guess it was just like that." Megan snapped her fingers. Peter saw it yesterday, too." She knocked on Peter's door. "Time to get up!"

"Unnh!" The sound came muffled by a sheet and a blanket.

"Come on, Pete. Mom made breakfast. They can see the fireplace."

Peter sat upright. "Is it still happening?"

"Yeah, big time. Mom and Dad are out here staring at the fireplace."

"Wow! Give me four hours to sleep and two minutes to get dressed."

"Forget the four hours," Megan grinned and closed the door.

After they washed up, they breakfasted around the hearth. "You guys say it was not just this house last night, but all over?" asked Susan.

"Yup, all over town. There are things I can't wait to tell you."

"We'll go over to the office and ask what they did. I'll bet these houses are built to be converted suddenly like sets at a theater," John surmised.

"Yesterday, this seemed to go in and out, or we seemed to go in and out of it. Peter and I have projects to work on to really help some people!"

Peter shot her a 'shut up' look. "Yes, we both found topics for school. I am looking at slavery and Megan is working on—what, Megan?"

"I learned the American Revolution was not about what we thought. There were secret deals among leaders in England and in the colonies to take land King George had reserved for the Indians. His governors granted the same land to soldiers who fought in the French and Indian War. Rich guys secretly bought up the land grants and sent servants who didn't know better into Indian country to clear the forests."

"Whoa, Megan. It sounds like a historical conspiracy theory. Pick an idea for your paper and work on it, but do research to be sure it's true."

"But Dad! I researched it last night and I haven't told you most of it yet!"

"First we have to find what happened to the bathroom!" John growled.

Susan handed John a mug of coffee and changed the subject. "It was a good sermon last night. Before Jefferson advanced religious freedom, everyone in Virginia had to attend Episcopal services and pay taxes to that church or be fined. Jefferson helped make this a country where we are free to practice any religion or no religion."

"If Jefferson was really for freedom, why did Lincoln still need to free slaves almost ninety years later?" Peter objected.

"Pete's right. Over half the people in Tidewater were slaves, and many whites were bonded servants. Free men who owned no land couldn't vote either. Almost half the free people were women who did not get to vote for over a hundred years. Whose freedom were they fighting the Revolution for?" asked Megan. "I want to show you something..."

Her father interrupted. "Wait just a minute! They fought for us! They gave us freedom and launched the greatest country in the world!"

"True, John," Susan agreed, "but we heard yesterday that taxes had been repealed long before the Revolution. The burgesses mentioned that some leaders in Britain agreed with our Founding Fathers. Maybe war was unnecessary."

"That's what I'm trying to tell you!" interjected Megan.

"Not now," warned John, controlling himself. "Later, if I find a library they haven't converted to a chicken coop, I'll do some reading myself."

"This sudden change is a shock. We need to find out what happened," said Susan. "There are other strange things. I saw the woman who talked about peace again in church last night and she looked terrified. At the Capitol she looked around as if someone was following her."

Peter thought of Annie. "I can look for someone I think can help with this problem."

"I don't know if it is a good idea for us to split up when…"

"When things are so weird, Mom?" Megan asked.

"The office will explain this. Peter, don't take reckless risks and look both ways before you cross the street. Let's meet here at noon."

"OK Dad, see you then." Peter gave his parents and sister a hug and left.

John was surprised. "He hasn't hugged us in a long time."

"There's nothing like the overnight appearance of a warm hearth to bring the family together, Honey."

"Mom, I'm going to learn about who was fighting who and why."

"Who was fighting 'whom'," Susan corrected.

"Yeah, that too. They were all fighting each other." Megan went to her room and dressed faster than her parents had ever seen. She was about to leave when her mother asked John, "Are we sure it is safe out there?"

"I've been in bad situations," John added, seeing Susan's concern. "If I hadn't spotted dangers, I wouldn't be here. This feels safe. Let me finish my coffee, and then we'll see what happened. Megan, you stick with us."

"What for!"

"We aren't sure what's going on here and if I hadn't been sleepy and stunned by the sudden remodeling, I would have kept Pete here, too."

"It wasn't remodeling, Dad. We've gone back in time," Megan insisted.

John saw his daughter's intensity. "Come on, Megan, that's impossible!"

"Meg, you saw this change before we did, so you can help us figure it out. Stick with Dad and me until we understand what's happening."

The idea she could help appealed to Megan. She sat to eat the last muffin. "If this is anything like last night we won't find an office."

Outside the door, sounds and scents assaulted their senses. From a porch, a merchant's son called out a list of goods just arrived from the docks. As they walked, they winced at strong smells of smoke and horse manure, the reek of sweat, and the stench of urine in the lane beside a tavern. There were as many people on the street as the day before but everything was different.

"Everyone is in period costume," John noted, "Old worn out costumes."

Susan sniffed. "These are smells I sensed yesterday but today it's …"

"Really up our noses, Mom!"

Most people wore faded rough garb: shirts of osnaberg—a fabric as tough as canvas—pants of worn leather, and coarse dresses. Those in carriages wore fine hats, linen shirts, wool trousers, or dresses. Ladies in carriages held handkerchiefs over their noses and mouths against the dust and smells.

John looked up and down the street. "This must be a special program. Why didn't they tell us?"

"A program? Maybe it's a Williamsburg version of *Brigadoon*. The town shows up one day every hundred years. Soon they'll start singing and dancing or…" Megan looked at the ragged people shuffling out of the way of horses and their droppings. "Or, uh, maybe not."

The Sinclairs walked toward the office amidst a rush of strange sights. They arrived at a building they had never seen. Where yesterday there was fresh paint and contrasting trim, they now saw weathered clapboards. Unshaven, unwashed travelers, some with more gaps than teeth, sat on steps near a board scrawled in charcoal: "NO MOR BEDDS TONITE."

John struggled with an impossible conclusion. If he had found himself alone back in time, he would have assumed that post-traumatic stress had snapped him at last. However, his family saw the same things he did. Looking around, he realized there was nobody to talk to about the shower. "We need to sit a moment." They walked away from the crowds to a garden in bloom. John sat on a bench and took a deep breath. "Is this crazy or are we crazy?"

"Are there any other options?" asked Megan. "What flower is this?"

"Those tiny pink and orange flowers are milkweeds, great for attracting butterflies. I think those pretty yellow ones on the stalks are wild indigo."

"Mom, I thought indigo was, like indigo, blue-purple."

"For dye, they used leaves, not flowers. I saw a documentary. They soaked and fermented the leaves then dried the sludge and added lye.

"Hey! Why are we talking about dye? We have a problem!"

"We are getting settled, John. We need to be calm to figure out what to do." She recognized her husband's stress and put her hand on his arm.

"Yes we need to stay calm. Sergeant Sargon used to say, 'Stop, breathe, and get right here, because like it or not, right now we're nowhere else.'" He took a deep breath and exhaled slowly, looking at Susan. "This doesn't feel dangerous, but it's crazy. Megan, you and Peter saw this last night?"

"Yeah. The bathroom was gone. I found better light at a tavern. On the way home, I ran into the Indian chief I met. He told me the man I saw running away hit his head and died. His name was Simon. That wasn't program."

"There must be another explanation. We're in a place full of historical reenactments. I'm going to ask." John walked to the street. Picking out the best-dressed man, he asked, "Excuse me, Sir. Could you tell me the date?"

"Have you just come out of the wilderness? 'Tis May 13th, 1775."

"I was traveling and lost track of time, Sir."

Three men nearby were in a heated discussion. One waved a newspaper to make his point. "'Tis here in *The Gazette*. The British fired at Lexington and killed eight then advanced to Concord. Three hundred militiamen were waiting and opened fire. The Redcoats retreated to Boston fired upon from behind walls mile after mile. Some stopped to loot houses and were shot by farm wives as they filled their satchels. By the time they reached Boston, over seventy were killed and one hundred and seventy wounded. The militia had fifty killed and forty wounded and laid siege to Boston."

"Excuse me," interrupted John. "When did this happen?"

"April 19, 1775, about three weeks ago. The news came on a fast ship before fair winds. Some are calling it the shot heard round the world."

"Thank you, gentlemen." John walked slowly back to the garden.

"Williamsburg, we have a problem. It's May, 13th 1775."

"Cool."

"Not cool. How do we get home from here or from then? In battle, time seemed to slow down. Sometimes there were flashbacks…" John stopped himself. "If this is real, a war is starting. This is a bad time to get hurt."

"Maybe this effect will pass soon, John. Megan and I can look around to learn what's happening. I want to find that troubled woman."

"And I could get first-hand comments for my paper. My teacher may flunk me if I say my sources were interviews with real people in 1775."

John punched his palm with a fist. "Alright—Pete will meet us at noon. We need to get back to our time whether we're imagining this or not. This may be nuts, but let's split up. You two find out what you can and I'll do the same. We'll let each other know at lunch."

"Oh, Dad! With that colonial currency, we're rich. I bought hot chocolate last night for pennies. Dinner for us all will cost less than a dollar. Being in 1775 is not all bad!"

Susan and Megan walked back to Duke of Gloucester Street. "Mom, don't you think I'm old enough to look around on my own?"

Susan gave Megan's hand a squeeze. "Be careful, Honey."

Day 2-2:   Peter Finds Field Hands Planting Tobacco

Peter strode off the stoop and tripped on a brick. Stumbling forward he planted his right foot into freshly dropped horse dung. "Shit!" He looked up and gasped at a team of horses bearing down on him. He jumped back—as the driver pulled hard on the reins to bring the carriage to a stop. The flank of a horse was one step from Peter's face and a large wagon wheel next to his right shoulder.

"Are ye all right?" asked the passenger with a gold-trimmed tricorn hat.

"He's sound, Mister Mercer," the driver grinned, "but he messed his boot."

"Aye, I can see that. Glad ye are unhurt lad. Mind where ye step or ye could be maimed. 'Tis good we were moving slowly."

"Yes, Sir. Sorry," mumbled Peter.

"I have not seen ye before. Your attire is foreign. What is your name?"

"Peter Sinclair."

"Hugh Mercer." The man touched his hat. "Mind ye look both ways when crossing the street." He waved as the carriage pulled away.

Peter took a deep breath. "Good advice at any time."

He wiped his shoe on the grass and hurried to the Powell House. No reenactors welcomed visitors. In the garden, a woman stooped to weed between the rows with a hoe. It was not Evie.

"Excuse me."

"Yes, Sir?" Rosie the cook was startled.

Peter hesitated; a white man asking after a slave woman might arouse suspicion. "Evie asked about laundry soap, and we have it in stock now."

"Evie shoppin' wit' Missus Powell 'til noon." Rosie resumed weeding.

"Is that you, Mister Peter?" Dilli limped to the gate.

"Yes, I've been me since I woke up this morning, Dilli. Is that you?"

Dilli giggled. "I be me, too. I been waitin'. You been gone a week."

"Didn't I see you last night?"

"Mister Peter, you funny. That was a week ago you came by here."

"I'm glad to see you again. Say hello to James and your Mama, Dilli."

Peter was mystified that a week had slipped by. Could Annie explain this? Ramshackle shanties huddled along fence lines. The pasture where he first met Annie was empty but for a pair of tethered sheep.

The air carried scents of blossoms, fresh cut hay, and pipe smoke. The sound of a distant two-handled crosscut saw moving back and forth through a log blended with laughter of children in a garden. Crickets chirped, a bird called, but absent was the hum of fans, lawnmowers, and vehicles, the drone notes of the soundtrack Peter lived by. Now there was space between the sounds. Peter smiled, remembering how Annie paused when he was thinking. She seemed to know his thoughts as if they were part of the conversation. He would follow this path where it led.

He walked out of town toward where he had parted from Augustus. Beyond a pasture where Guernsey cows grazed serenely, the rustic huts of the quarter came into view. Skinny, dusty chickens pecking for bugs in the grass ignored him. "You lookin' for Mister Jack, I s'pose?" called a voice behind the rail fence, where garden greens were past knee high.

"Mister Jack?"

Molly stood from weeding to address this unusual visitor. She had taken off her apron and was in a long dress and yellow head wrap. "He in the fields wit' the gang." She pointed, "Follow yonder road a quarter mile, go right at the fork 'til you see a gang workin'. He'll be there."

Peter was intrigued. The next steps seemed to open up as clearly as a trail marked with chalk on trees. "Look both ways and don't take any reckless risks," he muttered.

He retraced his steps up the road he had run on after the Hush Harbor a week before. Before the woods obscured his view, Peter looked back at the barracks. The buildings were seven yards by five, made from boards nailed to upright posts, chinks pointed with mud and straw to keep the wind at bay. Wooden clay-lined chimneys were separate from the building, so when a chimney fire broke out slaves could pull the chimney away to save their house. Peter shook his head. What a life those slaves endured!

*   *   *   *   *   *   *   *   *

In the barrack a week earlier, the morning after the Hush Harbor, the fires dwindled to warm ash and glowing embers. Outside, the overseer shouted, "Up you get now! Get movin'! We got ourselves a big day."

"One more day 'till Sunday." A voice sounded in the dark barrack. There were coughs, sniffs, and scuffs of callused feet on the dirt floor followed by a burst of light as the first of the five slaves in the hut opened the door.

Augustus opened his eyes. At the foot of his pallet, a box held his simple belongings: a small knife for whittling and skinning, a ball of twine, one brass shoe buckle found by the road, and an osnaberg canvas shirt, not torn like his work shirt. He had won this prized possession in a foot race.

"We don't know what we're doin' today." Robert stretched at the far end of the barrack. "I ain't wearin' my boots to stand in muck."

"I ain't putting no boots in muck, neither," Claudius declared.

"You ain't got none, mister barefoots. I'se goin' for grits while there's grits to get." Robert laughed as he and Claudius jostled at the door. Augustus followed them out.

Jack Read, the overseer, stood next to Molly the cook at the head of the line. Augustus held back. "If he catch me for gettin' back late, no breakfast today," he breathed to himself, trying to look like he was just waking up rather than dragged out from dancing and running. He kept his eyes down but his ears told him there might be nothing to fear.

Jack reminded Molly, "Mister Carter says a special portion of mush and cube of sow belly. You all want to be hardy today. We got work to do."

Confidence rose as Augustus held out his wooden bowl. "Good mornin', Mister Jack. Mornin' Molly."

"Mornin', 'Gustus." Molly plopped a ladle-full of corn mush from the iron pot into his bowl and rapped the edge of the ladle handle on the side of his bowl so the dollop on the back plopped in. She placed a cube of salty bacon fat on top. With a ration of two gallons of corn meal a week and a bit of meat, fat, or fish only three times a week, this was a treat.

"Thank you, Mister Jack. Thank you, Molly." Augustus ambled to the large logs alongside the quarters where the other men sat eating.

"Must be heavy work' today." Robert spoke with a mouthful of corn.

Augustus bit into the bacon fat, eating quickly. He would need strength. They ate breakfast in ten minutes. Augustus swiped two fingers over the bowl and licked them. Jack called out, "Put your bowls away and grab a hoe. We're heading to Partridge Quarter to put tobacco in the ground."

Partridge Quarter was a hike northeast across the York County line. The road passed lands owned by several better-sorts men who were called Gentlemen, not planters. Planters were middle-sorts landowners with few or no slaves. They did the hard physical work of tending fields themselves.

Robert muttered as they walked to the pile of tools Jack had laid out. "It be too late in the season for pullin' up hills."

Claudius was thinking about it too. "Hills was washed out. We got to hoe then plant. This gonna be a hard day."

Up the road trudged five pairs of callused bare feet and four pairs of worn boots. Two men pulled a cart filled with tobacco seedlings from seedbeds, carefully covered in wet burlap to keep the moisture in. Upright sticks protected the shoots from being crushed. The men had

73

ragged shirts and pants torn at the knee. Some wore tattered coats and some had rags around their neck as a scarf. A few stalked opportunity, guarded eyes scanning for any chance to improve the narrow pens of their daily lives. Others were bent, their eyes retaining no light of hope for a better life.

One pair of feet was warm in wool stockings darned at the heels inside boots with brass buckles and thick new soles. Jack Read had a second pair at his cabin, with small silver buckles. He wore them with pride to church and on rare visits to the main plantation house to signal his first step up the ladder of society. He had a better waistcoat for those occasions. He got few such invitations but gentlemen did show favor to their overseers from time to time to motivate these agents of productivity on the plantation.

Jack's britches were fastened at the knee with five buttons a side, each punched from horn and hand-drilled for the thread holes. The oversized hunting shirt kept him warm and his white shirt clean. His tricorn hat would have fallen off his head were he as stooped as the slaves his age, but he carried his head high.

Hoes over shoulders, each slave carried a ball of corn mush wrapped in a rag for lunch. They passed the cornfield Augustus had crossed at dawn and then tobacco fields on the right and woods on the left. The sun was behind a pall of low gray clouds. The damp air clung to their skin.

Tobacco crops had saved the struggling Jamestown Colony 150 years before but tobacco wore out the land after several seasons. Plantation owners accumulated up to ten times as many acres as were under cultivation in tobacco at any one time. The slaves trudged past a patchwork of fields, and a few tracts still forested. There, semi-feral hogs rooted and ate acorns in season and were roasted and eaten themselves. Newly cleared land yielded sweet tobacco. As the soil tired, owners tried to renew the soil with manure. Tobacco from those fields was of a bitter inferior grade.

Augustus followed behind an older slave, a good tactic since an overseer would often yell at the man in front for setting too slow a pace. He looked down and rested as he walked, and did not notice the deer in the woods to the left, alert and ready to leap away from the men on the road. Nor did he notice Mister Jack drop back from the front to walk on his right. The deer suddenly bolted and Augustus looked to his left.

"How ya feelin', 'Gustus?" The words from so close gave him a start.

"Wha? Oh, Mister Jack. Sorry, Mister Jack, I… I didn't see you."

"This morning when I stepped out of my cottage, I saw someone run across the field to the barrack. Did you see anybody before rising time?"

"Uh, no suh, Mister Jack."

74

"Maybe it was just a dream about a fast black buck and a young white buck running next to the road through the corn stubble."

Augustus became very worried.

"I thought it was a dream, but walking by the field, I saw two sets of footprints. One set led to the quarter and the other followed the road to town. So maybe 'twasn't no dream at all. But 'twas not light enough to see clearly who they was. How long have you been at this quarter?"

"'Bout twelve years, Mister Jack."

"How long has it been since you had any kind of trouble, 'Gustus?"

"Well, I got a bad croup last winter and that infected foot a while back,"

"Did you ever need a whippin'? I don't recall givin' you one."

Augustus felt the threat. "Oh, no suh, Mister Jack, I does what I s'posed to do, and I don't do what I ain't s'posed to do." He tried not to show fear but he began to sweat. Last year he and other slaves were forced to witness a slave get a savage whipping from an overseer at a nearby quarter. Tiny knots at the tip of the lash tore the man's back open and he screamed and bled until he fainted. Augustus threw up in the trees when it was over.

"I suppose runnin' to the quarter ain't as bad as runnin away from it."

"No, suh. You want me to ask around to find out who might have been runnin' in the dark wit' the son of a gentleman?" His voice was too shaky.

"A young gentleman eh? No 'Gustus, Nobody will tell anything but stories. People make up stories when they think they are in trouble."

"Yessuh."

"'Gustus, we got to hoe up hills to get plants in the ground before a rain comes." He looked at the overcast sky. "We'll pray the rains ain't heavy."

"Yes, suh."

"I need the boys to work hard today and no leanin' on the hoes, you hear? I need a strong boy to stay out front and help me keep everybody moving. If we get all the hills planted, I could forget that dream I had. What do you think 'Gustus?"

"We gonna work strong, Mister Jack. Pork belly will keep us hoppin'."

"That's good, 'Gustus. I brought more and if the work is done well I can cut off a piece for every man here to have with his corn at mid-day."

Jack moved to the head of the column moving up the road. "Step quicker now," he barked. "We ain't carrying a casket! Not today."

Augustus let out a slow breath. "Ran into a snare and out again wit'out gettin' skinned," he murmured.

The slaves and their overseer were on a long hike before starting work. As he walked barefoot, Augustus thought about the long loop of the seasons. In February, he had shivered as he sowed tobacco seeds in beds hoed, raked, and picked free of stones. When the seedbeds were threatened by night frost, slaves covered them with straw. The straw was pulled back by day to give sun to the seedlings.

In spring, fields were prepared for transplanting seedlings and for planting corn and wheat. Wheat was planted in rows, tobacco and corn in mounds a yard apart for drainage. Large plantations had thousands of mounds, hoed, raked, and planted by slaves. The backbone of the plantation economy was a multitude of backbones, stooped in servitude. The gentry saw slave labor as the key to prosperity. Each good field hand could work five acres. This gang could raise over forty acres of tobacco.

Augustus did not look forward to May when tobacco seedlings were transplanted from seedbeds to waiting mounds. He recalled the never-ending strain on his back, bending over the hills to make holes with a stick, inserting a seedling, and filling the hole. He did not look up at the other men or women with mud caked past their knees, streaking their faces, and matting their hair. They would wipe their eyes with the backs of their arms, spit grit, and keep their heads bent, from early morning to sunset as the ache of muscles increased through the day. The owners had learned to give them water to avoid fainting or worse from dehydration.

Augustus preferred planting corn. He stuck the pointer finger of his left hand into the earth to his second knuckle to set a constant depth, made a design of holes, and dropped a kernel into each hole patting it shut. He was the fastest planter in the quarter, which partly explained the lack of whip scars on his back. Even when he felt sad or angry, planting corn brought him peace.

He carried a piece of canvas to kneel on to reduce the pain of hours of stooping. He focused on the pattern of holes and the rhythm of dropping a seed in each hole. When two dropped, he would say, "Friends," pat the hole shut and keep planting. He knew how big a handful of seed to grab from the hemp bag tied at his waist to go quickly without spilling. He recalled the preacher reading, "As ye sow, so shall ye reap." As he put seeds in the ground, knowing corn would come made him happy. Sometimes he had nothing on his mind but the smell of soil. Planting corn made him feel at home and this was the only home he knew.

Augustus saw the owner and overseers watch the fields like hawks hunting mice. What they saw determined the slaves' tasks six days a week, nine to twelve hours a day. If they spotted an attack of the tobacco fly, the slaves would rush to cover the plants with straw until the danger passed. Heavy rains brought orders to dig drainage ditches and replant washed out hills. Drier weather brought weeds the slaves would hoe or pull.

If rains were right and worms scarce, Augustus found the hot days of summer less grueling. Slaves girdled trees or cleaned tobacco and horse barns. In a drought there was little to do but hear the planters pray for rain and complain the rest of the time. In church when the preacher prayed, "Give us this day our daily bread," Augustus pictured abundant yellow corn bread. He believed the easier days of August, with the varied work of mending fences, hauling firewood, and walking fields looking for worms and not finding any, were a gift in the month that carried his name.

When worms were spotted, the field gang stooped all day, picking caterpillars off tobacco leaves and crushing them between thumb and fingers. It was easier to lie on the ground to spot worms under the lower leaves. When slaves were lying down, they had to put the worms in a canvas bag to show they were not resting.

In late August, slaves cut tobacco. They chopped stalks with a half a dozen leaves each and left them to wilt in the sun. Then the stalks were carted to tobacco houses, placed on long stakes, and hung high in the beams. While tobacco dried, slaves harvested corn. It was stored in cribs with gaps between the boards where breezes passed through to dry the corn for grinding. Augustus enjoyed husking in a circle with the others. They chewed on corn kernels so they were never hungry those days.

The slaves planted rye, barley, and wheat. After first frost, another burst of work occurred as tobacco was covered to "sweat" or ferment the leaves. The stalks were stripped and women tied leaves in bundles or "hands." These were prized, which meant packed into hogsheads in presses weighted by stones to squeeze more tobacco into the four-foot barrels. Fully prized, a hogshead weighed half a ton. Overseers gave meat or coins to slaves to prize barrels all night in an excited, exhausting rush when a ship was due at the wharf. The seductive smell of tobacco that Augustus liked on his fingers was the fragrance of prosperity to his owners. To a few slaves, the extra rewards of packing tobacco provided a scent of freedom.

The men skirted a swamp to arrive at Partridge Quarter. Dead trees girdled the previous year stood in the field, lower branches stripped for firewood and the rest reaching out gnarled fingers on blackened dead limbs, foreboding silhouettes against the cool slate sky.

Jack stepped into the field. "Listen well, boys! The rains washed these hills out bad. We'll hoe them up then plant seedlings. Leave the pebbles on the sides of the hills. We ain't got many big stones, but if you find any, throw them into piles carefully. Don't knock each other senseless. Some of you ain't got sense to spare. We'll start here… here… and here." Jack dug his heel into the soil of the first three hills then he pointed. "Work up that rise. Hoe them fine but hoe them fast. Show 'em what I mean, 'Gustus."

"Yessuh!" Augustus stepped to the nearest heel mark and swung the blade of the hoe down through the cover of twigs and leaves blown in from the woods. The hoe imbedded itself into the earth with a thunk. He pulled the clod of earth over, and as it fell from the hoe, he swung the hoe up and hurled the blade down into the earth again a hand-span to the left. He pulled each clod toward him, bending to toss a large twig to the side.

"'Gustus showed you how. Now, show me you saw what he did!" The slaves moved to the hills and began to hoe. Jack assigned Robert to separate the seedlings. "Don't poke each other with the hoe handles. I don't want nobody hurt. Poke enough to stay awake!" Jack laughed and watched the quick movements aimed to impress. "Settle down, boys. Keep it smooth and steady so you last all day. How about a song, Claudius?"

Claudius began. "Hmm, hah! Hmm, Ho! Lord, show me the way. Hmm, hah! Hmm, yes! Lord, show me today." The 'Hmm' on the upswing and 'Hah' on the downswing to chop the earth masked the groans of toil. 'Hmm, Ho!' was for pulling the clod of earth over and the melodic prayer line marked a momentary rest after the pull. Other men joined in, first in unison, then branching into harmonies and syncopation. Claudius sang to help men find a flow and to ignore sore muscles and blisters. Sometimes the songs passed on messages or stories the overseer did not understand.

Jack walked to a stump and sat to load his pipe. A peaceful smoke was a morning ritual. He was far enough away to see the slaves and appear to be paying attention. No slave dared look at his eyes closely enough to know.

Augustus sang along. When the soil was chopped, he pulled the hoe back and forth to flatten the hill and made cuts for the seedlings Robert brought. He placed a seedling in each cut and patted it closed. He stepped up the rise two paces to the next mound and began again with a swing of the hoe. "Hmm, Hah!" His legs ached already. It would be a long hard day and a long hard summer. He moved with the hoe and the soil and the song. He would sleep tonight.

    *   *   *   *   *   *   *   *

A week later, Peter heard singing as he approached. He slowed his walk when he saw the slaves. He witnessed how hard the men worked, stooped under the gaze of a white man sitting on a stump smoking a pipe. He figured the white man must be Jack the overseer and decided to stick to his story of being a trader from a northern colony. Peter boldly walked into the field toward the overseer. As he got close, he recognized Augustus, Claudius, and Robert at work, but knew he could not speak to them.

"Hello Mister Jack. Someone told me I could find you here."

"Hallo." The overseer took off his hat assuming from Peter's confidence and strange but fine clothing he was at least middle-sorts, perhaps better-sorts, but certainly a strange sort.

"I'm Peter Sinclair." He extended his hand. "We don't grow tobacco up north, but we enjoy a pipe of sweet Virginia now and again."

"Jack Read." The overseer chuckled with pride and shook Peter's hand.

"I came out to see that miracle of Virginia tobacco done well."

"No trouble, Mister Peter." Jack smiled. "Today they are cleanin' up them hills around the young tobacco plants." Enjoying Peter's interest, he explained the cycle of how tobacco is sown, grown, cut, cured, packed, and the barrels pulled down the rolling roads to the docks. Barrels were hitched to a horse and rolled like a giant wheel.

"Those are fine field hands. How would I buy two for my farm?"

"Slaves are mighty expensive and these ain't for sale. There are auctions and you can buy what's on the block. You can buy them in Williamsburg or go to a port like Norfolk or Alexandria and buy them at the ship for less money. But those don't speak English and sometimes they get sick and die before you can say 'wasted money.' You could make an arrangement with an owner, but that could be more expensive I reckon."

"Why more expensive?"

"A rich man might like money, don't you think? He might name a high price as if they are good slaves and they might be or they might not. He would know which, but you wouldn't."

Peter smiled at the bargaining advice. "How much does a slave cost?"

"A slave costs from twenty-five to one hundred pounds sterling depending on age and skill. That is more than I earn in several years. For these good field hands without a trade, you might pay forty pounds for the young ones, and twenty-five for the older ones, who have less time left to work. Slaves cost much more than virgin land to the west where I hope to buy someday. Even if you have money to buy a slave, you have to feed him, give him blankets and heavy shirts so he don't freeze to death on you, and you have him build himself a quarter. You give him boards, nails, and the time to do it. All that costs money, too, and I don't have any."

"What if I need a cook or say, a laundress, how much would that cost?"

"A good cook costs more than a field hand but less than a man skilled in wood or brick. A laundress, who could keep you alive with her cooking, could cost 30 pounds. A pretty wench costs more. 'Tis, easier to get her bred and increase your slaves." He winked and did not notice Peter wince.

Talking about people as property was distasteful but Peter needed information so he pressed on. "Some Africans are free. Can we hire one?"

"Yes. When Master Carter has work like fancy plaster for the parlor or new windows, the work is done by an undertaker with a gang of men under hire. Some are free black men or slaves hired from others. One African joiner had his own slave working with him on a window job."

Jack pulled on his pipe and they fell silent and watched the slaves put tobacco plants into the hills making slow, steady progress, singing in syncopation and harmony. Peter hummed a few notes along with the gang and Jack looked at him, surprised.

"Catchy tune, isn't it, Jack?"

"They can have their ways as long as they get the work done."

Augustus saw the young white man who had run with him last week talking with Jack Read. "I wonder what they talkin' 'bout." Augustus was grateful that today was Saturday and he had heard that tonight Jack would bring them home early so he could clean up and put on his good waistcoat and shoes with silver buckles for dinner with the better sorts.

"By the way, I heard an African woman named Annie comes 'round these parts. Do you know her?" Peter asked.

"I heard of her. She cheered up some of our slaves when they was dejected. Some slaves kill themselves when they get like that. She is a kind of preacher. Like I said, they can have their ways if they get the work done. She don't cause harm nor stir them up or nothin'."

"Good to meet you, Jack. I must get back to town now."

"Mister Peter, you could get sunstroke wanderin' around with no hat."

"Good idea. I'll get a hat." Peter started down the road thinking about the irony of an overseer with a touch of sympathy for dejected slaves and strangers without hats. He watched Augustus working as he passed.

Day 2-3:   John is Amazed at the Raleigh Tavern

John felt urgency to solve their "time-zone problem" but had no idea where to look. He pushed past men arguing on the stoop of Wetherburn's Tavern and entered a room filled with loud voices, smoke, and more men than chairs. Some stood with bread and coffee or beer. Those who had a coin to spare breakfasted on a meat pie or bowl of stew. A sudden cheer came from a table near the back where a roll of the dice had just changed one man's month for the better and made this a dark morning for three others.

Seeing no spare seats John threaded his way through the crowd, barely avoiding beer spilling on him when a serving girl swerved to avoid the intrusive hand of a drunken patron. Men slept upstairs, several to a bed or on the floor. A few had splashed water on their faces but none washed to the standard John was used to even when camped in a jungle or desert. He heard threads of conversation as he made his way through the crowd.

"We may soon see if ye stay calm enough to shoot a bright red coat as well as you shoot a squirrel. Unlike squirrels, Redcoats shoot back at thee."

"Tobacco prices are down at the Liverpool docks, I canna offer ye more."

John looked for breathing room and saw space by the window. He was taller than most in the room so he could scan without obstruction.

"Here's a toast to Liberty, Wilkes, and the 45!" Even at ten-thirty in the morning, twenty men stood and raised their glasses.

"There's a rumor the King will offer George Washington a title and lands in England. He is so ambitious I wager he will take the bait. That would dampen the firebrands among us."

"Washington does not need a fiefdom from the King. He has lands aplenty here in Virginia, and some say he has much more land west of the Proclamation line."

"No one heeds that Proclamation of '63 or the Importation Agreement. The lucre from tobacco shipments brings fine china to tables and a fine lining for pockets! Imports have risen during this non-Importation Agreement. It is an agreement few wish to keep."

"We sent petitions to the King. Some towns are casting lead statues of His Majesty to honor him in hope he comes to his senses and ignores the bad counsel of his governors."

"We might have to use the lead to make musket balls. Those royal statues may melt away."

John felt dizzy. He disliked crowded noisy bars, even after a beer on a Friday night, and this was cold sober in the morning. He left the tavern and crossed the street to a bench. His mind was full of questions: If we considered ourselves Englishmen and had friends in Parliament, why did we fight a war? Why did we get into the wars I fought?

He noticed he was sitting near the Raleigh Tavern and went in. It was cleaner and less crowded than Wetherburn's Tavern. In the large Apollo Room, he found an empty table in the rear corner and ordered a cup of coffee. Five men near him were playing a game of cards for high stakes, but they were more refined and quieter than their compatriots were across the street.

Suddenly a hush swept over the patrons as a trio of men walked across the room. Patrons whispered. All eyes were on the young men taking seats at the vacant table next to John. One of the men was six feet tall and had a long face and prominent forehead. He wore an ill-fitting brown wig tied at the nape of his neck with a brown ribbon, his auburn widow's peak showing. The second man was taller, John's height, and boney. He wore no wig, and with his freckles and red hair tied back, he would stand out in any crowd. The third man was not much older than Peter.

A man stood and doffed his hat, "Good morning, Mister Jefferson, Mister Henry," giving a respectful bow. "I thought this morning would find you in Philadelphia."

Patrick Henry pushed his spectacles to the top of his head, almost dislodging his wig. "You are correct. The Continental Congress began a few days ago. I depart after this farewell breakfast with my friends."

"Will we have a war, Sir?" called out a man at a nearby table.

Burgess Henry stood to reply. "The distinctions between Virginians, Pennsylvanians, New Yorkers, and New Englanders are no more. I am not a Virginian, but an American! So, Sir, we have no election. It is now too late to retire from the contest. There is no retreat but in submission and slavery! Our chains are forged! Their clanking may be heard on the plains of Boston! The war is inevitable and let it come!"

"Just so!" called out a vestryman. "We were not subdued by unjust taxes. Nor do we accept port closure or giving land to Catholic Quebec."

"What about the Olive Branch Petition to the King?" asked another.

"It is natural to indulge in the illusions of hope," Henry replied. "We are apt to shut our eyes against a painful truth and listen to the song of that siren. Is this the part of wise men, engaged in a great and arduous struggle for liberty? Are we disposed to be those who, having eyes, see not, and having ears, hear not, the things which so nearly concern their temporal salvation? For my part, whatever anguish of spirit it may cost, I am willing to know the whole truth, to know the worst, and to provide for it."

Men in the tavern applauded. John recognized some of Henry's words.

"William Pitt told parliament that the colonies are 'equally entitled to all the natural rights of mankind and the particular privileges of Englishmen'. No man in Britain would lay down his rights or liberty voluntarily or under duress. Then should we, gentlemen?"

"No!" called out a dozen men in chorus.

"A year ago, Burgess Jefferson and I, and ninety others met in this room when Governor Dunmore suspended the House of Burgesses. We planned a Day of Prayer and Fasting to protest closing the Port of Boston. We resolved to call other colonies to meet in general congress, at such place annually as shall be thought convenient, there to deliberate on those measures which the united interests of America may require.' The place chosen was Philadelphia in the midst of the colonies from north to south. The Continental Congress is now a reality, so no one should doubt our capacity to triumph in our cause!"

"Huzzah for Patrick Henry!"

"Have you heard Pitt's words to Parliament four months ago?" Henry asked without losing his rhythm. "Lord Chatham, to use his title, addressed the Ministers, 'The whole of your political conduct has been one continued series of weakness, temerity, despotism, ignorance, futility, negligence, blundering, and the most notorious servility, incapacity, and corruption!'" Patrick Henry paused and looked around the room. "Now why did he not come forth and say openly what he thought of the ministers and their policies?"

The roomful of men, including John, laughed.

Patrick Henry pulled a folded paper from his vest pocket and opened it. "A few days later when Parliament decided to send more troops against us, Liberty's friend, John Wilkes…"

"You mean our libertine friend?" called out a regular patron.

Henry laughed. "Indeed. Wilkes admits he uses his sense of humor to befriend as many women as are willing to tolerate his homely face. In order not to have anyone mistake his words for mine, and hang me for it, I will read his words to Parliament received in a letter."

"In the great scale of empire, you will decline, I fear, from the decision of this day; and the Americans will rise to independence, to power, to all the greatness of the most renowned states, for they build on the solid basis of general public liberty."

"These words of Wilkes resound with truth. Thank you, Gentlemen."

The men in the Apollo Room cheered. "Huzzah for Patrick Henry!"

83

"May we hear from Burgess Jefferson?" asked a portly man in an expensive wig.

Thomas Jefferson stood, obviously uncomfortable to be called upon. He kept both hands on the table, causing him to look stooped. When he spoke, all but those near his table strained to hear him. John could scarcely believe he was seeing young Thomas Jefferson—just over thirty.

"Other business keeps me from departing for the Congress until June." He stopped, as if looking for something else to say. "With regard to the adversity in Boston, I agree with Burgess Henry. The spirit of resistance to government is so valuable on certain occasions that I wish it to be always kept alive. It will often be exercised when wrong, but better so than not to be exercised at all. What country can preserve its liberties if its rulers are not warned from time to time that their people preserve the spirit of resistance? There will be differing views. I say in matters of style, swim with the current; in matters of principle, stand like a rock."

"Huzzah for Thomas Jefferson!"

"I shall present my friend and neighbor from the Piedmont who serves on the Committee of Safety for Orange County, Virginia, Mister James Madison. I believe he will contribute to the governance of our country some day." Madison, at twenty-four, hoping his wig made him look older, stood and nodded to the patrons of the tavern as Jefferson quickly sat down.

"What say you of Congress, Mister Madison?" called out a militia officer.

"If men were angels," Madison responded, "no government would be necessary. If angels were to govern men, no controls on government would be necessary. In framing a government, which is to be administered by men over men, the great difficulty lies in this: you must first enable the government to control the governed, and in the next place oblige it to control itself. A dependence on the people is, no doubt, the primary control on the government, but experience has taught mankind the necessity of auxiliary precautions."

Patrick Henry applauded. "If our struggle for liberty takes us on an independent path from Britain, perhaps Burgess Jefferson's friend, Mister Madison could write a Constitution."

John was sure that he had read some of those words of Henry, Jefferson, and Madison in school. If I ever get home, who will believe that I actually heard them say those things in a tavern before they included them in speeches, he wondered. Would I dare to tell anyone?

Day 2-4: Susan Gets a Coiffure and an Earful

"You are here to sell your hair? Do you speak English, Meine Frau?"

Susan nodded, somewhat puzzled.

"Did you come to sell those long lovely auburn locks? I can give a fair price. We have gentlemen customers who can afford a wig made from human hair. I know a lawyer with auburn hair who wears a brown poorly-fitting wig. I might be able to persuade him to invest if I had your tresses to work with." The wig maker was a petite, prim, middle-aged woman.

"No Madam, but if I ever cut it short, making a wig is a wonderful idea."

"Terribly sorry, Missus, I mistook you for a new arrival. You never know what those Germans, Swedes, or Dutch will be wearing. They often have no funds to begin their new life and the women folk sell their hair. But your fine speech shows that you are a lady of the better-sorts."

"Please forgive my clothes... uh, for the voyage. I'll soon buy something more appropriate. I'm a middle-sorts wife—no need to be deferential."

"If you would like hair dressing, we are happy to serve you. My husband imports perfumes and soaps we can offer you. Most of our goods are not from England, so we are not interrupted by the non-importations agreement, which we ardently support, of course."

"Of course you do. We all do!" a woman in a chair joked as her hair was being powdered with a product rowed ashore by Dutch smugglers.

"Are you going to the Governor's Ball tonight?" asked the wig maker.

"Governor's Ball?"

"The woman in the chair explained, "Even with rumblings of war, there remains a place for social graces. I hope higher culture will prod men loyal to the King and supporters of the Congress to settle their differences, rather than scrap like wicked schoolboys. The ball may be the idea of Lady Dunmore, the Governor's wife, who wishes the stubborn men of all sides to take the pot off the fire before it boils over."

"Hush, Amanda. You may offend the lady."

"I'm not offended," Susan assured them. "Like you, I'm troubled our leaders resort to war when war is usually worse than what provoked the fighting. We proudly wave flags and pray for victory. Our enemies do the same thing to their people. On both sides, people get rich selling arms. We fight for years, and many people die. Oh, sorry! I made a speech."

"You speak well. Are you a preacher's wife?" asked the wig maker.

"No, my husband is not a religious man."

"Madam, if you wish us to dress your hair for the ball, we can help you now. We have promised the time this afternoon to several ladies."

Susan chose to go to the ball on the spot. "That will be lovely."

"I can give you delightful ringlets with your beautiful hair. May I ask your name? My husband likes me to put the first letter of the customer's name in the book."

"I'm Susan. I can write the whole word if you like." She printed her name imitating the lettering the wig maker used for the initials.

"The name Susan reminds me of sunshine," said the woman in the chair.

"The name has been in my family for a long time."

"My daughter is expecting her second child. I won't be an interfering grandmother but if it is a girl I shall gently insist she name her Susan."

"I overheard you called Amanda, a lovely name. May I call you that?"

"As prisoners here, we should use our personal names." Then Amanda asked the wig maker, "Can you extend my respite away from the house?"

The wig maker laughed and peeked at her book. "Most days, you could linger, but Missus Byrd is next. She insists upon being prompt."

"By what name might I call you, Madam?" Susan asked the wig maker.

"She is Charlotte, like our Queen," Amanda said.

"My husband is George, like the King. We are the not-royal couple."

"Charlotte, speaking of the Queen, have you seen a print of her portrait?" Amanda lowered her voice. "Some say she is an octoroon and the portrait makes plain her African features from her connection to black lines of Portuguese royalty. Others say her painter is an abolitionist and the image promotes an end to slavery. 'Tis three years since slaves were set free in England."

"Were there troubles when the slaves were freed?" Susan asked.

"None. They became servants and got wages and that was that."

"Perhaps slave owners here fear violence because they know in their hearts that slavery is wrong . . ." Susan caught herself and stopped.

"I hope you are not an abolitionist," declared Amanda. "I remind you that slavery is still legal in the Colonies and the British slave trade is thriving. We own but one slave and treat him well. If we set Caesar out, where would he go? We don't confine him yet he chooses to stay with us."

Susan forced herself to repress the urge to counter what to her were outrageous ideas. She did not want to provoke an argument.

Not meeting resistance, Amanda admitted, "We made it through hard years without slaves and we have only one now. At prayer meetings, Africans are among us singing hymns. It no longer seems quite right to own another soul in bondage for their whole life."

"But Amanda, you have other servants in bondage."

"Yes, our servants are Scots. Ethan is free now, gets wages, and has a small cottage with a glass window. Mattie has time left on her bond and cooks and washes at our house. They have clean, warm beds, we feed them well, and when they have paid off the sum we gave for their contracts, we give them money so they can start out on their own. Mattie may continue working with us for a wage, maybe to marry Ethan."

Amanda continued, "I try to live as a Christian each day, not just on Sunday. My parents suffered hard lives under a selfish master and both died when I was fourteen. I worked to feed myself until my husband married me on my seventeenth birthday. Knowing what unkindness feels like, I want to be kind. Perhaps we should begin to pay Caesar a small wage and give him manumission when we pass on."

It was almost impossible for her not to comment, so Susan changed the subject. "Do you both go to Bruton Parish Church?"

The women looked at each other and Charlotte shrugged, "Amanda and I differ on religion. I attend Bruton Parish Church every Sunday."

"My husband and I come once a month to town." Amanda explained. "We shall go to Bruton Parish Church tomorrow. We have friends there like Charlotte and her husband but we draw spiritual sustenance from the Presbyterian Meeting House. We obey the law. Our minister has a license to preach given to him at the Williamsburg courthouse."

"Amanda and I agree on many points. 'Tis wrenching to see families torn asunder and preachers beaten and jailed. Not all preachers are sincere and some are deluded. A man was brought to the gaol for preaching without a license. His wife sits outside the gaol crying because she has naught to give him."

"What about those who practice no religion?" Susan asked.

"Without redemption they are doomed to perdition. I do not take it upon myself to judge their blindness. They are in God's hands," Amanda pronounced. "Charlotte and I disagree yet we are friends. Men seem feeble on that point, because they have not been mothers. What Church do you attend, Susan?"

Susan, not a churchgoer, thought a moment. "I believe in tolerance and trusting the wisdom of Spirit to beckon us all to the Divine on the path that is best for us."

"You are not a preacher's wife, but you have heard many sermons."

"Yes, but my path is a personal one. I support giving space to everyone."

The women looked puzzled. "You are not a Quaker?" asked Amanda.

"No, I'm not. I think we should give everyone an opportunity to find inspiration meaningful for them." She decided the less said the better.

The women sat quietly as Charlotte and her helper worked. Amanda took her leave. Charlotte held up a hand mirror for Susan to see the hair piled above her head and the ringlets beside her face and on her neck.

"I like it very much. My husband will be surprised. How much is it?"

"I'm afraid our costs have gone up. It is ten pence without the powder."

Susan pulled out a small bill of colonial currency. "Can you take this?"

Charlotte looked at the bill. "Yes, we were paid in ready money for a wig this morning. She counted out the change carefully, checking twice, and wrote the total in the book, slowly, one digit at a time, biting her lower lip. "There!" She exhaled after the effort.

"Thank you, Charlotte. Will I see you at the ball?"

"Yes, this is my first ball. There has been no ball at the Palace for months, and until recently, my husband and I were too poor to be invited."

The door opened and Missus Byrd glided into the shop.

Susan walked slowly looking into faces of people in the street. Each had a story, a struggle. She wondered if any were her ancestors. Perhaps her hair had been styled next to a relative.

Entering the Prentis Store, Susan gazed at felt hats, baskets, wooden mugs, weights to close garden gates, flasks, and fringed hunting shirts of coarse blue-green osnaberg. There were whale products from New England: whale oil for lamps, candles made of spermaceti, a wax from the head cavity of whales, strips of whalebone for corset stays, and ambergris to retard evaporation of perfumes. At the back of the store, she eyed women's clothing. Next to a rack, two women spoke about the man in the gaol for preaching without a license. She recognized one as Missus Powell. A slave woman stood behind them, well practiced in being non-intrusive.

Susan looked over the dresses and picked a pink one she liked for everyday wear but saw nothing for the Governor's Ball. Then it occurred to her that if they were stuck there for a while, she should get something for John and Peter so they would fit in better. She looked at men's clothing and picked out hats and hunting shirts.

Loaded down with packages, incongruous for a woman with such elegant hair, Susan made her way down the street toward the Capitol and home. "Hi Mom!" Megan appeared from a shop door. "Wow! What... an amazing hairdo! Are you going to the Academy Awards tonight?"

"I'm going to the Governor's Ball tonight and got my hair done. I have tickets for your dad and me. I thought you'd prefer not to go. I've done some serious shopping following your example of dressing to fit the times. You always told me I was living in the past."

"I had no idea you were so good at it. May I help carry those packages?"

"That would be nice, Honey. There is another favor I would like to ask."

"I'll do anything short of actual help."

"I'm hunting for a bargain on a gown and I have a hunch where to look. Would you buy lunch and meet us at the house. I'll give you the money."

"That will be fun. Let me treat with the colonial currency Dad gave me."

"I'm glad I had children." Susan hugged Megan and hurried to the milliner shop. There in the window crossed-legged on his board was the bushy-browed tailor. She was excited to see him and tapped the window. He waved back and she entered.

"Hello again. I'm happy to find you in."

"You might find me here at any time." The tailor had a knowing look. "In the high season we are open seven days a week."

"Good. I have a problem and I hope you can help me. I'm going to the Governor's Ball."

"That does not seem like a grave problem, Madam."

"The problem is I need a dress and I remembered you were working on a gown to wear at a ball. Is that gown already promised to someone?"

"No one has come forward as yet. Perhaps, Madam, I was working on that gown for you. It is not completely finished so if you would like it, you may try it on for a final fitting and I can have a perfect fit ready for you in about five hours. Would you like the mantua to wear against the brisk evening air and stun the overly proud ladies of the large estates?"

"Oh, that beautiful cape with the embroidered trim! I can't afford it." She stopped as the tailor smiled. "Oh. Last time I was here you said if I had come in 1775, the mantua would cost a few pounds."

"I did — six pounds to be exact. It is waiting for the perfect customer."

"I'll take the gown and the mantua. I have money of several countries."

"Rather inconvenient how the British increase our dependence on them by forbidding us to have our own currency and limiting the supply of theirs to a trickle. It makes commerce difficult and ingenuity inevitable."

"I agree and I have a question for you."

"I am a tailor and do not know physics or time and the like."

"My question is, what is your name? I am Susan Sinclair."

"Ha! 'Tis my turn to be surprised. I find my name embarrassing."

"Why embarrassing?"

"Alwyn means 'friend to the elves.' I was short and children teased me. Taylor means tailor. It seems my height and my trade were preordained."

"Alwyn Taylor is a charming name. Speaking of charm, I have another question. Since you became a tailor as a result of your last name, did you become a friend to the elves because of your first?"

"Susan. I have yet to meet my first elf, assuming you are not a tall one. You could be a tall elf. It is a rare thing to meet a customer at this time."

Susan smiled. The tailor was mum about the mystery of being in the past, and probably did not know how it worked. Nevertheless, it was a relief to know that she had seen him in her time and now in the colonial era and he was clearly enjoying it.

Alwyn smiled. "I'll take a break from being the window dressing to alter the gown for you." He measured Susan and then marked the gown with a chip of soap and pinned the fabric, which he called tissue, in a score of places. "I'll have it ready at five."

"In what year?" joked Susan.

"Today, in time for the ball, I promise."

"Alwyn, I have another problem."

"Oh dear, Madam Susan, you certainly seem beset with them today."

"Yes, it's been dreadful! This time it's my shoes."

The tailor looked down. "Ah yes, verily you have an acute problem there but providentially one that has a ready solution. Three blocks down is a shoemaker's shop. Alas, George Wilson died last fall, but Elias, his Scots-Irish journeyman and a capable cobbler, bought the shop from George's widow. Tell him I sent you."

"Thank you Alwyn. Goodbye until this afternoon."

"God be with you, too."

"I forgot goodbye means that."

Day 2-5:   Megan Roams the Market

As Megan approached Market Square, her thoughts turned to Mark the blacksmith. She expected he was getting ready to escape again and guessed Standing Elk would help him. She veered suddenly to avoid walking headlong into a man carrying a wooden crate of fresh eggs. Dodging him, she collided into a woman holding a leather pail half-full of fresh milk. The woman cried out in surprise and dropped the pail splashing milk on their dresses and the pants of the man carrying the eggs.

"I'm sorry!" Megan squatted to grab the pail before it was completely empty, saving a ladle or two of the milk. "I was not paying attention."

The woman looked stricken. "Oh, I spilt the milk! My children hav'na had a cup for days. My husband just spent six days cutting firewood to get money. He will be displeased."

"Your kids are hungry?" Megan had to do something. "Sorry, it was my fault. Let's go back to where you bought the milk and buy more."

"But my last coin was spent on wilted vegetables."

"I'll buy the milk. I bumped into you. I have coins."

"But your dress, Madam and your pants, Sir..."

"We'll give them a rinse," the man assured her. "Don't worry, Missus. 'Tis kind of the lady to buy milk for you. How many children have ye?"

"We've three, Sir, three living."

"My hands are full but Missy please take six eggs for the Missus, one each for her husband, herself, and the children, and one for the pan."

"Oh, no, I couldn't, Sir!"

"Missus, it will take me more than six eggs to repay the miracle of my angel mother feeding my brother and me in a hut after our pa was killed. Please accept and help me happily make this payment on my debt."

"God bless you, Sir. You are a kind of angel yourself."

Megan carefully put eggs into the woman's basket.

"I must be off to the inn, and Missus, we are not stealing eggs. My master told me to buy a shillings worth. I bargained for a dozen extra. My master will get half a dozen more and will be happy. Farewell, ladies."

Megan took the woman's arm and they pressed into the dense crowd in Market Square. Holding tightly to keep from being separated, she muttered, "Did absolutely everybody forget their deodorant this morning? Somebody ought to tell them to wash!"

The market ran every day but Sundays and holy days. Live sheep, pigs, and cows were tethered to stakes, chickens and ducks squawked from baskets as hawkers shouted. Slaughtered animals hung from tripods — quarters of beef, sheep, and pigs. Megan was revolted by flies gathering to drink at the bloody spots until vendors waved them away. Plucked chickens hung by their feet, heads swinging. Live oysters from Chesapeake Bay, dried fish, fresh fish, and, by the odor, not-so-fresh fish, wrinkled carrots, potatoes, and beets stored all winter in root cellars were piled on rough tables. Eggs that had been carried in boxes of sand to keep from breaking over rough roads were neatly stacked.

They came to a stall where milk was ladled into whatever container the customers brought. Megan greeted the dairywoman. "We had an accident and I would like to buy more milk for this woman."

"I remember you, Ma'am. Seven ladles wasn't it?"

To Megan, prices were low and she could help this woman and her family for pennies. "There are still about two ladles in there — let's buy another seven ladles to give her more."

"Let us make it eight for the price of six. She has hungry ones at home."

Megan surveyed the goods on the table. "Very kind of you, Madam. I'll buy her some butter and cheese curds. She will be making eggs."

The poor woman showed surprise. "Bless you both for your kindness."

"I shall tie a piece of twine tight around the neck of the leather bag using a slip knot you can easily undo," the dairy woman offered. "If the pail falls again you won't lose the milk."

Megan thought about lunch. "I'd like two packets of the cheese myself. There will be three hungry mouths to feed at my house."

"Remarkable for one so young," the dairy woman marveled.

"Yes, I'm young. And even more remarkable, those hungry mouths are older than I am. This is lunch for my mother, father, and brother."

A smile found its way to the thin woman's face. "You are a kind daughter."

Megan paid for the milk and cheese and walked the woman to the edge of the market. Getting over her aversion to the crowds, noise, and smells, she looked closer at the faces of the sellers and buyers. "Are you and your husband bonded servants?" she asked the woman who still held her arm.

"No. I wish we could find a station having shelter and food we could rely on."

"How did you get to the Virginia Colony?"

"I was born here. My Ma died at my birth and Pa died when I was fourteen. He finished his servitude, but had no luck as a planter. My man, I should not say but you are kind, came to North Carolina as a prisoner at fifteen for stealing bread for his widowed mum in England. His master took him to clear land in the Piedmont near the Great Wagon Road. After two years, a gang of men killed his master and mistress while my man was off searching out a lost pig. They burned the house, shed, and cabin and left.

"My man found the bones of the couple in the ashes and buried them with what prayers he could remember. They were almost the only folk he had seen for two years. He cried and stayed there a few days. He wanted to tell someone but folk would not believe a former convict and he feared suspicion so he wandered off. When he came into the Tidewater, no one knew him and there was no record of his bond so he was free. He took work as he could find it.

"He found me after Pa died. I was fifteen and he was eighteen. We picked worms together alongside slaves in the fields or worked at drying time for food and a place to sleep. When our first baby came, we built a shelter but our baby died. We had other babies. My man has not abandoned us these five years, providing as well as he can. God bless you, Miss."

Megan worked her way back into the crowded market. Some vendors were animated and engaged with the passersby. At those tables was a sense of abundance and activity. At tables holding only tired root vegetables or spring greens wilted beyond freshness, the sellers were not hopeful this late in the market day. Megan sensed desperation.

She purchased biscuits, smoked ham after sniffing the meat, a jar of wild mulberry jam, and carrots with life left in them. From a vendor with a heavy German accent, she bought a bottle of "apfel cidah." From a wiry man who reminded her of the runaway, Simon, she bought an earthenware pot of honey sealed with beeswax. She felt a deep disquiet. What will happen to the people who don't sell much? They will eat their own stuff but they have no money to buy other things. Who will help if they fail completely? She had never seen deep poverty before nor thought much about it. Now it was right in front of her.

Megan came to a table displaying nothing but dusty root vegetables. A woman stood up with a spark of expectation on her tired face. Megan thought the woman was younger than Susan, but life had been hard. She pulled out two coins. "What could I get for this much?" she asked, showing the woman the money.

"For ready money, Ma'am, I can give an ox bone for stock, and greens to boil."

"Thanks, that will be..."

"Parsnips, radishes to pep it up, a beet, potatoes, and salt to make it savory."

"You have just given me the whole recipe. I will take all those things."

The woman wrapped the goods in a sheet from an old gazette and tied a piece of string around the bundle. "Thank you for your custom, Miss. I put in an extra beet root for ye."

On the edge of the square, a woman sat on a worn blanket by a pile of wild green onions. She had acorns in another pile and some dried mushrooms. Where the last woman had seemed tired, this one seemed frightened. She was skinny, her skin dry from sun and wind, and about Megan's age. "What would be good in soup?" Megan asked her.

"This wild onion gives flavor. I shelled and soaked these acorns in ash water for three days to get out bitterness. The mushrooms are from fallen trees and dried in the sun. An Indian woman taught me how. These tiny leaves from a pond are duckweed. All are good in soup."

Megan offered a small coin. "How much could I get for this?"

The vendors were used to customers with no cash. They bartered one foodstuff for another or exchanged what they had for a candle or a spoon—whatever the person had. Megan's coin got her a small bundle of each item and brought a rare moment of relief to the woman. "Are you a servant?" Megan asked.

"No, I am my own person. I have not found a master."

"Where do you live?" Megan asked.

"I live where I am, Ma'am, as best as I can. I hope to find a station. Last winter was hard."

"I have more carrots than I need. I shall give you two for your lunch. I wish you well, Miss."

On the way home, Megan passed a skinny horse and three shorn sheep foraging on sandy ground in a fenced yard. She tossed the most wilted greens, carrot tops, and half the duck weed over the fence. The animals approached and immediately began to eat her offerings.

Back home she got a pot of water, made a fire, rinsed the ox bone and put it into the pot to start simmering as she washed and cubed the potatoes, parsnips, carrots, and beets.

Day 2-6:   A Picnic Lunch at Home

"Hi, Mom! Looks like you've done some serious shopping." Megan was busy in the kitchen. "I bought ham, cheese, and biscuits and I'm making soup. I boiled a bone, salt, root vegetables, and acorns then moved it off the flame to let it simmer. I'll add the green stuff just before we eat it."

"Sounds great, Megan. Where did you get the recipe?"

"A woman sold me ingredients and told me what to do. Remember the story of the soldiers and the stone soup? We're having stone-free soup!"

"Good. Now I can go off duty in the kitchen and let you take over."

"Mom, that blacksmith I met, I think he was planning to run away. Hardly anyone makes it. People with no work have a hard time."

John came into the house. "I just saw Thomas Jefferson, Patrick Henry, and James Madison in the Raleigh Tavern. Wow… that's quite a hairdo!"

"I hope you like it. I wanted to surprise you. I got tickets to the Governor's Ball tonight. We haven't danced in I don't know how long. In college, I drank coffee while studying for history exams. Founding Fathers appeared then, too. Did you learn how to get back to our time?"

"No, did you guys?"

"Not yet, John. Megan was telling me about the blacksmith she met."

"Yeah. His name is Mark. He may run away. Runaways usually stay close to home to get food or help from friends. They usually get caught."

"But with the contract to pay his passage Mark owes someone money."

"I don't care if it's legal, Dad, it's way wrong! You condone indentured servitude?"

The door flew open. "What happened to you, Mom?"

"Great to see you too, Peter." Susan said. "How did you get along?"

"He's fine." Megan persisted, "How is it fair for Mark to be stuck as a servant even though years were added to his term as punishment?"

"Mark who?" asked Peter.

"The blacksmith I told you about."

"Megan, people should not work involuntarily. Maybe the contract was unfair, but if you help him escape he could find a worse situation."

"I'm worried he might get caught or get killed like the guy who ran past me yesterday, Dad. I'd like to help him not make a big mistake."

"That's a worthy goal, Megan. Who knows why we're here? However, we should not change the course of history."

"Who knows? If we change something we might go home to find Sylvester Stallone was never elected Governor of Pennsylvania." The others stared at Peter. "Just kidding."

"Megan made ham and cheese sandwiches, and the soup is ready."

Peter opened the back door. "Let's have lunch in the garden."

John and Peter moved a table near the well. "Dad, I saw a gang of slaves in a field this morning watched by an overseer. It was depressing."

"It took a big struggle to get rid of the abomination of slavery in this country," John reminded them. "Some people are willfully blind to injustice."

When they all sat down, John used a pocketknife to pull the cork from a bottle. "Whew, this is potent stuff! What did you buy?"

"The guy called it 'apfel' cidah. Wouldn't that be apple cider?"

"Yes, but it's fermented like strong wine. Do we have anything sweet?"

"I bought honey at the market, Dad."

John poured cider for everyone and added honey and lots of water.

"This drink is refreshing," said Susan.

"What are these little leaves in the soup?" asked Peter. "They're good."

"Duck weed. I fed half to animals on the way home. Who knew it was good? I made a poor woman happy by buying her stuff."

Susan handed John and Peter the tricorn hats and hunting shirts. "You guys are embarrassing Megan and me. This stuff should help you fit in if we're stuck here a while." She pretended she was not worried.

"Now we won't scare the neighbors." Peter admired his new shirt.

Megan decided that even though her dad was less stressed than in the morning, she would not bring up what she had learned about the taxes.

John got up from the table. "This afternoon I need to find a way out of here. I felt time slow down in wars, but never anything like this. I don't understand it."

"Remember the ball at the Governor's Palace tonight, Honey. Wait 'till you see the dress the tailor is making. Here's the cape called a mantua."

"It's very nice."

After John left, Megan said to Susan, "Dad seemed in a hurry to get out of here. He mentioned the army more today than I ever heard him in my life."

"He's fine, kids."

"OK, Mom, I'll take off now. Did you find the lady you worried about?"

"Not since church last night, Megan. I need to find her."

Day 2-7:   John Visits the St. George Tucker House

John explored the streets of Williamsburg for an hour, hoping to unearth a shard of understanding about their inconceivable slide into to the past. In Market Square, bustling earlier in the day, a few tired vendors tended sparse tables. Farmers and merchants dispersed toward home or, if sales were good, to join friends in a tavern.

He lingered in front of a store where a crowd of men shrouded in a cloud of tobacco smoke complained about non-importation agreements. "If our smithies are so damn good, why is there almost nothing on Greenhow's shelves where iron goods should be?"

"And who can afford whiskey?" asked a man who stitched harnesses.

"I don't drink away my money," scoffed a man in fine wool jacket.

"He brought money from England, that one," a man beside John muttered, "enough for a horse, an ox, two slaves to clear land, and a servant woman to cook and wash so his wife won't harden her hands."

"How did he do that?" asked John.

"He is the third son of a landed family. The first son will inherit the estate and the second went into the church. The old man gave this one a sum to start life here. They plan to ship tobacco to England to increase the family fortune. However, the only available large tracts of fertile land are far above the fall line where the river is not navigable to the sea. He has the added expense of transporting tobacco to the ships."

The man shook his head. "My old man died coughing when I was nine. When me mum died, I shipped over here in Pa's old clothes to seek my fortune. My auntie sewed shillings into my trousers. 'For your future wife and baby,' she told me. Though I shant see her again, I am grateful. My uncle paid half my passage and I got two years service to pay the balance. I was free at sixteen. Did your father leave you land or lucre?"

"My dad is eighty and still fit."

"Astonishing! A rare bit o' luck. I wish you the same longevity."

"May you also live long and prosper."

The voice of John Randolph, Virginia Attorney General, boomed from a porch. "In the House of Lords, William Pitt proposed withdrawal of troops and recognizing Congress's authority to levy taxes. The Intolerable Acts would be suspended. We can have our rights without war."

"John," a voice resounded, "We respect thee and thy brother Peyton. At your Tazewell Hall, we admired the tones of your violin. However, Pitt's motion failed and more troops are under sail. They cast the die and we are resolute. Our children may shake their heads in wonder of how we came so close to resolving this in peace. We pray they will be wiser than we."

Randolph answered, "If we threatened each other wielding knives, friends would pull us apart. However, nations taken by similar madness send young men to kill the youth of another nation. All march to a charnel ground under the misconception that negotiation signals weakness. How do sane men become so mad in groups? After great loss of life and great wealth to those who sell cannon, nations build monuments to the fallen heroes and praise God for triumphs that brought misery to others. Those monuments represent a failure of leadership.

"My friends, if not reversed, that defeat of Pitt's motion will live in history as a failure of civilized man. I will close Tazewell Hall and sail to England soon with my family to do all in my power to seek a peaceful outcome. I will correspond with Thomas Jefferson and others here."

"Three cheers for John Randolph," called out a man. John noted the huzzahs were less spirited than the cheers for Peyton Randolph.

Even under his tricorn hat, John felt dehydrated. He rested in the shade of a large sycamore north of the market. "Maintenance of the objective." He reminded himself to seek a way to his own time. The walk along hot, sandy streets evoked veiled memories and he grew edgy. He had been nineteen, barely older than Megan. At least this isn't the desert or tropics. "Enough of this!" He stood up. "I'm going back to my own time to get a lemonade." On the north side of Nicholson Street, he glimpsed someone entering a house on a broad lawn enclosed by a white picket fence. A small sign by the gate read St. George Tucker House and John assumed it was a tavern. He opened the gate and walked up the path.

He entered the house. A woman looked up. "It certainly is hot out."

Looking down at his disheveled state, John realized the woman was wearing modern clothing, and suddenly he was as out of place in this air-conditioned place as he had been on the street. He weakly returned her smile. "Uh... yes it is. Pardon me, but is there a rest room here?"

"The Tucker House is a rest stop for donors to the Colonial Williamsburg Foundation. We have sitting rooms and a library."

"I would like to donate to support this place."

"When you get back from the restroom you can register."

In the men's room, John splashed water on his face, looked into the mirror, and struggled to get oriented. Returning to the entrance, he made a donation for a year's membership, and the woman directed him to a salon. "Would you like lemonade?"

"Amazing! I mean, thank you."

He looked over the shelves, chose two books, and sat in a comfortable chair to skim them, occasionally shaking his head in disbelief at his experiences this morning. He read that at sixteen, George Washington found a benefactor in a distant cousin. Thomas Lord Fairfax had a domain of over five million acres in Northern Virginia when he employed young George as a surveyor. The only British Lord living in the colonies was a rare mentor for an ambitious young man at a time when land ownership was the path to wealth and power.

Lord Fairfax's predecessor, Thomas Lord Fairfax, the 3rd Earl of Cameron, commanded Parliament's army against the Royalists. Parliament worried that King Charles I sought absolute power so they overthrew and beheaded him. Four months later, the 3rd Lord Fairfax put down a mutiny by 'Levelers' who had the audacity to declare all men were equal! He then retired with a generous pension. His second in command, Oliver Cromwell, became the Lord Protector. What a perfect role model the 6th Lord Fairfax was for young George Washington who also went on to lead an army against the king!

In the French and Indian War, Washington rode with General Edward Braddock to the terrible defeat by the Indians at the Monongahela. Bullets tore through Washington's clothing. He wrote that he was saved by all-powerful dispensations of Providence. John smiled at the irony. Survivors of a battle might believe they had Divine protection, but if they were killed later in another firefight, survivors of that engagement thought the same thing. John shuddered. He could have been face down in the field and Danny Adamson or Sergeant Sargon could be here sipping lemonade, having a flashback to the colonial period — maybe thinking about him.

A man in a sweat-spotted blue shirt and button-pulling paunch sat down hard in an armchair beside him. "I'm too old for hiking in the sun."

"I got parched myself." John wanted to read but he was being polite.

"I'm from Shepherdstown, West Virginia," the man said proudly. "It was chartered in 1762, here in Williamsburg. My ancestor William Crawford came here on business just before the Revolution. We have a letter that mentions GW. Grandpa told us GW was George Washington."

"What was the business?"

"He registered land claims. It was secretive — maybe rival claims. There were no problems at the home farm — it's still in the family. I brought the grandkids here to show 'em where William Crawford, their great great — who knows how many greats — grandfather, came long ago."

"It's good you were able to keep in touch with your family history."

"Yeah. I'm in real estate too, so it's in the genes." The sweating man welcomed a glass of sweet iced tea from a volunteer. "I sell vacation homes along the Shenandoah. It's not easy to get permits near the George Washington National Forest but William Crawford had trouble with claims, too. History around here was all about real estate."

"I'm starting to get that idea."

"In the old days, surveyors used a rod sixteen and a half feet long. Four rods make a sixty-six foot chain. A tract two chains by five is an acre. People know there are 640 acres in a square mile but no one remembers what an acre is. Did you know George Washington made a fortune surveying land before he married a rich widow and doubled his holdings? Our Founding Fathers knew rods and chains."

"Sounds like they did."

The man continued, "Bees make hives, birds make nests, and people make buildings. I ought to hang a rod and a chain over the fireplace since they've been good for my family. Well, I should go make my grandson let his brother out of the stocks."

"Good talking with you."

John read that at the end of the French and Indian War, in the 1763 Treaty of Paris, Great Britain gained Quebec and French territory west of the Appalachians. From Spain, Britain won East Florida on the Atlantic and West Florida, on the Gulf Coast of what are now Florida, Mississippi, Alabama, and Eastern Louisiana.

He felt a presence and looked up. "Hello, Ma'am."

A thin dark-haired woman smiled at him. "Oh, Hello, I'm Frances."

"I'm John. Sorry, I did not hear you come in. Are you a docent?"

"I am a caretaker. You are reading about land in the West. You know the second half of that story but maybe you never knew the first half."

"I would like to hear it."

"The house closes soon so there is no time today. Can you come back?"

"I will. I'll use your plumbing again before going back to colonial times."

"There has been progress. Williamsburg these days seems miraculous."

When John stepped onto the street outside the gate, he was back in 1775. "I've got to figure out how this works," he muttered to no one.

Day 2-8:   Susan Hears of Scandal at the Randolph House

Susan and Megan strolled to the shoemaker's shop. Inside, a young bearded man worked on a pair of men's shoes. He greeted them. "A pleasant afternoon to you. How might I help you this fine day?"

"A fine afternoon to you as well. Would ye be Elias, then?"

He was surprised by Susan's accent, "How do ye know my name?"

"My name is Susan Sinclair. Me grandmother was from Belfast, and me grandfathers descend from the Scots-Irish. Alwyn the tailor said you might solve my problem with the Governor's Ball." She pointed to her shoes.

"And who is this lovely colleen here, your sister?"

"This is my daughter, Megan. No use resorting to flattery."

"You caught me. I have three pair of ladies' shoes. I hope one fits, as there is no time to make a pair in time for the ball. I promised the shoes I am working on to Carter Braxton. His old ones gave him bunions. See, I have them stretching on a last a half size larger than his regular shoes. Braxton hopes the soft deerskin lining will make him a better dancer."

The shoemaker placed the three pairs of fine ladies' shoes on the floor. It was obvious one pair was too small and another too big, so she tried on the remaining pair. "These fit perfectly. I'll dance in them at the ball."

"Wonderful. Shall I wrap them?"

"No thanks." Susan paid for the shoes and the shoemaker picked up an awl and with a smile, bent to his work on Carter Braxton's dancing shoes.

Strolling along Nicholson Street past the St. George Tucker House, Susan and Megan were unaware that centuries later, John was inside drinking a second glass of lemonade. They came to the red house from which Peyton Randolph had left for Philadelphia. A woman greeted them at the gate. "Welcome, Ladies. Are you here to join Missus Randolph for a chat?"

"Mom, I have errands to do. I'll see you at the house before dinner."

"You'll probably get to the shops in time to find some real bargains."

Susan joined other guests for a tour of the elegant Randolph House. Bold wallpaper in a pattern of columns, arches, and belvederes bedecked in garlands decorated the hallway. Upstairs, in wood-paneled rooms, canopy beds had curtains to protect against drafts and mosquitoes.

Downstairs, Susan admired the dining table, set with fine china and silver. She peeked into Peyton Randolph's office. On a worktable were candles, spectacles, a quill pen, and a long clay pipe lying there as if he had stepped away a moment rather than for eternity.

In a large salon were portraits of Randolph and his wife Betty Harrison Randolph. Susan thought the reenactor yesterday was a close likeness of Peyton but she was taken aback as two ladies entered the room. Betty Randolph looked as if she had stepped right out of the painting.

"Lovely to see you, ladies." Betty Randolph was a study in poise. "May I present my niece, Lucy Randolph Burwell. My husband inherited this house from his father, Sir John Randolph, the only native Virginian knighted by the King. My husband is at the Congress in Philadelphia."

"Will you be going to Philadelphia to visit him, Missus Randolph?"

"I should like to see Philadelphia. My husband says 'tis twelve times bigger than Williamsburg and the third largest city in the English-speaking world. Alas, this household is too burdensome to leave for any length of time, what with servants to oversee and supplies to manage."

A guest asked, "Missus Randolph, A preacher is in the gaol and will be tried in court for preaching without a license. What are your views on religious tolerance and the practices some call the Great Awakening?"

"This problem concerns me. Too much freedom to express whatever comes to mind leads to chaos, as I am sure you agree. Unschooled men who say the Lord called them to preach incite servants and gather up money. They are called more by their purses than by the Lord. The man in gaol will be treated fairly and his punishment will be a lesson to others that the Established Church is the proper way for people to worship."

Susan was shocked by Betty Randolph's views on religion but her musings were interrupted by the Randolphs' niece, Lucy.

"Dear Aunt Betty, I am unsettled by the discord in our community. I listen to Uncle Peyton, Uncle John, and my husband endlessly debate about it. We, who are established, hold power and economic privilege in one hand, while with the other hand we withhold freedom and prosperity. The poor face danger and sometimes lack food for their children. Is it surprising they seek emotional expressions of their relation to God? The Established Church and established society bring people outside the establishment neither prosperity nor comfort. Were not our grandfathers rough-hewn like people coming on the ships?"

"Lucy, those rough-hewn men educated their sons and their sons began to educate daughters so they could be articulate in their impertinence. Our commerce sustains countless freemen and bondsmen here and in England. Our husbands are leaders. Many of those men of integrity now gather in Philadelphia to ponder affairs of all the colonies."

"Auntie, yes, our families contribute and our efforts are compensated, but the word 'integrity' does not portray all acts in pursuit of prosperity."

"Whatever do you mean, Lucy Burwell?"

"Well, we could begin in 1766 with the death of John Robinson, long-time speaker of the House of Burgesses and treasurer of Virginia."

"We don't speak of him any longer, Lucy!"

"He was a friend and we must understand unseen currents underlying today's instability. Robinson took a fortune of £100,000 in currency due to be burned and lent it to prominent friends in the Tidewater. Many families secretly owe large amounts to Robinson's estate."

"Lucy, you are talking about a horrid scandal that is behind us now since John Robinson died nine years ago, may he rest in peace."

"And important families are grateful he rests in discreet silence. Well-known Virginians still carry burdensome debts to the Robinson estate, which in turn is in hopeless debt to the colony. William Byrd III, of the Governor's Council, had a debt of £15,000. Archibald Cary, a member of the very committee formed to resolve the Robinson estate, borrowed £7,500 so he is more interested in keeping it quiet than in solving it."

"Lucy, stop!"

"This is important, Aunt Betty. The corruption is kept secret or the leaders will lose their positions. The people abhor such hypocrisy. The men at the pinnacle of Virginia society were aware the money should have been burned. I grant that Richard Henry Lee with a debt of twelve pounds and Patrick Henry who owed only eleven may be innocent of complicity, but it will be fifteen more years before the large debts are cleared."

"How could you possibly know such things, Lucy?"

"A member of the committee to resolve the debt often visited Kingsmill. When he over-drank, which was on every visit, he strutted like a peacock displaying a fantail of gossip. He had dipped his hand into the public coffer. Last year, after gambling away his family fortune trying to clear his debt, he took an overdose of laudanum to escape his failures in the oblivion of death. His shamed and penniless widow lost the plantation."

"That is quite enough, Lucy Burwell. Our guests must find the subject tiresome. I surely find it so. I don't understand operations of the treasury."

To the contrary, Susan found it shocking that leading Virginia families benefited from embezzlement and covered it up for decades. As their carriages rolled past the shacks of hungry people, could the gentry not see? A network of cousins and friends held the reins of government, church, and economy. It was a puzzle to Susan how our democracy was born from a culture with so much injustice woven into its fabric. We have not solved the problem in our time either, she thought. Missus Randolph would be relieved that centuries later few knew of the corruption and those who took the money have streets and schools named after them still.

Betty Randolph was obviously displeased as she brought the salon to an end. Lucy would get a stern talking to when the guests departed. The shameful secret gnawed at the security and privilege of this home as well. Peyton Randolph's brother John had borrowed almost a thousand pounds of the expired currency and Missus Randolph feared worry over this matter could kill her husband. Had nervousness not contributed to his gluttony? She was not sure whether her husband was complicit or not, but if the scandal became public, they would be humiliated and, if he did have a debt he was forced to pay promptly, they could be bankrupt. The specters of shame and ruin pressed her like a vise.

Lucy stepped to the door to say goodbye to the visitors.

"I learned a lot from your account, Missus Burwell."

"I am afraid I badly overstepped the bounds of social correctness."

"Being socially correct is not as high a calling as having the integrity to tell the truth, however uncomfortable that is. You made your aunt uncomfortable but you gave us the truth and I thank you."

"I am grateful for your frankness. May I ask your name?"

"My name is Susan Sinclair. It is a pleasure to meet you, Lucy Burwell."

Susan shook off her reaction to the scandal and focused on the fine gown waiting to be picked up. She had not been this excited about a dress since her wedding. She spotted a woman in a brown cloak at a distance, quickened her pace, and dodged people coming the other way. This was her chance! Losing ground to the woman in the cloak, she veered into the street, lifted her dress to her shins, and jogged a block to catch up.

"Excuse me! Jane?" The woman turned. It was the gaoler's wife.

"Oh, I'm sorry! I thought you were someone else."

"At times I wished to be someone else but I'm me and shall make the best of it."

"We may as well be who we are," panted Susan. "Sorry to bother you." She continued to the milliner's shop to pick up her gown, wondering if she would ever encounter Jane in 1775.

Day 2-9:   Peter Stumbles upon a Library

Peter took a different road north toward the quarter where Augustus lived. Down a street on his right, he was surprised to see the opening of a tunnel. He felt compelled to walk through. The path beyond ran by a stream and a copse of trees. He followed it into bright sunlight. He squinted and heard a screech. He jumped back and gasped, "A car!"

The car was only going ten miles per hour at a parking lot entrance when the driver braked. He opened the window. "Are you OK? You have good reactions." The driver did not guess the extent of Peter's surprise.

"I'm fine. The sun was in my eyes and I didn't see you, sorry."

"The library is closed on weekends. Is that where you were going?"

By the entrance, a sign read John D. Rockefeller Jr. Library Parking. "Uh... yes, the library."

The driver thought Peter might be in mild shock. "Look, I've got to finish a project. Why don't you come in and read while I work."

"Great! I would like to research slavery."

"I'll park then let us in the side door. I'm Joe, by the way."

"Peter."

Inside the building, Joe led Peter to a reading area. "Soda, juice?"

"Do you have any orange juice?"

"Sure, I'll get a can from the machine. What do you want to research?"

Peter was confused to find himself in his own time. "I'm... studying slavery and want to learn how slaves got manumission. Also, with no Underground Railroad in 1775, how could a slave escape?"

"Have you heard of Dunmore's 1775 Proclamation? All slaves and indentured servants belonging to owners in rebellion were freed if they took up arms on behalf of the King."

"Wow! I would be very interested to read about that."

"I'll get your juice and help you pick out something. That gives me ten minutes to procrastinate before finishing this budget I need to complete."

Peter looked at the bookshelves. Filing cabinets held information on the history and contents of each building managed by the Colonial Williamsburg Foundation.

Joe returned with two cans of juice and pulled a book off a shelf. "You'll find what you are looking for in here. The men's room is down the hall. If you need anything, I'll be in my office — the one with the open door."

"Thanks, Joe."

Peter sipped orange juice as he read that John Murray, Earl of Dunmore, the last British Governor of Virginia, abandoned Williamsburg in June 1775. From a ship off Norfolk, he ordered attacks on rebel towns. In November, he issued Dunmore's Proclamation. Peter was excited to read:

" I do hereby declare all indentured servants, negroes, or others, (appertaining to rebels), free that are able and willing to bear arms, they joining His MAJESTY'S Troops as soon as may be, for the more speedily reducing this Colony to a proper sense of their duty."

Men, women, and children from rebel and loyal plantations had streamed toward Norfolk seeking freedom. "That's it!" Peter said aloud. He read on to learn that the real British intent was not freedom for slaves but rather, to break the revolutionary leaders economically. The fate of most slaves who joined the British was tragic. Many died of illness or fighting. Some were captured and sold. Some voluntarily returned to their masters because they had nowhere else to go. Despite those dangers and snares, of one hundred thousand escaped slaves, as many as ten thousand made it to freedom in Europe, Africa, or the northern colonies.

Peter reflected on the risks of altering the past. "I could change one thing and that might mean I was never born, or the Continental Army lost the Revolution." He took a sip of juice. "Maybe it's safe to help people do what they want to do. I won't persuade Evie to run if she doesn't want to."

Joe walked in. "I finished my budget. How is your research going?"

"I'm learning lots! Do you mind that I took copy paper for notes?"

"Not at all. Glad this was helpful. I'll be ready to go in ten minutes. Just leave the books on that table and a librarian will put them away Monday morning. They're careful about getting history in the right order."

Peter thanked Joe in the parking lot and walked to the opening of the tunnel under some railroad tracks. He stopped. Now that he had knowledge of Dunmore's Proclamation, would he return to 1775 through the tunnel or stay in his own time with only a memory of strange experiences? He felt a pull toward the tunnel.

"What do you want?" He heard his own voice within. He clearly wanted to return to 1775 and help Evie and her sons find a way to freedom. The pull to the tunnel became insistent. He stepped out of the sunlight and strode to the other end of the tunnel, where the scent of wood smoke immediately struck him. Two men rode horses across his path fifty yards ahead. He walked into town without looking back.

Day 2-10: Megan Shops for Contraband

Megan thought her mom's Irish accent was cool. While they looked at shoes, an idea had occurred to her and she was impatient to act on it. She left her mother at the gate of Randolph House and hurried to the John Greenhow store. She planned to shop in several places so no one would see all her purchases. Next, she went to the Prentis Store before taking the packages home. She started again at the other end of town at Tarpley's Store and continued on to the wigmaker. "Oh-oh! Sticker shock."

"Pardon me?" asked Charlotte, the wigmaker.

"Oh, sorry. Do you have cheaper wigs? My uncle is not a fancy man."

"Yes, those human hair wigs are expensive. You remind me of a woman with auburn hair who came this morning. Miss, we have several good middle-sorts wigs made from horse hair."

Megan chose a distinguished-looking white wig with a black bow.

She dropped off the second batch of packages and returned to Market Square where vendors loaded their wagons for the ride home. Megan studied men loading the wagons and spotted one in a nice waistcoat.

"Sir, I have an offer to make to you."

"Lovely. I have not packed the honey or corn meal away yet."

"I see you're a man who appreciates a fine vest."

"A fine what?"

"A waistcoat like the one you're wearing. The Prentis Store has new ones with carved buttons of deer horn—very stylish and only two pounds."

"Oh, you are seeking customers for Mister Prentis? Well, I like my waistcoat fine. My wife bought it didn't you, Maggie?"

Packing up the next table was the milk and cheese woman. "Oh, hello, Miss. Did your friend get home with her milk all right?"

"I hope so. You were kind to give her extra milk."

"Bartholomew and I help where we can. We were often hungry and rose from a lowly station to a life of sufficiency for which we are thankful."

"Maggie, this miss wants me to buy a waistcoat at Prentis store but I am satisfied with this one you picked for me. She says the new ones have horn buttons," he winked, "but two pounds is a bit rich for us."

"I'm not selling waistcoats. I'd like to surprise someone with a waistcoat to cheer him up. I like yours, and I'll give you the two pounds to buy yourself a new one."

"An astounding offer! Why not buy the new one for your friend, Miss?"

"I'm Megan. My friend might draw attention to himself if he wore a fancy new waistcoat. People might be hard on him for putting on airs."

"He's a bonded servant, I would imagine."

"I'd rather not say. It's a surprise."

"I understand. This is the strangest offer I've heard in seventy Saturdays, but if you think it to be a good idea, Maggie, I shall do it."

Maggie looked at Megan. "Bartholomew, Megan was kind to a worried woman this morning. This is to help someone, I reckon. Megan's offer is beyond fair. Give her your waistcoat for one pound fifteen shillings. We shall pay the balance of the new one."

Bartholomew helped count out Megan's diverse collection of currencies taking two shillings less than his wife had suggested. "I shall bargain them down at the Prentis Store." He unbuttoned his waistcoat and gave it to Megan.

"Thank you so much!" Megan left them to their packing and returned home to lay out her treasures. She yanked the top sheet off the bed. Wrapping everything in the sheet with a loose knot at the top, it looked like a laundry bundle and that would attract no suspicion as she walked. "Perfect!" she declared.

Day 2-11:   Mustering the Militia

On the north side of Market Square, men mustered for an infantry drill. John recognized the sergeant in charge as the wheelwright. He wore a blue double-breasted tunic with bone buttons. The citizen soldiers around him wore old red coats from the French and Indian War or fringed pullover hunting shirts. John moved into the shade to watch.

The sergeant called to bystanders, "If Tommy Redcoat comes marchin' in, ye best move as an army not as a herd of goats rushing a pile of corn, or worse, dashing or freezing at the sight of the enemy like rabbits from the shadow of a hawk. Step up, lads, and muster with the Second Virginia Militia."

He got louder so the crowd could hear. "The Virginia Militia Law calls for an annual muster in each county. We humbly demand all able-bodied males from sixteen to fifty to step forward. A Virginia infantry company has 68 soldiers commanded by a captain, two lieutenants, an ensign, four sergeants, four corporals, and a drummer who also bears the colors. Do ye see 68 men here? Neither do I. Step forward and be lively about it."

To the gathered men he shouted, "Company, fall in! Form ranks!" The men in uniform shuffled quickly into ranks; the newcomers fell in behind them. "Dress right!" The experienced men in the front rank raised their arms to the side, turned their heads, then shuffled forward and to the side until their arms almost touched the shoulder of the man beside them. In seconds, the row was straight. The men in the front rank carried a mix of flintlock rifles and muskets while the men behind had no arms. Two corporals distributed oak broom handles to the men behind.

"To the front, face! Attention! All right ye future sharpshooting, quick marching, seeds of a Continental Army. Listen carefully. If ye do not know what to do, follow the man in front of ye. The front rank has done this many times, and every man-Jack one of 'em lived through the worst war had to give. If ye pay close attention, so might ye."

"Port arms!" The men in the first rank held their muskets in front, their right hand on the butt and their left around the stock near the trigger. The following ranks fumbled to get the hands in the right position.

"Shoulder arms!" The men brought their muskets to their shoulders. "LEFT shoulder arms unless I say otherwise, you newborns! Do it again, but this time do it with a snap. Port arms! Left shoulder arms!" Even broom handles went crisply to the left shoulders.

"Company, forward march!" Onlookers in front of the formation scurried out of the way but there was no hurry, for a second later the sergeant shouted, "Company, halt! Have ye ever heard the words 'Left right, left right' in that order? If you set out on any foot you like, you will trip and land on your snouts while bayoneting the bottom of the man in front of you. That is bad for morale and gives aid, comfort, and entertainment to the enemy! Lead with the left foot, shall we soldiers? Company..." he paused and looked along the ranks, "Forward march!"

Again, a noticeable difference occurred as the company moved forward in unison. As they marched past the tree, John recognized Peter in the fourth rank. He stepped out to fall in beside him. "Hello, soldier."

Peter was surprised but kept the pace. He could hardly wait to tell his father that they were not stuck in the past.

The sergeant shouted, "Company, halt! Take the terror off your faces, lads. We drill and fight as a unit. Failing to work together makes ye less effective and puts ye in grave danger. Grave danger means danger of being put in your grave. Be calm. No one is shooting at ye. In battle, enemies will be shooting. By then ye will know what to do."

"Company, forward march!" John hoped his son marching beside him would never have to kill, see his friends die, or die violently himself. He was relieved his family was not stuck in the past permanently but he felt the pain of foreknowledge that many of these young men would be killed.

When they arrived at the Magazine, the sergeant called a halt. "Ye'll be good soldiers before long, men. Ye have done well. The corporals shall collect the weapons. Company, dismissed!"

Peter and John walked toward the house. "Dad, I've got something huge to tell you. We're not stuck here. I walked into our own time this afternoon. After a couple of hours in a library I walked to the past again."

"Were you at the St. George Tucker House?"

"No, I went through a tunnel. I learned amazing things in the library."

"It's a weird situation, Peter, but I'm not worried. It seems we can leave when we want." He was less surprised by the news than Peter had hoped.

Chowning's Tavern was east of Market Square. "Hey Dad! We talked about having dinner here tonight. We could book a table now." They were told a table in the garden would be open in twenty minutes at six o'clock.

"Peter, this experience is bringing memories back. I need a walk. Book a table and I'll meet you here at six."

Peter jogged back to the house, his concern about his father eclipsed by his excitement to tell Susan and Megan about his walk through the tunnel.

Day 2-12:   Dinner at Chowning's Tavern

The Sinclairs were led to their table in the garden of Chowning's Tavern. Susan ordered the Welsh rarebit. "I'll have that, too," decided Megan.

"And what about you, Sir?"

John looked over the fence. "Me? I'm not hungry. I'll have today's soup."

"Did you have a nice walk before dinner, Honey?" asked Susan.

"It was all right."

"Peter walked through a tunnel to our time. I'm relieved we're not stuck. I'll bet we can find our car in the parking lot and drive home."

"I'm sure we could, Mom. I learned that in 1775, Governor Dunmore is going to proclaim free all slaves willing to bear arms for the King against the rebels. The British freed as many slaves as the Underground Railroad!"

"How was your day, John?" asked Susan, concerned about his mood.

"In a donor center library I found myself back in the 21st century."

"You found a way back to our time, too?"

"More like an island in time. I learned that young George Washington worked for Lord Fairfax, Earl of Cameron whose predecessor overthrew the king. Fairfax may have influenced our revolutionary general."

"John, I learned that leading families borrowed currency stolen from the Virginia treasury. Being found out would have led to scandal and ruin, so they kept the debts secret as they slowly paid them off. The pressure of those debts led to several suicides. It seems the financial mess of the large estates tempted them to throw off the authority of the King."

"Mom, there was lots going on. Indentured workers sent west to clear Indian land didn't know that their greedy employers ordered them to do illegal things that could get them killed."

"Megan, be respectful of our Founding Fathers."

"I am respectful, Dad. We need to know the reasons for the actions of our government and business leaders. You said I should learn something. I'm learning if we don't pay attention, we deserve what we get."

"Everyone knows the Revolution started because people were against taxation without representation. You can't just make up history."

"I'm not making this up! Parliament passed the Stamp Act in 1765, but the colonies resisted and it was repealed the next year. In 1767, the Townshend Duties Act was passed and repealed in 1770. Dad, you were a soldier. Would you go to war over taxes repealed five years ago?"

"Of course not!"

"Well, neither did they, Dad! Almost all unpopular taxes had been repealed. Who would fight about something already over for several years? No one would risk their lives, fortunes, and sacred honor for that!"

"Where did you read this, Megan, a conspiracy theory online?"

"No, in history books I brought—one got a Pulitzer Prize. The truth is easy to find if you look. The outbreak of war followed implementation of the Intolerable Acts, passed in 1774. That should give us a clue. What was so intolerable? The Boston Port Act closed the port. I wrote them down... here they are. The Administration of Justice Act allowed British officials to have trials moved to England. The Massachusetts Government Act revoked the charter and shut down elected government. That was tyranny, Dad. The Quartering Act put British troops into taverns and empty houses, but people feared they would have soldiers in their homes. And a big one for Virginia, Pennsylvania, and the Southern Colonies—the Quebec Act gave control of land west of the mountains to Quebec."

"Hey, just because somebody wrote a book does not mean it's the truth. Why are you arguing against what everybody knows to be true?"

"Rich families needed new lands as they depleted their land with tobacco. They persuaded people it was something else. Sound familiar? Quebec was far away and had only sixty thousand people compared to two million in the thirteen colonies. By having Quebec manage the western lands, the King tried to stop settlement to avoid more war with the Indians. Land developers did not want to be prevented from taking Indian land. Ordinary people didn't know what the fight was about!"

"You don't think a war was necessary?" Susan's eyes widened.

"No, everyone had hidden agendas. Peter told us the British freed slaves and servants. That was not because the Brits cared about the slaves—they tried to ruin the disloyal slave owners. There were no good guys."

"Why are you riled up, Megan?" asked John.

"It still goes on in our time! Wealthy people and giant corporations hire lobbyists to draft laws and push tax cuts in their favor. Rich talk show hosts support even richer guys by telling people this all benefits everyone and they mock opponents. The government bails out big business when they fail and taxes working people to pay for it. Follow the money, Dad."

"You know who you remind me of, Megan?" interrupted Susan.

"Who?"

"A young man I met a long time ago who took a stand for justice even at personal risk. His name is John Sinclair. Now let's enjoy dinner."

Day 2-13: Annie's Journey from Africa

Peter left Chowning's Tavern, determined to find Annie. He walked only half a block when he passed a great oak tree. There on the other side of the tree Annie sat on a wooden crate — her back against the trunk.

"Oh!" Peter was startled. "I was looking for you, Annie."

"Looks like you found me waitin' for you. We found each other by me feelin' where you was comin' from and you feelin' where I was waitin'."

Peter was perplexed. "I didn't feel you waiting. Mind if I sit down?"

"Try it and see if I mind." She broke into a warm smile. Peter got a crate.

"Move 'round behind the tree, Peter, so no one see us talkin'. I know you confused by what you seein'. Most folk don't know they's confused. Somebody comin' here soon so I gonna tell my story like I promised."

"That would be good, Annie."

"I was born in West Africa of a Bambara-speakin' mama from grasslands. Folk lived by rivers and grew rice in the sun. Daddy spoke Dogon and came from the forest. They lost three babies 'fore I was born so they held me close and talked 'bout how good life was, prayin' I would be healthy and not die like them other babies. I started talkin' 'fore one year and my folks forgot somethin' important.

"If babies talked early, the tribe s'posed they was possessed by a dead relative or a devil. Some wondered if clever children might grow up smarter than the chief, but they was 'fraid to say that very loud. Fo' whatever reason, bright-eyed babies who talked too young was taken from they mamas and sacrificed in ceremony for the good of the tribe."

Annie took a long breath. "One day, the chief came by. I talked to a doll Daddy carved for me. Mama hushed me but the chief kep' lookin' over.

"Mama cried into the night. Next mornin' Daddy took me far up river. After many days, we found the camp of Fulani people who move cattle wit' the seasons. His cousin married a Fulani man and Daddy told her I was a year older than my real age. He axed her to take care of me for a few years. She wouldn't have no trouble if I was short, but talkin' too soon was dangerous.

"Auntie was good to me. The Fulani is nomads wit' herds on pastures so wide it takes a month to cross. Gazelles, deer wit' straight horns, live on them grasslands. A big cat called a cheetah chases the gazelle fast-fast-fast. The gazelle leap and race off in another direction when she land. Nothin' here, not even a gallopin' horse, be as fast as a cheetah and a gazelle.

"We saw long-necked giraffes hunted by lions. The she-lions disappeared and the male stood high so the giraffes could see him. The giraffes stared to see what that golden lion was gonna do. All of a sudden, the she-lions ran from a gully to snatch a giraffe starin' at the male. When lions was near, men herded the cattle into a circle and stood outside wit' spears, while women and children stayed together by the herd.

"We camped near towns wit' people of many colors and tongues. I spoke Fula wit' Auntie and learned Hausa words used in town markets where we traded milk, yogurt, cheese, and meat from our herds. I milked cows and goats. I got cowpox like all the women do. They joke that we is leopard ladies 'cause the marks left on the skin is pretty.

"In dry times we moved the herd south into forests to forage. We did not swim in rivers 'cause bama was in there. Bama is Bambara for crocodile. There was big animals we called mali and you call hippopotamus. They look funny but they be dangerous. A mali can kill a crocodile. The men watched out for mali and bama before we crossed a river.

"One night we was sleepin' when men wit' spears attacked. Our men was surprised and some was killed. The rest of us was tied wit' leather strips and made to walk many days down a dry river bed wit' little food.

"We reached where they done hid canoes and we floated wit' the men pushin' on long poles. I heard men speak Dogon and the words of my daddy came back. They thought I was Dogon taken as a slave by Fulani.

"After two weeks the little river flowed into a wide river through forests. On the bank, many men sat by cookin' fires while they ate and drank, pointed to us, and argued. Auntie told me we was bein' sold to work in rice fields. When the tradin' was done, the new men strapped us together at the wrists and dragged us into canoes. We drank from the big river called the Gambia so we was not thirsty, but we got only enough food to keep us alive.

"When I prayed, I felt Spirit move in the water. The men paddled and kept to the middle of the river. They watched the shore but they was too worried to be huntin'. Maybe somebody was huntin' to steal us. When we camped, men stayed awake while the rest slept and once we slept in the canoes driftin' past sleepin' villages. We could feel the danger. They kept arrows in they bows and watched the huts."

"A month after we started down the wide river, we came to an island wit' a big stone building called Fort James. Some sick or weak folk was stabbed and they bodies thrown in the river. I was so sick to see it I threw up. We was taken to rooms wit' iron bars over the holes.

"After two days men grabbed me away from my auntie. I cried and she screamed and prayed. That was the last time I saw her. Outside was a big boat wit' white cloth rolled on long poles hung across high masts. The men on the boat was paler than the lightest skinned North Africans in the market of Timbuktu. A few wit' fancy hats was pale as better-sorts ladies here. They put iron rings on our ankles and pushed us into wooden racks inside the boat. I thought they was blind in they heart. They had no feelin'.'"

"Next day they brung us on deck and we got a surprise. The river banks was gone and everywhere was rollin' water. The boat moved wit' nobody paddlin'. I wondered if the pale men was magic, but no light shone in them like in magic people. I was scared, hungry, and thirsty, but I felt Spirit in the wind pushin' us over the waves. It whispered in the sails, 'Everythin' is deeper than you see, prayers is always heard.'

"People cried and moaned. The smell in them wooden racks from pee and shit and vomit would make you gag. Every day they splashed the racks wit' buckets of sea water but people got sick and died and was thrown into the sea wit' no songs or words. Some folk tried to jump but they was chained to people who wanted to live so no one was able to kill they self. When a bad storm came, the pale men did not bring us up top or feed us for three days. The boat bounced so hard two people broke bones from bangin' against walls. A man on the ship set the bones, but he was not kind and smelled like fermented grain.

"Finally one day a man up high on the mast shouted and we saw a green line of land in front of the ship. At Annapolis, we was washed wit' fresh water and fed to look better at auction. At the sale they stood us up naked so people could see if we had sores or wasn't well and strong."

Annie looked down the street. "Yonder come 'Gustus. You say hello. Then I gonna finish my story when he gone."

"Hello, Annie," called out Augustus. "The overseer sent me to town on an errand and I been lookin' for you."

"Looks like you found me waitin' for you," Annie winked at Peter.

"Say hello to Mister Peter, 'Gustus. You 'member him."

"Hello Mister Peter. You the best runner I ever seen for a white man. I saw you again this mornin' talkin' wit' Mister Jack.

"I was asking how to buy slaves so I could set them free."

Augustus looked astonished. "Is that a fact? Well, the gentry all talkin' 'bout freedom. It must be good for them so I gonna get freedom myself. Annie you is the only free African I know. What do you say?'

Annie tilted her head to the left. "Runnin' away be very dangerous."

"True Annie, but stayin' be dangerous, too. My life be more than half over, and if freedom be so good, I want a taste 'fore my life be done."

Annie took another long look at Augustus. "Maybe wisdom comin' to you, 'Gustus. You want to try for freedom even tho' it be dangerous and you ain't sure you can succeed?"

"Yes, Ma'am"

"What be the chance your massa might set you free some day?"

"Annie, Massa don't know me 'cept on a list of his property. The chance he gonna set me free when he alive or dead be betwixt none and not any."

Annie quietly asked Peter, "What would you say if 'Gustus axed you?"

"I don't know."

"Peter, you must find your own knowin' or waste a very long trip."

"Well," Peter began, "Augustus, freedom is worth working hard for. Even so, life is precious and you can help people using the herbs as Annie taught you. So you might do well to be patient, do your best, and watch closely for a better chance to be free than we can see now."

"You think somethin' will happen to make it easier to run to freedom?"

Peter felt restraint new to him. "Maybe so. You're a good runner, but you need a good path. Remember how the wild turkey tripped you?"

"Yes, I do. Well, Annie always told us to be patient until a gate opens. I can do that. Maybe I is a slave you be plannin' to buy, Mister Peter."

Peter paused. "There are some people I'd like to help but slaves are expensive, precious actually, and sadly I don't have enough money."

"That be sad, Mister Peter. I will watch for chances. Please don't tell."

"I promise I won't."

"I'll be hoppin' past a gibbet on just one foot! A white gentleman makin' me a promise! I never thought I would hear that. Annie, you got wonderful friends. Well, I got to get back. Thanks for the good words, Annie. You too, Mister Peter. I wish I had a massa like you."

"Didn't I hear you say you want to be free without a master?"

"That be true, Mister Peter." Augustus was off, running.

Annie tilted her head to the left for a long look at Peter. "You done well. Now I gonna finish my story. I got bought as a slave by a planter four days' west of here. I cleaned and helped in the kitchen. His wife taught me English. When her eyes got weak, she taught me to read her Bible to her.

"After Massa died, his widow grieved and despaired of runnin' the plantation. I read her the Bible, and when she felt prayerful, I told her she

116

treated folk kindly and they could work wit'out bein' forced. It was they home too and they had nowhere else to go. The Missus looked at me wit'out a word. Saturday she had me make up a big meal for all the field hands. She told them she did not want to sell the plantation and break up the families. Death broke up her family and she knew how bad it felt.

"The Missus had some good years. She let folk keep gardens and chickens and gave us meat when a hog or calf was butchered. Folks got food and more free time.

"I watched what Massa did when slaves was sick. I learned 'bout herbs used by the Pamunkey Indians, and healin' ways African folk remembered from home. When a doctor came, I watched what he done. I looked at Massa's books on physic and read papers that came wit' powders from the apothecary shop. I axed questions and like you do, I kept them in my mind and watched and listened until I got an answer wit'out axin' out loud."

I do that? Peter thought.

"Yes, you do." Annie smiled and continued, "I helped people when they got sick and folks from nearby plantations came when they needed help. The Missus got sick two times, and two times I healed her. Because she was kind, the field hands never made no trouble when she was feelin' poorly. Everythin' hummed along like bees on a flower-bush."

"How can you tell what I am thinking?"

"That ain't part of this story, but I can say they ain't no walls betwixt people's minds 'cept what they put there they-self."

"But...

"The second time I nursed her, she was grateful I kep' things smooth on her plantation. She tol' me she would give me manumission in her will."

"I heard the word manumission yesterday. What does it mean?"

"Manumission is papers that make a slave free. I told her slave or free, I would stay to help her because she been so kind to me, and this was my home. Well, this good woman cried. 'Annie, I would have lost everything and died if not for you. I never had children and you is like a daughter.' She went to town to do the manumission. It don't happen often. A year later, she died of a fever I could not cure.

"I grieved for her and so did the other folk, even 'fore they learned she freed them all in her will. Maybe she freed them because she had no children, or maybe the plantation had no debts to be paid by sellin' slaves, but they was freed just the same. I think her hearin' the Bible in my voice helped her see wit' her heart. In Africa, my family still prays for me and I pray for them. Maybe the missus felt them prayers.

"Her brother did not break the promise to set them free. He was happy to inherit the land, 'cept for twenty acres apart from the rest which she left to me. It had a small cabin on it and was by a creek. I grew food and kept chickens. Many folk stayed in their quarters even though they was free. They was paid for their work in his fields. The next year, I sold my land to the brother. I set out alone grateful to be free at twenty-two years old.

"I talked' wit' wise people wherever I found them. I met folk who could cure people by prayer or kindness in they hearts whether they was Christian, Indian medicine folk, African healer, or some other path. I met a Dogon man captured by the Yoruba in a war. He told me the wisdom of our ancestors." Annie paused. "Is there anythin' you want to ax me?"

"Annie, you were kind to your Missus and she was kind to you. What can Evie do? I have a feeling I'm supposed to help her and the boys."

"That may be why you be here, Mister Peter. Maybe somebody prayed you would come. But Evie ain't made a choice in her heart to be free."

"But if she was prayin' someone would come to help..."

"I did not say Evie was prayin', I think maybe somebody was. I ain't guessin' who, but if you feel somethin' callin', you should follow that call."

"How are you able to tell what I'm thinking? I don't understand that."

"I tol' you there ain't no walls betwixt souls. You came a long way here to do somethin' that looks impossible. The path may be hidden. If you don't pay attention you ain't gonna see it." Annie looked at Peter and her eyes got wide. "You already found a way to help slaves get free ain't you?"

"Well, today I went through a tunnel and read in the library. Later this year, Governor Dunmore will issue a proclamation freeing slaves loyal to Great Britain who are willing to take up arms."

"See what I mean? You done gone through a tunnel that ain't there to a place that ain't there and read 'bout somethin' that ain't happened yet! Those must be powerful prayers brought you here. Keep lookin' and you gonna find somethin', but maybe not what you expect. Now, I got to go to another place and a woman this big don't wander fast," Annie stood up.

Peter thanked her and started up the street. When he turned around, she was already gone. Again! How does she do that? Peter had forgotten to ask Annie about the shift in time. He decided to go to bed to make up for the lack of sleep the night before.

Day 2-14:   Susan and John Dance the Minuet

The reception line at the Palace moved slowly as Susan and John approached the Governor and Lady Dunmore. As she was introduced, Susan curtsied and said she hoped peace would return soon to all the colonies. Lady Dunmore complimented her mantua and her new shoes. "Are those from Europe?" she asked.

"Thank you, Your Ladyship. They're made by an inspired tailor and gifted shoemaker in town."

They entered the ballroom to chamber music played by a string quartet and harpsichord. Elegantly dressed couples from prominent families were enjoying the dance. It was coming to an end, so Susan did not coax John onto the floor.

The first violinist stood to welcome everyone. "It is an honor to play at the Governor's Palace. Tonight we have contra dances, which are European versions of English country line dances. You will hear familiar music by Vivaldi and Scarlatti. As a special treat, we have a minuet by the young Austrian composer Wolfgang Amadeus Mozart. At nineteen, he has been popular in European capitals for several years. The music for this work arrived last month from London and we practiced ardently to play them tonight in their Virginia premiere."

"Mozart is nineteen? The whole world is in 1775!" whispered John.

"This is 1775. We are the strange ones here," Susan whispered back.

John surprised Susan when he squeezed her hand and took her onto the floor for the next dance. "It would be a shame to wear that beautiful dress without dancing. How often do we dance at the debut of a minuet by Mozart?"

A diminutive man gave a brief minuet lesson. He took a portly woman by the hand and went over the steps. "That was perfect, Missus Byrd," he gushed. He asked each couple in turn to try a few steps. "Well done Mister Braxton!" He flattered an elderly awkward man in soft new shoes with a deerskin lining.

"It's one thing to encourage people, but this fellow is obsequious," Susan whispered. She took a dislike to the man. "There's a slithery insincerity about him."

As the ensemble launched the minuet, several couples who had not joined in the lesson were surprisingly good at it, evidently having danced at many such events before. Susan noticed Charlotte the wig maker and her husband George near the edge of the floor, not masters of the dance but doing their best.

"When is the last time we danced together, Susan?"

"It been a couple of years, but this is our first minuet. Isn't that romantic?"

At the end of the dance, the first violinist called for a short break. John went to the restroom and Susan took a glass of apple cider from a side table. The dance instructor approached. "Good evening, my lady. My name is Randall Weaver. Forgive me, but I do not think we have met before. You and your husband dance nicely. Are you recently arrived from Great Britain?"

"I'm Susan Sinclair. I live to the North. This is our first visit to Williamsburg."

"At a Governor's Ball on your first visit? You must be from a renowned estate."

"My family prefers restraint, Mr. Weaver. We are happy to be unknown."

"That is refreshing, Lady Sinclair." He lowered his voice to a conspiratorial level. "One finds the pretentions of the so-called great houses here in Virginia to be tiresome, doesn't one? I often miss the refinement of real gentry back in England."

A middle-sorts planter at his first ball at the Governor's palace was standing next to the dance instructor and asked, "What is so different in England?"

"Sir, this house which people call a palace would not be called such in England. This is the only residence worthy of the name 'house' in this colony. The dwellings of these so-called 'gentlemen' do not compare to the hundreds of great houses of England. Most are grander than this palace.

"And palaces? Compare this humble building to Blenheim Palace in Oxfordshire built for John Churchill, Duke of Marlborough, after his victory over the French. Such architecture, statues, elegant gardens! People here would faint at the sight. That stately palace shall inspire leadership in the Churchill family for generations to come. We shall not bother comparing this place to the least of the royal palaces.

"The Governor puts the best face on it," Weaver allowed, "but this village must feel like an isolated outpost to him. Just think; there are two thirds of a million people in London! Compare that to the mere two thousand in Williamsburg." Susan grew increasingly uncomfortable as the dance instructor mocked the people from whom he earned his living.

"When do you plan to return to England, Mister Weaver?" Susan asked.

"As soon as I gather up a decent purse from these rural pretenders for a comfortable existence in my native land, I will hie me thither to civilization again."

Good riddance, Susan thought as she smiled thinly and wandered across the room to where John was standing.

He took her aside. "I liked dancing with you but I need a walk to work out some memories this is bringing up. I'll walk you home first." He took her arm.

"I understand, John. Dance one more dance with me." They stepped onto the floor for another dance but Susan could see that John was preoccupied. When the contradanse was over, Susan said, "I would like to stay a bit longer, you go ahead."

"Are you sure you will be all right? You should not walk back alone."

"It's only a few blocks to the house and I will walk with others. I'll be fine." For the first time in years, John kissed her on the cheek in public.

"He'll be all right," she whispered as she watched him edge past people gathered near the main door, each vying to catch a moment of the Governor's attention.

She walked to the wigmaker, who was standing next to her husband just beyond the dance floor. "Hello, Your Majesties. You look elegant tonight, Charlotte."

"Hello, Susan." Allow me to introduce you to my husband, George. George, this is Susan Sinclair, the woman I told you about."

"I am George, no relation to the King." He bowed awkwardly.

"Oh Susan!" Charlotte exclaimed. "I saw you and your husband on the dance floor. That is the most beautiful cape. Fit for a queen it is!"

"Alwyn, the tailor across the street from your shop made it."

"Maybe someday he will make something for me in barter for a fine wig."

The men standing near them grew loud. "Quakers were traitors in time of war."

"They are not fighters and will remain on the sidelines. I am more concerned about those German speakers in Pennsylvania. Will they remain loyal to their fellow German, King George III, or will they follow the dreadful Leveler's ideas that claim all men to be equal?"

An elegant woman walked across the room to Susan. "Madam, that is a most stunning mantua. Wherever did you find such a masterpiece?"

"Alwyn Taylor, here in town, is an excellent dressmaker. Excuse me, but I saw you today at the home of Peyton and Betty Randolph. You are Lucy Burwell?"

"Oh dear, yes! You witnessed that unfortunate conversation I had with my aunt. You offered frank but kind words to me as you departed. The secret has troubled me for years, and I felt I would explode if I did not finally share it. Thank you for not judging us harshly."

"There is nothing to judge, Missus Burwell. We all have our crosses to bear."

"Please call me Lucy. And your name is Susan?"

"That's right, Susan Sinclair."

"You don't live in Williamsburg, Susan. I would have noticed you. Oh dear, my husband is signaling me to meet a new Burgess. Would you write your address in this booklet so I may invite you to a party at our plantation? It is refreshing to meet someone of an unpretentious nature and like everyone living in the countryside; we are hungry to welcome visitors."

Susan wrote her local address. "How do you know I'm not a horse thief?"

Lucy laughed. "You are the only person here able to say such outlandishly funny things without blushing!" She crossed the ballroom back to her husband.

A man nearby exclaimed, "Virginia will stay loyal to the crown. Even when Cromwell was in power, Virginia stayed in the hands of the loyal Cavaliers and ruled itself for a period."

"They did until the first British ship arrived. We think the Cavaliers were sympathetic to the Papists," muttered Charlotte's husband George.

"They are Loyalist, drunk, opinionated, and intolerant," Susan commented.

Charlotte's husband whispered in her ear and she nodded. "Susan, we are ill at ease here. I am happy to see you looking so beautiful, but we are going now."

"I understand, Charlotte. I am ready to leave as well. Let's make our dignified exit and we can walk together."

Day 2-15:   Old Soldiers Tell Stories over an Ale

The walk had done him good. John put his elbows on a table in Shields Tavern, rested his chin on his fists, and stared at the candle in the hurricane lamp. The flickering flame entranced him. He sipped a beer.

Susan had said during their courtship that his emotions were bottled up. "You're a wonderful man," she told him, "but it's not easy to touch your heart." What did that mean? He talked it over with an Army psychologist on his return from the First Gulf War. Having a lid on his feelings was not a problem. It was self-control. He did not want to blow up. Anyway, she married him, didn't she?

John did not think about the wars and that was best. He had experienced combat in sweltering Nicaraguan jungles and cold, dry Central Asian mountains. He knew the heart-pounding rush of adrenalin, the surreal focus, and the slowing view of rapid events seen through the borehole of intense concentration.

There were places in the world he had gone before he married, places he could not talk about because the United States had not officially sent combats troops. His clothes, weapon, and gear had not been American and he had carried no American ID or currency. Had he been killed, a field examination would not have confirmed his nationality. With his dark hair and tanned skin, he could be from any number of places. The army would have declared him lost in an accident. He was told it was in the national interest and he had volunteered.

Like places he could not admit to having fought, he had places in his mind he did not venture. Stress? Yeah. Post-traumatic stress? No, he was sure he was fine. Sure, there was pressure at work but he was running again and doing Tae Kwan Do. Not the combat martial arts he learned from Uncle Sam, but it was relaxing and kept him fit. Punching a heavy sack was a good release—release of what?

The beer was bitter, like the beer in Malta on his weekend off, before he was dropped into the North African desert. Don't even think about it. No one knows we were there.

"May I join you?" The voice had a Scottish accent.

"Have a seat." The wheelwright had been the drill sergeant on Market Square. The uniform was replaced by a woolen waistcoat.

"Lass, I'll have an ale with my friend," he called out to the serving-girl.

"I'm John Sinclair."

"I'm Bruce Wallace. Sinclair? Are ye a Scot then?"

"My ancestor came from Nova Scotia to Ohio and married a widow."

"I dinna know settlers were in the Ohio territory long ago but Nova Scotia has many Scots." Bruce raised his glass for a Scottish toast. "Here's tae us, wha's like us? Damned few and they're all deid. Slainte!"

"Slainte!" John knew the toast.

The serving girl came back to take their food order and set a basket of warm corn bread on the table. John asked for the Yorkshire beef and cabbage pasties.

Bruce was a regular. "I'll have my usual shoat pâté. Liver peps me up.

"We spoke at the militia camp, John, and in the wheelwright shop. I learned me first trade back home in Glasgow, apprenticed in the shipyard. When I came to Virginia, I grew fond of working with wood. Maybe I saw too much iron in battles..." He paused. "I built my own cabin and then made a cart. Making a good wheel was the hardest part. I made money from fur, firewood, and timber. Once I had my cart, I was my own transporter, so I saved enough to buy a wee cottage on the edge of town and some land beyond. Then I found a good woman. Now as wheelwright, I work in both wood and iron. What is your work, John?"

"I install things more than make them."

"You are a joiner or a wright then?"

"Not exactly. I send out... wrights to be sure machines are installed properly." John changed the subject rather than attempt to explain to a wheelwright in 1775 the work of an information systems integration manager. "You were right when we spoke yesterday. Like you, I was a soldier. Where did you serve?"

"In 1742, as a boy of fourteen, I fought in the Highland Rangers under James Oglethorpe at the Battle of Bloody Marsh in Georgia. Do you ken Bloody Marsh?"

"Do I ken... no, I don't know of the Bloody March."

"That would be 'Bloody Marsh', John. I am surprised you have'na heard of the victory. It is why we still speak English in Virginia. Fifty years before the English came, the Spanish destroyed a French fort in Florida and a colony in the Carolinas and hanged the prisoners for being Protestants. Two centuries later, they planned to crush the Protestant English colonies one by one. An invasion force of fifty ships filled with soldiers set out to start at tiny Fort Frederica on St. Simons Island.

"We were six hundred Redcoats and a small militia of new arrivals in the Province of Georgia. The colony was a new chance for people down on their luck and their militia was ready to fight to keep that precious chance alive. Do you know of James Oglethorpe, then?"

"No, I don't know much about the history of Georgia."

"As a Member of Parliament, Oglethorpe envisioned a new province to help debtors and others in difficult straits that would be a buffer between the English and Spanish colonies. He named the proposed colony "Georgia" to win endorsement from King George and the tactic worked. Oglethorpe was Governor of Georgia before returning to England.

"As a junior officer, Oglethorpe was at the successful siege of the Ottoman Turks at the White City or Belgrade in the Slavic language. From that experience, he knew we could not hold Fort Frederica against the Spanish, so he took a bold gamble and sent most of us out of the fort to lay an ambush along the trail from the sea. 'Twas a noisy day and as a soldier ye ken my meaning. With few losses on our side, we defeated the Spanish at the outset of their campaign to conquer the British colonies. Spanish armor still snags a plow blade now and again to remind us how close we came to oblivion. Only later did I think about the mothers, wives, and children in Spain and Florida waiting in vain for their men to come home."

Although it was a pivotal moment in American history, John had not heard of this threat before. "You had an important victory." They clinked glasses.

"Johnny, I tasted defeat as well and saw my friends' wives widowed. After Bloody Marsh, I returned to Scotland and Oglethorpe returned to Parliament in London. Three years later at seventeen, I joined the Rebellion supporting Bonnie Prince Charlie. You've surely heard of him?" John nodded. "Good. I am named Bruce Wallace after Robert the Bruce and William Wallace, so 'twas my natural choice. Have ye heard of them?"

"Yes, I saw *Braveheart* the movie..." John barely caught himself. "I mean I know the moving story of brave Wallace and Robert the Bruce."

"At Culloden, we formed our lines on an exposed moor betwixt stone livestock enclosures, a bad spot at Culloden chosen by O'Sullivan, the Prince's adjutant general. Other officers complained, but Prince Charlie did not overturn the order. We were tired, hungry, and soggy. Many men out foraging did not hear the call to battle. Disputes among clans led some to leave and others to refuse to charge when the fool order came.

"Lowland clans ranged against us on the English side and artillery under Major James Wolfe hit us as we waited for an attack, but it never came."

"The same General James Wolfe killed as he defeated Montcalm at Quebec?"

"Aye, the same, he was not a general then. Our men were cut down like oat stalks by artillery on the hill and muskets behind stone walls. The

Prince ordered the first line to charge. As those reaching the British line raised their broadswords, the Redcoat to their right, bayoneted each man under his sword arm. 'Twas the first trained use of the bayonet in history and a lake of Scottish blood was spilled.

"In the second line we waited for an order to charge or retreat but if 'twere given, I never heard it. Musket balls, cannon balls, and rain fell upon us, and men turned to run. The British carried out orders to kill even those who surrendered.

"Some things we do not talk about when we return home, but I see in your eyes you know battle, so I will tell you 'twas the gift of Robbie McDougal's last thoughts and prayers that saved me. He stood forward to my right when a cannon ball swept away his head leaving his body to fall limp to the ground. I was showered by a horrific splash of brains. I wiped my eyes and turned to run when I felt a sting in my leg. The whack of falling to the stony ground saved me from being shot again.

"From where I lay, I saw the Redcoats bayoneting Scottish wounded. When a bayonet got stuck in a man, they fired a round so they could pull back their weapon. I lay 30 yards away, not bleeding much from my own wound but with Robbie's brains on my face, I looked deader than most dead men and no one checked me before they moved back to refresh themselves and celebrate their victory. Too many men died there, John.

"I heard the whistles of musket balls sentries fired at men attempting to crawl away. I slowly pulled the arm of a dead man over me face, the folds of his wool cape over me chest. Amongst the dead and dying, I carefully sipped water from me flask. I prayed for me mother and sister and the soul of me father. I prayed for clouds to cover the moon but none came. In the morning, the soldiers camped far from the stench of corpses. When the moon passed behind clouds the next night, I crawled away. Two thousand Scots were slaughtered at Culloden and the victors butchered people in the highlands. They plundered food and livestock and burned buildings. Many survivors of the massacres starved.

"I was taken to Hugh Mercer, a doctor for the Scottish forces. He saved my life by disinfecting and sewing me leg. He asked if I would come to the colonies. 'I've been in the New World' I told him, me at seventeen being the one with experience.

"I heard that Major General James Oglethorpe led four cavalry companies at Culloden. One company proudly bore the name Georgia Rangers. I found it, how do they say, ironic."

John asked, "How did you get back to the Colonies?"

"With the help of sympathetic Scots, including many who had not joined our cause, hundreds of us made our way to the Hebrides Islands as did Bonnie Prince Charlie, helped by Flora MacDonald. The Prince took a boat back to his exile in France but we found ships carrying refugees to Nova Scotia, Pennsylvania, and the Carolinas. Flora went to North Carolina with her husband Alan MacDonald.

"Mercer moved to the western frontier of Pennsylvania where he fought in the French and Indian war. Wounded, he was left for dead by his retreating mates. He found his way home, moving alone for weeks through Indian country dressed as one of them. Mistaken for an Indian, he was almost shot by sentries as he limped toward a fort. He became known for this adventure and he accepted Washington's invitation to move to Fredericksburg, Virginia, to open an apothecary shop.

"Like Mercer's, my life has settled. I am 47 and happy as a wheelwright. I am also a cooper. I like coaxing soaked hardwood to bend into wheel rims and barrel staves. If I push too hard, the wood snaps just to spite me. Johnny, tell me of your service to Mars the God of war. How did it come to be I am supping here with ye and not your lonely widow?"

"Well, Bruce, I served in more than one war."

"You speak like a man who has had schooling. Were you an officer?"

"No, I was a sergeant like you. I went to college when I came home."

John was stirred by Bruce Wallace's stories and for the first time, he told his own stories without naming the countries where he fought. American secret advisors to the Contras in Nicaragua were not officially in combat. Nor were men inserted into Afghanistan to support the Mujahedeen in the fight against Russians in the eighties.

John told Bruce of losing his friend Danny to friendly fire in the Gulf War. "Our own artillery took him down. As Danny lay dying, our sergeant, we called Sargon, was furious as Hell. He saw Danny blown open and he jumped up to wave off our guns—a bad mistake. A round from an enemy sniper took him through the head. Like your friend Robbie, Sargon was dead before he started falling. That moment I became acting sergeant. I yelled at the men to drop down and crawl among the rocks closer to the enemy to get out of the target area of our artillery. I ordered them to cease firing to avoid drawing enemy fire and we wriggled forward like salamanders. Near the enemy, we lay still. They pulled back to avoid the artillery fire which was finally landing forward of our position."

It was good medicine for John to open up to a seasoned warrior with graying temples like his. Bruce understood the sudden loss of close friends. "Who was it you fought? And what is a sniper?" He looked at John with curiosity.

"A sniper is a crack rifleman. We fought uh… in Spanish colonies and later I battled Russians and fierce tribesmen in the mountains of Asia."

"'Tis strange I have'na heard about your wars. 'Tis not easy to defeat people on their own territory. How did those wars end?"

"We won most battles but our leaders tired of the dying and expense, and brought us home. Years later we made peace with our old enemies."

"Maybe the English will win most battles until they get tired and go home."

"Maybe so."

"Well, John, we are living quieter lives these days although perhaps for not much longer. People on both sides of the ocean seem eager to offer up the lives of young men to win an argument. Will ye be here long?"

"In a few days, I'll return to where I come from."

"Well, since ye will be here a few days let me warn ye about taverns around here particularly at crossroads outside town. They can be as violent as a battle field."

"What should I watch for, Bruce?"

"There are bad apples baiting drunken buckskins from the frontier into a fight for money against a man who has stayed sober. They gouge and dismember. They might pluck out a man's eye or tear off his privates as the betting crowd cheers. Pay special mind to a pair called Dancer and Dagger. Dancer fawns upon the better-sorts with dancing lessons. He also talks young men into fighting Dagger."

"I heard the name Dagger before. My daughter met him chasing a runaway servant for bounty. I hope for their sake I don't run into them."

"Stay sober if ye mean that. Ye shall need wits and skill. He is wily."

"We are closing the tavern now," interrupted the serving girl.

"It's time to go home, John. I have enjoyed your company."

"Likewise, Bruce." The former sergeants made their way to the door of the smoky tavern and set off in opposite directions in streets dimly lit only by oil lamps on a few porches.

128

Day 2-16:   Megan Finds Mark's Hut

Wary from her experience walking alone the previous night, Megan waited until two couples came by on foot and fell in behind them for safety. She looked back several times to be sure no one was following. She ducked down the walk to the blacksmith shop. The forge was dark.

She quietly crossed the yard past piles of coal. Nothing behind the forge looked like a dwelling. By the back gate, she smelled pigs as she had her first time in this yard. Grunts and high-pitched squeals came from beyond the fence where a large sow lay on her side with new piglets squirming over each other to vacant teats. "You're all so cute," she whispered.

She gently opened the gate but it squeaked loudly. She froze before silently easing it closed behind her. In darkness, she edged down a path, feeling her way a step at a time. Sudden, savage barks of a large dog burst out beside her. An image of angry fangs leapt into her imagination, and she let out a cry stifled by her own hand as she realized the dog was behind a fence. A canine chorus began, and she rushed along a hedge hoping she would not trip on a stump.

Around a corner, dimly lit by a lantern, two men stood up. Standing Elk chuckled. "I think this is the screech owl we heard frightening the dogs."

"Oh, it's you! That was scary! The dog was right next to me and..."

"'Tis all right now," assured Mark. "Please sit." He indicated a log standing on end, its bark removed and top sanded smooth.

"I told you going out alone is dangerous," said Standing Elk.

Breathing too hard to respond, Megan handed Mark the bundle.

He placed the present on a log. "Would you like a cup of broth?"

"Yes, please."

He stepped into a lean-to set against a wall and was back with steaming chicken broth. Megan sipped and her breathing and heart rate slowed down. Crickets chirped and cicadas added a rhythmic rasp.

"Go ahead and open your present, Mark." As he looked over the clothes, Megan explained her idea. "The posters describe runaways by the clothes they wear. There are no drawings of their faces. If a person were in different clothes, no one could recognize him from the description. You worked a long time and have more years left, so I wanted to help."

Mark studied the white wig. He was moved by her generosity but awkward about expressing gratitude. "This is most convincing. No one would suspect a bonded blacksmith to be so well attired."

Megan sat quietly. A crow squawked from a roost beyond the wall. Green katydids high in the canopy joined in with the cicadas.

Standing Elk broke the silence. "Do you think Mark should run away?"

"I thought escape was what you two were talking about so secretively." Mark looked at Standing Elk. They did not answer.

Crickets carried the conversation. Moonlight filtered through the boughs of a tall pine. Looking up, Megan saw fireflies high above. "Look up!" She pointed. Pulses of light moved among the branches, tracing dots when they hovered and dashes as they moved. "It looks like many fireflies but there are five. You can trace their paths by their flashes."

Mark cleared his throat. "Megan, your generosity, and these gifts are… well, even with these clothes, the success of an escape is not guaranteed."

"You have to take a chance to make a change." Megan hesitated. "I know a secret. My brother Peter found out that Governor Dunmore will proclaim free slaves and servants who take up arms on the Loyalist side."

Standing Elk studied her. "There are eddies in the river of events these days and anything could happen. Mark has never seen such a gift Megan. I am sorry we seem secretive, but danger is afoot. I'll tell you something that may explain why Mark and I are concerned.

"West of the fall-line, up-river beyond where ships can go, the land has been filling up with settlers. Since the French and Indian War, new arrivals and freed servants seek unclaimed land with land titles in hand or none. Brigands attack settlers on the trails. They steal and make the massacres look as if we Indians were the perpetrators. My people and yours hunt down as many of the cutthroats as we can. Along the frontier, soldiers skirmish against Indians twelve years after the war. Escape for anyone in that direction is not easy.

"Now in many places, Loyalists and patriot rebels have begun to fight, sometimes settling scores with old enemies that have nothing to do with politics. These are not good times to set out into any violent areas."

"What are you saying, Standing Elk? Should Mark work until he earns his freedom or follow the Proclamation and get free by being loyal?"

"Megan, I live in a Mattaponi village north of here. We have gardens and animals, fish in the river, and live in peace. If my people become entangled in the rage sweeping the colonies, we could be swept away even if we pick the winning side. Just as we must be careful, servants, slaves, settlers, and gentry all face difficult choices in the months ahead."

Megan wondered why Mark did not respond himself to the suggestion he run away. Maybe Standing Elk was trying to distract her. "How did you manage to keep your lands during the French and Indian War? Weren't people afraid that you would fight on the other side?"

130

"Since the mid-1600s we pay an annual tribute in deer skins to the Governor of Virginia. We stayed out of the last war. It helped that many of us are part European, part African, or a mix of all three. When times were tense, to protect our families we went to town looking as much like the other people as we could or we stayed home. There is too much suffering in our history to risk breaking the peace now."

Megan turned to Mark. "Something is troubling you. I don't want to complicate your life. The clothes are a gift whether you run or not."

"Thank you, Megan. This means more to me than I can say."

"You're welcome." Megan hesitated, "Mark, I'm not pressuring you for a relationship. If you ran away, I knew I would not see you again."

"Megan, you are the most honest, direct woman I ever met. We don't know of a proclamation freeing servants and slaves but if it requires taking up arms, I have never killed anyone and I hope I never shall."

They slipped again into silence. The insect songs sounded new to Megan. Individual creatures sent out each chirp or rasp. The fireflies high above signaled to each other. She was absorbed by the rhythm in the sounds and patterns in the flashes of light. "Wow! The insect sound and light show is beautiful. I have been mean to them. Bugs have short lives and they are doing the best they can."

"They are born into the same world we are and share this day with us."

"I see that Standing Elk. Settlers take land from the Indians. The King tried to stop the fighting by reserving land for the Indians but the plan is not sincere. The rich use the poor, and people kill each other because they think the others are wrong or they are afraid of them. They do not see the gifts of Creator. They do not notice that we all fit together.

"Mark, you told me to be quiet about your meeting Standing Elk because it was dangerous for me and you might be hanged. I was not listening, but now I think that you and Standing Elk are talking about how all the problems fit together. I don't want to put you in more danger but I hope you don't mind that I will pray for you to be safe."

She stood up. "This is a special evening for me. I'm learning to notice what is happening not just what I want for myself. See you again, I hope."

Standing Elk rose. "Megan. I shall walk you home."

Megan and Standing Elk stepped into the darkness. Mark sat quietly. After a minute, he heard barking of dogs but no shriek.

Day 2-17:   Safely Home for the Night

As Susan got to the door of their house, she was startled by a figure hurrying up to her.

"Hi, Mom! I recognized your luminous cape in the moonlight."

Putting a hand over her heart, Susan relaxed. "Oh, you scared me, Megan! Did you have a good evening?"

"I learned how little we know about history, especially Dad! How was the ball?"

"We made history. Your father danced the minuet with me. He left early to go for a walk. Don't be mad because he didn't accept what you learned about the taxes. You are saying different things from what we were told all our lives. If what you say is true, it will take him time to work through it."

"If it's true? Mom, don't you believe it either?"

"I'm adjusting to a new way of looking at things. We are all learning here. I believe you."

Inside the house, Megan headed to her room and Susan looked in on Peter through his open door. Tired from the gathering at the Hush Harbor the night before, he had fallen asleep on the bed with a book beside him and the oil lamp still lit. She gently placed a blanket over her son, put out the lamp, and smiled, thinking how fast twenty-one years had gone by.

She lit a candle and started a small fire in the fireplace. As the kindling crackled and three small logs began to burn, John arrived and she could tell he had had a bit to drink.

"Hi, Honey," she welcomed him. "Did you have a good walk?"

"I met the sergeant again. It was good to talk with an old soldier."

Susan saw that the conversation with the sergeant had a salutary effect on John. Something in him was loosening up. She gave him a hug and he returned the squeeze. She was disappointed when he slid into sleep within seconds of his head touching the pillow.

Day 3-1:   November 1775

"Rise and shine! It's time to get up!" Susan called to Peter.

"What time is it? I mean what year is it?" Peter yawned loudly.

"It's still 1775 it's already November and chilly out there—that's crazy. Megan and I found out when we got coffee and scones at the Raleigh Tavern bakery. She went off to study her notes."

At breakfast, Peter said, "I won't take food for granted any more. Virginia had hard beginnings. By fifteen years after the founding at Jamestown, only two thousand people survived of fifteen thousand that landed since 1607. They faced starvation, disease, fights with Indians and each other—lots of disasters. A ship from Bermuda saved them at the beginning, and later tobacco provided income."

"Two out of fifteen surviving is worse odds than a battle or an outbreak of bubonic plague." John took a sip of coffee.

"I'm praying our survival rate is four out of four," said Susan.

"This is not the 1620s. We'll survive," Peter assured her, hoping it was true. "Slaves and servants are poorly fed. Settlers moving west try hunting and gathering, but many don't know how to hunt or what to gather."

"Megan says the local Indians are friendly and that helps," John added, "but soon His Majesty's Royal Artillery, Infantry, and Grenadiers will be very unfriendly. This is a much more violent society than the one we live in." John finished his breakfast. "Let's meet here at noon. How will Megan know?"

"One of us is bound to run into her. This is not a big town."

Day 3-2:   Peter Sees Augustus off to Norfolk

For an hour, Peter read the notes he took at the Rockefeller Library. It was not going to be easy. Over the two generations, the Underground Railroad led tens of thousands of slaves to freedom mainly into Canada. The British freed a hundred thousand in six years—but rarely helped them. Only ten per cent of those who ran during the Revolution made it to a new life.

The downside could be death for Evie or her sons. Was it worth the risk? A slave's best chance seemed to be to get to loyal colonies, or Britain, France, or Africa. Should he tell her Dunmore's coming proclamation was a rare chance for freedom and let her make up her own mind?

Peter stepped into chilly November air. As he walked to the Powell House, he grew excited that Dunmore's Proclamation could be a way for Evie to escape. She would have to beat the odds and avoid the consequences of failure. By a tavern, he learned he was not the only one excited. On the porch a citizen called to passersby, "A week ago on November 7, Dunmore freed slaves who join the British cause. He ordered attacks on rebel towns and plantations. We have war in Virginia as in Massachusetts. What a calamity if slaves attack their masters! Make haste to spread the word lest the news reach the slaves first."

Now it did not matter if Peter told Evie about the proclamation because it was announced already. Farther on, he saw Augustus marching toward him, a canvas sack on a pole slung over his shoulder like a musket.

"Hello Augustus," Peter called in a failed attempt to avoid startling him.

"Oh, Mister Peter. I ain't seen you since we was wit' Annie. It turned out like you said. I waited for months and then this proclamation came."

"Are you off to Norfolk?" asked Peter.

"Please don't say nothin'. If I leave town beyond the College and walk like I does when I'se fetching something for Massa, and don't look scared like a rabbit, then I'se hopin' nobody will ax me my business."

"That sounds like a good plan, Augustus, but planters and the county militia will be watching the roads to Norfolk like an owl eying a rabbit hole, and you could be their rabbit. The closer you get to Norfolk, the more you should keep to the woods. Would you like help?"

"I'se tryin' not to look like a rabbit, but inside I'se jumpy."

"Is freedom worth this danger?"

"Yessuh! If Annie and you be free, and Moses freed the Hebrew children, then the Lord who delivered Daniel from the lions can deliver me!"

"Sit on this bench, Augustus. I have an idea." Peter took a piece of paper from his wallet and wrote, "The bearer of this note is my trusted servant, Augustus. I gave him five Spanish dollars to take to his former master, my cousin George, near Smithfield, to buy medicine. Augustus will return to me at Williamsburg carrying a package." He signed it with a flourish.

"What do it say?"

"It says you are taking five dollars to my cousin at Smithfield for medicine."

"Is he sick?"'

"I don't have a cousin there. The money is for you and the note shows anyone who stops you that you have a reason to be on the road. Smithfield is across the James River toward Norfolk."

"I cain't take five whole dollars of your money!"

"I saw you become a healer, and now I see you setting out on a challenging journey. Augustus, you can help others with the money and with your healing skills. Don't take a boat to Norfolk. The boat owner may sell you. Go up river toward Richmond until the river narrows, and then find a bridge or swim it."

"I cain't swim."

"Find a shallow ford if there's no bridge. From there keep to the woods and head east, the direction of the sunrise, to Smithfield then Norfolk. If someone stops you, find out which side they're on. If they are Tories, say you're joining the forces loyal to the King. If they are colonial militia, show them the note. Pretend to be stupid. Maybe they won't shoot you. If they point a gun at you, don't be nervous. It will make you look guilty."

"Don't be nervous? I'll die of nervous 'fore they shoot me even once! But I been pretendin' I'se stupid all my life. That part be easy for a slave like me."

"You're not a slave, 'Gustus. Not because I say so, but because you say so. You just ran away, remember? Slavery is in their minds, not yours."

"I hear that and I believe it be true. Praise God! I'se a free man!"

Peter shook Augustus's hand. "Good luck, Mister Augustus."

"Mister Augustus... *Mister* Augustus! Thank you, Mister Peter. I will always remember this." He set off down the road.

Peter watched him disappear down the road. He stood to walk to the Powell House as two militiamen and a man in a cap caught up with him

"This is the fellow!" The man in the cap pointed at Peter.

"Halt right where you are," a militiaman brandished his musket.

Peter stood still and raised his hands. "Did I do something wrong?"

135

"This fellow says he saw you talk to a slave. He says you gave the slave a note and money. What did the note say and what was the money for?"

Peter worried Augustus had been captured. "He is taking a little money to my cousin in Smithfield where he is going on an errand for his master."

"We have a lot of trouble with slaves these days. It ain't right you talking to another man's slave. Are you sure he ain't running away?"

"I hope not. Then Mister Carter will not get the errand done."

"You hope not? You gave him money and with that, he could go farther and feed himself until he was long gone. We cannot have that going on."

"Let's put him in the stocks to teach him to be careful about the slaves," said the other militiamen. They each grabbed one of Peter's arms and marched him to the nearby courthouse. There was already a man sitting with his legs in the stocks outside the building so they called for the bailiff who opened the heavy upper board of the pillory and placed Peter's head and hands into the holes and locked him in.

The soldiers and man in the cap left Peter in the pillory, standing bent over in an awkward position. "What did you do?" asked bailiff.

"They saw me talking to the slave of a friend. I guess that was the wrong thing to do." Peter did not want to get in any deeper.

"Well," pondered the bailiff. "Those militiamen are short tempered these days." He pulled out an old pocket watch. "I don't want to go against what they ordered so I'll keep you here only an hour. I hope no more young ragamuffins come by to throw rotten fruit or dog shit at you. Time in the pillory or stocks can be dirty."

The man in the stocks whimpered, "Look what the ruffians rubbed in my hair this morning! Can you let me out in an hour too?"

"Not 'till sunset, Alfred. The merchant you insulted was sorely angry at you." The Bailiff walked back into the courthouse.

"I apologized for what I done!" the man in the stocks called out.

If what Peter did for Augustus were known, he could be sitting in a cell and facing a questionable future. He bent his legs slightly to take the strain off his back. After a few minutes, he grew extremely uncomfortable. He hoped no one would come to harass him during his hour in the pillory. His hope would not be fulfilled.

Day 3-3:   John at the Magazine and Masonic Hall

John approached a noisy assembly near the octagonal powder magazine. "When Dunmore seized our powder and threatened to cancel land grants to veterans, he almost provoked insurrection!" a man shouted. "Patrick Henry called up militiamen and Hugh Mercer prepared to ride from Fredericksburg with a company of light horse."

"But Peyton Randolph negotiated a settlement. Dunmore paid for the powder and maintained the grants."

"'Twas settled poorly!" shouted a third man. "We need powder more than money! Let's march to Norfolk, sink Dunmore's ship, and chase the Redcoats off!"

"We should not widen this conflict! Britain is the world's strongest military power and does not fight alone. Do you want to fight the Loyalist militias of the Floridas, Maryland, Nova Scotia, Quebec, and loyal counties in New York, New Jersey, the Carolinas, and Georgia at once?"

A man in the back of the crowd called out, "There is news from up North. Benedict Arnold and Ethan Allen raided Fort Ticonderoga and captured British cannons to fire at Redcoats in the siege of Boston."

"No wonder our King declared those colonies in rebellion! His forces will thrash them!" exclaimed a man from across the Chesapeake. "Our Maryland legislature began its recent session with an oath of allegiance to His Majesty. Last year, John Adams said we do not seek independence. We want our rights as Englishmen just as our forefathers in Britain struggled for their rights since the Magna Carta!"

John wondered how the Founders kept people together and how they survived years of fighting. The chances were slim. With so many links to Britain, was the war necessary? Were my wars necessary? His mind spun. It seemed simple in school. We were the good guys and they were the bad guys. This was much more complicated.

He wandered away from the rancorous group and found himself in front of the Masonic Hall feeling a strong urge to bang the brass doorknocker. No response, so he tried the handle. Locked! He turned to leave when the door opened behind him. There in colonial dress was James Walker, the Episcopal priest. "Oh, it's you!" he stammered, "I'm John Sinclair. I was at your sermon Friday."

"You sat in a front pew next to the woman I met in the bookstore. The Hall is closed but step in a moment. I'll get out of costume before church."

"Your costume?"

"Yes, the Lodge hosted a breakfast this morning in colonial dress."

"I... I am confused about the time. The reenactments seem so real that..."

"I understand. Sometimes I imagine we are in colonial times. This is an active Masonic Hall but we occasionally have public tours. I'll give you a quick look around." They climbed the stairs to the Lodge Hall where Reverend Walker pointed out highlights in the room including the intricately carved Master's Chair, a gift of Governor Botetourt in the 1760s. "If his successors had been Masons perhaps the colonists and Britain could have settled their differences without a war."

"Who is the Master today?"

"I am—for three more months, and then I'll be a Past Master. In Freemasonry we rotate through the chairs, moving up gradually so that many have the opportunity to take responsibility when they are ready."

"You called this a Masonic Hall. I've heard it called a Masonic Lodge."

"Technically, the building is a Masonic Hall or Temple, and when we are in session the assembly is called a Lodge. People get that confused."

"How did you become a Mason, Reverend Walker?"

"Please call me James. To join the Freemasons, you ask a member of a Lodge to invite you. You'll be welcome if you believe in a Supreme Being whatever your religion, or even without a religion."

"Can an Episcopal priest be a Mason?"

"Certainly. The Reverend James Madison, a cousin of the President, was a member here and later became the first Episcopal Bishop in Virginia. In the 1920s, W.A.R. Goodwin was rector at Bruton Parish Church and a Freemason when he enrolled John D. Rockefeller, Jr. into restoring Williamsburg. Many luminaries were members—Peyton Randolph, President James Monroe, St. George Tucker..."

"St. George Tucker? I was at his house reading and drinking lemonade."

"They have a good library. You may meet a wise woman there named Frances. She knows history and seems to know a lot about intuition."

"She does? I met her briefly. I'll go back this afternoon to talk with her. Reverend Walker, I heard that Masons were involved in the founding of America, that they know deep mysteries, and that some of their symbols are part of the Great Seal of the United States. How much of that is true?"

"Many Freemasons helped form the nation. George Washington and Benjamin Franklin were Masons. At least nine of the 56 signers of the Declaration of Independence were members and probably more. However, many Founders, including John Adams and Thomas Jefferson, were not Masons.

"There are abundant myths about Masons. I could lower my voice and speak of a Divine Plan to bring forth a New Order of the Ages. Some talk

138

of secret crypts hiding treasures or ancient scrolls. I could whisper those things but as a long-time Freemason and Master of this Lodge, I have not run into secrets like that while studying Masonic traditions or participating in our ceremonies. In my experience, men in the Lodges learn to work together, become more virtuous, and contribute to their communities. A popular Masonic slogan that sums up the point of our practices is, 'We take good men and make them better.' I think we do that, with support from each other and from the Supreme Being, whatever name we use for it.

"There is a spiritual quality to all we do at the Lodge and all we aspire to in daily life. A deep and glorious potential within every one of us may be the real yet best-hidden secret treasure. There are Divine secrets around us and within us. They are secret because we do not turn our attention to notice. In the outer world, no one was keeping radio waves secret when Moses led the Israelites out of Egypt or when Christ preached the Sermon on the Mount; we just did not notice or know about them back then. Radio waves are still invisible but they are not a secret anymore. Our inner qualities are revealed with a similar gradually growing awareness. People the world over use prayer, ceremony, and spiritual practice to notice what previously was unknown to them.

"We use symbols in ceremonies that we don't make public. Why not? Realization of the meaning of symbols or parables is a personal experience. We prefer not to weaken the effectiveness by talking about them. If someone learns a new concept without experiencing the deeper meaning, a new obstacle is placed on the path to realization. They think they know the truth because they have a new belief. That false certainty gets in the way of observing the depth of the practice in life. For that reason, some of what we do is secret, at least until the member is ready."

"That sounds like a wise approach. Can you tell me whether the Great Seal of the United States is a Masonic symbol?"

"There are Masonic, Egyptian, and Hebrew symbols on the Great Seal that we can see on every dollar bill. Charles Thomson, Secretary of the Continental Congress, did the final design of the Seal in 1782. He was not a Mason. Some design elements were suggested by three earlier committees that included Masons and non-Masons. As a young man, Thomson was adopted by Delaware Indians. Perhaps the tribe provided the symbol of the eagle that for many native peoples is a carrier of their prayers to the Creator and a messenger from the Creator to the people."

"So what really was the Masonic influence on the birth of America?"

"One third of Washington's Continental Army generals were Masons. Perhaps it was Freemasons' confidence in one another that led to those promotions. I would also say Freemasons' ideals and aspirations supported the Founding Fathers' commitment to liberty. Whether a Royal Governor like Botetourt who lived in the Palace or the jailer Peter Pelham, who lived at the Gaol, as 'Brethren in the Craft' they met as equals in the Lodge. They called it 'on the level' and respected each other as men rather than ranked by titles, wealth, or station."

"I heard men talking about 'levelers.' Is that related to 'on the level'?"

"Not directly, but men who grew accustomed to treating each other 'on the level' might well begin to wonder about the foundations of their society such as the Divine Right of Kings and the hereditary rights of nobility in Europe and of the wealthy landed class here in America. For the very wealthy those are revolutionary, dangerous ideas."

"Revolutionary, indeed! Reverend, I know you have to change for church. I'm still confused about the imagination at work around here but talking with you helped."

"Good to see you again, John."

John stepped back into the street amidst the smells of wood smoke and horses.

Day 3-4:   Susan Tours the Public Hospital

Susan set out to search for Jane wearing layers to keep warm in the nippy November air. She stopped at the millinery shop. "Ah, Lady Sinclair, I have wondered how the dress and mantua were received."

"They were a big hit, Alwyn. People assumed I came from a highborn family. My husband danced with me for the first time in a long time."

"A long time you say. It is not easy to keep track is it?"

"No kidding. It seems like yesterday I bought that mantua. You're a tease, Alwyn! You know more about time than you are letting on."

"Susan, I work here in the midst of history. I have an active imagination and on rare occasions, I meet someone who experiences the same things I do. Not a good explanation, but that's all I know about it, verily."

"That's a bit helpful, Alwyn. Do you know a woman named Jane who wears a cloak and speaks about peace? I'm anxious to talk with her."

"I don't know her but I have seen her many times in public places."

"Thanks for everything, Alwyn."

Susan carefully crossed the street avoiding the horse droppings, and entered the wig maker's shop. Charlotte turned around and gaped.

"Hello, Charlotte! It was wonderful to see you at the Ball. Today is the first day I have been in town since then. How are you?"

"Lady Susan! I worried all these months." She hugged Susan then stepped back. "Oh, Milady! Forgive my impertinence!"

"I told you I'm a middle-sorts wife like you." Susan smiled.

"Susan, my husband and I are fearful of war. Friends on both sides are ready to hang each other. George says everyone has gone mad. I pray your family is safe. A customer is coming for trimming, so I can't chat long."

"I understand. I just dropped by to say hello. Do you know a thin, shy woman named Jane who wears a brown cloak even in warm weather?"

"I know who you mean, Susan. On occasion, I see her walking to the Public Hospital. That place gives me the shivers!"

"There are many people in distress. Thank you, Charlotte. I will look for her there."

The door opened as Charlotte's next customer stepped in. "Thank you for visiting, Susan. In topsy-turvy times 'tis nice to have friends."

Susan walked past the church and turned south. Her thoughts turned to Jane when she reached the path to a two-story brick building topped by a cupola and weather vane. By the door, a sign read "Public Hospital for

Persons of Insane and Disordered Minds." She paused at the entrance wondering if they would let her in, then smiled. More importantly, will they let me out? She knocked on the heavy door using the fleshy side of her fist. A key turned in the lock, and a slave opened the door a crack. "Are you here to visit Doctor John de Sequeyra?"

"Uh, he's not expecting me. I am Susan Sinclair. What's your name?"

Surprised to be asked, he responded, "I am Sal. I can tell Doctor you is here."

Susan felt a shudder as the great door closed behind her and the key turned in the lock, but Sal's kind manner put her at ease.

A man with his hands pressed together walked by, slowly repeating a phrase. Susan could not make out his prayer until she realized it was not English. *"In manus tuas commendo spiritum meum. In manus tuas commendo spiritum..."* his murmured prayer faded down the corridor.

Sal returned to say the doctor was doing a ducking and she could follow him to see the doctor at work. They passed heavy doors with barred windows and the murmuring man going the other way, *"In manus tuas commendo spiritum meum..."*

They came to an immense barrel full of cold water. A chair was suspended above by a chain running over pulleys into the hands of a slave. In the chair, restrained by leather straps, a patient, gagged to keep her from biting her tongue, attempted to kick her bound legs. Her wet hair matted to her head and her eyes were filled with rage. "No more! Cold!" Susan made out through the woman's gag.

A dark-haired man in linen shirt and woolen waistcoat, stood beyond the range of splashing. He nodded and the slave lowered the chair.

"No, no!" The woman's shouts became a stifled bubbling.

My God! Susan thought, do they think this woman is a witch?

The man in the linen shirt nodded again and the slave raised the chair. "What do you say, Missus Jackson? Enough for today?"

"No more! Cold, cold!" coughed the bedraggled woman in the chair.

"Well done! When you stop shouting all night, there will be no more ducking. Daniel, you may lower Missus Jackson. Sal, escort her to her room where Rachel shall dry her. Do what you can to calm her." The man turned to Susan. "Welcome. I am John de Sequeyra, the doctor here."

"I'm Susan Sinclair." She gathered herself after what she had witnessed.

"It is damp here. Let us adjourn to my office." Susan followed the doctor, surprised at his relatively kind manner with Missus Jackson. On their way to the office, the praying man passed them again.

In Doctor de Sequeyra's small office Susan sat where he gestured. "Thank you for coming to the hospital. I rarely get visitors. How may I help, Missus Sinclair?"

Susan started with a new question. "What is the man in the hall saying?"

"He is repeating in Latin the last words of Jesus Christ according to the Gospel of Luke. Jesus was quoting the 31st Psalm, which is better known to me than the Gospel. It means 'into your hands I commend my spirit.' He may be a secret Catholic but he never talks about it. If so, it may be safer for him here among the insane than out there with so-called sane people who might kill him for his beliefs. His prayers calm the other patients."

The doctor smiled. "You appear to be of sound mind. Troubled persons do not knock on our door of their own accord. Oh, except for one woman. We are the only such hospital in all the colonies. A need was noted by the Council of Burgesses and we were fashioned after the Bethlem Royal Hospital near London. Its nickname 'Bedlam' has come to mean chaos and madness. Did you come to visit a patient?"

"Thank you for seeing me, Doctor De Sequeyra. I am a teacher and mother from Northern Virginia. I came to ask a question and to look for someone. But first, can you tell me the benefit of the treatment you administered to that woman."

"The four humors, Earth, Air, Fire, and Water, make up our bodies. Air is represented by blood, Fire by yellow bile, Water by phlegm, and Earth by black bile. That woman has too much yellow bile as evidenced by her anger and shouting. We duck her to douse the fire to balance the humors. With the coming of winter's own damp, that should not be needed."

"I see. For her sake I am glad of that."

"It is for her sake that we administer the treatment. She shows signs of recovery. I suspect the insane manage problems by retreating into unhealthy states of mind. We use compassionate restraint so they cannot hurt themselves.

When treating other ailments, we use tulip tree bark to reduce fever, lavender flowers as a sedative, and rosemary to stimulate blood flow. We bleed patients to reduce pressure on the brain."

Susan winced, she hoped not visibly.

"Besides sparing people the cruelty of being chained in barns or smothered by those who fear madness is demonic possession, we release one in five back to their homes. We hope to cure more troubled souls."

"Doctor de Sequeyra, I have a question about problems of ordinary people. I am a schoolteacher. What can you advise for a person who is agitated or depressed?"

"I see such patients in my practice on the main street. I administer laudanum or a ration of brandy to relax them. Since you teach children, I shall share a professional secret. Humors have cycles, and moods change with circumstances. I find good results come from simply listening to what a distressed soul, young or old, wishes to say. When people share a burden, adverse feelings fade. I may suggest herbal tea or walks in nature. If they are devout, I suggest they pray for support. Are you religious?"

"I'm an infrequent churchgoer. Do you attend the Established Church?"

"Like everyone in the colony, I pay taxes to the Church of England and attend services once a month or face a fine. However, that is not the faith of my fathers. I am most familiar with the first five books of the Old Testament we call the Torah. I am the only Jew I know of living in Williamsburg."

"There are no other Jews here? How does an eligible Jewish doctor find a bride? Where I come from, many young women would love to marry a Jewish doctor."

"I must live in the wrong town. I join Jewish families in Richmond or Norfolk for the Day of Atonement or Passover. I gave slaves here names from the Torah: Rachel, Samuel, and Daniel. A few months ago, Samuel renamed himself Sal, which he says reminds him of his youth in Africa when he was free. At Passover, we Jews remember our Exodus from the wretched condition of slavery in Egypt, which is also in Africa, so I am happy that his name reminds him of freedom. He is skillful at caring for the hard to reach and he recently learned to read."

"As the only Jew in Williamsburg, you didn't spring from a burning bush. Are you from Pennsylvania?"

"I was born in Holland where my Sephardic ancestors moved to escape the Spanish Inquisition. I came here to experience the New World. Speaking of experience, do you care to walk through the hospital? Some of our patients walk in the halls, and help by cleaning or by serving food."

They walked slowly past the twenty cells of the hospital. Through barred windows, she saw some patients in chains tethered to the wall. Others lay arms and legs akimbo or in a fetal position on a straw mat. Two were restrained in a head brace to prevent them from biting themselves or others. The cells were cleaner and better lit than those of the gaol.

A patient shuffled toward them with eyes piercing yet vacant. His voice demanded and pleaded, "I don't want to be stuck in eternity. Day after day, it stretches forward and back in time. It always was and will always be. It is frozen but not cold. I am locked in a scream with no sound." He opened his mouth in an expression of anguish and stood motionless.

"Ask the Lord to help you, Nathan."

"I don't deserve help!" he snapped. "None of you know a thing! You are lost in eternity like me. You believe religious fairy tales that disperse like steam in a windstorm! Day after day it stretches..."

Sal returned from escorting Missus Jackson to Rachel. He put his hand on the patient's shoulder. "Walk wit' me, Nathan, to the end of the hall and back. Swing your arms when you walk and you will not be frozen. Listen for the heavenly music. You know it never be far away."

Nathan looked startled by the physical contact on his shoulder. Without another word, he set off slowly swinging his arms just as the praying man came past again, "*In manus tuas commendo spiritum meum.*"

"He certainly has a way with patients," Susan noted. "Doctor, I'm looking for..." At that moment, a cell door opened and Jane emerged, carrying a soiled blanket. "I was going to ask where I might find Jane."

Jane was startled to hear her name, "Doest thou know me?"

"We spoke by the Capitol a few months ago. You said you lost your family in a war. I told you my husband was troubled by war."

"Forgive me. I speak to many people. I don't remember thee."

"Jane Harding, this is Missus Susan Sinclair," the doctor said. "She came to learn about the hospital. Please take a few minutes outside in the fresh air to explain to her what you have learned here."

"Oh, I would like that very much." Susan saw Jane's hesitation.

"Go ahead, Jane. The fresh air will be good for you both. Oh, look! Here comes Sal with Nathan. He shall open the door and you two can talk."

Sal opened the door. Nathan continued past, swinging his arms and humming heavenly music. "Rachel will launder the blanket and you may come back to help another day," the doctor assured her.

Susan set a slow pace down the walkway. She judged it better to walk in gardens rather than crowded noisy spaces. "Jane, it is kind of you to help at the hospital. I'm sure you ease the doctor's burden."

"I strive to do what I can. There are so many troubles in the world it is hard to know where to start, and there is no end. It seems so dark."

"Jane, I care about the spiritual life. I know you work for peace and help the tormented. Are you a member of the Society of Friends?"

Jane tensed.

"I attended a Friends' Meeting House for a wedding and was moved by the spontaneous voices speaking after periods of silence," said Susan.

"Hast thou been to Meeting? Most call us Quakers. Yes, I was born into the Society of Friends, but I have not been at Meeting for years. If I seek Inner Light, fear and loneliness come upon me. Long ago, Friends were willing martyrs when Puritans hanged them for preaching after being banned. I serve in small ways and have not found a deeper service."

They came to a bench by an oak tree, boxwood hedge, and a rose bush offering a few late blooms. "Jane, let's sit a moment in silence." Leaves trembled in a light breeze. Their fallen brethren rustled on the path. Clouds soared slowly, shapes transforming. Jane sighed.

Susan recalled her deep calm the first morning by the fire. Was that months ago? She listened, watched, and felt herself slow down. The words came to her again.

"The extraordinary — extra ordinary, forever underlies the apparent.
Beneath habitual, behind familiar, all form animated,
All pattern emerging, resolving, and dissolving."

Jane raised her hands in an attitude of prayer, put them to her face, and trembled. She sat in silence. Then words came:

"The Light within illuminates eternally through seeming darkness.
Beneath the known, behind the dream,
light causes all that moves, sustains all that is still.
Source of all becoming and all slipping away.
All come, all go. The Light is ever and forever so."

After several minutes, Jane looked into Susan's face. "It has been so many long years. I was but a girl the last time I felt touched by the Light."

"You have been in pain a long time, Jane Harding."

"I wandered in fear without solace. Thou has gifted me, Susan Sinclair."

"We both received a gift, Jane. I have a pain I've never shared with my children." She drew a long breath. "Many years ago my older brother Richard was called up to war. He told me he was afraid to die or be maimed, but even more, he worried he would kill a person who did not want to go to war either and was as afraid as he was. I was stubborn, naïve, and almost crazy from wishing I could stop the war. While my brother was in training, I joined protests on the streets of our city. When the time came, he went off to war... and he never came back to us."

"Did he die in the war against the French?"

"It was a far-away war, at another time. A week before he was to come home, he was ambushed in a forest. Some men in his platoon survived and got back to their base. No one saw what happened to Richard. His body was never found. I think I married my husband partly to help a

146

soldier. I saw my own pain in your eyes by the Capitol, and I looked for you."

"That was a kindness thou did for thine husband. My grief led me to the edge of madness, and I visit the Public Hospital to help poor souls and seek peace. I witnessed what happened to my family when I was twelve."

"What happened? When you were at the Capitol, what did you fear?"

Jane sighed. "This is not Pennsylvania, and sixteen years have passed. Doctor de Sequeyra told me many times that no one wants to hurt me, but I never mentioned even to him that I was from the Society of Friends or those Paxton Boys who committed that horrible deed."

"I haven't heard of the Paxton Boys. Do you want to tell me?"

Jane watched a squirrel harvesting acorns. "That squirrel is making ready for a hard winter. A hard winter is coming to us all. I don't know how I shall bear it."

"You said, 'The Light within illuminates eternally through seeming darkness.'"

Jane sighed. "During the French and Indian War, a group called the Paxton Boys came west and slaughtered Indian villages that had long lived in peace with us. People in the Society of Friends warned Indians they knew and urged them to escape over the mountains. My people sought to save lives but..." Jane took Susan's hand to compose herself.

"Rather than escape as the Friends hoped, a village was reinforced by Indians from the West. The Paxton Boys were ambushed, and some killed." Jane wiped away tears with her sleeve. "My father was one of the men who warned the Indians. Months later, after my mother died from fever, I was gathering berries by a stream. As sunlight sparkled on the water, I felt my late mother's presence and did not want to leave just yet. When my basket was full, I followed the path through the woods toward our house and saw smoke.

"When I ran home, I fell to my knees and wailed. My father and two brothers lay bloodied on the ground, their hair cut away as hostile Indians do. The roof of the house was gone and one of the burning walls fell in as I stared. I was horrified and ran along the wagon road to the east to get help from my uncle and his family.

"I saw their house in flames and white men loading a cart. I crawled near through the bushes. One man called out 'Let's ride lads! We have one more visit to treacherous Quakers today. I hope they are poor because we have no room in the cart.' They laughed, Susan Sinclair! Dead children lay on the ground and they laughed! Another said, 'Tis a tragedy the

147

savages resorted to butchery. The militia will ride west to take revenge.' He cleaned a long blade on my auntie's apron torn from the line."

"I heard one say, 'Come on, Roger. You shall use your dagger again today.' The last of them mounted and rode away down the wagon road."

"I don't remember walking home. The shovel was gone but using pointed rocks, I scraped shallow graves for my father and brothers and covered them with stones as we had done for my mother. Over the next days, I buried the poor souls at the other houses and bathed in the stream where my mother saved my life by causing me to linger. I walked to southeast Pennsylvania finding food where I could. I worked as a maid for a German family for four years. They were kind to me.

"Where the Susquehanna empties into Chesapeake, I worked in a tavern. Men would not leave me alone, so I went to Alexandria and found a family that needed a maid. I was not free from fear of the Paxton Boys finding me, so I moved on to Williamsburg. I thought my fear was silly because the bad men never saw me. But a few months ago, I thought I saw the man with the long knife here."

"Fear is not silly," offered Susan. "My husband taught me courage is not the absence of fear—it is willingness to face that which we fear. I am inspired by the courage of the girl you were. You and I seek peace so people won't have such horrible experiences in the future. The Light was in you all along. No need to call me Susan Sinclair. Call me Susan."

"In the Society of Friends we don't use mister and missus so we use the full name. Thou sayest the Light is always near. It came through today."

"Jane, I feel a calm I have never felt. My brother is at peace and I can be at peace about him. You and I experienced something wonderful."

"I thank thee for this, Susan."

"Jane, my family and I have met wonderful people here. I can introduce you to them. With friends you might feel less alone."

"Wilt thou be my friend?" Tears came to Jane's eyes.

Susan hesitated. "Yes, Jane, I will. I live very far from here, but know that I will always pray for you and we will be friends from afar."

"Susan, there is a trial this afternoon at the Court House. I fear an innocent man is being persecuted, and I will be there to pray for him. Art thou free to join me?"

"I will join you at the Court House and we can pray together."

Jane took Susan's offered arm and they walked back toward Market Square.

Day 3-5:   Megan Sees Patterns in the Pasture

Fortified by tea and scones, Megan found a path through a pasture to a spot in the sun. She sat on a log with her back against fence boards already warmed by morning rays. A trail into town passed on the other side of the fence. She read her history text and added to her notes. "Oh boy!" she exclaimed. "Wait till Dad hears about the Boston Tea Party!"

The sunlight shone through the thinning leaves of an oak tree as a dancing mottled veil. Megan noticed her surroundings. Bees were still at work in November. A lone swallowtail butterfly visited wildflowers, its open black wings shimmering with a patina from purple to light blue with vivid orange spots. The pattern changed with the angle of light. She smelled grass, soil, and traces of wood smoke.

A birdcall heralded an approach on the trail. When the sound of footfalls was close, she looked up to see Standing Elk walking toward town. He smiled when he saw her and vaulted the fence. "Hello, Megan. May I sit?"

"Sure." Megan hid her text under the notebook. How is Mark doing?"

"He is doing well and still at the forge."

Standing Elk looked across the meadow to a line of trees. Megan was not used to silence and she spoke. "The scenery here is beautiful,"

"It is beautiful like the fireflies you saw in spring."

"I remember how the flashes of fireflies and the sounds of crickets all fit together. We were part of that pattern as we sat in a circle by Mark's hut."

Standing Elk smiled. "What do you see in those white flowers?"

"Clusters of tiny white flowers, petals pointed up making cups with yellow at the center. The top leaves are narrow and dark green. Near the ground they are drooping and gray." She felt a leaf. "Fuzzy underneath."

"We call it rabbit tobacco. Settlers call it 'everlasting' because it blooms into winter. We use it in tea to treat pain or coughs or burn the leaves for aromatic smoke for purification. We put it into pillows for a good sleep."

Megan crushed a leaf in her fingers. "Oh! Nice fragrance—it's... astringent, like a persimmon that's not quite ripe." She touched the edge of the leaf to her tongue. "Yup, astringent like witch hazel."

"Good. You use all your senses. That shrub by the sycamore is witch hazel. It has unusual flowers, little green pots with yellow ribbons. We make a poultice of its bark for bruises. That plant with pointed leaves by your feet is Virginia Spiderwort. In spring, purple blossoms come and go in a day, a short beautiful life, but flowers keep coming for two months."

"I'll bet you use that plant for something, too."

"Yes, we eat shoots as greens and when the leaves are old we boil them for a poultice for bee stings and mosquito bites. The tea is good for the stomach or kidneys. Mixed with other herbs it helps women on their moon. It was taken to England a hundred years ago. Our purple friends are now in many English gardens. See those yellow flowers?"

"Those are dandelions!" said Megan. "We can use the greens in salad and kids like to blow the seeds when the flower becomes a fluffy ball."

"Our children blow those seeds, too. Our ancestors did not. Dandelions were not here yet. Colonists brought them to eat as an early spring green. The plant moves west faster than the white man, and Indians who have seen not a white man now know dandelions. We did not have honeybees before they were brought by Europeans.

"Megan, there are designs in the veins of leaves, in wings of insects, and in the many mirrors of a dragonfly's eye. There are patterns you see, patterns you hear, and patterns you feel. Everything is part of moving patterns. You and I are part of the whole. We receive food and medicine from the Earth and warmth and light from the sun."

"I'm beginning to get that."

"Bees, deer, flowers, and worms in the earth, we all strive to live and grow. Our bodies go back to the Earth. That is a flowing pattern, too. We feel separate but we take in from each other and give out to each other or we would cease to be. Most do not notice but you are waking up. What keeps people deaf, blind, and alone is that they do not listen, look, or touch. We live in closed worlds we imagine instead of using our imagination to explore the world as it is. You are moving outside that pouch to be open."

"I am?"

"Waking to the patterns of life may be why we are here. We learn from each other. My people receive both benefit and bane from the Colonists. We buy iron goods, muskets for hunting, and other useful inventions. And they buy from us. South Carolina settlers get rich growing rice, but they also have a major export of deerskins traded with native people.

"New plants, animals, and people can be good for this land, but some are greedy for more and hurt other life. Colonists brought English Ivy vines that invade the land and kill trees by blocking light and weighing down the branches. Some colonists are like that. Their hunger for land and misuse of it hurt all life. They clear trees for iron works and rain carries away living soil to clog streams. Their tobacco depletes the soil. Powerful families and new arrivals seek new land in the West to begin the destruction again by girdling trees."

"My brother told me about that."

"Take a walk with me and I will show you." He vaulted the fence, Megan climbed over, and they walked together.

"My parents named me Standing Elk to remind me that we Pamunkey and Mattaponi are still here. Sadly, the Manahoac, Moneton, and Occaneechi tribes are gone forever from the land you call Virginia. They no longer tend ceremonial fires, though their blood may flow in a few people who remember a grandparent with love. My tribes found a way to remain. In the Treaty of Middle Plantation, now called Williamsburg, signed by Charles II, we agreed to pay a tribute to the Governor every autumn. We swore loyalty and kept small lands and the right to carry arms."

Standing Elk led Megan to a field where the trees had a ring of bark cut away, leaving blackening branches reaching toward the sun but no leaves to receive the light. Around them, mounds of soil with corn stubble were evidence of a harvested crop. "This is terrible." Megan shuddered.

"Now look at the field over here."

"It's full of bare patches and weeds and washed out gullies."

"Forty years ago that land was a forest. The trees were girdled by cutting a ring of bark and they died. The land was used for tobacco without letting it lie fallow. The crops failed. Now the soil is barren. These planters do not see the destruction because they are blind to life. When they ruin their land, they ruin themselves. This using up land cannot continue forever. However big this world, we will run out of land someday as more people keep coming. When the land is used up, all people and all life will suffer. It happens slowly over generations and most people cannot see the pattern.

"Men are even pillaging the seas. What will those Yankee whalers do for oil when the whales are gone, thrust harpoons into Mother Earth herself?"

Megan looked surprised. "That may be a prophecy, Standing Elk."

Standing Elk sighed, "I struggle to find the will of Creator behind this destruction. I know everything comes and goes but when whole tribes go and whole forests go, it is not easy to see a purpose. Maybe someday we will finally learn that what we do, what we say, what we think, always comes back to us. Always. There will be great beauty when we all learn that. Let's walk to something else I want to show you."

They came upon a ravine and he pointed to a tree. "Here is a good thing Colonists brought. The white mulberry was carried to Georgia to feed silk worms. Black mulberries have been here forever but white mulberries are new to us. The berries are pink and delicious and come in abundance for weeks. They are something sweet for your people and ours."

"Do you think people will learn to take care of the land?" asked Megan.

"They might," Standing Elk replied. "Wiser land owners like George Washington and his neighbor, George Mason, put manure, ash, and bone meal onto the soil to replace what they are depleting. They let fields lie fallow alternate years to build up again. It helps their plantations remain prosperous, leaves a better estate for their children, and slows the race to use up the land our Creator placed in this world for all creatures and people to share.

"Many owners are so squeezed by debt they plant every year until crops fail and they abandon their farms. Land beyond the proclamation line is being cleared against the command of the King. Secret investors in the Ohio Company and Vandalia Company send servants who do not know better into Indian country. Colonial leaders take land from the tribes because they ruined the land they took in the past. They think about getting wealthy quickly, not about tomorrow, not even about their own grandchildren. They give no thought to the future when there will be no new land to take. Megan, this is dangerous talk."

"Taking that land is not only illegal but also unfair."

"It is unfair to us and to our grandchildren and theirs. They do not look deeply into the present so they do not see the shape of the future. We all have some of this blindness. Prayer and ceremony help us see what is in and around us. When you saw the fireflies' paths, it was like a ceremony."

"I saw something I'd never seen before."

"Megan, today we are having a ceremony called a Spirit Lodge or Sweat Lodge. I would like you to come. You could learn about how people keep in balance and how we practice seeing what is deeper but always here."

"Yes, I would like to come."

"Good. I must go to complete my tasks in town. Mark will come to the Lodge. Go to the blacksmith shop and ask him to take you there."

"But I..."

"See you tonight!" he called over his shoulder as he walked up the trail.

"Right! Back to Mark this afternoon." On the way to the house, Megan thought about what to say to her father and how she could ask Mark to take her to the Sweat Lodge after not seeing him for months.

Day 3-6:   Early Plans for Union

John and Susan ran into each other late in the morning and stopped into Charlton's Coffee House. Peter passed by just as his parents came out. "Peter!" his mother cried. "Are you alright?"

"Good God! What happened, Pete?" John ran to his son. "Where's the wound?"

Looking seriously injured with dry blood matting his hair, Peter insisted, "I'm fine, Mom and Dad. Some kids by the market poured bull's blood on my head."

"Why did they do that to you?"

"I was put in the pillory for an hour after I was spotted talking to a slave. The kids played a prank. Two of us were locked in and they poured half the jar on each of us. The other poor guy has to stay like this until sunset. He may get other visits. I'm hurrying to wash up at the house."

They walked quickly. Peter wiped his face with a handkerchief Susan gave him.

"That's just awful, Peter. Who put you in the stocks?"

"A couple of militiamen told the bailiff to do it, Mom."

"I shouldn't have to tell you not to take reckless risks, Peter," John reminded him.

At the house, Megan greeted them from her room. Susan laid out lunch. Peter rinsed off with well water outside before going to his room to finish washing up.

It was too cool to eat outside so they gathered to eat their sandwiches by the fire.

"Peter, you look better without blood all over your head. An injury or death can happen that suddenly. There are real risks here."

"I'll be more careful, Dad."

"This is a dangerous time," Susan said. "I learned a terrible thing from Jane, the woman I've been looking for. She volunteers at the Mental Hospital. I sat with her in silence like the Quakers do and it was beautiful. Then she told me her family was massacred by white men who made it look as if Indians did it. She was twelve when she found their bodies and buried them herself. No wonder she worried about war."

John shook his head.

"What did you do this morning, Megan?" Peter questioned.

Megan was happy he asked. "I learned that getting rid of the Stamp Tax and Townshend Duties helped the colonies practice cooperation, but getting together was not a new idea. Way back in 1697, William Penn proposed a Plan of Union of English colonies for defense and business — like settling trade disputes or preventing people from running to another colony to avoid a debt or taxes."

"Nothing is certain, except debt and taxes."

"Come on, Peter! That was death and taxes!"

"*That* was a joke."

"I'm trying to make a point. In 1754, an Albany Congress of nine colonies discussed common defense. Benjamin Franklin suggested a federation like the Six-Nations Indians had done. His plan was approved unanimously at the Congress, and then sent to London and the colonial assemblies. They all rejected the idea."

"So what about the taxes?" John persisted.

"That's the point I'm trying to make! The colonies were thinking about union long before the problems over the taxes and they started the Revolution several years after the taxes were repealed so it was about much more than taxes!"

"What about the tax on tea? Everyone knows about that," challenged John.

"That's true, Dad." Megan was ready to spring a trap. "A small tax on tea was left when the Townshend Acts were repealed. The Boston Tea Party was in December 1773, with a bunch of guys dressed up as Indians. Here is the cool part. If the small tax on tea was there for way more than a thousand nights, why did those guys suddenly decide to throw that tea into the harbor that night?"

"I don't know, Megan."

"Why that night? Look at what happened just before. In May of that year, 1773, the Tea Act was passed..."

"You see..."

"Yes, I do see! That Act was not a tax. It allowed shipments of tea by the East India Company direct from India to the colonies without reloading in England. It lowered the duties, which were much higher than the tea tax."

"What has that got to do with anything?"

"It had everything to do with it! The Tea Act undercut the price of tea brought in by smugglers rowing out to Dutch ships. Those British ships in the Port of Boston were the first to arrive carrying tea direct from India. The tea was due to be unloaded the very next morning and show up in stores at half the price people had been paying on a luxury item."

"So?"

"So obviously, it was the guys who made money from tea smuggling who threw the cheaper tea into the sea. Because it never reached the stores, the people never knew it was cheaper. They were told it was because of the taxes and they cheered. We still think it was about the taxes but it was not about helping the people, it was for profits! The Tea Party movement in our time got it completely backwards!

"Why didn't the smugglers throw tea into the harbor a year before or two years before? I'll tell you why. Expensive tea was not a threat, but they were about to be put out of business by lower prices. They pretended to be Indians and pretended the reason was taxes. They would not get public support for throwing tea into the harbor to keep prices high, would they? We are not so dumb as to think Indians did it. So why do we still think it was about the tax? Why do people think the Boston Tea Party was a patriotic act when it really was a rip off of the people of Boston?"

"There's no reason to get upset."

"I'm upset because that kind of stuff still happens in our time! Some tax cuts or reductions of environmental and health protections increase profits for some industry but hurt working people, old people, and young people. How can we get a fair deal if we don't look behind the scenes? Follow the money, Dad!"

"Decisions were made by the elected leaders of the colonists. It was fair."

"No way! In 1775, there was no secret ballot. The vestrymen and burgesses for the county sat at the table when a person walked up to vote. An ordinary guy—I say guy because women couldn't vote—a ordinary free guy who owned property would have to be brave or dumb to vote against powerful rich men sitting right in front of him."

"We don't have a system that unfair in our time," insisted Susan.

"I agree it's not the same, but big money pours into elections on behalf of the interests of the donors. Like I told you yesterday, some guys on radio and TV tell the people what's good for them and mock anyone who disagrees. Listeners don't think for themselves but smugly think they're in the know when they hear the show!"

"You're upset for nothing! There's more to it than that!"

"You're upset, too!"

"I'm not upset but I don't think what you're saying is correct!"

"In Virginia it wasn't about taxes either. The King's proclamation that Indian land in the West would be managed by Quebec was a big reason for the fighting. The leaders wanted to take more land from the Indians! How come we didn't learn that in school?"

"Maybe because it didn't happen that way!"

"Fine! I'll go do more research! I won't be back for supper. I've got an invitation." Megan jumped up and was out the door with half a sandwich in hand.

John went to the door to call her but she was already down the block.

"She'll be all right, John," Susan reassured him.

"Do you believe what she was telling us?"

"It's not the history we learned, but she didn't make it up. We are finding out things we didn't know. The Burgesses talked about this our first day here."

"They were way off in their interpretation." John snapped.

"Based on what happened the next day, maybe they weren't interpreters."

Peter quietly ate his sandwich. Things in 1775 were not what he had learned either.

Day 3-7:   Peter Follows Evie to the Bridge

After lunch, the November air lost its chill. Peter found a sunny spot on a bench with views along Palace Green and Duke of Gloucester Street to watch for Evie returning from her errands. Was it his imagination or did the well-dressed people of Williamsburg look nervous today? How many slaves like Augustus were on their way to Norfolk already? He worried again about signing his name on the note he gave Augustus. At least no one knows who Peter Sinclair is.

"Good afternoon, Mister Peter Sinclair."

"Evie! You startled me. I didn't see you coming."

"I was behind you so 'less you got eyes back there it would be hard to see me comin'. Nice to see you, Mister Peter. I got to hurry to the post office on an errand."

"There are important things I want to tell you."

"Don't walk close. People will notice us talkin'."

Peter had learned a lesson this morning. He stepped back. "How's that? Better?"

Evie smiled and started walking. "Walk one step closer," she said without looking back. "If you far away you gonna shout and the whole town will hear."

"I want to tell you about Dunmore's Proclamation freeing the slaves."

"The Governor done made us free?"

"Not exactly. He proclaimed that slaves on rebel plantations will be freed if they go to Norfolk to take up arms for the King."

"Well, that don't help us 'cause we ain't on plantations and we ain't takin' up no arms. I could shoot my foot or my head off just touchin' one of them muskets."

"I know, but many are running to Norfolk, not just those who can take up arms and fight. This morning I ran into Augustus, running away. I helped him by sending him the long way around up the James River."

"Gustus ran away? Dear Lord, I hope no harm befalls him. He is my boy Dilli's daddy. Oh, maybe I should not tell you that."

"I knew that already, Evie. Augustus is on a dangerous path. He will fight on the British side to get his freedom. He told me if all goes well, he'll help you and the boys."

Evie took a breath to calm down. "Here we are. I got to mail this letter for Massa Powell." Peter followed Evie in and pretended to look at quill pens for sale. The clerk weighed the letter, looked up the rate in a tattered folder, and carefully counted out the coins Missus Powell had given Evie. Peter left the post office first.

"Is this is a good time to get free?" Evie asked when she came out.

"It's a dangerous time. Soldiers are raiding plantations, and there is fighting in many places. Williamsburg is at peace so you and the boys are safe for now."

"I am 'fraid to run to an unknown fate. Did you talk to Annie?"

"I went looking for her and found her waiting for me. Can we look for her now?"

"We ain't goin' to find Annie just like that."

"I didn't say we'd find her. Just looking for her could help us think clearly."

"That be true, Mister Peter. We can take a back way home through a pretty place I go to be quiet. Follow until we get to where no one can see us." Peter watched Evie slip into a small passage past the grocer. He paused to look in a shop window then followed down a stairway and path into a beautiful miniature world.

A tiny waterfall splashed from a pipe to become a stream flowing over shining pebbles, past lilies, Queen Anne's lace, an ash tree with drooping boughs, and lush ferns in the damp rich earth. Peter heard bird songs and saw two squirrels chase one another on the roof of an outdoor press used to make paper for the printing office. Beyond, Evie stood on a little bridge over the stream and Peter joined her there.

They both jumped then giggled at the loud "Harrumph" of a bullfrog, wide eyed and alert on a sandbar. A stalking cat approached, interested in the birds but paying attention to Peter and Evie. The cat suddenly looked up and there was Annie coming down the path.

"Oh, Annie!" blurted Evie. "Mister Peter said we should look for you, and here you be!"

The cat disappeared into the ferns seeking salamanders.

Annie was beaming. "I'se happy to see both of you, but let's get out of sight." They walked a short distance to a log bench well hidden behind bushes.

"Annie, what should we do? It ain't safe to stay and it ain't safe to run. Our lives was easier before these choices. If we run one night, death could take us by morning. My boys' life ain't so bad. They has food and clothes. Even shoes!"

Peter felt as if he had disappeared.

"Child, don't be so 'fraid about dyin'. We all die one day. You don't live by hidin' from life. You watch wit' your eyes and ears and mind open to which way everythin' movin' and not movin'. You 'member Old Julius? He stepped in front of horses and was broken up and gone by sunset. Maybe he stepped past the first horse and ain't seen it was two horses, or maybe he didn't look both ways 'fore he crossed the street." Peter recalled his own near miss in front of his house.

"But how do I know the right thing to do? We could get found by Continentals and killed or brought back in chains. We could die in the forest. We could be catched and sold to a bad Massa. We don't know if English soldiers will let us on a boat or how life might be if we go. How would we see anyone again that we love?"

Annie tilted her head slightly and studied Evie. "This knot has many threads, and to untie it ain't simple. Listen, child, you cain't die seven ways on the same afternoon. You worry about so many things happenin' all at once. Someday you gonna die anyway so why fill your head wit' frettin'? Even if you die of one thing, it will save you from the other six that had you 'fraid."

"But that wouldn't help me!"

"It could save you worryin' every precious day about seven ways of dyin' when you could be prayin' 'bout ways of livin' well."

"I know you ain't wastin' breath, but I don't see the point in it."

"Listen. Every day you see them hoops the chillun' play wit' on the street."

"You taught me somethin' usin' hoops, about leavin' the burden to the Lord."

"Yes, child. Everythin' that moves and everythin' that stands still can teach us 'cause Spirit is in everythin'. You remember when I told you some hoops in life is heavy, and you should not try to lift them or step in front like Julius did wit' the horses?"

"Yes, I remember."

"You roll a heavy hoop down the road wit' a tap-tap of a stick and run alongside as it rolls. Well, them hoops have more stories to tell and it be time you knew another. When you look at a hoop lyin' by the road how many hoops is they?"

"I don't understand."

"Child, this is the easy part. When a hoop is lyin' still, how many do you see?"

"One?"

"True. One hoop lyin' on the ground. When the hoop rollin' down the road how many hoops do you see?"

"One?"

"That ain't exactly so. You never ran beside a hoop to see how many. When the hoop goes 'round in a circle as it fallin' down, how many hoops is they?"

"I don't know what you mean."

"You don't know how many hoops because you never looked. This is a big choice you makin'. How things move and how they stop is how things come to be like they is, and you pay no mind to that."

"I don't understand, Annie, but when you tell a story I know somethin' is there."

"I want you to go home and heat up water and wash yourself all over like when you go to a weddin'. Pray for clear eyes and a clear mind to see a path through the brambles. Maybe you ain't got much time to choose a road for you and the boys. Then go roll a hoop and use wise owl eyes to look close as it rolls. Look close 'cause this world happenin' fast. You look when you hits the hoop and look when that hoop is fixin' to stop. You come and tell me what you seen, and we gonna talk about what to do and what to don't."

"Where will I find you?"

"Where you always do, right where I be and no place else." Annie walked off.

Evie stood quiet a long minute. "You know what she talkin' about Mister Peter?"

"She's saying it's complicated. You should look at a hoop. Evie, this is confusing to me, too. But I'll visit you with a hoop if I can find one."

"Will you come around tonight after dark to help? I gonna go to Nicholson Street and you wait 'til I'se gone to go the other way." She squeezed his hand and left.

Peter made sure he was alone and left the garden the way he came, pausing to listen to the water falling onto the rocks. He was about to have another surprise.

Day 3-8:   Megan Cantors to the Countryside

Megan stomped three blocks up the road gripping the half sandwich. I'll just drop in on Mark who hasn't seen me for six months and say, 'Hi Mark, take me to a Sweat Lodge.' This is not going to work. She sat on a bench and finished her sandwich while staring at the ground. She wanted to prove her research had revealed something, but no—Dad's stuck on what he learned years ago.

She looked up at the slow drift of a cluster of cumulus clouds. Watching their lacy fringes dissolve into invisibility, she slowly cooled down. Standing Elk's words about struggling to see beauty and purpose behind the pattern of difficult situations came back to her. There's a pattern here too, she thought. I blew up at Dad like I always do. All his life, he has known things to be a certain way. I didn't give him space to let in something new. I'll apologize when I see him next. For now, I look scraggly and I'm in recovery from a hissy fit. It's not a good time to visit Mark and ask him to take me to the Sweat Lodge but I have to do it! This is part of a pattern too, I guess.

It was a short walk to the blacksmith shop. Framing and trusses were in place for a major building expansion. She sidestepped the construction and entered the shop. "Here goes..."

There were no customers and three smiths were hard at work as she approached Mark. He looked up. "Oh! Megan, you are a refreshing sight."

"I... thank you."

"When did you get back to Williamsburg? I have not seen you since May."

"I was away and uh, just got back today." For her, it was the truth.

"I've looked for you, Megan. I am grateful for what you did for me."

"I was happy to do it, Mark. What's all the construction here?"

"With the fighting, the shop is becoming an armoury to make musket barrels by the hundred for the militias. I am afraid we're going to be busy."

"I wish the war wasn't coming, Mark, I saw Standing Elk this morning."

"You did? So did I. He invited me to a Sweat Lodge. Will you go with me?"

"I..."

"Sorry to be so bold, Megan. You are probably busy doing something else."

"No. I mean, yes, I would like to go to the Sweat Lodge with you, Mark."

"Truly? Splendid! Mister Anderson is sending me to take a message to an iron works that is on the way. I want to stop for food for the feast, so we must leave in fifteen minutes. 'Tis an hour's ride from here."

"Fifteen minutes? An hour ride?"

"Yes. The Lodge will be this afternoon and we shall return not too late in the evening. I have to finish this quickly. Can you wait for me?"

"I... yes. I'll be back in fifteen." Mark resumed hammering and Megan walked to the street. There was no time to get home and change. She found a bench.

"Hi, Megan! I saw you come out that gate. How are you doing?"

"Wow! Hi. Peter. I'm in shock right now."

"Was the argument with Dad so bad?"

"It's not that. I should have realized that people can't let go of what they thought they knew the first time they hear something different. I want to apologize to him."

"I think you're right about the taxes."

"So do I but I don't have to be a rebellious teenager all my life, do I?"

"My, my. Little sister is growing up fast."

"This place is turning my head around, Pete."

"Mine too, Meg. I heard a strange riddle about a hoop today. 'When a hoop is lying still in the grass there is one hoop but when that hoop is rolling down the street and spinning around to come to a stop, how many hoops are there?"

"What's the prize?" asked Megan.

"The prize is freedom and the risk is disaster."

"That's a high-stakes game. I can find you a hoop so you won't have to guess."

"You can? Where?"

"Wait right here and I'll be back. I have two surprises." Megan hurried back down the walk toward the blacksmith shop.

Peter had waited only a few minutes when he heard Megan call him.

"Hi, Pete!"

He stood up, astonished to see his sister rounding the corner high on a white stallion, sixteen hands at the withers, behind a young man wearing a black leather jerkin over his linen shirt. She brandished a large iron tyre ring in her right hand.

162

"Here's your hoop, Pete." Megan held out the tyre. "Mark says you can borrow it to solve the riddle. Mark, this is my brother Peter."

"Good day, Mister Peter. Megan speaks well of you."

"Hi Mark. Nice to meet you." Peter reached up to take the hoop from Megan.

"Listen Pete, Standing Elk invited us to a Sweat Lodge an hour's ride from here."

"Who is Standing Elk? What should I say to Mom and Dad?"

"He's Mark's Indian friend. Please tell Dad I'm sorry I got mad. Tell the folks not to worry. I'll be with a group of people and I should be back before nine."

"We must be off." Mark nudged the stallion into a trot. Megan waved.

Peter watched his sister ride away. "In 1775, she rode off on a white horse behind a handsome blacksmith to an Indian ceremony. What am I going to tell Dad?"

At the edge of town, Mark cued the horse to the three-beat motion of a canter. Megan had ridden before but only at a walking gait or trot. They rolled in smooth arcs as the surroundings streamed by. "We're flying!" she called out.

They rode for twenty minutes on a dirt road; then Mark slowed the horse to a trot and turned down a long wagon track to a two-room log house. A neatly built livestock shed and corncrib stood behind it near a root cellar dug into the side of a hill. In the back was a huge pile of composting leaves. Mark dismounted and led the horse through a narrow point in the worm fence. "I want to buy a food offering for the feast after the Sweat Lodge. It won't take long."

Megan was happy to stretch her legs. She was surprised when Maggie, the milk seller from the market, stepped out next to her husband Bartholomew.

"Well, Mark, you brought a friend along. She is the kind young woman I met in the market in the spring. She got Bartie a nice vest."

"Hello, Maggie. Hello, Bart. Megan got a nice vest for me, too. I'm riding to the iron works on an errand, and then Megan and I are going to a Sweat Lodge at the Brown place. What have you got I can buy for the feast?"

"You've picked the perfect time to come, Mark." Bartholomew recognized his old vest but did not mention it.

"You say that every time."

"I do, because 'tis always the perfect time, Mark. We have corn meal, wheat flour, and salt for the fry bread the Indians like, butter or lard for frying, and we began pressing corn and sunflowers for oil."

"That oil is healthier for us. Animal fat makes us fat animals, I say." Megan added.

Ignoring Megan's comment and his paunch, Bartholomew continued, "I can kill a chicken for you fresh. Do you have time for us to blanch it to pluck the feathers?"

"They won't have time to cook a chicken. We will take the fixings for fry bread. What vegetables are left?"

"Carrots and cabbage and we have smoked sausages made this week."

"Good, I'll take sausages, a large cabbage, and some carrots."

Bartholomew went to the root cellar door and stepped down as he entered. He had dug the cellar underground into the hill to keep produce cooler.

A cow wandered from behind the livestock barn with a yoke around its neck. Fixed to the front of the yoke was a short wooden picket pointing forward.

"Why is that cow wearing a wooden tie?" Megan asked Maggie.

"Wooden tie? You are a funny one. That is a cowpoke. The cow cannot jump a fence when she is wearing it."

Bartholomew came back with a bunch of carrots and the biggest cabbage Megan had ever seen. "Wow! How did you grow a cabbage that big?" she asked.

"Mother Nature's secrets child. Maggie and I labored many years to turn a sow's ear into a silk purse. Mark, do you have time for me to tell Megan our miracle?"

"Give the short of it, Bart. Standing Elk can smell sausages frying already."

"Well, Megan, the short of it is that Maggie and I were cheated into prosperity. During our servitude, she cooked food for a tavern for ready money. I became known as a capable wright. Owners of expensive tools were happy to pay good money when I repaired them.

"By the end of our bondage, we had saved money and we bought land in spring already sown with tobacco plants. Maggie was doubtful. She can smell a dead squirrel better than I can, but I saw those tobacco plants and got greedy. Within weeks, the whole crop failed. We lost five years of savings. We learned the same thing happened on that land the previous year and the owner left to go west. An agent without scruples bought the land for nothing and rented slaves to transplant tobacco seedlings into the

164

depleted earth. He sold the land quickly to us at what seemed a good price before the truth became clear. We had no recourse.

"We cried and then set back to the cooking and repairs that gave us money in the first place. 'We did it once, we can do it again,' Maggie told me. Half my courage lives in her strong heart. We thought about why land that looks good can have nothing left to feed a plant. We heard that large estates put manure on their fields but tobacco was bitter in those fields. I spoke to planters and visited Standing Elk's village to learn about their gardens of corn, beans, and squash growing in the same field. I prayed in Sweat Lodges, as you will tonight. I prayed in church and I pondered while walking my land and in the forest.

"It was in a Sweat Lodge that a question came to mind that changed our lives: 'What did God put on the land that made it so rich before we got here?' I thought about it for days and answers kept coming. Animal manure, yes, but in small quantities. Ash from campfires and more from forest fires over the years. What else? What else? Then it hit me like the blue end of a brick. 'Leaves, Bartie, leaves!' Every autumn the ground is covered by countless leaves and twigs that rot into the soil. The trees give back.

"For two years I cleaned fireplaces and stables in town and carried ashes and manure home in my cart. I was paid to chop firewood and I brought home bark and chips. Some paid me a penny to clean out a ditch. The mud and leaves in the ditch were a banquet for our land. When I had no work, I filled my cart full of leaves. We covered our land acre by acre with the treasures in my cart and we planted clover to leave the land fallow for a time. The third year our miracle began. We planted grasses for the horse and cow and the next year beans, squash, and corn like the Indians grow."

"He said the short of it, Bartie," urged Maggie, wrapping a packet of corn meal.

"I'm done. We never planted tobacco, Megan. Only a third of the fields in Tidewater are tobacco anyway. The rest is crops for subsistence and for sale in the markets. We never bought a slave or bonded labor. At planting and harvest time, I hire people at fair wages including slaves on Sundays. We feed them well to let them know we appreciate them. We tell them how we succeeded so they find confidence to succeed someday themselves. Now that I know how to do this, I bought other spoiled land at low prices and we are bringing life back there, too."

"That's a hopeful story, Bartholomew."

"What do I owe you, Bart?"

"Nine pence, a low price to help with the feast."

"Here is a sixpence. I want to contribute, too."

"But Megan, sixpence is most of it. I have to pay my share."

"You gave me the ride on the horse."

"'Tis Anderson's horse. You are generous, Megan."

Mark and Megan paid Bart and Maggie and they all wished each other well. Then Mark rode out the wagon track to the dirt road. In fifteen minutes, Megan saw black smoke billowing ahead of them.

They approached the source of the smoke, and long before they got there, Megan smelled charcoal and an acrid sharp odor. Air pollution that isn't horse poop, urine, or lack of showers, she thought. More like home, but I don't like this either.

Crossing a treeless wasteland, they rode beside a river to a row of buildings where chimneys poured out smoke. Wood was piled high next to what looked like cabin-sized beehives of brick and earth. Great piles of coal stood next to the river. Mark tethered the horse to a post upwind of the buildings and dismounted. Megan jumped down. "What is this, Mark?"

"This is an ironworks. Would you like to step through the gates of hell?"

"Not really. Will I come back out?

"That depends on what the Devil says."

Megan followed Mark through a wide opening and immediately covered her mouth and nose. The air was smoky and hard to breathe. Six shirtless men in the haze shoveled from three piles into an opening as tall as they were. Their skin glistened orange near a raging fire in a great stone furnace. They were streaked with black dust. Two were African, three European, and the youngest was Native American. One of the white men had rags around both ankles held in place by iron shackles joined by a chain. The fire roared and the spades scraped as the men shoveled from one pile then another.

Behind the furnace was a bellows much bigger than those at the blacksmith shop. It pumped air into the furnace and was opened and closed by a piston driven by river water flowing through a sluice. The creak of the piston, past due to be lubricated with whale oil, and rushes of air from the bellows added to the noise. "What's happening here?" Megan shouted near Mark's ear.

Mark stepped away with her toward a side of the building open to a yard. "This iron furnace is like the one I worked in. The men load the furnace with layers of charcoal, lumps of bog iron found in swamps, and oyster shells as a flux to separate out impurities. Molten iron flows through channels in the stone beneath the fire into sand molds to cool as pigs."

"Pigs?"

"Blocks of pig iron to be smelted into cast iron or better quality wrought iron."

"Why does one man have chains on his legs?"

"The man in shackles is a convict. He put rags there to keep the shackles from hurting his ankles. Convicts get longer bondage to begin with. The price for a convict's bond is less than for indentured servants. If he works well, he gets better food. If he tries to escape, more time is added and his life made miserable."

"Can we get out of the smoke?"

"Yes. I have to find the proprietor. He is probably upwind of the smoke. No one stands long near a furnace unless he must through bondage or need of money."

"What are these brick and dirt domes in a row? They're smoking too."

"These are charcoal ovens. The men stack wood over a fire then seal the doors. The heat bakes wood into charcoal since there is not enough air for wood to burst into flame. The moisture and impurities in the wood leave as smoke or drippings. The charcoal that remains burns cleaner and hotter than wood in the iron furnace."

"The word 'furnace' suddenly sounds like 'inferno'," said Megan.

"Here is the owner. Hello, Mister Toliver. James Anderson sends a message."

"I saw the stallion and thought 'twas Anderson. You work at his forge?"

"Yes, I am Mark, a smith for Mister Anderson. He is occupied with building an armoury. He offers to buy triple the iron at a price suitably reduced for the increased volume. He would provide his own cartage. I am not authorized to propose a price. He asks if you will be in town over the next fortnight. If not, he will ride out to meet you here."

"I have news in return. The forests here are gone and nearby bogs low on iron so I will move the furnace. I have an agent riding north and south, looking for suitable property with access to bog iron and forests. Another reason to move is to get out of range of British naval guns. I suggest Anderson do the same. If the British come, he will make muskets for Redcoats or hang, depending on their whim. I am busy arranging this move. If Anderson wants to talk he should ride out here."

"I will pass on the message, Mister Toliver. On behalf of my employer and myself I wish you success and safety for your family in the coming difficult times."

167

"Thank you and the same to you and Mister Anderson. Congratulations also to you for having a comely wench sharing your horse. What is your name, miss?"

"Megan Sinclair."

"'Tis a pleasure to meet you, Miss Sinclair."

Mark and Megan mounted and rode away from the furnace and bad air.

"A comely wench?"

"He meant it as a compliment. The negotiations have begun. We shall be at the Lodge soon and you can sweat the soot off. This furnace reminds me of a hard time in my life."

Day 3-9:   John Gets the News from Frances

John signed the registry in the St. George Tucker House. Just as he settled into a chair he looked up to see Frances in the dress she wore the last time he saw her. "Oh, hello, Ma'am. I'm glad to see you."

"Please call me Frances. It seems like only yesterday we met, but was it not in the spring on a hot day. I have been hoping you would return."

"Yes, it was in May. I find the passing of time confusing around here."

She smiled. "People do have special experiences in Williamsburg."

"Frances, you wanted to tell me a story. Do you have time now?"

She sat on a chair across from him. "I have waited a long time to tell you. In the 1760s, the Ohio and Vandalia Companies began to survey land in the Shenandoah and Ohio Valleys. Investors included prominent citizens in Britain and the colonies, like Pennsylvania printer Benjamin Franklin and George Washington and his two older brothers. Land in the West was cheap, less than two pence an acre. A wealthy person got fifty acres free as a 'head right' for every settler whose passage he paid. Those settlers worked in servitude to pay the passage, so investors got both land and labor as a return.

"In the Proclamation of 1763, the King forbade expansion west of the Appalachians but investors were unwilling to stop. The Indians knew the Proclamation reserved the land for them, so on occasion they attacked those cutting trees west of the mountains. Survivors ran crying havoc back across the mountains.

"The King sent Redcoats to keep settlers out of Indian Territory as much as to keep Indians there. Since the treasury was depleted by the long war against France, Parliament imposed the Stamp Act in 1765, followed by the Townshend Duties to cover the costs of protection and to assert its authority. You have heard the next part of this story.

"When the colonists shouted 'No taxation without representation!' the British were stubborn and stupid. If they had given the colonial councils authority to decide which taxes to levy, a main argument against the taxes would have melted away. Many in Parliament supported the colonies so after encountering resistance, most taxes were withdrawn."

"My daughter Megan told us that. I told her everyone knows the Revolution was over taxation without representation."

"She is wise. What 'everyone knows' is not always true. Sometimes we humans are no more clever than a fence post. While colonists protested the Stamp Act and Townshend Duties, larger taxes gave more revenue to the Crown than all offending taxes combined and no one noticed."

"What taxes were those?" asked John.

"High taxes were placed on sales of tobacco in Britain. Why did the British use the Stamp Act that hindered every business transaction? Maybe because there was already a stamp tax levied in Britain without protest. The reaction in the colonies was doubtless a surprise to Parliament."

"What triggered fighting in 1775?" asked John.

"In 1774, the Quebec Act guaranteed Indians their lands west of the Proclamation Line by attaching the lands to Quebec. A survey of the line finally began. Investors feared Carleton would launch evictions. The Quebec Act threatened the fortunes of leading citizens. Not only that, but Governor Guy Carlton ruled Quebec not with an elected assembly but with a council of Catholic landowners that he himself appointed. When elected government was also revoked in Massachusetts, it was a threat to the sovereignty and rights of all the English-speaking Colonies. They feared a similar fate and leaders throughout the colonies cried "Tyranny!"

"I'll be damned! My army friend Danny joked we were fighting for our lives, our honor, and the sacred fortunes of those who sent us to war. In the Revolution, sacred fortunes played a big role too? Why wasn't land mentioned in the Declaration of Independence?"

"Oh, but it was. Please open that book to the Declaration of Independence." John did and she pointed to a section. "Read that."

John read aloud, "... *abolishing the free System of English Laws in a neighboring Province, establishing therein an Arbitrary government, and enlarging its Boundaries so as to render it at once an example and fit instrument for introducing the same absolute rule into these Colonies...*"

"The Declaration did not name Quebec nor make clear the significance of *'arbitrary government'*, or *'enlarging its boundaries'*, but fear of absolute Royal rule and enforcement of the Proclamation Line triggered fighting. 'Taxation without representation' was an old issue, but that victory gave the colonies confidence to try again against the Intolerable Acts."

"How do you know this story so well, Frances?"

"Staying in Williamsburg keeps me connected to my roots." She nodded to John and left as silently as she had come.

John read about the colonial economies. A third of British ships were built in the colonies with plentiful white pine and skilled labor. That enabled Americans to launch naval vessels of their own. The colonies exported iron, tobacco, grain, and fish. Some years George Washington made more money from Potomac River fish, dried, and shipped to the Caribbean to feed slaves, than from all other production on his estates.

However, there were grave economic problems. A flood in 1771 destroyed stored tobacco and hurt prominent Virginians. Good prices in 1773 saved many from bankruptcy, but in 1774, a frost followed by a drought hit them again. They were desperate, John thought. With the survey of the Proclamation Line starting, they would be tempted to overthrow the authority that could take away their lands for debts and prevent them from expanding west.

John looked up John Wilkes, the populist leader opposed to increasing royal power. Wilkes' four elections to Parliament were voided, infuriating his supporters. There were parallels in Britain and the colonies. The Saint George's Day Massacre in Britain, a rallying point for voices for liberty, happened two years before the Boston Massacre roused passions here.

Others supported the colonies. In February 1765, in the Stamp Act, debate, Colonel Isaac Barré spoke in the House of Commons in response to Charles Townshend, who later sponsored the Townshend duties:

"...They planted by your care? No! Your oppressions planted them in America. They fled your tyranny to a then uncultivated and inhospitable country... they met hardships with pleasure, compared with those suffered in their own country, from the hands of those who should have been their friends.

"They nourished by your indulgence? They grew by your neglect of them: as soon as you began to care about them, that care was exercised in sending persons to rule them, ...sent to spy out their liberty, to misrepresent their actions and to prey upon them; men whose behavior on many occasions has caused the blood of those Sons of Liberty to recoil..."

John realized that colonial leaders took the name 'Sons of Liberty' from Barré's speech.

American resistance waned once most of the onerous taxes were rescinded. What else sparked the uprising in 1774? What about New England where land was not the issue? The arrival of ships direct from India without the need to offload, pay duties, and reload in Britain, would have meant tea at half the previous price for this desired commodity even with the remaining small tea tax. Megan was right again. Half price tea would hurt smugglers and merchants including John Hancock and put more 'sacred fortunes' in jeopardy. Our textbooks did not get this right, John thought.

John looked up the Battle of Culloden where Bruce was wounded. The Duke of Cumberland ordered massacres, but James Oglethorpe ignored the orders and called off the troops. Through his mercy, many Scots escaped. At a court marshal for disobeying, Oglethorpe was exonerated but Cumberland's reputation was tarnished for his brutality. Oglethorpe voted in Parliament against sending troops to crush the rebellion in America. Significantly, he declined an offer to lead British forces to put down the Revolution. That decision left the post to less competent generals and was thus a big contribution to the American cause. James Oglethorpe's decision perhaps made all the difference.

He noticed Frances standing near him. "Oh! I didn't hear you come in. Frances, the last couple of days my family and I have felt we were actually in the past. Reverend Walker suggested I ask you about it."

"He did? Well, imagination can enhance what we notice. You may not be practiced in how to sort it out. Consider it lucky. Did anything dramatic happen that might have opened up your perception?"

"Not that I know of. Oh. We almost had an accident on the way here."

"It can happen in different ways. I knew you were observant from the moment you saw me. Tell your family not to worry and enjoy it while it is happening. The meaning is in your experience and not in any explanation I could give you."

"Frances, I don't think about such things very often."

John turned to replace a book to the shelf. When he turned back, Frances was gone. "She talked about it as if it were normal," he thought. "What did she mean she knew I was observant from the moment I saw her? Didn't she get that backwards?"

John left the Tucker House reflecting on how events often happen in our lives without our understanding the underlying circumstances. Danny and Sergeant Sargon did not know why they were fighting. It ended for them zipped into a body bag. "Follow the money," Megan told us. She's smart, like her mother. However, I'm not happy with what I'm learning.

Day 3-10:   Susan Attends Three Trials

Susan arrived at the Court House amidst a gathering crowd. She looked for Jane. To be sure to get a seat, she moved past the pillory where Peter had been held and edged toward the entrance. Near the double doors, a familiar-looking woman with a troubled expression stood with eyes closed, lips moving slightly, and hands clasped. When she opened her eyes, Susan asked, "May I join you in prayer?"

"Missus, many souls could benefit from prayer at this Court today. One is my husband, who finally has his trial for preaching without a license."

Susan recognized the woman she had seen carrying a basket to the gaol. "But Ma'am, I saw you carrying food to your husband at the gaol six months ago. Has he not had his trial yet?"

"No, Missus, 'twas a long wait. Lord knows why we endured this."

"I have a friend coming today. If you like, we will sit with you."

"I would appreciate your company. My husband has had his Bible and it gives him comfort to hold it when he prays." The woman began to sob and Susan put a hand on her shoulder as Jane found them in the crowd.

"Thou found another soul to comfort, Susan, as thou hast done for me."

"My friend Jane Harding will join us. I am Susan Sinclair."

"I am Dolly Cook. I pray my husband Arthur will be freed."

The attorneys for today's cases, in robes and wearing white powdered wigs, pressed through the crowd. The public was held back until the lawyers and clerks were at their places, then the doors were fully opened and Susan, Jane, and Dolly squeezed onto a bench. As three judges in robes entered and took seats behind a wooden rail at the front of the courtroom, everyone rose. Susan assumed the man in the center chair with the stained-hardwood panel behind it was the lead judge.

The first prisoners led in were two runaway convicts accused of stealing a cart on the Great Wagon Road and killing a family in a manner to make it appear Indians had committed the atrocity. They were spotted the very next day moving east in the ill-fated family's wagon.

Jane reached for Susan's hand, her attention riveted on the witnesses.

The deceased woman's brother testified that he recognized the wagon that day. He shot one man, who was holding a rifle, in the chest at close range. Then, as his wife pointed a musket at the other two men, he demanded their surrender. With their friend twitching on the road beside the wagon and their rifles under canvas behind them, they complied. The brother rolled the dying man into a swamp beside the road and brought the brigands to town, bound like cargo in the wagon they had stolen.

The brother identified the culprits. Another witness identified them as convicts from the docks at Norfolk. A third, also a prisoner in the gaol, swore he overheard them express regret, not for their victims, but for their own predicament. The men were asked if they had anything to say.

One blurted, "Billy killed them, not us. We should not be here."

Because this was a capital case, an appointed lawyer argued, "My Lord, these men risk hanging for this crime, so we suggest this trial should not be held here but at the Capitol."

The lead judge conferred with his colleagues then looked from one prisoner to the other. "You, your lawyer, and the judges agree that you should not be here. You should not have killed innocent people. You are convicts so your trial is here rather than at the Capitol. We do not know how many others you murdered, but we can ensure you will kill no more. You are found guilty and sentenced to be hanged tomorrow. Then, as you requested, you shall not be here. Bailiff, take these men away!"

The two men were led from the court in stunned silence. Jane gasped. "Just five minutes and gone! The trial took less time than the murders."

The next case involved a man accused of stealing a dairy cow. He had retained a lawyer, a graduate of William and Mary, who explained that his client purchased the cow, and agreed to six monthly payments. Because of hard times, the fourth payment was late. He went to the bench to show hand-written receipts for the four payments.

The Judge grew irritated. Speaking to the man who sold the cow he intoned, "This court does not take lightly wasting its time on false charges. This is not a case of a stolen cow. It is a partially unpaid debt."

He addressed the defense lawyer. "You have presented evidence of four of the six agreed-upon payments. Have you other evidence?"

"My Lord, my client has not paid the full debt. He commits to do so."

"This case should have been settled outside of court. We rule the plaintiff is to be paid two remaining payments without interest because of the prevarications and exaggerations of his claim. The next payment is due in a fortnight and the final payment one month later. Next case!"

The next case was that of Dolly's husband. As he was led in, Susan slipped from her seat and spoke to the lawyer who defended the man who bought the cow. The lawyer nodded and Susan handed him something.

"Who represents Arthur Cook?" called out a clerk."

"With the help of God I will speak for myself." Arthur hoarsely cleared his throat. Having nowhere to spit, he swallowed.

The young defense lawyer rose. "Your Worship and Mister Cook, I have been retained by the defendant's wife to defend him in this case."

Confused and surprised, Arthur smiled at his wife and nodded.

"Is that your wish, Mister Cook?" the judge asked.

"Yes, Honorable Sir, I agree."

"When called upon, address us as 'Your Worship' or 'My Lord'."

"Yes, my Worship, I mean Your Lordship, I agree."

"That seems a very good idea. Well then, let us proceed. You are charged with preaching without a license. Article 23 of The 39 Articles of Religion of the Church clearly states the following with respect to Ministering:

"It is not lawful for any man to take upon him the office of public preaching or ministering the sacraments in the congregation, before he be lawfully called and sent to execute the same by men who have public authority in the congregation to call and send ministers into the Lord's vineyard."

"We cannot tolerate the name of God invoked to pass a basket and deprive the Established Church of funds needed to minister to the flock."

"Can they cite an Article of Religion of the Church of England as the basis for a charge in the public court?" whispered Susan.

"Yes, the Church and the Law are intertwined," Jane murmured.

"Heaven save us," murmured Dolly, a little too loud.

"No talking in the gallery," ordered the Judge, "or I will tell the Sergeant at Arms to clear that row. Many standing would happily take those seats!"

The judge continued, "How do you plead, Mister Cook?"

"My Lord, my client pleads 'Not Guilty.'" Then the lawyer asked, "May I question my client to clarify the case?"

"You may."

"Mister Cook, have you been to any seminary school or has any man ever called you Reverend, or Pastor, or Minister?"

"No, Sir, none has."

"Do you own a Bible, Mister Cook?"

"I do. I pray over my Bible each and every day."

"Can you tell the court whether you are able to read your Bible?"

"No, Sir. But I spent Sundays in church and heard what is in the Bible."

"You are neither able to read the Bible nor write a sermon. Is that true?"

"Well, I don't write but I speak out powerful when the spirit moves me."

"I am sure you do, Mister Cook. When the spirit moved have you ever administered sacraments such as baptism, communion, or funeral rites?"

"Spirit has not called me to do that, and I have not learned how."

"How long had you been in this county when you were arrested?

"Two days, Sir. I was arrested speaking about the Bible at a crossroads."

"Did you pass a collection plate at the end of your talk?"

"No, Sir. I do not have one. I preach because I love the Lord. When I finished, only my wife, a boy, and his dog were standing there."

"That may have been an inspiring homily, at least for your wife who has stood by you these months while you languished in jail. The boy and his dog may have benefitted as well."

There were chuckles in court. The Judge shook his head.

"My Lord, I submit that Mister Cook gathered neither a flock nor contributions. He cannot read his Bible nor write a sermon. His unfortunate choice of a public place to speak put him in our gaol for eight long months. Surely, that is sufficient burden on the public purse and sufficient discouragement to Mister Cook. The prisoner's wife offers a fine of one pound to go to the gaol or the Church at the discretion of the court. Mister Cook apologizes for any trouble he has caused and agrees to leave the county if the court should offer mercy in this case."

The head Judge looked at the downcast defendant and the three women praying. The one in threadbare attire was doubtless Missus Cook in the company of a better-sorts lady, one not to offend. He briefly conferred with the other judges then cleared his throat with a loud harrumph. "The noble bard wrote 'The quality of mercy is not strained. It droppeth as the gentle rain from heaven upon the place beneath.' Mercy may not be strained, but I am. We sent two men deservedly to the gallows, redeemed a milk cow oblivious to these proceedings, and we now release a misguided man who dwelt eight months in a cell for insignificant harm. The court directs the fine to be divided between the gaol and the Bruton Parish Church. Court is recessed for fifteen minutes!"

"That's wonderful!" whispered Dolly as they stood up. "But how can we pay a fine of one pound, and how can we pay the lawyer?"

"The fine is already in the hands of the Lawyer as is his fee." Susan moved toward the doors. "Here's ten shillings to help you and your husband get started when you get to a place more welcoming."

"The Lord surely sent you, Ladies!"

"He sent us all," Jane agreed. "May we be worthy of his purposes."

The Sergeant at Arms removed the shackles and sent Arthur Cook outside to his wife. She introduced him to their benefactors.

"Arthur Cook," said Jane, "some of my people met a worse fate for preaching where they were not welcome. May the Light guide thee to do the Lord's work where it will be of benefit. Where goest thou now?"

"We shall walk to New Jersey where Dolly's sister is prospering on a farm. She will give us work until we are steady again. I will pray to serve without provoking anyone. Thank you, ladies, for what you have done."

They watched Arthur and Dolly begin their journey north. Susan took Jane's arm and asked, "Would you join my family for dinner?"

"Would I not be an imposition?"

"Not at all. I would like them to meet you, Jane."

An open carriage pulled by two horses approached from the opposite direction and stopped. Behind the driver, a woman wearing a hat and a white scarf protecting her face from the dust of the road called out, "Susan Sinclair, you are back in town!" The woman removed her scarf. It was Lucy Randolph Burwell.

"Oh, hello Missus Burwell" said Susan. "I did not recognize you."

"Sorry about the highwayman's mask. The dust on these roads is dreadful. I am happy to find you through the lucky coincidence of coming into town for last-minute purchases. We are having a ball at our house tonight and I would be pleased if you and your husband could come and stay overnight at our house."

"Thank you but I don't know how to get there and..."

"Susan, I will send this carriage. Where should it pick you up?"

"We live near Christiana Campbell's, but my friend Jane..."

"Please bring your friend. The carriage will be at Christiana Campbell's at eight. I apologize for being hurried but I must get back. I need to speak with you, so I look forward to tonight. Home, Obadiah!" The carriage driver uttered a single low syllable to the horses and the carriage was off.

Susan and Jane turned to avoid the dust. "Jane, you're going to a party."

"I have never been to a great house before. I have no clothes to wear."

"You are my size, Jane. We will solve that clothing crisis when we get to my house. I have experience dealing with this kind of problem."

Day 3-11:   The Virginia Militia Drill

Susan spotted John walking on Palace Green and waved him over to join them. "John, this is Jane Harding. She will join us for dinner."

"It is my honor to meet thee, John Sinclair."

Soon Peter came down the road. "Hi, guys. This is a tyre... for a science experiment." They shuffled to make room for Peter.

"Jane, this is my son Peter. Peter, say hello to Jane Harding."

"Hello, Jane. Dad, Megan says she's sorry she got upset."

"She did? I want to apologize to *her*! She was right about the taxes. Where is she?"

"That's the other thing. She was invited to a Sweat Lodge by an Indian chief. The blacksmith gave her a ride on a horse. He's a good guy."

"She rode out of town with a guy?" asked Susan. "Will she be all right? I thought when we leave here..." She stopped because Jane was there.

"I'm sure she'll be fine. She says she'll be home early."

The sound of drums approached and high-pitched fifes began to play. "What's happening?" Susan asked a man standing nearby.

"The Virginia Militia is marching to fife and drum to get in the spirit."

The music grew loud as the militia wheeled in straight ranks onto Palace Green. For generations, European men marched to martial music, which raised passion and muted fear. Susan felt both exhilaration and foreboding.

The militia was unlike the rag-tag muster in May. These citizen-soldiers were disciplined. In white shirts, tricorn hats, belts for cartridge pouches and bayonet sheath—most were younger than John was when he went to war. For America's Independence, did we have to pay such a price?

Bruce's voice startled John. "Soon many shirts will redden with the blood of wounds. How proud I used to be to march! Now I ask why we pay such a price. Is there is a better way? His Majesty's regiments drill like these lads and prepare for the sea voyage. Some will never go home."

"Bruce, this is my son Peter, my wife Susan, and her friend Jane. We are having dinner at a tavern after the drill. Would you care to join us?"

"Good to meet you. My wife's sister ran with her children from the fighting in Norfolk. My wife roasted a goose to raise her spirits tonight." Let us talk soon, Johnny."

"Not easy times, Bruce. Be careful." The drill seemed to John a display of defiance and a claim of victory when the fight was just beginning.

178

Day 3-12:   Dinner with Jane Harding

Over dinner, Susan and Peter found it awkward to talk openly with Jane present, though it was not really an issue for John because he said little.

Susan ordered the chicken soup and a salad of fresh greens.

"That sounds just right." Jane closed her menu quickly, not embarrassed. In her world most women could not read.

As the server left, Susan turned to Peter. "I hope Megan is all right."

"She's fine, Mom. She's in good company."

"Good company may not be enough if there's real danger."

Jane joined in. "These are difficult times. It hurts me to think about people being overwhelmed. Where is the light?"

"Mom told me you're worried about the war. I know someone, a free African named Annie, who may be able to help. Have you heard of her?"

"I have not. I keep to myself for the most part."

"I'm busy with this hoop tonight but I'll find a way to introduce you. She's wise and kind and knows more about the Light than anyone I met."

Susan saw a change in her son. The food arrived and there was little conversation. Jane enjoyed her meal. "I appreciate thy kindness John and Susan Sinclair."

"John, we've been invited to a ball and to stay the night at the Kingsmill Plantation. Lucy Burwell is sending a carriage. Will you come with us? We'll be back after breakfast tomorrow, the day we planned to go home." Susan did not say more in deference to Jane's presence.

"Thanks, but I won't go to the plantation with you. I need a long walk."

Peter leaned over to John and asked quietly, "Dad, may I use the car?

"The car? Did I hear you correctly?" John whispered.

"I want to check roads to Norfolk to find a route for an escaped slave."

"You can't go for a drive in our time, and see what is going on in 1775."

"I can't drive in 1775 but I want to learn the terrain along the James River. I could give bad advice if I don't know the route."

John studied his son. "Reconnaissance of the terrain is important. Here are the keys."

"Thanks, Dad. And I know you want to tell me not to take any reckless risks." Peter was shocked to get his father's permission.

Day 3-13: Peter Takes the Hoop to Evie

Peter ran to the Powell House holding the iron tyre, slowing as he approached the side gate, trying not to crunch loudly on the gravel.

"There you are." Evie spoke from the bench in the shadows. "I put the boys to bed early so we could talk." Evie had braided her hair and put on her Sunday dress. Peter caught his breath.

"Hello, Evie. You look beautiful. I brought you all some cookies."

She opened the bag, inhaled the scent of oatmeal, raisins, and brown sugar. "Thank you, Mister Peter. The boys will eat these in the mornin'."

"My sister found me something else."

"You got a sister here?"

"Yes, and a mother and a father. We're staying not far from here."

"Your whole family came on this voyage? Why ain't you said befo'?"

"Sorry. Uh, Evie, this is a family voyage. Maybe that's why I took such an interest in you and your boys because you are a family like us."

Evie was quiet a moment. "My daddy got sold away before I knowed him. When Mama passed, I was brung to the Powell place." She sighed. "I ain't seen James' daddy but one day in my life. I don't know where he's at. Dilli's daddy, 'Gustus, stayed one night and along came Dilli the next year. 'Gustus ain't paid us no mind until that Hush Harbor meetin'. You a grown man and you still has a mama and daddy. I heard only one slave child in three has two parents to raise them up. My boys and me is our family."

Evie pressed her sleeve to her eyes to absorb tears that welled. "Sorry, Mister Peter. I'se afraid 'bout this fightin' and folk runnin' away lookin' for a new life. I don't want to make a mistake and lose what life we got."

Peter put his hand on Evie's and she trembled. She pulled out a handkerchief and blew her nose.

"Done like a champion, Evie. You could play trumpet with Gabriel."

Evie laughed. "Mister Peter, you be a kind man."

"Let me show you what I brought."

"I see what you brought. It be a tyre or a cooper's ring for a hogshead."

"Evie, tonight, it's a hoop we can watch to learn what Annie meant today. Do you have a strong, straight stick?"

"Let me get one." She ran to the kitchen and returned with a wooden spoon. She was more buoyant than Peter had seen her.

They walked to the end of the lane and made sure no one was around. Peter gave the hoop a whack with the handle of the ladle. It fell over. On

180

the next try, he shoved the hoop to get it rolling, and then they hurried beside and tapped it forward. "It looks blurry when I hit it, Evie. Do you think that is what Annie meant?"

"Maybe so. When it look fuzzy, we don't know 'zackly where it at."

"Now we'll let it fall and watch what happens!"

The hoop slowed and they jumped aside as it leaned to the left and rolled around in smaller and smaller circles. It leaned more as it rolled in place, wobbling faster and faster. For an instant, they saw in the blur of motion, images of many hoops falling away from the point where each image touched the ground. There was a final vibration as the many hoops came to rest as one.

"Oh! Lordie! They was too many hoops to count, six or eight standin' out and goin' round as they fell and more dim ones in between. Ain't that Annie somethin'? And me tellin' her they was only one hoop!"

"But lying there still is one hoop," Peter observed. "What do you think it means?"

"You be a strange gentleman, Mister Peter, askin' what I think."

"Evie, Annie gave the question to you. I just brought the hoop."

"Let's go back to the bench out of the street. I ponder better when I ain't worried someone gonna catch me doin' somethin' I ain't supposed to."

"What aren't you supposed to do?"

"I ain't supposed to do much at all 'cept what I am told. I sure ain't supposed to be talkin' to you about runnin' away."

Peter sat next to Evie. She moved her hip and leg against his. He felt her warmth through her dress and his jeans. "Oh, God!" he thought to himself. "This is not what this visit is about."

"I know Annie enough to know this ain't simple. When we goin' along in life it be like a hoop rollin'. But when a big change come like the hoop fallin' over, ain't no way to know which way it gonna fall. So you watch close, and pick what to do near the end when you see better how it gonna fall. Even then, be ready to change quick if it fall another way."

"How do women see so clearly sometimes?"

"Because we have babies we need to watch over real close, I s'pose."

"You're amazing, Evie. There are many ways this could turn out, so we should pay attention before making a move, and then choose. I hope Augustus is all right."

"I hope so too, Mister Peter. I hope he finds the freedom he wants."

Evie leaned close and Peter felt her left breast press his arm. "You bring me comfort, Mister Peter," she whispered. "When a man is nice to a woman maybe he want somethin'. Do you want somethin'? We can climb up to the loft. The boys be sleepin'."

Peter held Evie close. This was something he thought he wanted. He thought of Annie and what she might encourage him to do and his words surprised him. "Dear Evie, when I first saw you, I wanted to be with you so much I could hardly breathe. Annie knows about it. But you don't have to give yourself to me because I'm helping you. If I climb up in the loft, you might think I wanted to help just for that and it's not so."

"I know. What about me, Mister Peter? I been lonesome a long time and scared since this fightin' started. You holdin' me brings a warm feelin'. You feel like you is part of our family, too."

"Evie, I hear Annie in my head saying, 'Help her, but if your heart is true, help her find her own strength inside.' Evie, let me hold you here."

Lost in the pull he felt toward Evie, Peter held her tight and they were still for long minutes. The passion slowly ebbed and a deep peace came over both of them. "I think you came here from Heaven," she whispered.

Peter looked at her. "Maybe we all came from Heaven and forgot."

"This, I won't forget, Mister Peter. I will remember this always."

"So will I, Evie, always. Now get a good rest. You need to be fresh to make good choices. I'm going along the river tonight to learn the ways the hoop might land. Can you take this hoop back to a blacksmith named Mark at Anderson's shop and armory? I don't know when I'll get back."

"I will. First, I want to show my boys how the hoop rolls and how it falls. That will be a good teachin' for them. Bless you, Mister Peter. If you find a way to take me away, I want to go wit' you. You be our family, too."

"It's hard to explain, but I come from far away and I can't stay. If you go away, I can't go with you. You and the boys are family some other way."

"Please be careful tonight whatever you doin' and wherever you goin'."

"I will, Evie. Good night, mother of James and Dilli."

He felt her eyes on his back as he walked toward the tunnel with his hand on the car keys. He asked himself if he just missed an opportunity. No, he thought, I took the opportunity.

Day 3-14:   Susan at the Plantation House Reception

It took thirty minutes for Susan and Jane to make the bone-shaking four-mile carriage trip to Kingsmill Plantation. The house and dependencies — cookhouse, smokehouse, schoolhouse, chapel, stable, tobacco houses, servants' and slaves' quarters, corncribs, barn, and chicken house — together looked like a village. They walked through a groomed garden with chrysanthemums and trimmed, five-tiered topiary boxwood. The hedge was twelve feet high, and beyond a stunning vista opened to an expanse of fields beside the James River. Jane gazed at the faint lights of a house across the river. "Oh, see how wide the water is here!"

An herb garden was enclosed by a trimmed thorny hedge, dense enough to discourage rabbits. At the end of a footpath, at the large door of the main house, Lucy Randolph Burwell welcomed them. "I am so glad you are here. This is my husband, Lewis Burwell. Lewis, this is Susan Sinclair, the wise woman I told you about and her friend Jane Harding."

Colonel Burwell bowed. "It is a pleasure to meet you, Ladies."

"Excuse me, Lewis. I shall show Susan and Jane the refreshment table."

Lucy took Susan's arm and with Jane following, moved down a hall with portraits of Burwell and Randolph ancestors gazing at them. "Susan, I see you lent Jane your elegant mantua," Lucy whispered. "You are a kind woman to lend your best. These gatherings are important to leading families in Virginia. We feel isolated. Social occasions help maintain a sense of community. We welcome travelers to learn of news from afar. Anyone arrived from London is particularly attractive as a guest.

"I find a refreshing genuineness in you, Susan. You are more educated than any woman here but you do not flaunt what you know. I spoke of the false image that masks the debt of most leading families but you are not judgmental. Oh dear, more guests have arrived, I must greet them."

Susan and Jane used the facilities off the hall. The toilet was a chamber pot under a chair with a hole in the seat. For this social occasion, a slave stood outside the door, his job to replace the chamber pot, empty the used one in an outbuilding, rinse it, and stand ready to replace it again. The Burwell's did not want to impose unpleasantness on their guests.

Reentering the ballroom, Susan felt instant unease when she saw the dance instructor Randall Weaver leading a contradanse. Weaver offered obsequious praise at every opportunity. It was amazing to her that people did not see through him. He played in a practiced way to their vanity and lack of confidence learning the dances that were symbols of refinement.

The orchestra began an allemande in three-quarter time. Few guests were familiar with the new step. Weaver strolled to the side table to avail himself of the punch. Susan noticed him check a pocket watch.

A man stepped in front of Susan and asked her to dance. She raised an arm to shoulder height and they set off circling the floor. "My name is Richard Henry Lee, back from the Continental Congress on business. I am charmed that you know the allemande, Madam."

"Where I'm from, we call this a quick waltz. My name is Susan Sinclair."

"I see. I learned this dance at grammar school in England. I am surprised this orchestra can play it. Did you notice they include the cream of Virginia society showing off their skills? They include a Ludwell, a Byrd, a Randolph, two Carters, and a Marshall. The able violinist is Thomas Jefferson, also on a break from the Continental Congress."

"Since you call the delegate who presides over the Continental Congress the President, do you call the delegates Congressmen?"

"'Congressman' you say? I like the sound of that."

"Well, let me be the first to call you Congressman Lee. Do you think a war is inevitable?"

"Is it inevitable? We could call that which has already begun 'inevitable'. We are now at war and we are resolute in pursuing the changes we seek but these subjects don't concern a lady."

"I mean no disrespect. My concern is genuine."

"We reject the arbitrary government of an unelected Governor's Council, as we see in Quebec, being imposed upon us. Giving Quebec's Governor Carleton authority over all lands west of the mountains is an affront to free men and could ruin investors here and in England."

Susan assumed he had visited the punch bowl to be so forthcoming. The orchestra went into a crescendo and finished with a flourish.

"I shall return to my friends and endure less refreshing company. It was a pleasure, Madam."

Susan walked toward the side of the dance floor when another man stepped in front of her. "You honored my older brother with a dance. Would you offer me the same charity, Madam? My name is Francis Lightfoot Lee. I am sure my brother wasted no time before informing you that he is in the Continental Congress. I will not be so vain. I shall wait a moment and then reveal that I am also in Congress." They laughed.

Lee was an excellent dancer, and Susan asked if that is where he got the middle name 'Lightfoot.'

"You may withdraw the compliment, Madam, if one of my feet happens to alight on one of yours."

184

The dance ended and Susan walked with Francis to the edge of the floor. "Your brother is strongly against the Quebec Act. Do you agree?"

"We are all against the Quebec Act, Missus Sinclair, but our views differ on the remedy. My brother prefers independency as do some in Congress, but most people will not speak of it. They oppose the increase of royal power and Parliament's usurpation of our rights but consider themselves loyal Britons. As for me, I would consent to independency if we find no other way to remain free. Did Richard tell you our younger brother William Lee is Sherriff of London?"

"He did not mention that."

"Men work on these problems on both sides of the Atlantic. However, since the recent death of Peyton Randolph, who was a moderating influence, as is his brother John in London, I fear options grow limited."

"Peyton Randolph is dead?"

"Yes, of apoplectic stroke last month. His body awaits transport home."

"He was Lucy's uncle. Poor Lucy!"

"Lucy is in mourning but this event was long-planned so she went ahead to have friends about. She will not dance so soon after his passing."

Suddenly, there were cries from women across the room. Susan and Francis Lee hurried over to see Lucy lying still. Colonel Burwell dropped to one knee and took her pulse. "She has fainted." He urged guests to be calm as he hurried out and returned carrying his bag of supplies for administering physic to his family, servants, and slaves. "This will return her to the land of the living." He opened a little bottle with a brass top and waved it near her nostrils to let vapors waft in with her breath.

Lucy sneezed and awoke with a start. "What happened? I'm so sorry."

"Don't worry. You had a fainting spell. You can retire to your room."

"I don't want to lie down and miss our guests," she protested.

"Perhaps you would like to get some fresh air." Jane offered her arm.

The Colonel and Jane helped Lucy to her feet. Lucy saw Susan in the circle of concerned faces and asked, "Would you and Jane join me in the garden?"

"Yes, I would like that, Lucy."

Lucy's husband escorted them through wide French doors to a bench in the sheltered courtyard by what in spring was a magnificent wisteria arbor. He instructed a slave to bring blankets to keep away the chill. "Lucy. I leave you in the care of Susan and Jane, who seem able to put you at ease."

"Colonel Burwell, what did you use to revive Lucy?" asked Susan.

"It was spirit of hart's horn, Missus Sinclair. It is also known as sal ammoniac or smelling salts. The whiff of ammonia stimulates waking. We distill ammonia at Kingsmill from whittled flakes of deer horn. I shall attend to my guests and return shortly to see if you need anything."

"Thank you," said all the ladies at once.

Lucy sighed, "I am embarrassed to faint at my own party!"

"It's nothing to be embarrassed about, Lucy. I faint at every opportunity that presents itself in order to have a quiet moment. Handsome men rush to my aid and I feel better," Susan said with a straight face.

Lucy looked at Susan, then at Jane who covered her mouth to suppress a laugh. Lucy burst out laughing and they could not contain themselves. They laughed until tears flowed. Lucy wiped her eyes with a towel the attentive slave quickly fetched. "I have not had a good laugh for a long time. My husband thinks I am out of sorts because of the death of Uncle Peyton. I do miss him but given his age, girth, red face, and wheezing, his passing was not a surprise. I am sad for Aunt Betty's loss."

"I am sorry for your loss and hers," said Jane.

"You two have empathetic hearts."

Susan put a hand on Lucy's shoulder. "You have the strength it takes to move through. I know from experience the unforeseen happens. We are able to adapt to unwelcome changes."

"Lucy Burwell," added Jane, "all the help we could ever ask for is always right here waiting in patience for us to accept it."

"You two are so encouraging. I cannot linger because I must attend to the guests lest they leave early for my sake. I shall have someone show you to your rooms in a few minutes so that you may retire when you wish, have a good rest, and join us for breakfast."

The trio returned to the ballroom and Lucy greeted her visitors to assure them that she was not ill. Susan noticed Mister Weaver, the dance instructor, walking to the large clock to check his watch against it. He looked agitated and moved quickly toward the door where he bowed low to Colonel Burwell, excused himself, and left. Susan watched the door close wondering what it was about Weaver that she found so disturbing.

She saw Lucy take a seat near the windows and a slave bring her a small plate of food from the refreshment table. Two couples took their leave and moved toward the door. Soon Susan and Jane were shown to their guest rooms to sleep in canopy beds that had just been warmed by sliding a brass pan filled with hot coals from side to side between the sheets.

Day 3-15:   Megan Joins in a Spirit Lodge

Mark and Megan rode two miles beyond the iron works before coming to a tree of any size. He turned onto a path to a grove by a stream. Twenty people gathered near a cabin, some sticking long thin sapling poles into the ground. In the center of the circle, a young Indian dug a shallow fire pit. Standing Elk greeted them as they rode up.

"Hello, Mark and Megan. We are building the Lodge."

"I shall help," said Mark. "Why did you pick this place for the Lodge?"

"This place is upstream and upwind from where the foundry poisons the water and the air. There are no nearby neighbors and is only an hour's ride from Williamsburg. The Mattaponi and Pamunkey reservations are far up the York River beyond West Point. We need prayer and healing at this time, so we are holding the Spirit Lodge where more people can join us."

Megan whispered to Mark, "I'm hungry after that ride. Do we eat soon?"

"I'll wash some carrots for you. We have the feast after the Lodge."

"Megan, we use willow saplings to form the Madoodiswaan or Spirit Lodge in the shape of the womb of Mother Earth."

The men bent the ends of the saplings to the opposite side, pushed into the same hole as the base of the opposite pole, and lashed to keep them in place. A wider space between poles was left on the east side for a door. Flexible willow saplings were woven horizontally at one quarter, one-half, and three-quarters of the height of the Lodge and the grid was covered with deerskins but for a small opening in the top for spirits to enter.

"I chose an east door today because the day begins in the East and British soldiers are approaching from that direction. We pray light will overcome darkness and danger. My nephew Thomas will be fire-keeper. He will build a low altar and sacred fire east of the door. He chose Grandfather rocks of the right size with no cracks or holes to cause them to crumble or explode. I will lead the Lodge and be the water pourer. You can go to the cabin for a few minutes to get ready."

In the cabin, Roweena, Standing Elk's half sister told Megan, "I have a loose-fitting dress for you. You will sweat so wear nothing under the dress. It does not show your form. The Lodge is for prayer. Men think making love is their idea, and we can let them think so. But in that Lodge, pray to Creator. Don't use your mind to attract men."

Megan changed quickly and joined the others. Thomas had a fire going beside the altar made of earth and stones and he placed large rocks onto the coals. Several people gave offerings of tobacco to Standing Elk.

"No more talking until we complete the Lodge," Standing Elk announced. "Begin to let go of everything that has been disturbing you. We will pray for purification, for healing those who need it, for all creatures in creation, and for progress on the spirit road. Did anyone take strong drink in the last three days?"

"I had wine two nights ago," admitted one Indian man.

"You know we do not drink three days before a Lodge. We need a clear mind in there. You help Thomas at the fire and pray with us. You others form a line, women in front, men in back. Roweena will pass with cedar and sweet grass burning in a shell to smudge you. It is to purify you."

Megan watched people fan smoke over themselves with their hands as Roweena passed and she did the same. Roweena came back with a basket of tobacco. Standing Elk called out, "Take tobacco with your right hand, and hold it in your left because the left hand is closer to your heart. When you are clear what you are praying for, place tobacco into the sacred fire.

"Now, staying in prayer, crawl through the door into the Lodge and go left around the fire pit. The first woman will stop before the door leaving room for the Lodge leader. Leave a space between the men and the women so you keep your mind on the Grandfathers and on Creator."

The first woman got down on her hands and knees on a woven grass mat, and crawled into the deerskin-covered dome. One by one, they followed her into the dark and veered left of the shallow pit in the floor. Sounds of shuffling told Megan where the others were. When the woman in the lead completed the circle, she sat and uttered a satisfied "Hmm." Megan felt the edge of the pit a foot in front of her and sat.

Standing Elk took his place by the door. "We will do four rounds and bring in seven Grandfathers each time so it will be a hot Lodge. Thomas will open the door after each round. If it gets too hot for you, breathe closer to the earth or ask me to send you outside to pray. You may come back on the next round. This Lodge is for healing, purification, and connection to Creator, not to show how tough you are."

Standing Elk asked Thomas to pass in seven Grandfather rocks. Thomas lifted rocks from the altar fire with a pitchfork. He reached through the door to drop the rocks into the pit. Standing Elk arranged the rocks with a wet deer antler then pulled the flap closed and began to tap on a hand drum and sing a prayer to welcome the glowing red-hot Grandfathers. He sprinkled water on them and steam in the small space made it hotter. Megan experienced why one name for this ceremony was Sweat Lodge.

188

"Now," said Standing Elk, "we will go around the circle. Say your name. Then aloud or in silence, say what you are here to pray for. Listen to the others and support them in your prayers. Say, 'Miigwech', or 'Thank you', so the next person knows you are done."

It moved Megan to hear people pray from the heart. Some spoke their native language and others prayed in silence. When her turn came, she prayed aloud. "I'm Megan. I pray for everyone who has pain, loss, or illness, and everyone feeling anger, fear, or sadness. I pray the invisible patterns behind what we see and hear give them comfort and strength. Miigwech."

The door opened after each round, and more Grandfather rocks were placed into the pit. Standing Elk prayed for Creator to open vision to see paths through difficulties ahead. He put tobacco on the fire and prayed for all creatures that walk on two legs or four, crawl on their bellies, swim in the water, fly in the air, wriggle underground, or stand rooted in the soil. "All living beings are sisters and brothers in Creator's family."

The third time the Grandfathers were brought into the Lodge glowing red in the darkness, Megan had two realizations. When Standing Elk said, "Welcome, Grandfathers," Megan thought of her grandparents and their parents in a cascade into the distant past and envisioned her ancestors shedding animal-skin cloaks and sweating around hot coals in a cave in Europe. The ceremony connected her to her own deep roots. If our fire had gone out in winter many would have died. There is no lightning in winter to start a new fire. The fire-keepers helped the clans survive.

Megan also realized that deep in the Earth beneath her, other rocks were red hot at this moment, down where the lowest levels of igneous rock glowed with the heat of the magma below and the great pressure from the rock above. "These rocks were red hot millions of years ago and here they are glowing again. They really are our grandfathers!"

Standing Elk spoke. "On this fourth round ask a prayerful question and listen for an answer. You could ask 'How can I solve this problem?' or 'What do I do next to help others or to walk on my spirit journey?' Then wait for what comes." He sprinkled tobacco on the Grandfathers.

Megan thought about the incredible journey to Williamsburg and sat quietly with the question, "Why did we come back to this time?"

The glow faded from the rocks in what might have been minutes or millennia. Standing Elk's voice seemed to come from the distant past and from a future not yet imagined. "If you wish, say what came to you."

"The path goes on and on. Don't ever stop," a man's voice intoned.

"Forgive, be kind, and be firm in truth," said a man to Megan's right.

"Thank you, Creator, thank you," a woman next to Standing Elk said.

After a pause, Megan said, "Be present and be patient. The Unseen is here and Presence shows proof enough. Mysteries are unveiled in Creator's time."

Standing Elk asked the people to crawl out of the Spirit Lodge, out of the womb of Mother Earth, and circle the fire and altar, leaving an opening toward the door of the Lodge. He began his closing words: "Look into this sacred fire. Soil, seed, sunlight, moisture, and warmth together brought forth a sprout before English settlers landed at Jamestown. The sprout became a sapling then a towering sycamore until it was cut down last year. From wood, to charcoal, to glowing ember, to ash, this limb from a tree standing tall a mile from here, dissolves before our eyes back into light and warmth, minerals of the Earth, and vapors going into the air."

Staring as the fire dispersed elements that briefly had gathered to be a sycamore, Megan was at peace with the mystery of moving through time.

Standing Elk thanked everyone for being in the Lodge, and Thomas for keeping the fire. They filed into the cabin where Roweena and other women laid out the feast on a long table. Megan and the other women changed out of their dresses.

In the front room, people were served venison and sausages, vegetables, fry bread and corn mush. Conversation began gently and gradually became animated. "I am happy to see our people, Europeans, and Africans here together in prayer," said Thomas the fire keeper. "There were times when we were not together in peace. Before the Europeans came, our people sometimes fought against the Iroquois Confederacy. When white people came, we fought with them. Can you tell us about that, Uncle?'

Standing Elk leaned forward, "The memory of the past can help us build a future. When the first iron furnace began at Falling Creek, the Indians saw settlers cutting all the trees and taking all the land, not just a line of farms along the water. On Good Friday 1622, my ancestor Chief Opechancanough led the Powhatan Confederacy in attacks on the iron works and almost every English settlement in Virginia and Maryland at the same hour. Every soul at Falling Creek died except two children. Two Christian Indians warned Jamestown and they closed their stockade and repelled the attacks, but many settlements were wiped out. A third of the colonists in Virginia and Maryland were killed. The chief thought the rest would leave. Instead, more soldiers came to slaughter our people. The history is bloody so we seek peace for the years ahead. The Proclamation Line was the Indians' best hope in a century, but it is clear Virginia leaders will go to any lengths to get western land, including rising against their King."

"A new iron works opened at Falling Creek, Uncle, just as the trees have finally returned. Will that mean war again?"

"Thomas, our European and African brothers and sisters marry into our families and become our friends. This is what peace looks like. Native People in the Northwest are choosing to fight expansion, but in our painful experience, there is no victory when many die on both sides. We need peace-makers: strong leaders with no need to prove their strength by harming others, leaders who listen to their enemies and search for common ground."

"I pray it is possible," said Mark, "but I don't know how to find such leaders on the settlers' side."

"Change the order of your words, Mark. First, know it is possible then pray we find leaders to lead not on a warpath, but on a path of peace."

Megan and Mark listened to others share experiences they had in the Lodge. "Everyone likes the sausages, Mark," Megan whispered. "I thought you were planning to run away. Now I see that's not what you want. If I can help you, let me know."

"I know you want to help, Megan. I ran and it did no good. Standing Elk taught me that wherever Creator puts me, I can help people, help nature, and work for something bigger than myself. When I see a path, I shall follow it. I don't have to thrash in bondage if my heart is free."

"Have you seen a clear path?"

"I see part of it. Standing Elk's people near and far are in danger. Some are on the side of Britain and others stand with the Congress. Colonists are also divided. Even families are split. If fighting comes here, all men, women, and children are in danger. I choose to help people, the servants, the small planters, the native people, and the slaves. If I must support the King and the Proclamation Line, I will. If I must support the militia against an invasion of Hessians and Redcoats, I will."

"Will you fight?"

"Will I kill people to stop them from killing people? That is not an easy question. Men loyal to the King have been hanged, and Loyalists attack those who support Congress. Standing Elk says it is best to settle the disputes without killing. If you want to help, find the seasoned warrior who can lead us in that. Your brother knew about Dunmore's Proclamation freeing slaves and bonded servants before it happened. Does he know of something else, Megan?"

"He says that someday the colonies and Britain will be friends again. The idea to help people while staying out of the fighting is a good one."

As the feast ended, people hugged each other. Mark gave Standing Elk a packet of tobacco. Outside, as Mark and Megan mounted the white stallion, Standing Elk was suddenly next to them with a hand on the saddle. "Megan, your prayers lead to truth and depth. The Unseen is here and the veils are lifting for you."

"Thank you for helping us to see, Standing Elk," Megan shook his hand.

As Mark and Megan rode, the sky shimmered with a brilliant lattice of points of light. Megan stared up in awe. She imagined soaring into the dark empty spaces between the stars. She remembered that there were billions of galaxies, each with billions of stars beyond the range of her eyes in all those dark spots. "For each star we can see, billions more are out there. No, not out there—*right here!*" she whispered. Mark did not hear over the sound of the hooves and the wind.

Day 3-16: John Takes a Stand at the Walking Stick Tavern

Beyond the edge of town, the country road seemed to wind eternally through fields, woods, and wetlands as John walked in the dim light of a hazy quarter moon. A lantern's glow in a distant window glimmered through the trees. He hoped to step out of the past and find a bar where he could have a cold beer and think about the coming Revolution and his memories of war. He paused to listen and smell the air, scanning ahead and behind for any sign that someone was there. Keep yourself together, he told himself. This is not Nicaragua or Afghanistan. A sense of danger nagged him for the first time since arriving in Williamsburg.

After an hour, he came upon a crossroads tavern. The words Walking Stick were carved into a sign with a painted relief of a cane and mug. He pulled open the heavy oak door. The smell of sweat, smoke, and rancid tallow lanterns made clear he was still in the past. He sat alone at a small table. Compared to taverns in town, this was a rowdy roadhouse. Voices were loud, the floor dirty. He ordered a beer, certain he had to stay alert.

At a table across from his, a man with cruel lines around his mouth also sat alone, hardening the sharpened thumbnail of his right hand above a candle flame. He pretended to ignore what was going on in the noisy room. John knew this means to avoid drawing attention. The man reached behind his back and pulled a large concealed knife from a sheath. Holding it in his left hand below the table edge, he sharpened the long cracked nail of the middle finger on his right hand then hardened that nail in the flame.

He's ambidextrous—this does not look good, thought John. He sipped from his mug and slowly scanned the room without turning his head. There! Among a noisy group of men, playing at dice was a small man with cleaner, fancier clothes than most in the tavern. John watched him place small bets while observing other players, probably noting those who carried a worthy purse. John recognized him as the dance instructor at the Governor's Ball.

"I'll be damned," thought John. "The ones Bruce called Dagger and Dancer. There is an ambush, but not for me." His awareness shifted. He slowly rotated his shoulders, letting go of tension. He breathed deeply, settling into a calm that could abide in chaotic life-threatening surroundings. John's skills in karate and kendo, honed in hand-to-hand combat, had never been witnessed by his wife or children. Certainly, such fighting had never been seen in the colonies. He smiled. Like riding a bike, it comes back. He sat composed, vigilant, barely touching his beer.

Dancer switched tables and placed a few bets in a higher-stakes game. A few minutes later Dagger stood and walked to the table where Dancer

193

was about to roll the dice and sat down across from him. I missed the signal, thought John, but there had to be one.

Ten minutes later, a young man next to Dancer stood up suddenly, swayed, and pointed at Dagger. The man was from beyond the Piedmont. The locals called his kind "buckskins" or "shirtmen" for the deerskin jackets and hunting shirts they wore. In the noisy room, John could not hear what he shouted. Dancer spoke to the young man who took the bait and shouted again at Dagger, pointing to an open area in the room. Dagger stood and without a word walked to the open place.

Patrons heard the buckskin yell, "If you're so damn sure, bet those coins you won, and I'll match 'em!" Dancer leaned over to him again and the young man shouted, "Give them to the inn-keeper and I'll give the same. The winner takes the whole purse!" He swayed into a table and almost fell over.

The owner of the tavern cleared a table and counted the coins and notes in the leather bag Dagger gave him. Then he counted the money the young man was carrying for himself and four other families in the hills of western Virginia to buy tools and supplies. Dagger's purse was short so Dancer stepped up to cover the difference. The drunken buckskin struggling to take off his jacket did not notice.

"This is murder," John's jaw tightened.

Two men held the buckskin back as side bets were placed around the room. The owner called for quiet. "The man left standing will win both purses. If neither can claim his prize, the money will buy spirits for every man in the house." A cheer broke out. "Listen! When one of you wants to give up to save himself, follow the tradition and shout 'King's Cruise.' The winner must stop or we'll stop you with that bludgeon." His brother held a wicked club in both hands doing double duty as he stood between the crowd and the shelf lined with bottles of wine and spirits. "Is that understood?" Dagger nodded. The inebriated buckskin strained at the men who held him. The owner shouted into his face. "Understood?"

"I don't care!" shouted the man.

"You can yell 'Kings Cruise' to yield and get hurt no more."

"He can yell what he wants!" That satisfied the owner's sense of fair play.

When the men released him, the young buckskin charged. Dagger stepped aside and slapped the man's face as he raced by. The drunk crashed into a table and fell, breaking a chair. Men grabbed the remains of a lantern from the floor and stamped out burning oil to avert a tavern fire.

The buckskin staggered up, shook his head violently, licked the cut on his palm, and rushed forward. This time Dagger tripped him and sent the poor dupe sliding across the floor with a yell as he picked up splinters in his back. He would need help to remove them to avoid infection tomorrow, if he had a tomorrow. He came to rest beside John's table.

John helped the young man to his feet. "What is your name?"

"Luke."

"Luke, listen to me. Don't charge the wily old bastard. Go to him slowly and hit him hard." The young man nodded and spat.

This time Luke walked over and swung a roundhouse punch that Dagger dodged but the young man knew enough to follow with a hard left jab that landed on Dagger's shoulder and spun him to the side.

Dagger stood still until Luke moved to grab him but quickly turned and got Luke in a hold. John saw Dagger's right hand form a C shape with the two hardened sharp nails at the points. Luke from the mountains was about to become a one eyed man with no money.

John felt a surge of energy and shouted, "King's Cruise!"

The owner's brother raised the club and stepped forward. Dagger pushed Luke away but the young man lunged back before being restrained by two patrons. "I did not say 'King's Cruise,'" he shouted.

"No, but your second did. Give me the purse," Dagger demanded.

"I got no second!" Luke squirmed to get back in the fight.

"It was not for him," John watched Dagger. "I called King's Cruise for you. Innkeeper, please give Luke his purse." The innkeeper bit his lip.

Dagger's hand felt for the handle of the knife against his backbone. "That trick will win you nothing. Give me my winnings!" he snarled.

With calm breathing, John stepped forward, his gaze fixed on Dagger. He sensed motion on his right as Dancer swung an iron bar. He ducked and shot out a kick that landed on the side of Dancer's leg placing fifteen pounds of pressure in precisely the right spot to dislocate the knee and send Dancer to the floor with a scream. The iron bar clanked against the edge of a table.

"You won't be teaching ladies the finer points of the minuet now, I suppose," called out John without taking his eyes off Dagger.

Dagger lunged and as quickly, John slapped him across the face as Dagger had done to the buckskin. Dagger used every trick he knew, slashing the blade to the right and left with his left hand in arcs while seeking an opening for his right fist. He passed the knife to his right hand and moved in to jab without coming close to John, who taunted as he poked Dagger's ribs hard beneath his knife arm. "You're not good at this when your foe is sober. You need another line of work!"

Dagger roared and dove forward thrusting the knife. The knife found only air and Dagger got another slap across the face that spun his head to the side and raised a bright red welt. The crowd in the tavern was silent. The owner's brother stared with his mouth open.

"Yield or face a gory gasping fate, you corpse in stinky boots!" roared John.

A shot rang out as a lead ball from a .62 caliber single shot flintlock pistol tore through John's shirt between his chest and his armpit, embedding itself in a wooden column. In the moment it took John to glance at the man across the room struggling to reload, Dagger slashed and John dodged too late to avoid a cut on his arm. He whirled to face Dagger again.

A thud from the stock of a weapon sent the man with the pistol crashing unconscious to the floor. A tall man with a black beard pointed the business end of an old blunderbuss and shouted, "The next man to raise a firearm gets a belly full of bird shot. It's time we saw an even fight in this tavern."

"Thanks," John called out.

Crazed with rage, Dagger dove forward, making short slashes to keep the point of the knife between him and John. In an instant, he was spun around and immobilized in a lock with the knife still in hand. John dropped to one knee and held Dagger's wrist in a painfully tight grip with the honed edge of the blade across his throat. Dagger's left hand flailed in the air. It happened so fast that no one could say how John did it.

"Just one move and by your own hand your head will go east and your body west," John shouted in the loudest voice he had used in twenty years. Dagger moved and the keen edge of the knife stung and started a trickle of blood on his Adam's apple.

Dagger made another attempt to move. This time John twisted the hand to keep the knife away from his captive's neck but pulled Dagger's knuckles hard into his throat making breathing difficult.

"Why make a mess? Right, innkeeper? *Right, innkeeper?*"

The innkeeper stared.

A local man with a bet on Dagger reached for a musket leaning against the wall beside him. "Don't move!" shouted the bearded man. "If you touch it you won't live to point it. A second bearded man with a pistol in each hand stepped out from behind him. The local man put his hands on the table.

"All wagers are off except for the purse," shouted the innkeeper. Patrons with money on Dagger relaxed as did the man with the blunderbuss.

Dagger tried to twist free to no avail. John pressed hard and paralyzed his opponent. He could not yell, could not breathe. His eyes stared, his movements weakened. John eased the pressure and next to Dagger's ear threatened through closed teeth, "Stop struggling, or you'll never move again. What's your name?"

"Roger!" He rasped.

"An old man like me with bare hands is no match for a fighter like you holding a knife, Roger. But you like uneven fights, don't you? How do you think those men felt that you set up and cut down? Did they feel like this? Innkeeper, we'll take that iron bar Dancer found and stake Roger's head outside to attract customers. Once it rots away to a skull, you can rename the tavern 'The Jolly Roger'. No, that would ruin pirates' good name. What about 'The Thirsty Skull?' Perfect! Men who prey on others will be dying to come in."

Dancer, lying nearby, moaned. "Be patient, Dancer. I'll end your pain soon." Dancer moaned again, more in terror than pain.

John noticed luminous eyes looking at him from in the crowd. Frances, from the St. George Tucker House, was staring into him. He could feel something else. Could that be Susan over there? No, maybe not.

He drew a breath. "It was long ago," he murmured. "Danny and Sargon are gone. It's over." He stood up suddenly and pulled Dagger upright. "Roger, some people say I have a problem. I get irritated by people who maim and kill for financial gain. I don't like you — you hurt people."

John bellowed at the patrons, "Stand up if you're one of the best fighters here!" No one moved. "You drunken gamblers just got bashful. Come on, haven't you seen a head come off?" Dagger twitched. John nodded toward the men. "You there, and you, step forward. Innkeeper, you too! And your brother carrying the big stick — now! Or Roger's head comes off right here! You two big fellows at the table, who were betting on the fight, leave your musket there and step up next to the others!"

The man with the blunderbuss shouted, "Do as he says!"

John waited until the men were in a row. "You clever fellows figured out how to piss and how to blow snot out your nose, but you don't know much else. You own one shirt and you don't know what soap is. That's why you smell like a pig barn in July. If I swing Dagger's head by his hair, it will bloody up your only shirts. You will at least need to wash them.

"If you want to keep your shirts free of Dagger's blood and keep Dagger's head on his shoulders, raise your right hands." A few complied and after looking at each other and shuffling, all ten hands were raised.

"See, Roger? They love you more with your head on. Do you men swear that when baiting men into fights happens here, you'll keep the peace?"

A few half-hearted mumbles.

"Are you so blind you can't see that when Redcoats come for you with fixed bayonets twice as long as Roger's dagger, you will need every smelly one of you and all the buckskins to be fit to fight? Shirt-men can drop a squirrel for supper at ninety yards and you town-folk can't hit a man at fifty when you are sober and the man is fat and standing still. You need the mountain boys to keep both their eyes! And no dismembering! In battle, you will need both your balls and then some! Now swear to stop these fights before they begin and spend your money on something sensible like land, horses, women, or whisky!

"Aye," a few men mumbled.

"I swear," mumbled the innkeeper and his brother grunted agreement.

"And if one of you has a few tankards and forgets, the others remind him. I showed you fighting—now I'll show you something else." With a jerk, John cut off the hard nail on Roger's thumb and shoved him gasping to the floor at the feet of the men. He spun in a circle, putting the energy of his spin into the dagger, which he hurled into a beam above the door.

"Stand aside!" John shouted and he bounded onto a chair and the table nearest the door and leapt up to grab the knife handle in both hands. As he dropped back to the floor, the handle snapped off with his weight, leaving the blade imbedded in the beam, to remind patrons of this night until The Walking Stick burned to the ground eighty years later.

He stepped back to Roger, lying on the floor, and placed the carved antler handle next to him. "This is yours. What I'm showing you is called mercy. I lost too many friends in the big bar fights called war to put up with crap like this when I'm having a quiet beer." He grabbed Roger by the collar and pulled him to his feet. He walked him to the door and shoved him outside. "Go far, Roger, or someone you hurt will finish you!"

John closed the door and exhorted the patrons, "Whether war comes to you or you march out to meet it, stay sober, help your friends, and show mercy to your enemies. Today's enemies may be our friends tomorrow."

John went to Dancer who grimaced, sweating on the floor, his right leg at a painful, distorted angle below his knee. "No! Please!" he cried.

John spoke calmly "Let's fix that before it swells." He placed both hands around the knee and with a snap, relocated it. Dancer screamed at the momentary pain then looked with relief at his leg.

"There was some tearing, so stay off it a few days and bind it for support but not too tight. It will swell then begin to get better. What's your name?"

"Randall Weaver," Dancer whimpered.

"Randall, you'll be walking with a cane in a week, dancing with a limp in ten, and amazing the gentry with your recovery in half a year. Make an honest go of it." John looked back at the crowd but the women were gone.

He nodded to the tavern owner. "What do I owe you for the beer?"

"Nothing, Mister. I'll grant thee another if you have a thirst."

"No, thanks. I tend to get rowdy if I drink more than one. Please give our young friend Luke, his purse back and half of Dagger's purse. Use the rest to buy everyone a drink." The innkeeper complied.

"You won some money, but learn more sense," John cautioned Luke.

"I could have beat him myself!"

"No, Luke. Roger was about to gouge an eye. Did you come on a horse?"

"Aye."

"I'll walk you outside and send you on your way. Wait! The splinters!"

"Barman, I'll take two shots of the strongest whiskey you have."

John tore off his bloodied sleeve and winced as he splashed whisky onto the cut and used the sleeve as a bandage. "Luke, turn around and hold the table." John pulled Luke's hunting shirt up past where the large splinters had pierced him. He pulled them out, and poured whiskey on the wounds.

"Ow!" yelled Luke.

"Done! That was so it would not get infected, Luke. Now you need to get far away from here. Good night, Gentlemen." John bowed to the stunned crowd and ushered the young buckskin out into the fresh night air. Roger was nowhere in sight. Luke climbed onto his horse without help.

"Find a place to sleep and don't drink when you get there. If you make it back home, share what you won with the families that trusted you. Learn to read. They may elect you as their Congressman someday." John slapped the horse's flank and Luke was off down the road toward Williamsburg.

John turned to see the men with the blunderbuss and two pistols come through the door and a third man with a musket following behind them.

"Thank you for keeping the fight fair," John said.

"Roger maimed two friends last year," explained the bearded man. "We came to kill him but you saved us the trouble and perhaps saved us from hanging."

"I'd call that a good exchange."

"So would I, Mister. You took a reckless risk fighting Dagger alone. My brother was standing at my back with two pistols, and our cousin was across the room with his musket in his lap."

John looked at the bullet hole through his shirt. "Maybe I was protected by Divine Providence like George Washington was."

"Godspeed," said the bearded man with the blunderbuss.

It was a long walk to town. My wars are over, John thought, but their war is just beginning. He thought of the suffering and grief to come. When he reached the house, it was dark and quiet. He washed his face in the large bowl, put disinfectant and a bandage from his travel kit onto the cut on his arm and slipped into bed.

Day 3-17:   Peter Drives toward Norfolk

The engine started with a roar and Peter noticed his foot was almost to the floor. Calm down, he thought. I sense that this is where the trail leads and Annie advised me to follow the feeling. He decided to take Highway 5 past New Hope, cross the bridge, and follow the Colonial Trail east. He drove in silence and watched the woods and fields along the road.

After crossing the James, he drove until the highway curved south, then turned north on a narrow dirt track to the river. He parked and walked to the water. This is close to Norfolk, he thought. Maybe slaves passed by here in 1775 on their way to the British. He was glad to be in his own time and not in the past when armed men were in these woods. It would have been dangerous around here back then.

He sat on a rock and tossed pebbles into the river. I would have been scared, running away and being put into battle, he thought. I wonder if Dad was scared when he was a young soldier. The woods were so silent he heard pebbles of varied sizes make different sounds as they hit the water. Throwing a few stones high into the air, he listened to the notes. It was the first four notes of a spiritual. "All night, all day, Angels watchin' over me," he sang to himself. He walked east then stopped again to listen.

The sound of singing drifted over the water. He followed a path around the next point and saw a glow in the woods. Through a veil of leafless branches, he saw a circle of African men seated around a campfire. They sang in a major key with harmony and syncopation, similar to what he heard at the Hush Harbor. Could he really have stepped back into the past? Just behind his head, he heard a metallic click.

"Hands up!" a voice barked. "Forward march or get a hole by your ear!"

"Don't shoot!" Peter cried. "I came to listen to the singing." And I'm about to be shot if I don't think of something better to say, he thought as he neared the fire holding his hands in the air.

"Look who I found snoopin' 'round," his captor gloated. "Likely a rebel tryin' to catch us back." He shoved Peter forward so others could see him.

"Good job, Aaron! You be a good guard."

"Stand him up by a tree. We need target practice," proposed one man.

The votes started coming in. "Yeah, shoot him!"

"Wit' a prisoner, the Redcoats sees we be ready," the captor protested.

"Naw, we can do that wit' his body."

"Shoot him so we can sleep wit'out him gettin' away to tell where we is."

"You know what I think? No, you don't, so I'se gonna tell you. I say ax what he doin' here and ax him to 'splain his self good. I hopes for your sake you can 'splain yourself, young man," cautioned a man in the circle.

"Are you William, the brick maker?" asked Peter shakily.

Before William could answer, Peter heard, "Hey, Mister Peter, what you doin' here?" from Augustus on the other side of the fire.

"Oh, Augustus! It's you! I'm glad you made it over the river."

"This here is Mister Peter. He helped me escape," Augustus explained. "Don't shoot, he probably come to help us. Good job findin' him, Aaron!"

Peter's captor lowered his musket. "Lord, don't forget me! I swear I wanna capture a slave owner to give him a taste of how he done to us."

"Come set by me, Mister Peter," Augustus called out. "Say good evenin' to Governor Dunmore's Ethiopian Regiment. We make raids to get black powder the rebels hid. We follow orders, but no massa owns us."

"That's right," echoed a number of voices around the fire.

"I'm happy to meet you, men. Thank you all for not shooting me."

Some men chuckled. They had scant experience of camaraderie with whites. "How did you get here, Mister Peter?" asked Augustus.

"I came along the south shore of the James to see if the way was open to Norfolk in case I'm able to help anyone else get out of Williamsburg."

"Good thing you stopped 'fore you got there," William said. "The Governor sits on a ship 'cause Rebel militia is nearby."

"That's true," Augustus chimed in. "I met up wit' these men when I came along the shore like you told me. You want a sip of corn mash?"

"No, thanks. I have to drive... I mean go back later. Do you have water?"

Peter gratefully took a cup of water. Around the circle, bright eyes watched flashes of flame dance above glowing coals. Brown faces glistened, reflecting orange, red, and yellow light. Logs popped—showers of sparks gave a feel of celebration muted by foreboding that soon, with little training, they would be fighting for freedom and for their lives.

These newly freed men flashed grins of white teeth with gaps and broken corners. They told tales of dancing on a Saturday night, good food snatched somehow, and willing women they had known. Any over thirty were old, and even young men were sun-baked and bone-sore. Slaves were forbidden to carry a firearm unless hunting with permission on the master's land. A free black found with a gun off his own land risked being killed. Here, every man had a musket, powder, and shot at hand.

Augustus leaned close to Peter. "Have you seen Annie since I left?"

Before Peter could answer, Aaron sat heavily beside them and took a pull from a crock of corn mash. "I ain't on guard duty now. Mister, I ain't against you if you helped 'Gustus." He took a drink. "'Gustus been good to me since we joined up. Folk say I'se angry all the time, but white folk been awful cruel to me. When I looks at you, Mister, I remembers them."

"I understand. I'm sorry about how you good men have been treated."

"I ain't no good man at all." Aaron took a long draught from the jar. "No-suh not a good man no mo'. And I ain't all African neither."

"Was you daddy white and ain't 'cepted you as a son like what happened to me?" asked Augustus who was lighter skinned than the others.

"No, he was a free man from British India. He was a real Dilli man."

"A Dilli man?" asked a surprised Peter.

"Yes. Folk from Delhi is Dilli men. Daddy served table for a British sea captain. After they got to 'Napolis he served in a big house near the Potomac. My mama was a tall African, so I was a tall boy. But mama was a slave, so by law I was born a slave even though Daddy was free. When Massa died, Daddy did not have money to buy me, so I got sold away as a field hand and never learned to serve in a big house like he done. Stuck out sweatin' in the hot sun..." His voice faded as he stared into the fire.

"Is Annie still talkin' to people about runnin'?" whispered Augustus.

"She tells people to keep ready but not to rush off."

"I'se glad 'bout that 'cause folk who got to Norfolk got catched."

Aaron took another swig and shook his head violently.

"I'll let people know Norfolk is not safe," whispered Peter.

"Damn, how could they do that to a man!" shouted Aaron.

"What happened?" asked Augustus.

"I was thinkin' about it again, is all. I ain't no man. Them yellow dogs done it."

Augustus put his left hand on his leather pouch with herbs Annie gave him. He put his right hand on Aaron's shoulder. "We all been done wrong. That be why we'se side by side to fight for freedom."

"I tried to run. I didn't know what I was doin'. They catched me and... "

"You had the balls to try, Aaron. I was too scared to run."

"You say I had the balls to try. I ain't got them now!"

"You got balls, Aaron. You brave as a badger, big as a bear, and you the strongest, fastest man by this fire. I wanna be next to you when we fight."

"Them yellow dogs cut me, 'Gustus. They cut me and laughed at me. I almost bled to death 'cept for a big woman healer that found me the next day. She put on a poultice, and sewed me up so I did not die."

Augustus kept a hand on Aaron's shoulder. "They cut you?"

"It weren't my massa but the men who caught me runnin'."

"But Aaron, Burgesses made a law sayin' they cain't castrate slaves."

"That law made in '69 but Slave hunters cut me before."

Aaron looked into the fire. "I never was wit' but one woman. That be why I was runnin'. There was a pretty girl washin' laundry in a fine house by the Capitol in Williamsburg. Massa brought me to load up supplies for building his new house. He needed me to help drive the team home since he was sometimes deep in the grog jar wit' other gentlemen.

"He went to a builder to ax how to do his roof. At our quarters, the only time the roof don't leak is when it ain't rainin'. But Massa's house need to be just so. They talked 'bout slate or cedar shingles, and whether squarin' beams wit' an adze be enough or do we need to plane them. They had a cup of rum and they ax Massa to have bread and quail at the house."

Peter and Augustus grew very quiet as they listened.

"I was out by the kitchen, talkin' wit' the cook and a washing girl, eatin' greens and potatoes. They had no men folk. I liked talkin' wit' them. It was time for them to sleep 'cause they got up before the sun to start the fires but because I was there, they stayed up a little longer.

"The men sat outside so as not to wake the missus, so we heard them talkin' and drinkin'. They got louder and soon they wasn't fancy at all. One of them was such a fine gentleman he threw up over the fence.

"Massa done said he should be movin' on. But the builder tol' him, 'Joseph, you sleep here instead of in a crowded room at the King's Arms.'

"Massa Joseph remembered me, and ax'd, 'Can Aaron sleep in the kitchen?' The other Massa rubbed his head a minute.

"'Yes, we can take care of your boy,' he says. They came through the gate by the garden and me and the women stood up. The builder tol' Massa that his wife is gonna have a baby 'cause she started feelin' poorly in the mornin'. He said, 'Your boy can sleep in the loft. If he breeds wit' our laundry girl, we'll have a wet nurse here for the baby.'

"'Go on ahead inside you all,' the builder told us. They was laughin' and slappin' each other on the back as they went back into the house."

"You say a cook and a laundress. Where was the house?" asked Peter.

"I don't remember 'zackly. The Capitol was across the street."

Peter let out his breath slowly.

"Well, the cook says, 'She been wonderin' 'bout men for a while so you two go up into the loft and I'll sleep by the stove to warm my bones.'

"'What should we do?' the washing girl axed.

"'Do what I told you 'bout.' Then the cook went to the kitchen.

"So we went above stairs. Neither of us knew what to do but Spirit moved us and I started to like her. Then I loved her like she was my wife.

"Next day, we was drivin' the cart back to Princess Anne County, near the beaches. All the way home, I thought 'bout that girl and how close to her I felt. It was a deep feelin' like prayin' I never felt before. I wanted to jump off the cart and run back but I would not get far. So when we passed a fork, I looked back to see what it looked like goin' the other way.

"We got home in the evenin' and me and the stable boy unloaded the cart into a shed. Massa Joseph was tired and went to his house to sleep."

"I got to thinkin'. Massa Joseph would not call me 'til tomorrow. I could run all night and be far by mornin'. So when the cook gave me a biscuit and cob of corn, I wrapped them in a cloth. I took a few nails from the wagon. I was goin' to say if someone ax me that Massa sent me back to get the right size nails."

"You was smart to have a story, Aaron," Augustus said. "If that was the first time you wit' a woman, I see why you had a strong feelin' for her."

"Well, the story wasn't smart enough, 'Gustus. I walked all night thinkin' of takin' that girl to Spanish Florida or west to join wit' black Indians. Outside Williamsburg, men axed where was I goin' in such a hurry. I tol' them, 'To the store to buy more nails like this.' But they tol' me, 'The store opens Monday and this is Sunday, so why you runnin'?

"They tied me to a tree and beat me 'til I cried I was runnin' to see a girl while I was waitin' for the store to open. One man pulled out a knife, 'Let's fix him so he don't run after no mo' girls.' I was tied and couldn't do nuthin' but beg and scream. They left me but a lady healer came by and cared for me. The men came back when she was off getting more herbs. They took me to my Massa and axed for a reward, which they got since they was carryin' muskets. I got ashamed to look after that girl 'cause I ain't no man no mo'." Aaron sobbed.

Augustus patted Aaron's back and kept his other hand on his poultice pouch. Staring into the fire, he began to pray on how to help.

"You is a friend, 'Gustus. I been too ashamed to tell folk I ain't a man."

Augustus rubbed the pouch like a healing talisman. "Aaron, you be a brave man. That washing girl had a son after you was wit' her. Her name Evie and her son be James because his daddy lived 'cross the James River. She tell James his daddy pray for him every night. I seen her at a Hush

Harbor. She still washin' at that house by the Capitol. Mister Peter and me know Annie, the big woman who saved you. She teached me herbs for poultices so I can stop bleedin', ease pain, and keep wounds from festerin'."

"Evie! That was her name! The cook called her that when she say good night. I got a son? I gonna pray for James every night like his mama told him. If we live through this fight, maybe I can do somethin' for my son. What's he like 'Gustus?"

"He's a big boy like you but a bit shy. He need a daddy to help him."

"I met James, Aaron," Peter added. "You can be proud of your son."

"There be somethin' else I want to tell you, Aaron." Augustus confided. "Two years after she had James, Evie had a second boy."

"She done? Who is the daddy? Did they jump the broom together?"

"Naw. He was sent to the loft like you was, but he never paid Evie any mind. She call her second boy, Dilli. 'Cause she been thinkin' about you, Aaron, all these years."

"I must have told her 'bout Daddy the free Dilli man. I cain't be a man for they momma but maybe I can help them boys. Mister Peter, is that your name? Good thing I ain't shot you. But damn! I still mean to take me a prisoner." Aaron flung the dregs of the corn mash into the fire. He lay back and closed his eyes.

The flash of liquor in the fire reminded Augustus and Peter of Annie pitching rum into the fire at the Hush Harbor. "That was good, Augustus," whispered Peter. "Why didn't you tell him you are Dilli's father?"

"I thought 'bout Annie and the flash in the fire was a sign I done right. I done it to help Aaron. I ain't got no poultice for lost balls but maybe he can feel like the brave man he is. It feels good to help people. I ain't obliged to run home to avoid a whippin'. I am free." As the men around the fire had done already, Augustus nestled into the leaves and dozed off.

Peter lay back and looked at the stars, thinking about the beautiful woman two centuries older than he was. He was camped out with the fathers of her two children. This must fit together somehow. He drifted off to sleep.

Day 4-1:   Susan Breakfasts with the Better-Sorts

Susan woke to the sound of water pouring. Disoriented, she opened a curtain with a rose design. An African woman was filling a wash bowl. Room service, she thought. As she dropped her head back to the pillow, she remembered, "God, what an intense dream! I hope John is all right."

Susan washed, dressed, and knocked on Jane's door to find her already up. "Good morning, Susan. I have never seen such a bed chamber."

Lucy Burwell came into the corridor, "Oh good! You are awake! I rise before the sun to be sure the cook starts breakfast. Sorry we have no extra housemaids to help with your ablutions and dressing."

"Lucy, that's fine," Susan insisted. "We normally dress ourselves."

"Breakfast is almost ready. Most mornings we read the Bible with the children, but today is Sunday so we are going to Church. We will sit with Aunt Betty. Would you like to have a look at the kitchen?"

"Yes," Susan said. "We'd love to."

They descended the back stairs. "My husband insists on breakfast at eight. With coaxing and help from my daughters, meals are on time."

In a busy kitchen, pots of water for tea and coffee hung in a fireplace high enough to stand in. The cook, a large woman with a headscarf, directed the kitchen maids. "Effie, keep stirrin' and mind it don't scorch. Mornin', Missus Burwell. Mornin', Ladies."

Lucy pointed to the table at the heaping serving plates and bowls. "Today breakfast is leftovers from last night. Ice cut from the ponds and stored in the icehouse is limited so we cannot store fresh food long. After breakfast, I plan dinner and give the cook the expensive ingredients from a locked pantry. I supervise the house and gardens until dinner at 1:30. Let's step out of the kitchen so we can talk."

A girl ran in and hugged Lucy's leg. "Good morning, Mother."

"Good morning! We go to church after we eat so get dressed, precious."

"Do your children go to school?" asked Susan.

"They are schooled here. My daughters help me so they learn how to run households by the time they marry. All children learn gardening, raising chickens, and managing servants. The boys learn animal husbandry, fishing with weirs, commerce, and the dealings of a large estate."

"Doest thou produce your own food, Lucy Burwell?" Jane asked.

"We have vegetables fresh in summer and from the root cellar in winter, fruit from the orchards or in home-made compotes and jams, bread from corn and wheat, and milk, butter, and cheese from our dairy. We have beef, pigs, and sheep, chickens, ducks, geese, doves, and game. From the river and the bay, we eat oysters, crabs, and fish, grilled or salted and dried. We get honey and wax from our bees and herbs from the garden. We go to town to meet friends, visit someone ailing, or to buy molasses, a tool from the smith, or some imported fabric.

"We do laundry on Friday, so everyone including bondsmen has fresh clothes on Sunday. Many of our bondsmen will ride with us to church.

"The hour before dinner is busy. I keep a bowl of cold water near to freshen up before sitting at the table in case I do not have time to go to my chamber to change. We often have guests. After the meal, the men stay at the table for brandy and a pipe. The women move to the salon for coffee."

Lucy sighed, "I try to find time in the afternoon to help my children with their studies or to be alone. I might read or talk with a visitor. Let us go into the gardens together for a few minutes before breakfast." The three women strolled through the garden past a flowering tree and Lucy became uncharacteristically quiet.

"Forgive me," Susan ventured, "but is something troubling you besides your uncle's passing?"

Lucy nodded. "I love Kingsmill. I am grateful for all our blessings." She led them to a bench with an unobstructed view of the James River. The crescent-shaped garden of Queen Anne's lace, and pink and yellow yarrow bordered with blue salvia, was all still colorful in November. "All this... is at risk of slipping away. Our debts are greater than the value of our land, buildings, and bondsmen combined. Last night the carriage took you by a plantation taken over by Scottish factors who held the debt. There are many such disasters. My husband thrashes in his bed, worried a factor might ask full payment or that a poor crop will bankrupt us. If war comes this way, our home could be burned. If everything falls into ruin, what can I do for the children?

"You both show kindness that can only come from contentment and wisdom. I envy you." Lucy began to weep and Susan put her arm around her shoulder. In the distance, a three-masted ship glided upriver. Lucy sniffed, "Sorry. I criticize the hypocrisy of other families but we present the same false facades. I know not what to do." They watched the river until Lucy asked, "Is there anything you can tell me that might help?"

Jane offered gently, "'Tis not the telling that will help. 'Tis thy knowing."

"What knowing, Jane?"

"Know life is lived each moment and the Light within illuminates eternally. Some see it as light, some feel it as love, and some hear it in silence. It is all of those and more. It is the Divine source of all that is."

"I have lost touch with my Faith." Lucy looked at the mist lingering near the shore. "I keep busy so there is no time to dwell on the travails in our lives. I feel an empty place within."

Susan spoke. "Lucy, do not fear that empty place—it is an opening. You have strength and the light within that Jane pointed to."

"You are saintly women."

Jane shook her head. "No, Lucy, we are all pilgrims on a long journey. Life's hardships are neither punishment nor a sign of abandonment. They are part of the landscape we travel as we learn and grow."

Susan assured her, "I know what it is to have a husband thrashing in the night. If you can find grace within the empty place, you may calm him as well. You are blessed with a grand house full of laughing children. Let their joy lift you. Many people work hard in your kitchen and in the fields to support you and your family. Be grateful for their efforts as well. They are souls seeking happiness just as you are and everyone should be appreciated and rewarded for their contributions."

Jane added, "Good mingles with tribulations. If thy future station is humble, enjoy thy family, and be grateful."

"Truth resonates in your words." They watched the ship sail out of view. "I have not so looked forward to singing hymns in years. You have given me back my appetite for life. Let us go in and meet the rest of the family."

Susan and Jane joined the Burwells at the table for Sunday breakfast. Steaming warm breads, smoked ham, and corn meal grits with a pat of bacon fat were added to the leftovers. Lucy gave her husband and children hugs as she walked around the table to her place. The Colonel led the family in a prayer and the meal began.

The children were delighted at Jane's way of talking. They found Susan funny as well, especially when she told them a joke her students liked.

After breakfast, everyone bundled up and hurried out to two enclosed carriages and an open hay wagon, their teams of horses hitched and ready. The older children jostled to get seats in the second carriage with Jane and Susan. Colonel Burwell came back to the second carriage. "Ladies, your presence at Kingsmill has brought a salutary effect to my wife's heart. Lucy is in the carriage laughing with the children. You brought levity to our home." He made a respectful bow.

"It is an honor and pleasure to be welcomed in your home, Colonel. We will pray for your family in these tumultuous times." Susan bowed.

"We are grateful for your prayers." The colonel returned to his carriage and they pulled down the lane. The wagon followed, crowded with fourteen adult slaves wrapped in the blankets Lucy provided, excited to be on their way to Williamsburg and hopeful of seeing friends, or loved ones there. Bright-eyed children cuddled among them under the blankets.

When the horse-drawn convoy reached Bruton Parish Church, everyone clambered out into the bustle of the crowd. "Can you join us in our family pew, Susan?" Lucy asked.

"Thank you, Lucy, but I must check on my husband and children."

"I hope to see you again, Susan." Lucy rejoined her children.

Susan turned to Jane and gave her a hug. "God be with you, Jane."

Jane was embarrassed by the hug but could not suppress a smile. "I thank thee, Susan. Thou hast truly brought me back to the Light."

"Jane, please keep the dress as a gift to remember the times we had."

"Oh, Susan! It was wonderful to wear it to Kingsmill and touch the lives of the better-sorts including their suffering, but I cannot take thy clothes!"

"Jane, I insist. It makes me happy to think of you wearing it on special days. Wear it at the Hospital once in a while and cheer up the patients."

"I shall remember thee for all time."

When Lucy noticed Jane moving toward the church, she hurried back, took her arm, and prevailed on her to join her in the Burwell family pew.

Day 4-2:   Peter Encounters a Smallpox Epidemic

Peter drifted to the surface of a fathomless sleep. He was covered by two frayed blankets beneath stark skeletons of winter trees reaching into the cold moonlight. It took a moment to register where he was. Near his feet were the cold ashes of a dead fire, covered by a scattering of frosted leaves. His eyes widened. The Ethiopian Regiment was gone. He was alone near the James River. "How did the fire get cold so fast? If I drank corn mash last night, I would say I passed out like Rip Van Winkle, but I'm probably just totally out of my mind! All right—calm down. Crap! I've got to get to Williamsburg."

He stood and stretched. What year is this? He laughed aloud at his question. To the southeast, orange light glowed on drifting billows of black smoke. He wrapped the blankets around him and walked along a shore trail to get a closer look. Picking his way over rocks to a promontory, he found a vantage point. Downriver, a town was being consumed in a firestorm. Smoke rose from charred ruins of warehouses and homes by the shore. The rest of the town blazed fiercely as flames leapt above the rooftops and a steeple. He wondered what town it was. He moved a hundred yards closer and sat to stare at the conflagration.

When he stood up to hike back to where he hoped to find his car, he detected motion beyond the trees. Moving shadows resolved into two men lugging a blanket as a crude stretcher. In it, a third man swayed back and forth with the labored steps of his struggling bearers. Beyond them, Peter saw a house gutted by fire but other buildings seemed intact. He approached the men through the trees. "What happened to him?"

An exhausted black man turned empty eyes toward him as he trudged forward, oblivious to Peter's question. Peter moved to the back end of the blanket where another ashen man could barely walk, let alone carry, and took the bulky blanket from his hands. The man slumped to the ground.

"Where are we going?" asked Peter of the other ghost-like man.

"Yonder," came a mumbled reply, with a nod at the stables. A man emerged through the haze from an open door, gesturing to lower their burden next to the fire. The blanket and the man in front were down in two thuds before Peter had fully lowered his end.

The man from the stables crouched next to the blanket, "He is dead." Only Peter heard him. This was the first corpse he had ever seen. "We must get water into them or they shall join their friend. If they got muscle aches and puking they is already sick wit' it. I will tell Annie we have a man dead, one staring at the fire, and a third fainted away in the pasture."

"Sick with what? Wait, Annie is here?"

"You know Annie, Mister?"

"Yes, I do. Can you take me to her?"

"People is dying of pox. Best get as far away as you can. Maybe it is too late. Many who carried the sick, lie buried here. I was inoculated in '68 and felt sicker than a rotting hog, but I don't get pox now, praise God."

"The pox, do you mean smallpox?"

The man took a pot of boiling water from the fire to rinse mugs he used to give water to the sick. "Yes, smallpox. Cow pox and chicken pox don't put hundreds of souls into the ground."

"Hundreds! You're telling me this is a smallpox epidemic?"

"That's what we got and little we can do but give them water so they don't die of thirst and to keep the fever down. I wager them two will go soon and maybe you will follow."

"When I was very young, I was vaccinated for smallpox."

"Do you have the mark?" The man pointed to an ugly scar on his arm.

Peter rolled up a sleeve to reveal a pale circle on his upper arm. He was vaccinated as a toddler when his parents thought John was going to be stationed overseas. Regular vaccinations ended in the U.S. years before. He hoped his vaccination was effective against this colonial era smallpox.

"We was forced to get inoculated. People got sick and some folk died. There was riots in Norfolk against inoculations, but now God help those people who did not get one! Annie is in the stable." The man turned and walked in and Peter followed right behind him.

A nauseating stench assaulted Peter's nostrils. A low fire failed to illuminate the space as smoke drifted vaguely toward a gash hacked in the roof. Straw on the floor had surrendered to a thin layer of soupy mud. Diarrhea-fouled blankets were piled to be burned. Moaning, snoring, and shouts from men in fitful dreams added a chorus of torment to the smoke-veiled images of suffering. In the first stall, lay another corpse, mouth gaping in a face disfigured by scabbed pustules.

Peter felt his stomach turn and warm saliva ran into his mouth. He dashed out the wide door and vomited. He looked at the billowing smoke in the distance and took a few deep breaths of air. I've got to talk with Annie. He felt fear and aversion abate. Holding a blanket over his mouth and nose, he stepped with determination back into the stables.

Moving slowly past people laying two to a stall, Peter breathed through his mouth to reduce the smell. He almost tripped on another body. Living men lay next to those who had died in the night. The dead would be carried outside and others would come to this rough clinic to take their place. He got to the back of the stable, and made his way past the stalls on the other side. He spotted the silhouette of a large woman sitting next to a cot. Annie nodded to him then turned to the man she was attending. Under a blanket, his face covered with the same violent rash and open or scab-covered sores as the dead men across the room, was Augustus.

"Augustus!" exclaimed Peter in a voice too loud. "What happened?"

"Mister Peter?" Augustus rasped. "I got pox. Annie sendin' me over Jordan. Lord knows I'se glad to see you, but best to go 'fore you get sick."

"I had what you call the inoculation, Augustus, so I won't get the pox."

"I pray it ain't your time to die. We gonna meet again over yonder."

"You rest, 'Gustus, and say them prayers." Annie leaned close.

"I say them Annie, but I got to tell Mister Peter somethin' afore I go."

"Annie, I have two blankets," offered Peter.

"Set them over there. 'Gustus won't need them now." She nodded toward the cot. Peter squatted next to Augustus to hear the faint voice.

Augustus wheezed. "Mister Peter, a few weeks back you was sleepin' when Redcoats came in boats to fetch us. Aaron and me left blankets over you. We didn't want soldiers to see you and think you was a deserter."

"A few weeks?" Peter was astonished—but he focused on Augustus.

"We marched to Kemp's Landing on November 15 to fight the Princess Anne County Militia. They was in ambush but they fired too early. We fired our muskets and them Redcoats fired volleys fast like I never seen."

Augustus pulled a breath. "The militia ran but their commander shouted 'Liberty or death!' tryin' to get them to fight. When he heard that voice, Aaron flew out like a spark off a pine log. He put the tip of his bayonet at the Adam's apple of the militia commander and shouted, 'Was that Liberty or Death you want, Mister Joseph Hutchings?' We could not believe our eyes. Aaron done captured his own Massa.

"It looked like Aaron was gonna send a musket ball right through Joseph Hutching's throat, his hand was tremblin' so, but I hollered, 'Aaron, here is that prisoner you been prayin' hard to take.'"

Augustus whispered. "I felt the whole world hangin' on Aaron's trigger finger as I heared him say, 'I'se a free man now Mister Joseph. I can barely hold off from shootin' you dead, but if just once you call me Mister Aaron, you can keep your life and get liberty again like I got mine.'"

Augustus winced as he tried to take a deep breath. "You tell him, Annie. I got to breathe." Weak from smallpox, he was succumbing to pneumonia.

Annie looked at Peter. "'Gustus told me Hutchings didn't answer quick since a wrong word would be his last. He raised his hands up high and spoke real careful. 'Mister Aaron. I was always sorry they cut you.'

213

Aaron pulled back his bayonet and said, 'Thank you, Jesus.' Hutchings was surely thankin' Jesus, too. Aaron told him to march in front over to them Redcoat officers."

Augustus nodded and pulled a labored breath as Annie told the story. "The British captain made Aaron a sergeant. He axed his family name and 'cause he never had one, he tol' him it was 'Freeman.' The captain made a note in a book. 'Sergeant Aaron Freeman, when the war ends you will get land for your bravery and service to your King and country!'"

Augustus whispered, "Sergeant Aaron Freeman! I won't forget that day, not for the rest of my life." He smiled. "That be easy 'cause the rest of my life ain't long. Annie, tell Mister Peter the other day I won't forget."

"You rest, 'Gustus," Annie put her hand on his forehead. "On December 9, 'Gustus and Aaron met the Second Virginia Regiment at Great Bridge. There was more than two Virginians for each man on the British side. The British officers ordered a charge. This time the Regiment fired volleys from behind a barricade like Redcoats do. In minutes, they killed and wounded many.

"'Gustus tol' me Aaron charged out in front and took a musket ball through his forehead. He fell while stormin' forward. 'Gustus dove to the ground beside him. Hearin' goes last on dying folk so he called into Aaron's ear that he was a hero and goin' to heaven a free man. Droppin' to help Aaron got 'Gustus out of the line of fire and saved his life.

"The British signaled retreat and the Virginians cheered the Ethiopian Regiment for bein' so brave. That ended Dunmore's fight and he sailed off to New Jersey on a ship named *William* with a few men of the Ethiopian Regiment. Most was left behind. Because he was good at buildin' walls, they took William the brick maker. As they sailed, he hollered, 'You know why this ship called *William*? 'Cause that's my name.'"

Augustus tried to laugh but coughing raked spasms of pain in his chest.

"Be at peace, 'Gustus," murmured Annie.

"I'se almost done," he whispered. "I was on my own then came fever, pukin', and these pox all over me. Now I'se ready to join Aaron and the others over yonder." Exhausted by telling the story, Augustus closed his eyes. "I join them as a free man," he rasped. "Help Evie and her boys."

"I will. You can make it, 'Gustus." Tears welled in Peter's eyes.

A look from Annie told him this was not so. "Of eight hundred in the Ethiopian Regiment, five hundred is dead or dying from wounds or pox."

Peter put a hand on Augustus's shoulder. "Mister Augustus, when you get to Heaven, hold a spot for the only white boy who runs as fast as you."

Augustus smiled faintly and whispered, "Almost as fast, Mister Peter. I'se bound to get to Glory first." No one spoke for a few minutes. Then, with Annie beside him and Peter's hand on his shoulder, Augustus, planter of corn and tobacco, father of Dilli, healer, soldier, and free man, slowly exhaled for the last time.

"Annie, I have never..." He could not finish.

"Death be hard even when you 'round it as much as me. 'Gustus on his way home now. You would have come in even if you ain't been 'noculated, and it was good you was here, but I saw you puke beyond that door. You was prob'ly riddin' yourself of fear but we must go to the river to wash and pray. Half the folk here will die. Some will go blind."

"Why don't you get sick?"

"Ain't you seen the marks on my face? I got cow pox travelin' wit' the Fulani cattle herds. I tol' you we is leopard ladies. We don't get smallpox. You and I will surely die, Peter, but it ain't gonna be from pox."

Annie carried a pot of hot water to a rock jutting into the river. She pulled off her dress and a padded petticoat and stepped into the shallow cold water. Peter noticed with surprise that the petticoat was made to make her look heavier than she really was. She washed her face, and body with a chip of soap and a rag she rinsed in the hot water. "Now it be your turn. We don't want to carry pox to Williamsburg." She waded back onto the rocks. Peter had never seen such large breasts. He looked away after Annie handed him the soap and the rag. With her generous girth, he had thought her to be older. He guessed now she was only in her thirties.

"Don't be shy, Mister Peter. The Lord made us all about the same. Maybe He gave me a big bosom 'cause I got to comfort many folk. And yes, I tries to look too old and too fat to be 'tractin' attention I don't want to be 'tractin'. It ain't safe for a woman travelin' alone, so I make myself look like a granny. Men don't see fat grandmas as beautiful."

"You're plenty beautiful. Get dressed or you'll attract lots of attention."

Peter followed Annie's example, stripped, and stepped into the bracing river. "What's that fire over there? I've never seen anything like that."

"Nobody here never seen nothin' like that. That used to be Norfolk. The British burned buildings along the shore so the militia could not fire on British ships even though Norfolk was a Loyalist town. The patriots set the rest of the town ablaze New Year's Day. So the two sides fightin' for what they believe is right, done destroyed the whole town."

"Norfolk is destroyed and it's New Year's Day, 1776?" asked Peter.

"Yesterday was New Year's Day. Since Norfolk was where African folks was runnin', they be in a bad way. Them that ain't got smallpox are homeless in winter or gettin' caught. Many be desperate. Some goin' back to they massa sayin' they is sorry 'bout runnin', beggin' to be taken back."

"Didn't any get away?" Peter dried off and pulled on his clothes.

"Governor Dunmore took 'bout three hundred African folk on ships to New Jersey. Others be findin' their way along the shore or into the forest, but it be hard. I must go to Williamsburg to warn people not to run here. There may be other chances someday. It will take me days to get there since I got no boat for safe passage over. First, let us pray."

Annie took Peter's hand. He prayed to help people at this hard time. Annie prayed to get to Williamsburg quickly. "Amen!"

"I am not sure this will work, Annie, but I might know a way for us to be in Williamsburg this morning. 'Not sure' doesn't say it right. I am totally confused and have no idea how I slept for six weeks from November to January without freezing to death or dying of starvation."

"You ain't slept six weeks. You slid through again like you slid here in the first place, Mister Peter. I was hopin' to learn to do that. You let go of where you was and slid through a gate in the fence of time."

"Do you think we can do it again? I want to help warn people not to run to Norfolk," he replied, hoping it was not too late for Evie and the boys.

"I'se worried about many folk. For now, Evie, James, and Dilli are fine."

"Annie, you want to learn how I slid through as you call it, but I want to know how you know what I'm thinking."

Annie tilted her head to the left. "I cain't answer wit' words, but you don't hear much wit'out words yet. A few words might point you on the way, so listen careful. What we feel shines out from us even if we cain't see it like heat shines out from a fire. You cain't see heat but you feel it. I listen careful to people to feel what they mean. After a while, I began to feel what people mean that they ain't sayin'. Do them words make sense to you?"

"I get it about feeling heat from a fire even though you don't see it. Feeling what people mean when they talk? I know what that is. Feeling what they're not saying sounds possible. It's like radio. We can't see the waves but if we tune in we hear the voice or the music."

"Radior?"

"Sorry. If we are lucky maybe I can show you."

Peter led Annie west along the shore. They passed the site of the Ethiopian Regiment's campfire. "I hope this works, Annie. Give me your hand and close your eyes. Then we'll walk over that hill ahead."

"If you doin' what I think you is, you best know it will happen. Hope ain't enough."

216

"I know it'll happen if you close your eyes and listen to my voice."

"Good, Mister Peter. Don't wonder how you know, just know it, and let's go. I'll stay right wit' you." Annie closed her eyes and they walked slowly through the woods over the hill. Peter told her where to place her feet, advice she didn't seem to need even with her eyes closed. She listened to his voice and heard him catch his breath when he saw his father's car.

"What you see, Mister Peter?"

"Don't open your eyes yet. Come put your hand right — here."

"I feel cold metal, Mister Peter."

Peter stared at the car, and held tight to Annie's hand. "Open your eyes, Annie. Tell me what you see, and please don't disappear."

Annie laughed. "I see a tall fine lookin' man, holding my hand next to a... shiny metal carriage wit' a curved glass window."

"Welcome to my time, where you should just call me Peter." He opened the passenger side door and held it open for Annie. "We say, 'hop in'."

"Ain't we gonna need four horses to pull this carriage?"

"Over a hundred years ago this was called a horseless carriage. Now it's shortened to 'car.' I never thought I'd say this but wait 'till you see what this baby can do!"

Annie sat in the car and Peter got in behind the wheel, helped Annie close her seat belt, and started the engine.

"What that growlin' sound?"

"It's an engine with the power of many horses. Ready?"

"You do what you got to do to get us to Williamsburg."

Peter turned around and crept through the woods along the rutted track.

"This moves quick for a horseless carriage."

At the highway, Peter stopped and turned to Annie. "This will be faster than you're used to." He edged up to thirty miles an hour as the heater warmed them.

"Oh, my! This is fast! And the tar road is so smooth!" cried Annie.

"We will get there sooner if you can handle going faster."

"If you can, I can. I trust you Peter."

Peter edged up to fifty-five.

"My Lord! Someone comin' right down the road at us!" Annie heard the whoosh of air and the Doppler-effect eee-yuhh change of pitch as the oncoming car sped by. "We was almost killed!" she patted her chest.

"Don't worry. Everyone stays on his own side most of the time."

"Somethin' happened in this carriage, I feel it." She closed her eyes. "A few days back the road was wet, and you all was spinnin' 'round."

"That's true, Annie! On our way to Williamsburg, a car cut in front and we spun around. We thought we would die, but we did not crash."

"Let me be quiet for a moment, Peter. I need to sit wit' this."

Peter crossed the James River, and turned east. There was no great pall of smoke on the south shore of the James. Norfolk had been rebuilt over two centuries ago, its destruction not even a memory for most Virginians.

"That be how you slid through, Peter. When a hoop spinnin', ain't no tellin' where it gonna stop. When this carriage spun, your family could be hurt or die. So, you let go. Holdin' tight be a painful way to live and a painful way to die. But you stopped wit' nobody hurt. You was ready to fly away home but still here. That be a good way to live every day."

"You thought maybe I came because someone prayed for help. Was it 'Gustus?"

"'Gustus was happy to be your friend, but it wasn't him. Don't keep guessin'. I ain't tellin' nobody else's prayers. Hear them for yourself."

"That's fair." Peter turned on the radio and they heard Sunday morning gospel music.

Annie looked around. "Who be singin'? You got angels in your time?"

"That's a radio, Annie. It's a machine that picks up invisible waves from the air and makes them into the sounds they were in the first place."

Annie nodded her head. "Waves. Good word. Everyone sendin' out waves. In a crowded room, there be people you would rather stand close to than others. That come from what they thinkin', what they feelin', and how those comin' out as what you call waves."

"Can you feel those waves?"

"Everybody feel them, but most times people don't notice they do."

Very soon, from Annie's point of view, Peter pulled into a giant parking lot by the Colonial Williamsburg Visitor Center. Annie was amazed at the horseless carriages, their bright colors reflecting street lights. "This land used to be... oh, never mind! Everything changes." They walked over the Bridge to the Past, but Peter saw they were in a restored Williamsburg full of historic buildings that would open, in two hours, in the 21st century.

"This changed a lot." Annie looked around. "Where do slaves live?"

"In my time we don't have slaves and few people have servants in their homes or gardens anymore. Annie, we have a problem."

"What problem? You ain't got no slaves or servants?"

"No, Annie, ending slavery was a good thing. You and I have a problem. We are in my time even though we crossed that bridge. I don't know how to take us back."

"You the best slider I ever saw, but seems like you had to almost get killed first," Annie teased. "Come wit' me, I got an idea."

They walked to the pasture where they first met. "I never slid over like you done but I come here and sit quiet. Some days, I see people in strange clothing walk by. They talk like Williamsburg was a long time ago. Almost nobody sees me 'cept once in a while someone dressed like people in my time looks at me and keeps on goin'. Then half a year ago, a young white man in strange clothes walked over and asked me if I was preparin' food. That never happened befo' so I knew I should talk wit' him."

"Half a year ago for you. For me it was three days."

"Didn't I say you been slidin' all over? Now sit here, hold my hand, and close your eyes like you done wit' me. Imagine you and me is back where you want to be and where I belong." Peter sat on the grass, took her hand, closed his eyes, listened to the hum of a distant truck engine, and relaxed. The engine faded away. Peter was startled by the shrill cry of a jay nearby.

Annie squeezed his hand. "Here we be, right where you left off. I ain't gonna forget that car ride. I got to hurry off to do many things."

"When are we? I mean when is this? You know what I mean."

Annie scanned the sky. "It be dawn the day after you rode to Norfolk."

"We are back in November, 1775?"

Annie stood up. "That's a fact. Best you hurry because for you, it will be later when you wake up. There be many folk I got to warn not to run. Can you tell Evie that for now it be best for her to stay where she is?"

"Yes, I will." Peter gave her a hug. "Meeting you changed my life."

"I feel the same but if you hug me 'round here, we goin' to gaol."

Peter jogged to the Powell House. It was dark so he entered the yard quietly and climbed to the loft where Evie slept next to her sons. "Evie," he whispered. She did not stir. He reached into the dark and felt a small foot.

Dilli sat up with a start. "Mister Peter! You come to run away with us?"

Evie sat up. "What you say, Dilli?"

"Mister Peter be here to take us to freedom."

Peter climbed into the loft. James sat up. "I'se ready, too, Mama."

The impact of what Peter had witnessed during the night hit him again. "I just got back from near Norfolk."

"What happened?"

"War is coming to Norfolk and the town will burn to the ground. Dunmore will leave on a ship. Right now, there is nowhere to run."

"Did you see 'Gustus, Mister Peter?" asked Dilli. "Did he get free?"

Peter looked into Dilli's bright inquisitive eyes. "Yes, Dilli, we can all be very proud of him. He became a brave soldier. And so did Aaron."

Evie twitched at the shock of hearing the name. "You saw Aaron?"

"Yes, Evie. Aaron became a soldier, too. He led a charge and took his massa prisoner on the battlefield. An officer promoted him to sergeant."

"Aaron..." Evie put her hand on James' shoulder. "He tol' you?"

"Yes, Evie, he told me. Years ago, he was caught trying to get back to you. The men hurt him badly. He never got another chance to come back, but he never forgot you. He was happy to hear you and the boys are well. I need to tell you that life is very dangerous for Aaron and 'Gustus now. Only three hundred runaways were... uh will be taken on the ships when Governor Dunmore leaves. One of them is William the brick maker. It looks hard for the others. There is fighting and smallpox."

A moment of silence passed before Evie asked, "What should we do?"

You and the boys stay here—maybe for a long time. Pray for those who ran. They are on a hard road. Some find their way back to be slaves again."

"But Mister Peter, Annie and you tol' us we should be free."

"Annie is warning people this is not a good time to run. The hoop can fall in many ways. It landed in Norfolk in a way that shows us you should stay. You and the boys are safe here. Soon I will have to travel far and I don't know if I can come back. Boys, mind what your mama says." He took them all in a hug. "Keep your eyes open. The hoop rolls every day and another chance will come. You can be ready then."

"Mister Peter, you be family to us."

"Evie, you're a good family to be part of." Peter climbed down the ladder and walked home. Exhausted, he quietly entered without waking his family and slipped into bed. In seconds, he dropped into a deep sleep.

Day 4-3:   John and Susan Sleep In

John opened his eyes. "Good morning, Mrs. Sinclair."

"Sorry I woke you. I was sneaking in for a nap." She kissed his cheek.

"I've warmed it up for you. I looked in on Megan when I got back. I was worried about her, but she was there, fast asleep. Peter wasn't home yet."

She got undressed. "They're both asleep. He must have come back late."

"Good. How was your visit to the better-highfalutin-sorts?"

"They are good people, John, living with privilege and with difficulties at the same time. They have a house full of great kids."

"Good people own slaves? Who kidnapped my civil rights activist?"

"She still believes all women and men are created equal. She is learning the only way to move ahead is to start from where you are. Interesting you mention dreams. I had a vivid dream about you in a fight in a tavern."

"That's amazing!" He stretched, feeling the sting of the cut on his arm as he sat up. "There was a fight in a tavern last night. Don't worry—I'm fine. Uncle Sam trained me for that contingency, so no one was badly hurt. A guy with a knife and that puffed-up dance instructor we saw at the Palace were preying on buckskins from the hills. They won't do that anymore."

"Did the guy with the knife hurt you? Did you hurt them?"

"Nah, his knife wasn't loaded. They were not hurt seriously. You wish it were a dream, don't you? But there is a small cut on my arm."

"You've always been my hero, John." Susan gave him another kiss. "Let's not wake up the kids yet." She slipped naked into bed.

John and Susan made love for the first time since coming to Williamsburg. She felt a communion uncommon even in the exciting sex of their early days together. Something was shifting. An hour later, John woke and kissed Susan on the forehead. "Mmm," she murmured.

John got out of bed and headed to the outhouse in his robe. On the way back, he saw Peter and Megan still asleep. "It's warm out there—more like when we arrived."

"So it is hot in here. I thought it was just me."

"Both—hot in here and you're definitely hot. I'm a lucky man."

"Oh you! John, that was beautiful and tender. Such a connection!"

"Thank you, Mrs. Sinclair. They're both still sound asleep." He ran his fingertips lightly on the skin of her shoulder and along her clavicle. "There's no hurry."

Day 4-4:   Plain Truth and Common Sense

"Good morning, Megan."

Megan opened her eyes to see her father sitting on the side of her bed. "Good morning, Dad. Sorry I was so crabby."

"Megan. I apologize, too. You were right on the taxes. They were repealed long before the revolution broke out. I was stubborn."

"I was in a hurry to show you what I learned."

"I'm proud of you, Megan. How was your time with the Indians?"

"Thanks, Dad. The Sweat Lodge was awesome. I felt our ancestors sitting around a fire and the Earth deep under me—glowing rocks and magma."

"That's extraordinary, Megan. Mom thought we could start out together this morning. But if you'd rather be on your own..."

"No, I would really like to be with you guys this morning."

They ate in the garden. "Let's pack so we're ready to go," John proposed.

"Are you sure we can just walk out of here and find the car? I rode an hour on wagon trails and stayed in the past."

"I drove near Norfolk last night, Megan, mostly on asphalt highways. We'll cross the bridge to where I left the car this morning."

"This morning? Did you stay out all night?"

"Almost all night, Mom. I camped with a platoon of freed slaves."

"Pete, you don't do that every weekend! Can I put it into my paper?"

"Sure, Meg, but it's not a happy story."

They packed up and Susan suggested, "Let's start at Market Square."

"I'll find you there after I take the bags to the car," Peter offered. He left carrying the bags as the others walked toward the market.

"Sir," John asked a passerby walking by, "can you tell me the date?"

"Why, yes. 'Tis May 15, 1776."

"The Declaration of Independence is seven weeks away," John calculated. "Last year, few wanted independence. I wonder what did it."

"I'll meet you guys at Market Square in a few minutes." Megan hurried ahead and disappeared down a walk to the blacksmiths.

Mark noticed her come in. "Megan! It has been months! I was worried."

"I'm so sorry, Mark. My family left suddenly and we just got back this morning. I wanted to thank you for taking me to the Spirit Lodge. I've been concerned about you too, Mark. Is everything all right?"

222

"I cannot talk now. We are rushing to finish an order Mister Anderson got from the Virginia Militia. We shan't stop for lunch today, but I might be able to step out in the afternoon. Can you come by again later?"

"I'll come back. We must leave today but not without saying goodbye."

"You are going again? It was hard when you vanished. We must talk."

"I'll be back before I vanish," Megan promised.

By the market, a man holding a pamphlet in each hand paced on a sturdy table. Pamphlets were stacked precariously and a helper strove to keep the speaker from kicking them over. "We hear more talk of independence than people dared utter before. This pamphlet is a reason for that. In January 1776, my employer, Robert Bell in Philadelphia, published *Common Sense* by Thomas Paine, an Englishman recently arrived in the colonies. Paine says of the power of kings:

'How came the king by power which the people are afraid to trust, and always obliged to check? Such power could not be the gift of a wise people, neither can power which needs checking, be from God.'

"Paine's views would have been treasonous a year ago:

'To the evil of monarchy we have added that of hereditary succession... an insult and imposition on posterity. For all men being originally equals, no one by birth could have a right to set up his own family in perpetual preference to all others, and though himself might deserve some degree of honors... descendants might be unworthy to inherit them. One of the strongest natural proofs of the folly of hereditary right in kings is that nature disapproves it, otherwise she would not so frequently turn it into ridicule by giving mankind an ass for a lion.'

"This pamphlet is shaking the ground from Florida to Nova Scotia."

Peter spotted his father, and pressed through to join his family. He went to look for Evie first but Rosie told him she was shopping.

"Two months later, in March, my employer published a response to *Common Sense — Plain Truth*, by Candidus, a successful Maryland planter loyal to the crown:

'If indignant at the doctrine in the pamphlet, entitled 'Common Sense' I have expressed myself with ardor; I entreat the reader to impute my indignation, to honest zeal against the author's insidious tenets... I love my country.'

"Patriots and Loyalists both love their country. Candidus also says:

'Demagogues, to seduce the people into their criminal designs, ever hold up democracy to them... examine the republics of Greece and Rome... No government is so subject to civil wars, as that of the democratical form...'

"This pamphlet by Candidus can be purchased here."

"Are you here to gather shillings or take a stand?" shouted an onlooker.

"Well, let me read an excerpt I personally like from Tom Paine:

'Small islands not capable of protecting themselves, are proper objects for kingdoms to take under their care; but there is something absurd, in supposing a continent to be perpetually governed by an island...'

"Huzzah!" shouted several men.

"As I travel south, another man goes north. He heard John Adams call *Common Sense* a poor, ignorant, malicious, short-sighted, crapulous mass.'"

"Why? We love Tom Paine's words!"

"Paine rightly challenges the misapplied power of the Crown but envisions a society in which each follows his own fancy without any government. Our leaders benefit from Paine's arguments for independence and I expect they shall declare it so that France, Spain, and the Netherlands can support them without all-out war against Britain. As Paine says:

'... instead of gazing at each other with suspicious or doubtful curiosity, let each of us, hold out to his neighbor the hearty hand of friendship... of a good citizen,... and a virtuous supporter of the RIGHTS of MANKIND and of the FREE AND INDEPENDENT STATES OF AMERICA.'"

"Huzzah!"

"Many are still loyal to the Crown. Were we not all loyal a year ago? Buy pamphlets to reason with your neighbors rather than tar and feather them."

A few men moved forward coins in hand.

"We should get fifty of each, signed by Founding Fathers, and sell them to museums when we get home," Peter advised. "We could set up the Sinclair Institute for American Studies and have money for nice houses."

"That's not why we came here, Pete," Megan objected. "If this weekend were a movie, the script writer would not let us get rich carrying anything home."

"I was kidding. Why do you think we came here, Dad?"

"I agree we should not interfere. I hope I did not mess up history when I got into the fight to save a guy from getting hurt at the tavern."

"Maybe that's what happened all along, Dad, and no one in our time knows what you did. Can I interview you about it?"

"Yes, but you just gave me an idea, Megan. Some mysteries happened in the Revolution. We might be able to help. I'll tell you more at lunch."

Susan had an idea. "Let's have lunch at the Brick House Tavern. It does not operate in our time and this will be our chance to try eating there."

Day 4-5: Reunion in the St. George Tucker House Garden

John settled into an armchair in the St. George Tucker House with a mug of coffee. He was troubled. How did the colonies prevail against the strongest military power on Earth? Could independence have come without war as it did in Canada, Australia and other British colonies? He was surprised by Frances standing near. "Hello, Frances. Did I see you in the tavern when I fought with Roger?"

"Did you see me? That depends. You have a vivid imagination. When we focus our imagination, we can experience directly through the mind, skipping the physical senses. Imagination is not just for fantasy."

"You were there, but then you were gone..."

"John, there is someone who cannot come into the house, shall I say, at this time. Please come out to meet him." She turned away.

John put back the book and through a back window, saw Frances was already outside. He followed her along a path between tall hedges to a clearing not visible from the street. Bruce Wallace waited on a bench and stood to clasp John's hand. "Damn good to see you, Johnny! Frances told me she could find someone to help. I dinna know it would be you."

"How can you be acquainted when you are...?" Frances stammered.

"John and I are old soldiers," Bruce explained. "We met properly over a glass of ale. John, Fannie Bland Randolph manages two large plantations while raising three children. St. George Tucker seems to have an eye for her."

Frances held a finger to her lips. John accepted her unspoken request not to mention the future time in which they met. "Frances, what's happening here is unknown to most people. Servants are sent to clear Indian land and people are entering a war without knowing why. I fought in wars people did not support. I did not think about it before I flew — uh sailed over and did what I believed was my duty. When you called people clever as fence posts you gave too much credit."

"Once we notice what is going on, we get smarter, John. You and Bruce did your duty, learned much, and built character while you served."

"Aye, but we lost friends, were wounded, and killed men who were good lads aside from the fact that someone ordered them to shoot at us."

"Be thankful peace always comes, Bruce. Divinity underlies all."

"John, I heard you met Dagger a few months ago. Two militiamen told me your style of fighting was astonishing."

"I trained in fighting from China and the islands you call 'the Japans.'"

"Methinks there is more to your story than what you tell."

"Some stories are best not told in their entirety." John saw Frances smile.

"John, I dinna ken how ye did that at the tavern nor have I heard of your wars, but I believe we share distaste for what we once did so well."

"Concern about the loss of life in war brought me here today, Bruce."

"People have gone mad. A quarrel is now reason enough to kill a man. A friend of mine was hanged in Maryland for refusing to take the test."

"Take the test?"

"They force men to swear an oath to support Congress against Britain. My friend stood with his neighbors against the Stamp Act, but chose to be loyal to the Crown that recently had the loyalty of those who hanged him. Where Loyalists are stronger, they attack Patriots, burning farms. Mayhem is spreading. There are raids on the Loyalist Floridas and 'tis rumored Congress invited Spain to take the Floridas back, to deprive the King of bases to the South. This after all we did to win those colonies from Spain!

"A Virginia planter named Charles Lynch runs a mock trial of loyalists. They are whipped and their property seized but none has been hanged yet. People call his mockery of justice 'getting lynched.' I do not wish to shoot a hole in a man's head because of what he might be thinking inside it. If I kill him, how could he be persuaded to change his mind?"

"What will you do, Bruce?"

"John, arguments against the Intolerable Acts are sound but choices are muddled. In the Carolinas, loyal settlers fight revolutionary landowners who oppressed them for years. People in Quebec sided with their old enemies the Redcoats. Congress sent an army there under General Montgomery but he was killed. His second in command, Benedict Arnold, was wounded taking Quebec. He asked for support but Congress failed to send it and Arnold seethed when the campaign was abandoned. Recently he was passed over for a promotion. He is proud and now bitter. What will he do next?

"No one from the Caribbean joined the Congress, except Henry Tucker who went to trade gun powder. His son St. George loaded powder onto boats on a cloudy night. They profit from smuggling." Frances shuffled noticeably.

"More British fell taking Breed's Hill and Bunker Hill than in any battle since then. Even so, Washington complains about the discipline of the men who dealt that blow before he took command. Congress has trouble raising an army. I canna' blame men for not making war on their countrymen. Congress voted letters of marque for privateers, authorizing piracy against British ships. The Royal Navy will send our ships to the bottom.

"I thought I was done with war; done with time slowing amidst the havoc, done with my heart racing, except in the company of a willing lass, pardon me, Fanny. I am too old to rush up a hill as musket balls whistle past my ear. Friends have joined both sides. We are fools to kill each other."

"Time slowing down—I remember that feeling." John folded his arms. "Maybe the pain of bad decisions will teach us to stop making such foolish choices."

"How much pain does it take?" Bruce asked. "New fools aplenty are born every morning. They get a spank to start them breathing, but it seldom cures the foolishness. The idea of democracy that New England Sons of Freedom shout about is combining with the Virginia gentry's wish to form a nation. Since Thomas Paine made the notion of independence popular, that combination makes sense to me. We canna' win this without help of other countries, but none will take the daring leap to support us unless Congress declares us independent. It should come to fruition soon.

"There was a vote for leader of the 1st Virginia Regiment. Patrick Henry, with little military experience, narrowly defeated Hugh Mercer. They chose a maker of fiery speeches over an officer and doctor forged in fires of battle! Someone called Mercer a 'North Briton' because he is a Scot. Fortunately, Mercer was later given command of the 3rd Virginia Regiment. The King also has trouble fielding an army so he hired regiments of soldiers conscripted by his German cousins. Those Hessians are a quarter of the invading troops. The Continentals worry about a German colonel named Johann Rall who takes no prisoners. King George also asked Catherine the Great of Russia for twenty thousand troops, but she turned him down, God bless her!"

"What drives this, Bruce? How big is the land issue?"

"I shall show you something important. My wife's sister is the widow of a soldier maimed in the French and Indian War who sold his veteran's land grant to one William Crawford. She cooks in a house near Mount Vernon. One evening, a guest left his coat on the chair when he went to bed. She searched the pockets to learn the owner so she could return it. In a leather sheath, she found a letter from George Washington to William Crawford. Her husband died believing the grant to be of no value since no one could settle west of the Proclamation Line. She knows how to read so she wrote out a copy of the letter and sent it to me. It is dated September 21, 1767. Would you like to read what she copied, John?"

227

"I would, Bruce. I heard of William Crawford from a member of his family right there in the St. George Tucker house." John began to read:

"I can never look upon the Proclamation in any other light (this I say between ourselves) than as a temporary expedient to quiet the minds of the Indians. It must fall, of course, in a few years, when those Indians consent to our occupying those lands… If you will be at the trouble of seeking out the lands, I will take upon me the part of securing them … and will be at all the cost and charges surveying and patenting the same. My plan is to secure a good deal of land."

"It goes on...

'*… this can be carried on by silent management… and carried out under the guise of hunting game, which you may do at the same time you are in pursuit of land. When this is fully discovered advise me of it, and if there appears a possibility of succeeding, I will have the land surveyed to keep others off and leave the rest to time and my own assiduity.*

"This deal to usurp land from the Indians might be secret forever, Bruce. Investors in land are willing to have war in pursuit of personal interests."

"There are many investors, John, on both sides of the ocean. What they are doing is against the law but that doesn'a bother them a whit."

"You two can think of something," Frances offered. "You both know war and saw peace in the end. Can you imagine bringing peace into this?" John heard the word 'imagine' and knew it was not an accident.

"It sounds like a riddle." Bruce scratched his beard. "If I can help, I will."

"Bruce," said Frances, "you know many leaders in Virginia. You knew Governor Dunmore before he ran off, and served him well."

"Aye, Fannie."

"John, you have knowledge that could be useful to save lives."

John was studying Frances and thinking fast. "Bruce, can you meet me here later? There are others I want to bring into this conversation. I think... no, I know there are things we could do together to save many lives."

"I must work in the afternoon, John, but I can be here at four." Bruce took his leave and left between the hedgerows.

"Frances, will you be able to join us?"

"I have waited for this day a very long time. I shall be here. I know you have questions about me, John, but if I tell you now, it could be disturbing. I promise I will tell you after the work has begun."

"Am I crazy, Frances? Am I imagining you?"

"'Tis not what you think. You will find a way, just as you once did to save your men in battle." Frances curtsied and left around a hedge.

228

Day 4-6: Megan and Maggie Visit the Gaol

Megan left her parents and ran most of the way to the blacksmith shop.

"This is a rehearsal, Mark. I'm practicing not vanishing."

"I won't be free until four o'clock, Megan. Standing Elk just came by to give me the news that Bartholomew is being held in the gaol."

"Oh, no! Did he do something wrong?"

"A planter who tried to cheat him spread rumors that Bart is a Loyalist. When the county militia accosted him in the market, Bart told them he was true to Virginia. When he refused to take the test, they threw him into gaol. Maggie is in town today trying to get him out. Can you help her?"

"I'll go right over and see if I can find her. I'll be back at four."

Megan ran up to Maggie outside the gaol holding a basket of food, a crock of water, and a blanket for Bartholomew. "Oh, Maggie, I'm glad I found you," she panted. "We have to get Bartholomew out."

"Megan, whom I have not seen in months, arrives right on time. How do you propose getting him out when his bullheadedness put him in?"

"Why wouldn't Bartholomew take the test, Maggie?"

"Oh you heard. He refused because he is a stubborn old fool. He worked hard to finish his indenture and be free. He says he will not be cowed by young firebrands who do not think through what they are on about. He does not want to be forced to fight and hopes that facing resistance and lack of fighters, Congress and the Crown will have to negotiate. He has friends on both sides but most just seek to live in peace."

"Why do some choose the Loyalist side?"

"Megan, some feel Britain is their home country. Others think Britain will win and want to be on the winning side. Families given royal land grants think their claims safer if we stay loyal to Britain. Some wealthy Loyalists fear Levelers like us may end their privileges and take their property. There are about twenty-five loyal colonies and thirteen in rebellion."

"What about the Indians, Maggie? I'm angry that leaders want to take their land."

"'Tis unfair to the Indians. In addition, patriots push for freedom but have no intent to end the abomination of slavery. The British are freeing slaves but help few and leave the rest destitute without a way to escape. 'Tis not easy to see righteousness on either side."

The gaoler's wife arrived to let Maggie in. "My niece is coming in too," Maggie announced as she entered with Megan following. They found

229

Bartholomew seated on the floor of a dark cell shared with three other prisoners. No one was considered dangerous, so no one was chained.

"Hello, Maggie. Oh, 'tis the long-lost Megan. How are you, Ladies?"

"Bartie, I brought you food, water from your well, a change of clothes, and a blanket. It smells in here. I should have carried a wash tub as well."

"Thank you, Maggie. What brings you to my castle, Megan?"

"We're going to get you out of here today, Bart."

"Will you break the wall so I die running like a fox before the hounds?"

"You can walk out of here as soon as you choose, Bart. If Congress breaks with Britain, and they probably will, you and Maggie will help people renew their land and raise crops. If the Redcoats march in, and they probably will, you and Maggie will still help people renew their land and raise crops. This war is hurting people while you sit in this dark, stinky place. Maggie struggles without complaining. You are not helping at all except by creating manure for compost with these other gentlemen."

"Did you put her up to this, Maggie?"

"I did not have any idea Megan would come or speak so strongly. Megan, hush. Do you not see that Bartie enjoys being caged in here?"

"Bart, take the test," persisted Megan. "You're loyal to Virginia, so it's not a lie. We will leave this basket for your friends here. You are old enough so no one will drag you off to war. You feed and encourage people. They need what you offer."

Bart needed only a few seconds to think. "You are right. Maggie, please tell the gaoler, that I am ready to end my protest and take the test."

"Well, that was not hard." Maggie winked at Megan.

Another prisoner spoke up, "Tell the gaoler, I will take the test too."

"You stole a pig. You ain't no Loyalist!" chided a third man.

"I shall steal a Loyalist pig to repay the Patriot I stole from."

Laughter broke out in the cell, rare levity in that dank, gloomy world.

Maggie and Megan went to the Capitol to register Bartholomew's change of heart. The Secretary knew Bartholomew; he had hired him to haul away ashes. "That stubborn old oak tree is in gaol for standing up to young poplars?" asked the Secretary. "Let's give him the test right now before Lynch gets a coat of tar on him. Bartie should stop lazing in a cell and get back to work like the rest of us."

Bartholomew swore his loyalty to Congress in the courtyard. After washing and putting on the clothes Maggie brought, he was out of gaol in time for lunch.

Day 4-7:   Rowdy Lunch at the Brick House Tavern

Peter almost ran into Evie as she stepped out of a shop behind Missus Powell. She was surprised but shook her head. She could not speak with her mistress three steps ahead. He gestured in the direction of the Powell House. He would drop by later. She understood and hurried off.

Entering the noisy Brick House Tavern, Peter spotted his family on benches at a long table and squeezed in beside his mother. The pot on the table was coated with carbon and half full of chunks of venison, onions, and potatoes cooked in broth with bacon fat and salt. A basket of hand-torn bread sat next to the pot. "Welcome to the land of 'Be happy with what you get'," Megan said as Susan ladled stew.

John leaned forward so they could hear. "I think we're here to help."

"Dad, you were the first to say we should not change history."

"That's true, Megan, but your research has given me ideas. Amidst the hubbub here, I can tell you without being overheard. The Declaration of Independence that hardly anyone reads lists 'a long train of abuses and usurpations' and 'establishment of an absolute Tyranny over these States'. Taxes are one example, but Megan pointed out, those were repealed."

John paused until an outburst at the next table quieted down. "The Declaration says the King dissolved legislatures to deprive people of local leadership, limited immigration, and blocked appropriations of new lands. He kept standing armies here, making the military superior to civil authority. He blocked trade, imposed taxes, and transported citizens to England for trial far from their peers. It says the King abolished English law in a neighboring colony but neglects to name Catholic Quebec. He established an appointed rather than an elected government there, and enlarged its boundaries to enclose the English colonies on the west. The drafters of the Declaration feared Quebec was a test for absolute rule in all colonies."

"Wow, Dad! You did tons of research." Megan was impressed.

"I had to memorize the Declaration in high school. Once fighting started, the King 'plundered our seas, ravaged our coasts, burnt our towns, and destroyed the lives of our people.' He sent armies of foreign mercenaries, took citizens captive on the high seas to bear arms against their country, encouraged Loyalists to start insurrections, and invited Indian attacks.

"There are things it doesn't say," added Peter. "Jefferson had a clause about slavery in the draft of the Declaration. I wrote it down: '*He has waged cruel war against human nature itself, violating its most sacred rights of life & liberty in the persons of a distant people who never offended him,*

231

captivating & carrying them into slavery in another hemisphere, or to incur miserable death in their transportation thither.' It was deleted from the final draft at the insistence of slave owners."

"That's true. We know now the colonies survived against the strongest military power on Earth combined with Loyalist militias almost as big as Patriot forces. How did they do that? Next question—why were British casualties never again as high as at Boston at the beginning of the war? Why do official records of the Defense Department show American battle deaths in the Revolution to be relatively low?"

Megan jumped in. "How did the local Indians survive when the Revolutionary War was the biggest war on the Indians ever?"

"Good question, Megan. Here's another," John continued. "Many German troops were shipped here. One leader, Colonel Johann Rall, took no prisoners. He was killed at Trenton. Washington authorized land and freedom to German prisoners who changed sides. How did he think of that? Conditions for prisoners on both sides were grim. Ten thousand Americans died on British prison ships anchored off Brooklyn. Even knowing that, the Americans placed many Redcoat prisoners to work on farms, and many stayed after the war, married, and never returned to England. Who planted that idea?

"And Peter, our first day here we learned Patrick Ferguson invented a breech-loading rifle with superior range, accuracy, and speed. At Brandywine, Ferguson was wounded and most of the rifles disappeared. Where they went is still a mystery. We do not know how Washington kept out of the way of stronger British forces, choosing to fight when surprise gave him an edge. Did he have intelligence of British movements?

"My friend Bruce Wallace and I meet at four o'clock behind the St. George Tucker House. Do you guys have friends who could join us?"

"My friend Standing Elk prayed for a warrior on the path of peace. I think you are the man he is looking for. May I bring him to the meeting?"

"Perfect, Megan. You each can suggest folks you trust. Use your head, heart, and gut on this. It may be an unlikely cast of characters. Bring people you would trust with your lives. The lives of some of our friends here will depend on their being able to trust each other. We have only one shot at this—we leave today so we need to get the people together at four in the garden."

Day 4-8:   A Glimpse of the Freedom Sky

Peter stopped outside the Brick House Tavern. "Dad, I'm proud of you."

John gave Peter a hug. "I'm proud of you too, son. Be safe."

Peter jogged straight to the Powell House. A wagon sat in the lane and a white draft horse harnessed but without a bit, grazed on long grass along the fence. Inside the gate, Annie sat on the bench talking with Evie and she beckoned to him to enter. Neither woman looked surprised to see him.

"Annie told me you was back. We got to decide so I'se glad you here."

"What do you have to decide, Annie?"

"We heard a Loyalist ship is off Jamestown and a boat come ashore this mornin'. We talkin' 'bout gettin' on a ship up to Long Island. From there, a ship might go to England where there ain't no slaves."

Peter looked at Evie. "What do you think? Is it time to go?"

"The Powells ain't home so I could run, but I don't see where to go."

"What do you think, Annie?"

"A ship been in my mind but it was in the distance so I figured it was in the future. When I heard 'bout a ship I came to think on it wit' Evie. The distance could mean it be a small chance, but I don't feel danger either."

"How long does it take to get to the river by Jamestown in a cart?"

"It be four miles so about forty-five minutes."

"Annie, who owns the cart in the lane? Maybe he'd rent it to me for a couple of hours and I could take Evie and the boys to Jamestown. If the ship is sailing to New York or New Jersey, I could pay their passage."

"How 'bout me and the boys go home with you, Mister Peter?"

"In Northern Virginia there are many slaves—not a good place for you."

"The owner of that cart is ready to take Evie to the ship. The owner ain't visitin' the Powells. She sittin' on the bench visitin' Evie."

"You have a horse and cart now?"

"It make it easier to move around. Since we saw each other I made some purchases to help get the work done and help more people."

"If you lend me the cart, I could take Evie to Jamestown to check it out. I can write something that gives a reason to be going with three slaves."

"How 'bout a bill of sale?" asked Annie.

"I can't make an official bill of sale, Annie. My father is meeting people at four o'clock in the garden of the Tucker House. I was looking for you to invite you. My dad wants a group of people to work together. He fought in wars, lost friends, and he lives with the knowledge he killed people. He wants people to help during the war so fewer people are hurt."

"You found me right where I be, again. I want be at that meetin' wit' your father. Now 'bout that bill of sale; how do this one look?" Annie pulled a sheet from her bag and handed it to Peter.

It had "Bill of Sale" printed at the top, an official-looking border, and names, dates, and prices neatly written in on printed lines. It showed Evie, James, and Dilli were purchased by Annie a month before. Peter was shocked, "Did you buy Evie and the boys? What are they still doing here?"

"I never bought them. I got a paper an hour ago that says I did. I can say I'se sending Evie and the boys to help my half sister in Connecticut. She be white. We had the same white daddy and I had a African mama."

"You got a white sister, Annie?" asked an incredulous Evie.

"I ain't got no sister at all. What I got is a story to get you on the ship."

"I have another story," Peter proposed. "Annie, you're white and I'm your husband. I'll take the slaves you bought to put on a ship to work at your sister's house. You can easily pass for white if you're not sitting in the wagon next to me."

"But Annie, you ain't white and you ain't married to Peter."

"No I ain't but if I ain't on the wagon, no one sees what color I be. Peter look white. That helps his story. Now Evie, is you going or ain't you?"

"I'se gonna get the boys and we goin'." Evie hurried to the kitchen.

Annie walked to the wagon and patted the horse. "On a short trip he can go a bit faster, but don't rush him on the way home."

"Will this work, Annie? I have money to pay the boat captain."

"I'se gonna tell you if it work or not when you get back. Don't dawdle down there. This meetin' at the Tucker House be important."

"What did you mean when you told Evie I look white?"

"What color you think you look?"

"White."

"That be what I meant."

The boys scurried back carrying their belongings in sacks. They climbed into the wagon as Peter helped Evie onto the front bench. She looked back and instructed the boys. "Lie down in the back and don't make noise."

Peter pulled on the left rein and turned the horse back to Waller Street. Avoiding crowded streets, he found his way west to the Jamestown Road. Dilli lay on his back looking up. "Mama! James! Mister Peter! Look up at those clouds and that big blue sky! Each tree look different as we go by.
234

Being free feels good, don't it, Mister Peter? I'se gonna draw that beautiful freedom sky through the trees."

"It is beautiful, Dilli. I'd like you to show me that drawing someday. You boys enjoy the ride. If anyone stops us, follow what I say to them."

Dilli found a stick in the wagon. Tossing it into the air, he watched it turn end over end. He stood and caught it as fell. "Free!" he shouted.

"Hush, Dilli." Evie was stern. "Sit down and be quiet so you don't get us kilt."

They rode past the College of William and Mary, passed farms with livestock grazing behind zigzag fences, and beside woods. They passed The Walking Stick Tavern at a crossroads. Peter was tempted to look for the blade his father had embedded in the beam but it was already late to find the Loyalist ship, so he kept moving. He went over in his mind what to say in the unlikely event that someone stopped them. As they rounded a curve, ten militiamen approached from the opposite direction. "Halt!" ordered the leader. Peter recognized Hugh Mercer from the encounter with his carriage by the house. He had not rehearsed this possibility.

"Where are you going and why?" demanded Mercer.

"Mister Mercer! Good day, Sir. I appreciated your kindness in Williamsburg a few months back when I stepped in front of your horses."

"He is Colonel Mercer, not Mister," declared a lieutenant. "He commands the 3rd Virginia Regiment in the North under General Washington."

"Sorry, Colonel Mercer. It is an honor to meet you again, sir."

"I remember you. Ye wore peculiar attire and your thoughts seemed miles away. What do ye have in the wagon?"

"I'm on my way to Jamestown, Colonel. Sit up and say hello to Colonel Mercer, boys." Dilli and James sat up in the wagon and waved.

"Evie, these are good men, Patriots. Say hello to them."

"Hello, Sirs," Evie said weakly.

"We were just in Jamestown," Mercer disclosed. "A Loyalist ship put a boat ashore, and we rode down to see what they were up to. The ship left after briefly sitting at anchor. Our search of the area turned up nothing amiss. They may have spirited Loyalists away or they may have put an agent ashore."

"Thanks for the warning, Colonel. Bruce Wallace told my father how you helped when he was wounded and how you got away on ships from the Hebrides."

"Bruce Wallace? Do you know where he is?"

"He is still working at the wheelwright shop. Have you not run into him?"

"Not for some months. I could use his help in the Regiment up north."

"Is it dangerous for us to go on to Jamestown today?"

"We don't know," replied Mercer, "perhaps they put men ashore."

"Colonel Mercer, my business in Jamestown can wait for another day. I will turn around and go back to Williamsburg."

"That might be prudent, lad. Forgive me, but I don't recall your name."

"Peter Sinclair, Colonel."

"Peter Sinclair, if you see Sergeant Wallace before I find him, please let him know I am staying at the home of John Galt, the apothecary, for three more days. I would like to see Wallace before I return north."

"I will do that, Colonel Mercer."

Hugh Mercer signaled the men and they rode off.

Peter turned the wagon around. "Evie, you and the boys did very well."

"We ain't goin' to be free today, Mister Peter?" asked Dilli.

"You are free right now, boys. We tried it to see how you like it. Those men told us the ship left already, so this is as far as we go today. You can do this again someday. Meanwhile, don't speak of this to anyone. Running has to be a secret. Do you understand, boys?"

"Yes, Mister Peter. Mama showed us how a hoop roll and how it fall. It gonna roll again and I know we gonna find a road to freedom." Dilly was exuberant.

"I got scared when he axed where you goin'. Oh! Riders be comin' back!"

"Don't look afraid, Evie. Just sit here and be calm," Peter instructed.

Peter watched two men approach and saw they were Indians. He waved a greeting, which they returned.

Peter pulled up on the reins. "Good afternoon."

"I am Standing Elk and this is my nephew, Thomas. You look familiar."

"I'm Peter Sinclair. I heard your name from my sister."

"Your sister is Megan Sinclair. You look alike."

"This is Evie and her sons James and Dilli."

"Is you real Indians?" asked Dilli.

Standing Elk smiled. "Yes, young man, we are real Indians."

"I heard you know how to live free in the forest," said Dilli.

"We know how, but our life is different than that of our grandfathers."

"You is still free?"

"Yes, we have difficulties but we are free. Free is a good way to live."

"We gonna be free someday!" James spoke up, surprising his mother.

"Hush, James!"

"Your sons are good boys." Standing Elk nudged his horse.

"Good to meet you," Peter called out. "I'll tell Megan we met."

"I gets so 'fraid when men rides up to us. We could get catched."

"Evie, Hugh Mercer helped us and Standing Elk told Dilli and James they are good boys. It doesn't help to give in to fear."

"I gonna try, Mister Peter. Least we gonna get home before the Powells. I feel good we tried. It be scary but it ain't so scary like I feared."

"You and the boys have been free for almost an hour, Evie."

"I suppose we is."

Peter looked far ahead to a rider approaching at full gallop and he steered the cart along the edge of the road. As the horse thundered by, he recognized Megan leaning forward in the saddle. "Hey!" he shouted.

"Hi, Pete!" Megan called out as she hurtled past.

"Wow! That was my sister."

"She look like a fearless woman." Evie was amazed.

"I think of her as a little sister but seeing her ride, I guess she *is* fearless."

"Where she ridin' so fast?"

"It might be for a meeting later." Peter signaled the horse to speed up.

As they pulled into the lane, Annie greeted them. Robert and Claudius stood near her. Evie shooed the boys to the kitchen, said a quick goodbye to Peter and Annie, and hurried inside to finish the laundry.

Peter watched her go, wondering if he would ever see her again. "Annie, the ship left already. We ran into Colonel Mercer and the militia. Imagine if they had caught us trying to get Evie and the boys onto that ship!"

"I don't want to imagine it, Peter. Why use my mind to help that happen? I gonna imagine Evie and the boys bein' free someday. How did you stay out of trouble wit' the militia?"

"I hid nothing and I talked about something else."

"That be why I don't imagin' Evie bein' catched. Keep your mind on what you want to happen. Watch for problems but imagine solvin' them not fearin' them. We find a path through the tangle or live to try again like you helped Evie do."

"How did I help? They did not get far."

"Evie took a bold step for the first time in her life. Until now, if a chariot from heaven came by to carry her all the way to England, she be too scared to climb in. When she thinks on today and prays on it, courage gonna grow inside her like them boys did. Someday that idea gonna be born."

"Someday may be a long time."

"They safe where they is. Around the time them boys might be sold off, she may have a chance to move again. I pray she gonna be ready. Now, Peter, let me introduce you to some other folks."

They walked to the shade tree where Robert and Claudius waited. "How are you doing? I'm Peter." He remembered them from the Hush Harbor.

"We'se doin' good, Mister Peter," replied Robert. Last January, before tobacco plantin', Annie axed if we was willin' to take two whippin's to be free. We figured we could never be free. She tol' us, 'Time's a wastin' and there be much to do. What if I buy you from yo massa and you work wit' me?'

"We could scarcely believe it," Claudius told Peter. "We would take ten whippin's to work for her. She warned us, 'Workin' for me could be the most dangerous, hardest work you done, but you could do good for people.' Then she axed again if we was willin' to take two whippin's."

"We told her yes, we was willin', but why two whippin's? She 'splained she had money enough to buy one field hand but Annie wanted to buy us both. So we had to stop bein' good field hands and be failin' field hands so we be sold cheap. Failin' field hands gonna get a whippin'."

"We told Annie yes so when hoein' time came, Claudius and me pretended we was old and lame, not fast and strong like before. Poor Mister Jack! He shouted and shoved us, but for days, he did not whip us. He did not want to report to Massa that he could not get us to work 'cause that look bad for him, too. Finally, he whipped us but he gettin' older, too. I think he did not like to hurt us, so he ain't kept it up long."

"That be true. Robert and me prayed out loud and begged and the whippin' stopped. The next day we worked faster for two hours like we was scared of gettin' whipped again and then Robert pretended to be gettin' cramps in his legs. I fell over twice. Mister Jack reported us to Massa Carter, but another week went by before he gave us the next whippin'. I heard him say, 'They cain't help gettin' old.'"

Robert continued, "We got word to Annie that we been whipped twice, and she come by the quarter to buy field hands for workin' in her garden.

238

Massa was happy to be rid of us. In less than an hour Massa had a handful of ready money he needed so bad, and we was in the wagon wit' Annie holding a real bill of sale for the both of us."

Annie was obviously enjoying the story the way Robert and Claudius told it. "It be all right to tell Mister Peter what I got you workin' at boys."

"Annie taught me how to make a poultice for Claudius's whipped back, and she taught him to do the same for me. She been teachin' us healin'."

"Tell him all of it," Annie encouraged them. "He be our friend."

"After she bought us, Annie teached Claudius how to remember the long stories of a griot. She finished teachin' me letters so I could read the Bible. Annie and Sal showed me words I never knowed. Claudius and me got good at what we did then she told us the rest of her idea.

"She rents me out to the print shop. I set type for the *Virginia Gazette*. I sleep in a shed next to the print shop, and by livin' in town, I get to know slaves and servants here. The rent Annie get for me workin' helps all three of us and some other folk to get along," Robert explained proudly.

"Mister Peter, wit' Robert workin' at the print shop, Annie took me wit' her to tell stories at Hush Harbors and to listen to folk the way she do wit' us. I be learnin' to comfort and help folk when I can. I take messages across the county and I can do a Hush Harbor by myself now, so it be like Annie workin' two places at once. I take the wagon and go slow in daylight so I don't look like a runaway."

"Claudius and me listen to news we hear from print shop customers, slaves, and runaways at Hush Harbors. We talk over wit' Annie what we hear. Sometimes we help a person get to New Jersey or out to the Indians. We already helped folk."

"Have you helped people by printing false documents, Robert?"

"You real smart, Mister Peter!" Robert laughed. "I won't say where those manumissions and bills of sale be comin' from but I can say I'se gettin' pretty good at settin' type 'specially working alone at night as a favor for the printer when we is busy. He gives me a coin to do that while he sleep."

"In case I get stopped, Robert made me a paper to show what I is supposed to be doin' like you done for 'Gustus when he ran to Norfolk."

"Claudius, you men are amazing! Please be careful."

"We is, Mister Peter. Jesus helps us and we help other folks."

"I'm sure you can help at this meeting. Let's go together."

"Let's ride in my wagon."

Claudius and Robert rode in the back and Peter sat next to Annie up on the bench. "Where did you get the idea to buy them, Annie?"

"I was sad when 'Gustus died. I wanted to teach healin' to someone else. William was gone and Sal be busy at the hospital. These two is rooted in spirit and was learnin' from what life was givin' 'stead of givin' up. That be why I picked them."

Annie lowered her voice so only Peter could hear. "You heard them say they was sure they could never be free. They was born slaves and did not know how to imagine bein' free. People need help and those two need to get on with helpin' so I gave them the first step to be slaves for me. Las' month I tol' them I put their manumission into my will so they gonna get used to the idea of bein' free someday. I will set them free soon as they ready. I can sell them to they selves so they be part of gettin' free. I gonna use the money to buy more folks into freedom."

"I see the path you are inviting them to follow, Annie. It should work."

"I hope they will pass somethin' on to them who come after. I know Sal can, but he ain't stayin' here forever. He got business in another place."

"Sal's story and the girl Sally, who lives in a good home, stayed with me since the Hush Harbor that night."

"God touches Sal and he touches whoever can receive it from him. Haw! Haw, Promise!"

"Pardon me?"

Annie laughed. "I'se tellin' Promise, my horse, to go left to the St. George Tucker House."

Day 4-9:   Susan's Helpers from the Hospital

Susan pulled the bell cord at the Public Hospital. The bolt slid and the door opened to reveal Jane Harding in a middle-sorts dress. No longer wan, she looked happy. "Susan! I have not seen thee for months!"

"I'm glad to find you, Jane. Is there a place we can talk a minute?"

"I have a nook by the kitchen. Come let us chat over tea." In an alcove next to the kitchen, Susan took a seat by a bird's eye maple table. Jane reappeared carrying a teapot and two cups on a tray. "We should let it steep. It pleases me to offer thee hospitality, and tell you my appreciation for what thou hast done for me."

"I'm happy I could to help, Jane."

"Susan, I have good news. I enter silence each day and my mind has calmed. Doctor de Sequeyra noticed my changes. Recently he asked me to be matron of the female patients. I have my own room and I receive pay. I invite patients for tea. A bit of normal life is good for them. We talk about the homes they will return to, and calm their fears about the future or ease their pain about the past. I take them for walks or to help at the market."

"Congratulations, Jane. The doctor made an excellent choice for matron."

Jane poured the tea and Susan took a sip. "Ah, delicious! I have something to tell you. My husband John will gather people in the garden of the St. George Tucker House today at four. He hopes they will work together to reduce the loss of life. You should be at this meeting."

"Susan, I lived in fear most of my life. Now fear has receded and I look for ways to help others. Oh, here comes the doctor now." Jane stood up. "This is Susan Sinclair, the woman who took me to Kingsmill."

"Of course, Missus Sinclair. You contributed to a miracle. Jane and Sal have done much to make this a better place. Did Jane mention I purchased Sal from his owner? Previously I rented his service. He saves his wages to pay back the cost to buy him so our secret is that he is indentured rather than a slave. Jane paid for a month of the time he owes as a birthday gift so I did the same and will do that each year until he is free."

Susan had not decided about inviting the doctor, but she explored the possibility. "Doctor, my family is concerned that as war is spreading, the suffering will be great and losses heavy. My husband was a soldier and he is seeking ways that people could work together to save lives."

"Missus Sinclair, we share concerns. I observe at my office in town that many physical ailments begin when people are unhappy, confused, angry, or fearful. They struggle as if their life is at stake over status in the community, money, or non life-threatening conditions. I witness in individuals, families, and communities, the same delusions that we see here in the hospital. My diagnosis is that most of us are as crazy as crows in a windstorm. We dive and spin in the air if we do not fulfill a fantasy of what we think life should be. Rather than be grateful for what we have, we pine for what we do not have, or worry about what we might lose.

"I see the failure of Parliament and Congress to resolve their differences, and conclude that a county court could resolve such a dispute among plantations. Sadly, kings and congresses heed no higher authority, nor do men who dedicate their lives to amassing money and power, willingly surrender their ambitions to arbitration. We witness lunacy at the level of nations. It is not mad to pursue an ambition. What is insane is the manipulation and violence men use to have their way. They sacrifice the lives of others and lie about the reasons for sacrifice. They risk their sons as officers to demonstrate their commitment. Sons who survive are deemed qualified to lead estates or nations because they led men in killing others."

"What would you do, Doctor de Sequeyra?" asked Susan.

Doctor de Sequeyra sighed. "Ending war will take a long time. I have a small idea. More soldiers die of infections or disease, than die directly in battle. Current methods of putting a slice of onion or drops of a mercury compound on a wound are of limited help. If every militia unit had men trained to reduce festering of wounds with wine or rum, proper dressings of lint and oil, and who knew the importance of keeping their medical tools, the surgical area, and military camps clean, more soldiers would survive the madness. Some survivors would tell the truth to the next generation of how deranged it is to send young men to fight each other to the death. Do you consider it unpatriotic for me to speak this way?"

"No, Doctor. I would say you love your country and have compassion for young people. I want to invite you to a meeting at four o'clock beside the St. George Tucker House with others who seek to reduce the carnage."

"There will be a meeting of souls who care about this? I shall be there."

"I should be off. We leave on a long journey after the meeting. Thank you for the tea, Jane."

"Let us walk you to the door, Susan." On their way down the corridor, they were passed by a patient walking the other way repeating, "*Gloria in excelsis Deo, Gloria in excelsis Deo, Gloria in excelsis Deo...*"

"He changed his prayer." The doctor smiled. "This may be a step in the right direction."

Day 4-10:   Megan Gathers Her Friends.

Megan hurried to the blacksmith shop from the Brick House Tavern. She was told Mark would return in an hour.

She walked through town, hoping to run into Standing Elk, and toward the market where Bartholomew and Maggie were selling their wares.

"Bart, it's nice to see you back at work so soon. My dad is having a meeting by the St. George Tucker House. He asked me to invite people who can keep a secret and want to save lives and reduce the damage of the war. You were willing to sit in a stinky cell to try to slow the race toward war. Are you willing to join others even if it's dangerous?"

"I am willing to hear what the plan is, Megan. If we have a chance to save lives, we must give it a try."

"Have you talked to Standing Elk about this?" asked Maggie.

"I've been looking for him all over!"

"He left minutes ago, riding to the Jamestown road with his nephew Thomas," Bartholomew told her. "They had to stop at a farrier at the crossroads beyond William and Mary, so they will not have gone too far yet. You can borrow the Earl of Loxley to catch up with them."

"The Earl of Loxley?"

"He is a fast horse. Bartie, do you think she can handle him?" asked Maggie, concerned for Megan.

"Oh, the Earl of Loxley is your horse?"

"Yes. He pulls both cart and plow nicely but he loves to race the wind on an open road." Bartholomew glowed with pride. "You rode with Mark. Can you ride yourself?"

"I took riding lessons for two summers."

"Riding lessons? You are fit to be a cavalry officer in the Continental Army. To catch Standing Elk, you must leave now to reach him before he turns off the Jamestown Road and heads west. There's no tellin' which track he might take."

"I'll do it!"

Bartholomew unharnessed the Earl of Loxley from the cart, tossed a saddle over his back, and attached the stirrups. "There you are, Robin, a good run with Megan will do you good."

"Robin? I thought his name was the Earl of Loxley."

"Robin Hood was the Earl of Loxley and a supporter of the people, like you and your family, Megan. He is a spirited horse. Better to ride him astride."

There was enough material in the fabric of her dress for Megan to put her left foot into the stirrup and swing her right leg over the horse. "Thank you for this. See you at the St. George Tucker House at four o'clock."

"I hope we see you here before that with the Earl. We cannot pull the wagon without him."

"Darn! I wanted to keep him, OK, I'll be back." She gently guided the horse out of the market.

"OK?" Bartholomew looked at Maggie, puzzled.

"I heard her say it before. I think it means 'yes' or 'doing well' or 'that will be satisfactory, thank you.'"

"Young people today have their own language, don't they?"

Megan brought the Earl of Loxley to a trot and posted in the stirrups to avoid the bump, bump of her backside against the saddle. Reaching the Jamestown Road, she nudged the horse to a canter. There were no horses tethered at the farriers, so she knew Standing Elk and Thomas had already moved on.

She looked ahead on a long, straight stretch and saw no one else on the road. "All right, Robin Hood, Bartie says you're a fast horse who longs to race the wind. Let's see if you can race against time."

She made a clucking sound with the side of her tongue and cheeks through closed teeth, gave a subtle squeeze of her knees against the horse's sides, and a mild swish of the loose ends of the reins against the Earl of Loxley's right side. That was all the encouragement he needed to change his rhythm and lean into a full gallop.

Megan had never ridden so fast. She stood in the stirrups, knees pressing the flanks and entwined the fingers of her left hand in the Earl's mane. Her hair streamed behind her in the wind and a smile spread on her face. The smile widened when she recalled a slapstick cartoon image of a rider knocked off a horse by a low hanging branch, and she bent low, intently scanning the road ahead.

In the distance, a cart approached and without guidance, the Earl kept to the right. There was no sign of two riders and Megan looked west down each lane and track hoping for a glimpse of Standing Elk. As she passed the cart, someone shouted "Hey!" and she glanced left to see Peter at the reins with an African woman beside him.

She shouted, "Hi, Pete!" as she hurtled by.

The Earl of Loxley slowed to a cantor to round the next bend. Megan spotted two riders and pulled back slightly on the reins. The younger rider turned to see who was approaching and leaned over to say something to Standing Elk who looked back as well.

Megan slowed to a trot as she rode up. "Hello Standing Elk, Thomas. I'm glad I found you."

"We just passed your brother, mentioned your name, and here you are."

"I hope you're not disappointed."

"What brings you down this road at such a pace? And how did you get away with stealing Bartie's horse?"

"He lent me the Earl of Loxley to ride after you.

"Standing Elk, at the Spirit Lodge, you asked us to pray to find warriors who rise beyond fear and hate and can lead on the path of peace instead of the warpath. I prayed and realized I know such a man. He is my father."

"Megan, it is no surprise to me that a woman like you should have wise parents. Is he a warrior?"

"Yes. When he was a little older than I am now he fought in forests, deserts, and mountains far away. He managed to save the lives of many of his men. A while ago he stopped a fight in a tavern called the Walking Stick to save a man from getting injured."

"The man in the Walking Stick was your father? That tavern is on this road and that fight is a legend throughout the Tidewater. That was your father? He was a hurricane that did not harm. No man there had ever seen such a thing. He changed many men. I have prayed that I might meet him some day. What is his name?"

"His name is John Sinclair. I rode here to find you. If you come with me to Williamsburg, you will meet my father and others who choose to walk the path of peace. My father is having a meeting in the gardens of the St. George Tucker House at four o'clock."

Standing Elk was silent as if in prayer.

He turned to his nephew. "Thomas, I felt the Spirit Lodge today would be deep. Now we learn a sacred secret gathering will take place at the same time as the Lodge. This is a sign.

"Today, you will lead the Lodge and choose someone to be your fire-keeper. You will know who to choose when you see him. He may have been a fire-keeper before or perhaps not. If not, teach him the main points, help him to build the fire, select the grandfather stones, set the altar, and give him clear instructions. You are prepared to lead, and I am pleased.

"I will go to the gathering. Tell the people that I had to meet someone and that I send my blessing to everyone. Do not speak of the meeting. I will share what I learn with you when I return. Thomas, you are ready."

"Uncle, this is important. I feel it. Thank you for the trust you have in me. I shall walk the road I learned from you." Thomas nudged his horse and turned off the Jamestown rode down a wagon track.

"I'm glad I met you, Standing Elk. It is an honor. Now we have to go. Let's ride beside each other. I have many questions I want to ask."

Day 4-11: Making History in the Garden

John sat on a bench behind the hedges, savoring the scents of cedar and yew. His posture was erect, hands clasped and resting in his lap, mind calm. He listened to the rustle of wind in the tall trees. He mentally listed what to cover when people arrived.

With his footfalls crunching on the path rounding the hedgerow, Bruce carried chairs from the Tucker House. He arranged them next to the benches, saluted John, and sat near him without a word.

More footsteps sounded and Peter entered accompanied by three African Americans, two strong men in their late thirties, hair graying but eyes bright, and a large woman moving with a confident and kindly presence. "This is Annie and these are her helpers, Robert and Claudius. Folks, this is my father, John Sinclair."

John stood. "Welcome and thank you for coming. This is Bruce Wallace."

"You be plantin' precious seeds of peace, Mister John." Annie took John's hand. "The seeds you sowin' will save lives. We be happy to help this garden grow."

"Peter told me about you, Annie. Clear seeing will be needed in the days ahead."

Annie and her helpers sat together. Moments later, Susan arrived with Jane Harding, Doctor de Sequeyra, and Samuel Abdul Latif. Susan took a spot by John.

There was no awkwardness in the silence as they waited. John thought about one person he had hoped to invite but had not found. Horses stopped beyond the hedges and Megan entered with Standing Elk. Mark, Bartholomew, and Maggie walked in, followed by Frances who sat next to Jane. When all were seated, they formed a square of four people on each side.

John looked slowly around the square. "Greetings, friends, my name is John Sinclair. I live near the Potomac River. Frances, thank you for inviting us to this garden, a tranquil contrast to the turmoil of these times. Some of you know each other well and some have never met. Either I know you or my wife Susan, daughter Megan, or son Peter told me they would trust you with their lives. Their judgment is good enough for me. We ask you to trust each other, and to be worthy of that trust. We have all gathered here to work together to find ways to save lives. Does anyone wish to speak?"

Frances raised a hand and John nodded. "My father's ancestors included Pocahontas, who was of the Algonquin tribes as you are,

247

Standing Elk. My mother's line includes a black slave in Jamestown who completed his term of servitude and was freed. He married a white widow, which was permitted then. Their son's wife was a white servant whose freedom he purchased through his labors. Their grandchildren were pale as I am. All of you, red, black, and white, are my family."

"Thank you, Frances. Does anyone else wish to speak?"

"I would like to pray," offered Standing Elk, stepping to the centre. "Creator, we thank you for this gathering. Help us to be patient and generous, and please make clear the paths to walk on this journey together. Miigwech, Creator, for bringing together people of courage, skill, and energy to walk side by side on the path of peace." He turned to John. "Thank you for inviting us to this place, John Sinclair. My people will do everything we can to reduce the suffering of war and to live in harmony with all our neighbors."

"Thank you, Standing Elk."

"I have a question for thee." Jane stood up. "Thou sayest we are here to save lives. Will the war against Britain continue? Can something be done to stop it?"

"I expect this war will go on for years," John answered. "Blood has been shed already. Like all wars, it will end and enemies will gradually become friends. Meanwhile, we have ideas about how to reduce the harm of this war. First, we can reduce losses in battle by averting large direct confrontations. Casualties on both sides at Concord and Breed's Hill were heavy. If we warn General Washington when massed troops are coming, he could move out of the way to save lives on both sides. Bruce, can you get close to the British command?"

"To tell it true, though it pains me to see war come, I agree more with Congress."

"Bruce, you could let the command of the continental forces know you support them. You would become a vital contributor to their cause by informing them of major British movements. The task is dangerous."

"I suppose I could do that until the British hang me, but how can I build trust with the Continental Army? They will think I am on the British side."

Peter interrupted. "I know how you can connect with the Continental Army, Bruce. I chanced upon Colonel Hugh Mercer today. He asked me to tell you he is staying at the home of Dr. Galt, the apothecary, and he could use your help in the 3rd Virginia Regiment."

"Bruce, it's being served to you on a platter," John told him. "You can visit Colonel Mercer here. His 3rd Regiment is in the North with General

Washington. He will introduce you to Washington and you can offer directly to be an agent. Then meet the British command and remind them of your service in the last war and of your connections to Dunmore and Oglethorpe. Once you give the British Generals information and they see you were right, even though they arrive after Washington has left, you'll have credibility with them while helping the Continental Army."

"I can do that, John." Bruce decided.

"Keeping George Washington alive is worth a try, Bruce, and reducing casualties on both sides will be a great service. Do you have friends who speak German?"

Suddenly the sound of footsteps on gravel brought everyone to an anticipative silence. Into the opening stepped James Walker the Episcopal priest and Master of the Masonic Lodge. "Oh, sorry to interrupt." He turned to go.

"Reverend Walker, I was hoping to invite you to this meeting."

The Reverend turned around again. "Hello, John. I come to this sheltered place to imagine life in... Oh! Susan and Frances, you're here?" It slowly dawned on Reverend Walker what he was seeing.

"Reverend," Frances welcomed him. "I am happy you joined us today."

"This is astonishing. If you don't mind, John, I feel a need to sit down."

"Please take this spot and I will stand," John offered.

John asked again, "Do any of you know any German speakers?"

"*Ich kann gut Deutsch sprechen.*"

John looked around to see who had spoken.

Jane held up her hand. "*Ich arbeitete für vier Jahre als Küchenmädchen bei einer deutschen Familie in Pennsylvania...* Sorry. I worked four years as a kitchen maid, living with a German family in Pennsylvania after my family was killed. They were kind and I learned their language."

"Jane, that's extraordinary! Bruce can introduce you to General Washington. You could offer to circulate among German prisoners and, if you are willing to take the risk, among the German conscripts in British service. You could tell them they could end their serfdom and get free land here by joining the Continental Army as free men. Washington will like the idea. Otherwise, since Colonel Rall is taking no prisoners, the Americans could decide to give no quarter either."

"Thou hast a good idea, but I am busy at the hospital as the doctor can attest."

"Jane Harding, if you can persuade General Washington of the merits of this idea, you will reduce the greater madness in the world and will put into service what you learned as a result of the tragedy in your family."

"If thou thinkest it worthwhile, Doctor, I am willing to do it."

"You have my complete support. I shall continue to pay your monthly stipend so you may concentrate on the work rather than worry about sustaining yourself."

"That is generous, Doctor," said John. "Now, we need someone close to the command of the Continental Army to deliver information coming from Bruce and other sources directly to General Washington. Mark, you could travel with Washington, ostensibly to repair swords and bayonets. Runners could bring news and warnings to you without observers knowing the true purpose of their visit."

"I would like to reduce the loss of life, Mister Sinclair. However, as Mister Wallace agrees more with Congress, I lean to the Loyalist side. The large landowners are taking land from native people and have no interest in freeing slaves or servants. It seems they fight for personal gain. Besides, I am in bondage at the blacksmith shop."

"Thank you for your honesty, Mark. With Bruce near the British command, it would be perfect to have you with your Loyalist leanings in the service of General Washington. You will both work to reduce loss of life on all sides. You can hasten the end of servitude and slavery for volunteers on the Continental side. The army is short of men and will see the benefit of granting freedom to volunteers."

"Mark," Standing Elk stood again, "slaves and servants are here together and my people will support it. You can keep the freedom of all people in mind."

"The thought of speaking to the commander of the Continental Army frightens me. But good idea or not, I am not free to leave Anderson's forge."

Standing Elk studied Mark. "I will contribute money toward buying your freedom from Mister Anderson."

"I'll contribute," John added. "We'll all give the money to Bruce to buy the bond of indenture. When he explains to your master that you'll work for Washington and will be able to direct business to the blacksmith shop and armory, the answer will be an enthusiastic yes."

Standing Elk handed a leather pouch to Bruce. "Mark, you are my friend."

Megan walked over the Mark. "I will contribute to your freedom. Servitude is not fair."

"Maggie and I will give coins to unbind you, Mark," offered Bartholomew.

Whispers came from the bench where the slaves sat and Robert stood up. "Claudius and Sal and me been saving coins for our freedom. We will give some to you, Mister Mark, so you gonna be free to do this. This be a day to remember. Since we be bound for freedom, if we be slaves a bit longer, it don't matter."

"This indeed be a day to remember." Annie stood as Robert sat down. "'Bound for freedom' you say? Robert and Claudius, I be very proud of you. We will get your manumission now. You will carry papers saying you be slaves to keep you safe as you travel, but now you know that you be free just as God has always known it. Mark Smith, I gonna put in money to help you do this work."

Doctor de Sequeyra stood. "I shall donate. My people were Pharaoh's slaves and miracles set them free. Mark, this meeting is your miracle. And yours, Sal. I shall sign your manumission now. You are free to work on this however you choose."

Mark wiped his eyes. "I have never known such kindness. I should introduce myself honestly. This is not easy... My name is Edmond Brown. The words 'his mark' were next to the place to make an X on the indenture paper. I copied the letters M, A, R, and K, and ever since I use the name Mark because I can write it and because I feel less trapped in bondage having a contract that is not in my name." He looked around at the faces staring at him as if for the first time.

"Edmond Brown, do you accept freedom through the generosity of these friends and will you meet General Washington?"

"Mister Sinclair, I gratefully accept. Your confidence gives me faith in myself."

"And Edmond..."

"Yes, Mister Sinclair?"

"I suggest you continue using the name Mark. It will help you remember that you have a special mission to help those in bondage."

"Yes, Sir. I shall be Mark Smith as long as it is helpful."

John outlined his plan. "Now as Bruce Wallace moves with the British and Mark Smith is in service to Washington, they will need messengers to carry information between them. Look around this group. We have native people who can move freely, slaves who can travel for their owner, vendors of vegetables, and a travelling preacher woman. There is strength in your differences. Do not mention people in this group to anyone. Others can work with you without knowing anyone beyond the people they directly contact. Standing Elk, you have experience and wisdom to lead the work. You will find Indians on both sides throughout the colonies to recruit that you judge safe and helpful. Annie and her friends can work with you."

"I am honored by your faith in me, as we meet for the first time."

"Standing Elk, though few will ever know it because you will work in secret, you will contribute to all the peoples of this land."

"I have something to offer," Doctor de Sequeyra said. "Most who perish in war die of infection rather than wounds. I can teach methods that would save lives."

"I gonna share what I know about stoppin' infection, and other physic, Doctor," Annie added. "I been teachin' Claudius and Robert and they teach others."

Standing Elk nodded. "My people know leaves and barks that stop infection, slow bleeding, and ease pain. We taught those cures to Annie and she added to our knowledge with what she learned from African healers and colonial doctors."

The doctor spoke. "I can offer the Public Hospital as an indoor meeting place. People come to the hospital to deliver food or visit family without townsfolk taking notice. Superstitious souls avoid even looking at the hospital out of fear."

"That is a good idea, Doctor," John agreed.

Frances added, "These hedges offer shelter from curious eyes and you are welcome to use this garden as a place to meet as well."

"Thank you, Frances. The path will become clearer as you move along it. My family and I are going away today, so I leave this work to Bruce, Standing Elk, the Doctor, and Annie to lead. Whenever Annie has an idea, I suggest you all listen."

"Thank you, Mister Sinclair. I want to let folks know that we can get printed bills of sale, military orders, manumission, and whatever folks need to help them move freely. I would rather not say 'zackly how we be able to do that."

"Annie, the papers will be helpful. Thank you all for coming to this meeting. May God smile upon your undertakings. Bruce, may I have a word?"

Peter stood by Annie. "I will pray for the success of this work, Annie."

"We all got to do the best we can. We pray the leaders wake up and them who profit from war find more helpful ways to get rich. You helped more folk here than you know, Peter. We gonna meet again."

"Annie, knowing you has changed me. I'll remember you all my life."

252

Next to a hedge, John spoke to Bruce. "I learned that a Patrick Ferguson in Britain is designing a breech-loading rifle, accurate at 200 yards. It fires six rounds a minute standing or four advancing, and doesn't misfire in the rain."

"My God, Man! If that rifle works, the Continentals have no chance!"

"Precisely, Bruce. So an important, secret part of your work is to find and steal or destroy those rifles—whatever you need to do to remove them from the field."

"That doesna' sound like an easy task, John."

"It won't be easy, but you'll be close to the British generals, so you'll know when Ferguson arrives. The road ahead will be difficult enough without a superior weapon ranged against the Patriots. You will think of something. Oh, another thing—American marksmen are shooting British officers but see if you can persuade Ferguson not to shoot American officers."

"Is that all you need? If you like I could fly to Heaven and ask Saint George the Dragon Slayer and the Archangel Michael to help us."

"Saint George is patron saint of England, so chances of his joining you are slim. Ask Saint Andrew, patron saint of Scotland, and keep your head down when it gets noisy. Your position is too critical to sacrifice yourself in a heroic gesture."

"'Tis too late for me to die young, John, and the temptation to be a hero, like so many of life's temptations, is slowly fading."

Reverend Walker approached them. "Thank you for including me in the circle, John. I won't forget this experience and in church and the Masonic Temple, I will pray for success of the plan."

"I am a Mason, too." Bruce took Reverend Walker's elbow in his left hand and gave him a firm handshake with the right. "Where is your Lodge?"

Reverend Walker hesitated, not knowing what to say. "I... came far to be at the meeting and my Lodge is not easy to reach from here."

"Perhaps Reverend Walker can meet you again in these hedges, Bruce. I'm sure if he can find a way to help through the Church or through the Masons, he will."

"Yes, I will do what I can to help," the Reverend agreed. "Goodbye for now."

John put a hand on Bruce's shoulder. "I'm not usually a praying man, but I'll pray for you and the success of this mission."

"Thank you, John."

Megan followed Mark out of the hedges. "Edmond Brown!" He turned around.

"Yes, Megan? I am sorry I did not tell you my real name."

"You did what you had to. I'm proud of you." She kissed his cheek.

"Can you come with me to the North, Megan?"

"Mark, I'll always remember you but I can't go with you. I know you will find a wonderful woman."

"I shall never find a woman like you. Now I have reason to wear those fine clothes you bought me, and I will think of you when I do."

Only Frances and John remained in the garden. "Frances, can you tell me now how you are able to appear in my time when you live in the eighteenth century?"

"I can tell you, John, but you might find it hard to believe or disturbing."

"This whole experience is hard to believe, Frances."

"In 1778, I married St. George Tucker after he returned from Bermuda. I became distraught when I learned my new husband and his father supplied gunpowder to the Continental Army. I swore to Heaven I would find a way to reduce the suffering of the war however long it took. St. George and I had five children in addition to the three I already had. The war ended and we settled into our life. He spent time in Richmond conducting his law business, which left me time to pray to atone for people killed in the war. About ten years after St. George and I married, I died, as all of us eventually do."

"But..."

"This may not be easy to believe, but after my years of prayer to do something about the violence, I lingered here at this house, where my husband moved, and where my children grew up after my death. I have long watched for a way to reduce the damage of the gunpowder."

"Why did you decide to work with me?"

"It is unusual that a person can see me or hear what I say, because, of course, I am not saying anything, just thinking it. You saw me and heard me so I knew I should talk with you. Today in the garden is the first time I have been heard by so many. It is the fulfillment of my long-held prayer."

"That is amazing, Frances. You're telling me that you are a ghost? If I had not experienced so many strange things in the past few days, I would not believe it."

"Those who are alive would call me a ghost. I am a soul that has lingered for a purpose, longer than my body was able to live. I have two

254

small gifts to give you John to help you believe what I have told you. First, two men contacted me this morning and asked me to tell you they are well. They expressed their gratitude, 'For back then, and for now,' they told me. Their names are Danny and Sargon — does that second name make sense to you? They were soldiers. Danny was younger than your son and Sargon a few years older."

John was stunned.

"The second gift is that I want to leave you no doubt that there are things that are real beyond what most people know. It is finally time for me to move on. Goodbye, John. I deeply thank you for who you are and for what you have done for so many." Frances curtsied, turned, and glided straight into the tall hedge, disappearing without rustling a single branch.

John stared at the hedge where Frances vanished. A breeze rustled tree branches high above. He looked up. "Go ahead, laugh, Danny and Sargon. You put her up to that trick."

On the street, Susan waved goodbye to Jane, Doctor de Sequeyra, and Samuel Abdul Latif. John joined her, Peter, and Megan and they set out toward the bridge.

Day 4-12:   Virginia Declares Independence

As the Sinclairs walked together up North England Street, suddenly shouting and cheering came from several directions followed by the pealing of bells from the Capitol, the Palace, and Bruton Parish Church. "What's going on?" asked Susan.

"There's a crowd by the Palace," John pointed. "Let's see what it's about."

A man placed a chair by the Palace gates and stood on it waving his black tricorn hat in the air. He shouted out, "Hear ye, hear ye! History is made in Williamsburg! Today, May 15, 1776, the Virginia Convention, meeting at the Capitol, resolved to instruct its delegates to the Continental Congress to declare:

> 'That these United Colonies are, and of right ought to be, free and independent States, that they are absolved from all allegiance to the British Crown, and that all political connection between them and the State of Great Britain is, and ought to be, totally dissolved.'

"They have asked Richard Henry Lee to propose the resolution at the Congress in June. Three cheers for Independence and the Continental Congress!"

The crowd cheered. Celebration began as more people came out of their homes and patrons spilled out of taverns into the streets.

John stroked his chin. "It's rolling and we're here at the beginning. Now it's time to go home." They threaded their way through the crowd, crossed the bridge in silence, and walked to the car waiting for them in their own time.

Day 5-1: Return to Williamsburg

Megan burst through the front door. "Mom, I got an A on my paper! My teacher says I can get college credit if I explain how I did the research!"

"Great, Megan! Dinner's ready—homemade lasagna."

As Megan took her spot at the table, John complemented her, "An A on your paper? Excellent! Will your explanation of your research mention we went back in time?"

"I want to. I may write it as a story. Can we go back this summer to check a few things out, or should I do it using books and the web?"

"Colonial Williamsburg has a program the last week in June called 'Under the Red Coat,' a reenactment of the British occupation in 1781. Peter will be back for the summer and he'd probably come," Susan said.

"A British occupation? What happened to the people we met, Dad?"

"I don't know. I looked online. Doctor de Sequeyra really ran the mental hospital and Frances Tucker was a real person. Patrick Ferguson invented breech-loading rifles that disappeared after the battle at Brandywine and a militia leader named Joseph Hutchings was captured by his own slave. I couldn't find Bruce, Standing Elk, Jane, or Peter's friend Annie."

"How did they make out?" wondered Megan. "If we slid to the past only because our car spun, does something intense need to happen for us to get back in time again, Mom?"

"Good question. We can try. Peter's summer job has him working Saturdays, but I will book a room for that Saturday night so we will get an early start Sunday to check out the British occupation and look for our friends."

Day 5-2:   June 1781   Under British Occupation

The server returned to the table. "Here are the granola pancakes and the poached eggs with ham. I see you two already got to the buffet."

John asked for a fill-up on coffee.

"When we walk into the Historic District, British soldiers will be camped in town," Peter reminded his family. "If we find a way to 1781, our friends will be five years older. Some may be dead and some may have left."

"It's not likely we can go back in time again," John said, "but it wasn't likely that would happen last month either, so who knows?"

"I just looked up where George Washington was in June, 1781." Megan looked at her phone. "He was in Peekskill, New York, until July 2 then he moved to Dobbs Ferry. He didn't get here until September."

"So Mark Smith or Edmond Brown won't be here either."

Megan shot Peter a look to be quiet.

After breakfast, the Sinclairs walked through town together. In an open space near the Magazine was a large camp of reenactors in British uniforms and civilian dress. The air had the scent of sweet acidic smoke from a hardwood fire. A barefoot English woman had set a large cut of beef to roast in a reflector oven made at a forge in Williamsburg.

"What are you making?" asked Susan.

"Well, Love, we're cooking for a hundred men. Some like their beef salty and some do not. Some like potatoes with garlic and some without. I shall use a honey and pepper baste on that roast to make it tasty. I enjoy doing colonial cooking each year. I don't need to pretend to be English, I am English, but I like pretending we are in the past."

"Being here is like a journey to the past isn't it?" Susan said.

"Indeed, it is. We come for a weekend, and then back to our time we go."

A faint melody from a British soldier practicing a fife could be heard above the bustle. Redcoats polished their brass buttons and buckles, oiled bayonets and muskets, or made cartridges with powder and papier-maché musket balls. A trio of young men practiced marching together to be crisp for the drill. John scanned the area for familiar faces but saw none.

The Sinclairs walked north. "Hey!" said Megan, "I remember that zigzag fence; they call it a worm fence. It has no nails or fasteners except that rail wedged at an angle at each corner. I sat reading there. Come on! I'll show you!" She led her family to the spot by the fence where Standing

258

Elk opened her eyes to nature. "Maybe if we sit quietly, he'll come walking."

Megan described the plants and trees she learned from her friend. "When I sat here last month it was November. Isn't that weird?" They sat quietly, lulled by the buzzing of diligent bees and whisperings of leaves in the canopy. An unseen blue jay called from upper branches. They felt the warmth of the sun in a mottled pattern as it shone through the leaves.

"Let's go to other spots where we have a clear memory of being in the past. We may find a way through," suggested Peter. He led them to the stream behind the printing office where he and Evie met Annie at the bridge. Lilies grew by the water gurgling from a culvert. The Sinclairs stood on the bridge, watched, and listened. Frond-like branches of ash trees swayed gently. Out of sight a large frog rumbled.

Peter noticed a small apple orchard he had not seen when he was in the garden with Evie. All my attention was on her at this bridge, he thought wistfully. I wish I could have helped them get to freedom. I wonder what happened to her sons. He half-expected Annie would come down the path.

"Let's visit other spots," Susan suggested. "Where did you first see Annie?"

They left the garden and walked to the pasture where Peter had seen Annie preparing food. They sat in a row along the fence. Minutes passed without conversation. They were calmed by the sounds of nature.

"It's amazing how much life you can hear going on when you stop and listen or look," said Megan. "When I sat with Standing Elk and Mark behind the blacksmith shop and again in the Sweat Lodge, I had a sense of how connected we are. When I look at stars, I'm looking at something—either at the stars or the patterns people see in constellations like the Big Dipper or Orion. But when I look into the deep black space between the stars, I get a sense I never felt before. Space is everywhere, out there, around us, and inside us, too. It's hard to find words because the feeling had no words."

"You're doing a good job saying it," Susan encouraged her. "When I sat in silence with Jane Harding in a garden near the Public Hospital, and at the Kingsmill Plantation, looking at a flower or at a ship sailing by felt timeless, like looking at the Infinite—no, more like being in the Infinite."

"That's good, Mom. I might mention that in my paper. I had trouble finding a way to say this the first time, so I gave up."

"I feel relaxed," said John. "This could be like when we let go in the spinning car. 'Timeless,' you called it, Susan. It does feel timeless. When we aren't thinking about the past or the future, we are in the stream of moments. By being present now, maybe we can touch something bigger."

Peter closed his eyes and imagined Annie smiling. A warm feeling of well-being flowed through him, and he joined her in a wide smile. He did not see Annie but in that instant, it made no difference.

"What are you smiling about, Pete?"

"I'm happy to be here again. Let's check out some other places."

They reached the Benjamin Powell House. "I'll see if anyone is out back." Peter dashed down the lane but a woman at the gate was directing visitors out. No one was behind her in the garden. He rejoined the others and asked if they would be willing to go through the house again. "This is where the time change began for me."

"Sure, let's go in, Pete."

After a short wait, they joined other visitors. The hallway, living room, and front bedroom looked the same but there were no reenactors.

A woman in costume in the dining room welcomed them. She explained how food prepared in the kitchen was set out ready for a Sunday feast. "The Powell family had a large dinner on their return from church."

Susan looked over the table setting. "It looks as if they will be home any time."

Peter asked, "I was wondering about an African woman named Evie who was a laundress here last time we came. Does she still work here?"

"I don't know a reenactor by that name. Perhaps there was once a slave named Evie in this house. Were you here back then?" she laughed.

"I guess I was!" Peter laughed along with the woman—if she only knew. He was disappointed to see no sign of Evie and her sons.

They meandered to spots they knew and others new to them, asking reenactors about the people they knew. Progress had been made on the Public Armoury at the blacksmith shop and Megan went inside to ask about Mark Smith or Edmond Brown who worked at the forge long ago.

"Never heard of either one of them."

"How about an Indian named Standing Elk who bought iron goods?"

"Sorry, I've never seen an Indian customer."

"Thanks anyway." Megan followed her family to the bench by the Public Hospital where Susan sat with Jane. "Look, Mom! It's an art museum."

"It's good to see beauty at this place which housed many tormented souls. Part of it is a display of the old mental hospital. Let's sit here for a while." The Sinclairs sat in stillness, as Susan and Jane did long ago. A

260

squirrel peered at them from behind a tree and quickly scampered out of sight. "He looks like the same squirrel we watched last month."

"It was way over two hundred years ago, Mom. It's a descendant."

"You're my descendant, but not distant, Megan." Susan gave her daughter a hug. "Having you kids is the best thing that ever happened to us. I feel the memory of Jane Harding as we sit here. She seems near."

"It's strange being in these places again, Mom," said Megan. "Sometimes I think there's no way we can get back to that other time. But that's just an idea going through my mind. When my mind is quiet like the space between the stars, the past seems close, but how do we get there?"

"I get what you're saying. We didn't do anything to slip back in time. We just woke up, walked around a corner, or ran into someone, and there we were. So maybe it won't be our doing if we get back again."

"Good, Dad! It wasn't our doing. Annie told me we 'let go' when the car was spinning and slid back into her time. She was able to walk with me into ours. She also thought maybe someone was praying we would come."

"Right! Frances Tucker told me she had been praying for a long time, and at the end of the meeting in the garden I learned how long."

"Standing Elk was praying for a warrior who could lead on the path of peace, and that turned out to be you, Dad."

"So maybe we were called back and we did nothing in our time to make it happen other than 'let go.' Maybe no one is calling us now."

To avoid the crowds around the Redcoats' camp they walked north. John ducked into the wheelwright's shop. A young man fitted hardwood spokes into holes chiseled in the wooden hub. John asked him, "I'm looking for a wheelwright named Bruce Wallace."

"I've worked here four years and don't know him. He must have worked here quite a few years ago."

John thanked the young wright and joined Peter looking over a fence at colorful chickens in a yard. "Did he know Bruce?" Peter asked.

"No. Bruce retired 230 years ago. Where are the girls?"

"They stopped in to see the basket maker. Here they come now."

"Hi guys! Megan and I just learned something. Let's sit on Palace Green." Admiring the view of Governor's Palace, Susan began to explain, "When I think of baskets, I think of thin materials like grasses or vines. But here they wove baskets from six-foot long white oak logs a foot in diameter."

Peter was puzzled. "They might be a bit hard to weave."

"That's what we thought," said Megan, "but they split logs into shafts and peeled off strips. They soak the strips and weave them into a basket."

"What did you learn from that, Susan?"

"They take something solid, and slice it down into thin strips that bend. When woven together, it becomes strong. Something we thought impossible can be done by seeing the form differently."

"Something impossible like travelling back in time, Mom?" asked Peter.

"Right! Everyone knows it's impossible to weave a log into a basket or to go back in time. However, when the log is transformed, something unexpected can happen. I think there is a way we can do this."

"So do I," Megan said, "but that doesn't mean I know how."

"Me neither," said Peter, "and I went back and forth a couple of times when we were here last month. So, how do we transform ourselves?"

John had a thought. "There's a place where time never failed to shift."

"Why didn't you say so, John?" asked Susan.

He led them to the St. George Tucker House and took them to a comfortable parlor. They got lemonade and relaxed in the stuffed chairs."

"So is this where you always had a time shift, Dad?" asked Megan.

"Yes and it's working. Look around. When we were here last, every time I came in here I jumped right back into our time. And here we are again!"

Peter and Megan began to laugh. Looking at them, Susan broke out. John could not keep a straight face. "What a relief to be back in our own time."

"That's funny," Susan said, wiping her eyes. "A magic place that puts you in your own century without any effort at all—just click the ruby slippers and we're back in Kansas again. There's no place like home!"

"Well," said her father taking a breath, "there's another thing I didn't tell you because I didn't want you to think I was completely crazy."

"We wandered around here in the eighteenth century." Peter smiled, "Most people would say we're all crazy, so your story is safe with us."

"When we sat beside this house among the hedges it appeared that just four of us and Reverend Walker crossed from one time to another."

"That's true. What are you saying, Honey?"

"I first met Frances Tucker here in our time. I thought she was a docent but on our last day she led me out to the garden to talk with Bruce Wallace in May of 1776."

"So she slipped across time like we did? Do you think she's here now?"

"She moved in the other direction like Annie did with Peter. She was the widow of St. George Tucker; she moved to this house... after she died."

"She died? Then how..."

"I didn't know it at the time, but she was a ghost. I wouldn't have believed it except that when the meeting was over, she wanted me to know what she was, so she faded away as she glided into a hedge."

"Like going into the corn field in that movie?" Megan asked.

"Exactly like that!" They got quiet, wondering if Frances would appear.

John closed his eyes and leaned back in the chair. He recalled that he never saw Frances take a book from the shelf or move anything. She seemed to glide when she left the room. He thought at the time that she moved with the elegance of nobility. In contrast, he and his family had bodily experiences—they moved things and ate the food. He was in a fight. He recalled what Frances said about that fight...

"Did it really happen? You imagined it really happening."

"But you were there, too," he said to her.

"The imagination is not just for fantasy," she replied. "When we focus the imagination in a chosen direction, we can experience directly through the mind, skipping the physical senses."

John sat with that a moment before opening his eyes. "Listen, gang. We have identified several pieces of what it took for us to move through time. First, we completely let go, not by choice but through instinct when it seemed we were about to die. Then we used our imaginations to make the experiences more real. Next, we became more open—we could say more porous. I was unwilling to accept it, so naturally I was last to experience a shift. Finally, someone in the past was praying for or calling someone—and in our open state, we responded to the call and experienced the past."

"Do you think we can do that again?" asked Peter.

"It was not anything we did. It was what we were willing to experience. I have an idea that there are two kinds of 'willing'—opposite meanings in the same word. When we are 'willing something to happen,' we are focused, working at it, determined to make it happen. However, when we are 'willing *for* something to happen', we accept what happens and our acceptance shapes what happens like a mold shapes plaster. We allow it and welcome it like letting it flow into a valley rather than applying effort to force it up hill. I think we need both approaches in life."

"Sounds like masculine and feminine approaches, Honey. Are you saying there is nothing we can do to get back in time again?"

"It isn't about 'doing', Susan. But if we let go, use our imaginations, be open, and listen for the call, it will either happen or it won't."

"That definitive, huh? It will either happen or it won't?" asked Peter.

"And like last time, we won't know until it happens," said Megan.

Susan made a slow wave of her hand. "It could start subtly, like when I smelled tobacco in the Capitol, or suddenly and dramatically like when we woke up and our bathroom had been replaced by a stone hearth. Maybe we'll get just a hint this time and not a full-on experience."

"Speaking of a bathroom and kitchen, I could use both in that order," Megan said. "We travelled through time all morning and got to lunch."

Susan had an idea. "The finest dining here is at the Williamsburg Inn. Since we're stuck in our time we might as well enjoy it."

"Great idea, Mom. Let's go."

"One more thing," said John. "Last month, every time I walked out of this house, I stepped into the past on the very same day I left it."

"It's worth a try."

They slowly opened the front door and stepped out of the St. George Tucker House. The aroma of wood smoke was in the air and the large open space across the street was filled with bivouacked British soldiers and camp followers.

"You see? It worked again," said John as he opened the gate at the end of the walk. "We went straight to the day we were in when we walked into the house."

"But this time we came in from our time," said Megan, then she got it and laughed. "Like you said, it works every time."

They wandered south to the Williamsburg Inn. The Terrace Room would begin serving lunch in ten minutes.

"I'm happy we came back," said Peter as they waited, "but I wish we could connect with our friends to learn if they made it through. They've been dead since long before our grandparents were born. It would be nice to know how it turned out for them. I hope they lived happy lives."

"We know the big outcomes, like thirteen of the British colonies in North America won a war of independence," said John. "We know George Washington managed to evade the large concentrations of British troops through the entire war and the breech-loading rifles are still missing. But we don't know how our friends fared during the many years of fighting."

Day 5-3:   Modern Lunch at the Williamsburg Inn

"Sinclair, table for four," called the Maitre d'. She led them to a table by a window. John pulled out a seat for Megan, giving her the best view.

Megan broke open a roll. "It is better around here now than it was in the eighteenth century. We have indoor plumbing and we ended slavery and indentured servitude, but many people still don't earn a living wage. We still deplete our soil, fresh water, forests, and fisheries just as our ancestors did. After more than two centuries of democracy, we don't yet have fair elections without manipulation by those with money."

"Have you become a revolutionary, Megan?" asked John.

"I was leaning Loyalist until I learned their leaders were no more helpful to Indians, slaves, and settlers than many revolutionary plantation owners were. It bugs me that so long after the Revolution, most Americans don't know how big a role land profits played at the time."

"When people crave to increase their wealth, they can be willfully blind to the impact of their actions on others and on nature," said Susan.

"Our worth is not determined by our wealth," said Megan. "Needy people feel what they have is insufficient, however much they have. Money in politics, lobbying, and public relations aims to increase the assets of those already rich. We need honest and open democracy."

"Will public funding of elections help, Dad?" Peter asked.

"It will help if we the people of the United States, pay attention to what is going on, learn how it affects us and the nation, and decide what balance we want between personal freedom and prosperity on one hand and equity and well being of the whole community on the other," said John.

The waiter placed a hearty soup and a salad in front of John and grilled salmon in front of Susan. Peter and Megan had crab cakes. By the time they finished eating, the Terrace Room had diners at every table. Megan looked around. "We are the only ones in eighteenth century outfits."

"I feel out of place, as if we are from colonial times," Peter added.

"It's subtle, but I feel it, too," said John. "Check, please!"

At the entrance, Susan suggested, "I think we should go on our own and find what we can about our friends. Where should we meet — and when?"

"In this case, 'when' is a funny question," said John. "Redcoats will be marching on the square today at 5. Let's meet near the gate of the Governor's Palace after the drill. It will be a short walk over the bridge to the car."

Day 5-4:   Susan Sits in the Light

Susan sat near the Public Hospital, on the same bench where she was with Jane long ago. She relaxed, took a long breath, and imagined Jane beside her. A rustling noise brought her right back. There was the squirrel again. She laughed. It was a happy distraction.

She slipped into silence, lightly scanning for subtle impressions. She heard or sensed, "Susan, I sense thy nearness. It gives me comfort."

"I hear you, dear Jane," thought Susan. She felt a sparkle like laughter and heard Jane's voice, "That squirrel is such a happy distraction."

Susan looked at the squirrel, surprised. "Yes, she is. How are you Jane?"

"Well, thanks to thee. John and I talk of what we learn from Annie."

"John?" Susan felt a blush and knew the feeling was coming from Jane.

"John de Sequeyra," said Jane. "Neither of us is lonely any longer."

"Jane, that is wonderful! No need to feel embarrassed — I felt you blush."

"We are close as sisters."

"Jane, in the light, we *are* sisters. What has Annie taught you?"

"I see that the Paxton Boys who massacred us acted on fear and rage from their own wounds. I am learning how the circle turns. How art thou?"

"I finally came to peace over my brother's death. Did you see Washington?"

"Yes, I met the General. I wore the beautiful dress thou gave me. He encouraged me to circulate among German prisoners and the Hessian camps. When I was successful, we asked other German speakers to do the same. Hundreds chose to change sides for the promise of a homestead in this country. It worked so well we made the same offer to Redcoats."

"You are a courageous woman, Jane."

"'Tis getting late. John invited me to a reception tomorrow in Richmond. It will be the first time we present ourselves in public as a couple."

"I am happy for you both. I will reach out to you when I sit in silence. It may not always work so well. I am on the bench where we sat together."

"I am on the same bench, but when I open my eyes, I see thee not."

"I am speaking from a time not yet come to you. I pray it happens again."

"I do as well. Fare thee well my Sister Susan."

The squirrel raced to a shrub. Susan smiled and closed her eyes to slip back into the silence to listen for guidance for her life journey.

Day 5-5:   Annie, Evie and Her Boys

Peter closed his eyes and thought of Annie. What had she said when he went out looking for her one evening and found her sitting by the road?

"We found each other by me feeling where you was comin' from and you feelin' where I was waitin'."

"I didn't notice I was feeling where you were waiting," he had admitted.

"Then you wasn't paying attention to what you was feeling."

This time, Peter did notice a subtle feeling. He cleared his mind and an image of a quiet shady spot near a zigzag worm fence came to him. He walked slowly past Christiana Campbell's Tavern looking between the houses as he went. "I have a vague sense that something is present but hidden," he said to himself. "I'm looking and someone is waiting."

He paused and turned up a lane between the tavern and the Powell House. A street sign said Lafayette Street, but this was a long curved driveway to a parking lot. A busy parkway called Lafayette Street bordered the Historic District just beyond these pastures. This shady lane was a remembrance of an ancient street. He looked over the fence into the garden where he had gasped at seeing Evie in May 1775.

"Not here, but near." On his left, a solid white board fence penned a few sheep behind the Powell House garden. By the curve in the lane, an aged worm fence stretched off under the trees. Between him and the pasture was an unpainted gate. Looking around to be sure he was unseen, Peter opened the gate and stepped through, closing it behind him. A faint shift occurred in the tension that pulled him forward.

He turned toward the worm fence and closed his eyes. "Over the fence," he heard. He ran to the fence at an angle, placed one foot halfway up the sloping rail wedged between the ground and an end post, and vaulted into the next pasture. The murmur of female voices blended into the hum of other sounds—the insects, the birds. He climbed the steps of a style over the next fence and stood at the top.

Laughter came from behind an ancient tree. "I ain't laughin' at you. I'se laughin' at how many ways Mister Peter is goin' over fences to get here."

"Annie? Evie?" Peter came around the large oak and they stood to greet him. Evie hugged him and Annie put her big arms around both of them.

"I'm so happy to see you ladies again."

"You see, Annie. He calls us Ladies. I be poor African folk, not even free, and he calls us Ladies like we was better-sorts women." Evie turned to Peter. "Oh, Mister Peter, where have you been so long?"

"Evie, I had to come a long way to be here this afternoon."

"That's true enough, Mister Peter. You walked around town all day."

"You could feel me coming, couldn't you, Annie?"

"I knew you would be gone a long time, Mister Peter. But today I felt you when I sat behind the fence near the Brickyard."

"You were *behind* the fence? You smiled at me."

"And you smiled right back. You felt me, didn't you? It was about mid-morning. Now go ahead and tell Evie what you came so far to tell her."

Peter took Evie's hand, "I'm very glad to see you, Evie, and relieved to know you are well. How are James and Dilli?"

"The war been hard. Sometimes we ain't had much to eat. Massa Powell was rentin' the boys out to work. I worried he be ready to sell them away but when the British came, the Powells ran to Richmond. Maybe the Redcoats or militias gonna grab my boys to be soldiers. I told them they daddies was brave and fought for freedom. Now they say they be ready to fight for our freedom, too. I tell them the English left African soldiers behind when they sailed away. If you fight, you gonna hurt people and be hurt.

"I want my boys to grow up free," Evie continued, "but the only home I knows and the only folks I knows is right here in Virginia. My boys heard Redcoats is working on a dock at Yorktown and feedin' folk who help build it. They want to get work there then take a ship to England."

"Evie, they should not go to Yorktown. A ship is a good idea, but there may be fighting there. The French navy may be coming that way..."

Annie interrupted. "Evie, bring our watchmen to say hello."

"The watchmen? Oh, yes! I will fetch them."

As Evie walked away, Annie said in a low voice, "I have a bad feelin' about Yorktown too, and there be things I want to tell you quick. The folk who met your family in the hedges all doin' good. Mark Smith warned Governor Jefferson before General Benedict Arnold attacked Richmond early this year so Jefferson got away. After Arnold went north, Bruce Wallace learned the British is makin' a port at Yorktown 'cause troops comin' from New York. Why Yorktown be a bad idea for Evie?"

"Annie, I'll tell you straight out. Hundreds of Africans in Yorktown working for the British forces will be trapped. The British, short of supplies, will drive the Africans outside the stockade where most will be slaughtered by American and French artillery or die from hunger. It will be a greater horror than what we saw at Norfolk. New York may be a place to go because a few thousand Africans will sail from there to England but at the end there will be panic to get on ships and many will be left behind. The best chance is to get to Halifax in Nova Scotia, or to England. If they can't get there, they should go to towns in New England, far north of New York City. The future is grim for Africans in the South."

"I feel great pain comin', Mister Peter. The British pretend to help, but win or lose they forget about Africans. Oh, here they come."

Evie rounded the corner of the fence with two young men. Peter thought the 'watchmen' would be Robert and Claudius, but these men were too young. One walked with an irregular step partially overcoming a limp he had since childhood. Peter hugged them. "James! Dilli! You guys got big!"

"James fourteen now, Mister Peter, and I'se comin' to twelve. I knew you would come back some day." Dilli was bright and animated.

Peter turned to Evie. "Five years."

"Yes, Mister Peter, they be almost men now."

Annie clapped once. "Sit down everyone. Mister Peter come wit' things to say."

"Well," Peter began, "I heard you boys are ready to go to freedom like we tried five years ago when we went to Jamestown. Is that right?"

"Yes, Mister Peter. I still got the drawing I made of the freedom sky we saw above Annie's wagon. It be on the wall in the loft above the kitchen."

"We's ready to go." James was less shy than he was at eight.

"It's a good idea. But like last time, you have to notice which way the hoop is rolling. Many folks are going to Yorktown but the wind may blow British ships or French ships into the Chesapeake. There could be a raging battle and you would not want to be standing there in your bare feet."

"Where you gonna take us if Yorktown be dangerous?" asked Dilli.

Peter hesitated and Annie stepped in. "Mister Peter ain't goin' this time, Dilli. If you decide to go, my wagon sittin' in the lane wit' someone ready to drive the horses. Someone else gonna get on a ship to help you. Then he goin' much farther on, a very long way. Now we need to hear Mister Peter say what he think 'bout where the best place to go is."

"Well, you could cross the Bay to Maryland and look for ships unloading at the docks of loyal plantations. Do you have money for your passage?"

"We will put money in your hand if you get on the wagon."

"Annie! You don't need to..."

"Hush. Mister Peter been studyin'. He know what to do."

"Do you have papers that explain who you are and where you're going that will work if the Continentals or the British stop you?" Peter asked.

"We ain't got no papers."

Annie spoke again, "If you get in that wagon, I'se gonna give you three perfect passes on fine linen paper makin' you all look important, which you all is. One pass is to show the British. One is for the American militias, and one is for when you don't know who you talkin' to."

"Evie and boys, I have a feeling this is a big day for you. I told Annie that New York or New Jersey could be good places to go for a while. Better would be Nova Scotia, over the river into Quebec, or across the ocean to England. There are no slaves in England, and I have a hunch there will be none in the northern colonies soon. Whatever happens, do not get on a ship sailing to the Caribbean—no ship to Jamaica, Barbados, or other island colony. It doesn't matter if the ship captain is English, American, or Dutch. They will sell you back into slavery in the sugar cane fields where life is short and much worse than the lives you have now. Do not go south to the Floridas even though the Spanish fleet has taken them back."

"Why not, Mister Peter?" asked James.

"Because when the Americans win, I mean if the Americans defeat the British, they will get Florida back from Spain and will capture runaways."

Evie and the boys looked alarmed. "Besides, in Florida they don't have the freedom trees you saw from the wagon. I think you should go where you can see those trees, don't you?" The mood brightened noticeably.

"Even after you get away, be careful. The Northern colonies, should they make slavery illegal in a few years, might agree to return runaways. Farther north is best. Nova Scotia is safe and not as cold as Quebec."

Annie sat pensively. "I know a man named David George. He preaches down in Charles Town, which like here has British troops all over."

"Charleston, South Carolina?"

"It be called Charles Town at this time, Peter. Now let me finish. Things gonna be 'zackly the way they gonna be."

"But we can do something about it, can't we?"

"You cain't not do somethin'! We is all part of the 'it' you be talkin' about. What you do today is part of what gonna make it be like it will be tomorrow."

Suddenly that became clear for Peter.

"Now David George run away and been caught so many times he got good at both!" Annie laughed. "He is free again and plannin' to stay free by sailin' to Halifax later this year. Evie, if you get there seek out David George. There will be enough of your folk you won't feel alone."

"Will you be goin', Annie?"

270

Annie sighed. "Many folk 'round here troubled and weary wit' hurts and lacks. So I gonna wander these parts as long as the Lord let me do what I can to help the captive peoples and bring comfort."

"Mister Peter, will we see you?" asked Dilli. "You live up North."

"I'd love to see you again, Dilli. I will think about you guys for the rest of my life. I live far from where you guys are going so we will say goodbye when you get on the wagon. At least, I hope you get on the wagon."

"We goin', ain't we Mama? I can run to pee and get my things."

"Evie, watching you leave will make me sad, but knowing you and the boys can find a new life in freedom fills me with a deep happiness."

"This happenin' so fast I'se dizzy. Do we have to choose now?"

"That wagon is in the lane right now," Annie pointed. "So you got to decide. When the wagon leaves, it will be gone and another chance may be a long time comin'. Mister Peter come to help you get on the road to freedom."

"That's right, Evie."

"Come on, Mama, it be time for Dilli and me to grow up to be free men."

"You right, James, of course you right. Oh, sweet Jesus! I pray we gonna make it. Fetch your things, boys. Put them in a pillowcase and get in the wagon. Remember your picture of the freedom sky, Dilli." The boys ran to get their few belongings.

"Just like when we went down that road to Jamestown, Evie," Peter reminded her. "The moment you make that choice, you're already free."

"I feel scared, but I'se ready. I got to get my clothes." Evie hurried inside.

The conversation was short and the decision sudden after years of waiting. Peter would never see Evie or her boys again. He felt sadness but deep satisfaction to be part of something that would change the lives of a family forever.

Annie leaned on the fence smiling at him. "It ain't easy havin' love for people in your heart. Sometimes what feels like a broken heart is a heart breakin' open. There be so much space in an open heart it can feel empty. But light shine through that open space, Peter. Wherever you go, light shine through you when you let it. You won't never lose that."

"Annie, you opened up something deep I never thought about before. I would like a deeper faith in Spirit, but many people who say they are religious in my time are intolerant, narrow, or opinionated. Those folks

271

are not filled with love and don't have light shining from them like you do."

"It wasn't me who opened you, Peter. It was you openin' to the movin' Spirit, or the Light, or the Lord, whatever name you use. I know many folk who speak about heaven don't yet know where it is or what it feel like. But holdin' so tight to they religion help them be less afraid, and bit by bit, light will dawn in they hearts. You do more good by helpin' them than by fightin' them. They fight each other about which religion be true and they don't look around to see the real, right now, right here, love and light their religions reflectin' like a mirror.

"From Creation to Revelations and all the parables in between, the stories ain't 'bout something beautiful that happened five thousand or two thousand years ago, or some glorious time that ain't come yet. You is beginnin' to inkle that all them stories be 'bout what always is and always was and always will be, everywhere and every when. The wheel wit'in the wheel and the fire wit'in the fire never stopped after Ezekiel done seen them. They turnin' and burnin' right now. It takes time to open our eyes, ears, and heart to see and hear and feel. You know more about this than most folks, Peter. You will keep on travelin' on your journey."

They walked in silence as Peter let the essence of Annie's message find a home in him. He would practice its embodiment until the end of his days.

"You been gone five years and you still the same age. How much time done passed between when you left and when you came back?"

"Five weeks."

"You done lived five weeks and we done lived five years. I gots to learn more about time. Maybe I can visit you in your time again, Peter."

"You will be most welcome, Annie. Meanwhile we can feel each other in the space between the sun and its warmth on our faces."

"We will." Annie gave Peter a kindhearted smile.

They approached the wagon and there was Robert holding the reins. "Hello, Mister Peter. I'se happy to see you. Look who we got here."

Samuel Abdul Latif put a hand over his heart. "Thank you for being here to wish us well on our journey, Mister Peter. I pray that by the help of God your family will be blessed for all time."

"Thank you. It warms my heart to see you, Sal. Are you going north?"

"Doctor de Sequeyra gave me my freedom five years ago and last week surprised me with money to help me on this journey. Annie taught me to remember who I am and who we all are. Today I set out on a road that I pray will take me north to a place where I can help this family and others place roots in freedom. Then, by the help of God, is His time, I will find

272

my way to England to help former slaves seeking refuge there. In a few years, if it is God's will, I shall sail to the British territory on the Gambia River and travel into the interior all the way to Timbuktu. I am beginning my long journey home, Mister Peter."

"This takes courage, Sal, and a big heart to help so many along the way. I will think of you often. *In sha'Allah,* you will tell stories of your time here to young people in Africa. We need bridges among peoples of this world — bridges like you."

Samuel Abdul Latif smiled. "I will tell them about Annie and Doctor de Sequeyra, about Robert and Claudius, about the memory of Augustus and Aaron, and about you and your family, Peter Sinclair. Thank you for helping us all."

A sudden commotion erupted as Dilli and James came bumping through the side gate with Evie close behind, each carrying a pillowcase filled with their meager belongings. Evie carried a bag of food Rosie the old cook had hurriedly packed for them. Rosie limped out leaning on her walking stick to watch them leave. She had tears in her eyes, tears of empathetic joy that Evie and the boys she had known their whole lives were leaving to seek a freedom she herself would never know.

The boys climbed into the wagon with a hand from Sal.

Dilli had a piece of paper in his hand. "Here, Mister Peter. It's a present for you." Peter turned the paper over and saw a drawing of white clouds against a light blue sky seen through a lace pattern of branches, spring-green leaves sprouting everywhere. The Powell girls saw the pencil sketch and shared their watercolors so Dilli could finish it. They showed him how to print the words "Freedom Sky," at the top of the drawing.

"This is beautiful, Dilli. Don't you want to take it along with you?"

"We gonna see the freedom sky for ourselves. I gonna make another picture like it when we get there. I want you to have this one, so we have the same picture and think of each other."

"Thank you, Dilli. I am moved by this gift. You are going to be free and will make another picture."

Annie handed the passes to Evie who put them in the pillowcase and placed her things in the wagon next to the boys. She looked at Peter.

"Come with me, Evie." He led her to the porch where they first spoke.

"Peter..." Evie looked into his eyes. "There will be thanks driftin' to you through the mist from wherever we end up, for the courage you gave me to take this step." She took his hand. "And prayers will shine upon you from my spot in Heaven when I'se gone, for how you helped me find a path to freedom inside my soul. When me and the boys is on that ship, I gonna look for that water dipper in the sky and the North Star you told me about. The boys gonna teach their grandchildren about the pointer stars like your grandfather taught you."

Peter nodded. He took her hand in both his hands and pressed. They both would remember that moment, Peter more than he could now imagine. Evie held the steady gaze he saw on the porch long ago. "It still feels like you is family."

Evie returned to the wagon, "All righty, boys, let's say goodbye and get movin' before Robert leaves us here pickin' other peoples vegetables. We gonna get our own garden."

"Don't stop at New York longer than you must," Peter admonished again.

Evie was wide eyed. "I got to learn to read. The things you learn in them books turns my head to face another way. God be with you, Peter."

"May you and your family be blessed, Evie," Peter held up both hands.

Peter, Annie, and Rosie watched Robert urge the horses out of the lane onto the street as Evie, Dilli, James, and Samuel Abdul Latif waved goodbye. Dilli, laughing brightly, threw a smooth stick into the air, which turned end-over-end as it arched up and back down to where Peter stood.

He caught it and in that instant he was standing alone in the lane as the sound of Dilli's enchanting laughter faded away into antiquity. Annie, Rosie, and the wagon were suddenly gone. He drew a long breath, carefully wrapped the picture of the Freedom Sky around the stick, and walked through the Historic District to meet his family.

Day 5-6:   John Meets the Redcoats

John watched his family walk together to Francis Street where they hugged. Susan went left toward the Public Hospital, Peter headed east on Francis Street, and Megan walked straight to Duke of Gloucester Street. I'm a lucky man, he thought. I hope they find what they're looking for. Now, where do I find Bruce?

He decided to walk to the Capitol where he first had seen Bruce Wallace leaning on a post. He found a small military encampment manned by Redcoat reenactors. They had just finished a demonstration of loading a Brown Bess musket.

"Good morning. How goes the war?" John asked.

"The war is going well, if any war could be said to be going well," the older re-enactor told him. "Philadelphia was seized and the Continental Congress fled to Baltimore to hold its meetings. Williamsburg, Charles Town, Savanna, and New York are in British hands. General Benedict Arnold ended his treason against the Crown. He sacked Richmond, the new capital of Virginia, back in January. Governor Jefferson unfortunately escaped capture."

A younger Redcoat intervened. "I am uncomfortable when we burn a town, ruining innocent lives. Cornwallis is cleaning up the South but Clinton fattens his fanny sitting in New York and has not finished Washington up the Hudson nor engaged the Comte de Rochambeau's French troops in Rhode Island. Many in Parliament did not want to send troops and some generals offered command of this campaign declined. Some commanders here perform poorly. Clinton is not the first to enjoy soirées in the towns as rebels hold the countryside."

The older Redcoat got excited. "Finally, the rebels are hungry to end this nonsense, and we shall all go home soon."

The younger man had another idea. "We have been promised land for our service. If many stay, there will be less chance of future rebellion."

"You guys know your history. Stay safe through the war."

John strolled past the post where Bruce had stood the first time they met and approached Shields Tavern where they once had shared a long talk. He heard singing inside. The melody was unmistakably the *Star Spangled Banner.* He swung open the door and entered the tavern, dark, smoky, and full of off-duty Redcoats, jackets hanging over the backs of their chairs. Why were they singing *The Star Spangled Banner,* not written until the War of 1812? He listened to the words.

275

To Anacreon in Heaven, where he sat in full glee,
A few Sons of Harmony sent a petition
that he their Inspirer and Patron would be,
When this answer arrived from the Jolly Old Grecian:
"Voice, Fiddle, and Flute, No longer be mute,
I'll lend you my name and inspire you to boot,
and besides I'll instruct you like me, to entwine,
The Myrtle of Venus with Bacchus's Vine!"

When the song ended, a sergeant stood and raised his glass, "God Save the King!" The whole assemblage was on its feet shouting the toast.

A soldier grabbed John's elbow. "Don't gape as if you were gazing at ghosts, man. If you have no better offer, please join me."

"Thank you, may I buy us both a beer?"

"I took you for a gentleman. This confirms it."

"What song were the men singing?"

"Have you not heard it before? *Anacreon in Heaven* is a popular drinking song published in London three years ago. The tune is complicated and most people have trouble singing it."

John smiled and raised his glass. Most people still had trouble singing the melody of that old English drinking song when they sang the American national anthem. "To your health and long life!"

"Now there is a toast I can join without smirking." The soldier clinked glassed.

"How would you say the war is going?"

"Sir, His Majesty's forces are winning in spite of bad leadership."

"Why are you willing to share that thought with a perfect stranger?"

"I agree you may be strange but I doubt you are perfect."

"Are you committed to this fight?"

"What are we fighting for? The revolutionaries here speak of rights most Englishmen do not have. The English gentry seized the Scottish highlands and enclosed the common land for their private use, driving tens of thousands into exile or poverty in the growing cities where they must sell their labor cheaply to survive. The success of this expulsion leads the great and greedy families of England to enclose millions of acres in England as well. This will drive many more to flee here or to other colonies.

"That disease of many people, to covet ever more land and wealth for their private benefit, infects leaders on this continent as well. I do not say powerful people are more avaricious than a chimney sweep or

276

fishmonger. They are just more cunning at grabbing what they are greedy for. Big landowners here plan to seize vast lands from the Indians. Those men abhor the ideas of the levelers as much as the King does. John Adams does not like what he calls the 'notions of Southern gentlemen' and their reluctance to agree on a democratic republican form of government. Some woodenheads even proposed Washington become king. They don't know a better way."

The soldier lowered his voice. "Perhaps I should fight for the people against both the self-declared aristocracies of the colonies and the German potentate of Britain and the land-stealing so-called nobility at home."

"Perhaps, although I expect the manipulation of ordinary people who are uninformed about the maintenance of power and wealth will continue for generations to come."

"I agree, Sir. Fog is created by leaders to obscure their true motives and benefits, and the people's indolence prolongs their ignorance. Now that we find ourselves in agreement, I am waiting for you to say what brings you to a smoky tavern on a sunny day."

"I'm looking for Bruce Wallace, a Scottish wheelwright. Do you know him?"

"Aha! It *is* you. Bruce Wallace told me that if I met a man named John wearing unusual apparel mingled with normal garb, I could trust him. Wallace is no longer a wheelwright but an aide to General Lord Charles Cornwallis! I am a messenger on the General's staff. I tipped many a glass with Wallace after I saved his life at the Battle of Cowpens."

John was surprised but responded, "My name is not John. It's Roger."

The soldier almost choked on his beer. "That is funny, Sir. Wallace told me that you are the man who subdued Roger and his dagger in a tavern on the Jamestown Road. I had a few pints with Wallace there one night and he showed me the blade embedded in the beam. He told me Roger was shot dead soon after by a one-eyed man he harmed the year before."

"I'll be damned. Do you know where Wallace is now?"

"Cornwallis sent him to negotiate peace with Lafayette who is harassing the British near Richmond. That negotiation was unsuccessful of course. From there he went north to inform Washington. You and I just met and we've already said enough to be court-martialed."

"We'll swear we were drinking to the health of the King and Lord Cornwallis."

"Yes, and it would be an irrefutable truth with forty witnesses." The Redcoat stood and raised his glass. "To the health of the King and Lord Cornwallis!" The men in the room stood and echoed the toast.

"Sheep," the soldier murmured. "Most likely Wallace shall be back in a day or two. Where shall I tell him to find you?"

"I'll be leaving later today. In case I miss him, I have a message that may benefit you as well. Neither of you should go to Yorktown. If your regiment moves there, get sick, or take a long walk and change your coat along the way."

"Understood."

"Good," said John. "I must try to find Wallace. Keep your head attached."

"Thank you, and may they always miss when they shoot at you."

John stepped out of the tavern and walked to Palace Green. He was concerned the timing was off and he might not find Bruce Wallace even though he had found his way into the past.

Day 5-7:   Megan Sends a Signal

Megan had an idea. If I sit in the lane next to Mark's hut where we looked up at the trees that evening, maybe I will connect with Mark or Standing Elk. She crossed the yard and slipped through the back gate. The weight of the cannonball on a chain pulled the gate closed behind her. No dogs barked and no brood sow grunted. Instead, a squirrel chirruped a warning of her approach.

The layout was different from what she remembered. The huts were gone as was the large hedge, replaced by a fence that shielded a private driveway from view. Megan paced off to where she remembered Mark's lean-to had been and looked around for something to sit on. The nearest place was a wide stump. She sat and repeated to herself the steps her father had talked about. Relax and let go; use my imagination; be open, and listen for someone calling me.

She listened to the sound of her breath and the gentle wind in the trees. She remembered the paths of fireflies and visualized them again. The paths had been invisible in the dark except for the momentary points of light, but as a pattern emerged she saw that the fireflies' motion was not random like dust particles in a sunbeam. They approached and related to each other along those invisible paths.

Who is approaching me? Megan wondered. How do I flash a light so my invisible path will be known to another? What is the signal?

She sat in silence. Her thoughts calmed as she gradually became aware of the open space in her mind through which thoughts come and fade away. "The space between the firefly flashes, the space between the leaves, the space between the stars, the space between my thoughts..." Megan was calm and attentive.

She looked up to the pattern in the branches above her. It had changed in 230 years. Mark's lean-to had been over there against a fence. We were sitting twenty feet from here, looking up this way at...

Suddenly a thought flashed like a flare bursting in her mind. Right here was the tree with the fireflies! I'm sitting on it! She noticed sawdust around the stump of the tree. It had been cut down recently. It had grown for over two centuries to become so big around. This is part of the pattern; another twinkle on the path of time we saw that night, thought Megan.

Dragonflies hovered and cruised across the open spaces. They had seemed mystical to Megan since she was a child. She was grateful when she learned they could eat their weight in mosquitoes in an hour. They have cruised here for two hundred million years, a million years for each year we went back in time.

She closed her eyes to scan the sounds. What did a dragonfly sound like? She heard whispering leaves, a hymn from bees on pilgrims' rounds to flowers behind her, the high-pitched whine of a mosquito near her ear. She was about to brush the mosquito away but hesitated. The whine was cut short by a buzz of whirring wings and a whoosh. Her exhalations of carbon dioxide had attracted the mosquito and a great blue skimmer dragonfly swooped past her head to swallow the mosquito on the wing. This is the pattern too, mosquitoes, dragonflies—all of us. Standing Elk told us we turn and turn into what we are becoming.

Megan listened to the soundscape again—the breeze rising and falling away, her breathing in and out, the call of a blue jay in a nearby tree, hooves on a hard packed road, the distant responding cry of a second blue jay, the crunch of footfalls on a path, the scolding of a squirrel to warn others of an approach. Someone is coming, Megan thought. I'll close my eyes and let the person pass. A moment later a thought entered her mind as the quiet footfalls drew closer. "Could it be? I know the sound of those steps!"

The footfalls drew close and stopped. "Hello, Standing Elk," Megan spoke without opening her eyes.

"Hello, Megan. I was riding on Francis Street when I felt a flash of light. I asked Creator what it was and a line of dragonflies flew past me down this path. I hitched my horse to a post and walked in slowly, feeling the sacred. Where are the huts and Mark's old lean-to?"

"I've been waiting for you, Standing Elk." Megan opened her eyes. "I was also surprised to see the huts gone. I want to know how your people are and what happened to Mark."

Standing Elk drew a long breath and exhaled. "It is hard to tell you how much joy I feel to see you, so I won't try. Miigwech, Megan, I am grateful."

"I was praying we would connect."

"Megan, Mark has enjoyed five years of freedom and saved many lives including that of General Washington. If he survives the war, he will receive more land for his services than he ever imagined owning. He told me he will share land with my people. Every woman and man can learn from Mark's generosity. My peoples, the Pamunkey and the Mattaponi, are surviving through this terrible war and we are seen as friendly by all sides. We heal their wounded and sick. We help them gather and hunt when we find them hungry. Sadly, war has devastated larger tribes to the north and west. Many entered the war on the American or British sides in the hope of benefit. The costs have been high and the benefits few.

Fighting is not the way to prosper. The path of victory is the path of peace."

"It's not easy to point that out in a way warriors or nations can see or hear, is it?"

"You are wise for your age, Megan."

"Only when I calm down and pay attention, Standing Elk."

"Practice that each day and you shall be a wise old crone some day."

"Thank you, I think. Is Mark still at the forge for George Washington's army?"

"No longer. The messages he brought to Washington made him a valuable aide-de-camp to the general. When the Marquis de Lafayette came south to defend Richmond, Washington sent Mark to keep Lafayette informed."

"Mark is nearby? In Richmond?"

"Not far but a hard journey. This area is thick with Redcoats, and Richmond is back in American hands again. The lands between are filled with raiding parties and sharpshooters seeking to damage the other side. They are nervous and do not ask questions before firing."

"Is Mark safe?"

"He is not in combat, but we would not want the British to catch him as an agent. So far, that has not happened to any of us." Megan was about to ask another question when a low hum could be heard far away but getting louder. They paused and looked up. "What is that sound?" asked Standing Elk.

"It's just a plane flying over." Megan froze. Standing Elk had walked down the path into her time responding to her call rather than the other way around.

They looked up as the sound got louder and watched the twin engine Piper Seminole move slowly, high above the trees. "Is that a wagon that flies? Who has such a thing?"

Megan decided to tell him. "They are all over the world, Standing Elk, flying carriages called airplanes. Some little ones are named after Indian tribes like the Seneca and the Cherokee. Big ones have numbers like 747 and carry more people than a sailing ship. I flew on one of those all the way to London in seven hours."

Standing Elk sat on the ground next to Megan listening to the sound of the plane fading away in the distance. "Can you tell me what is happening, Megan? This is big medicine I am feeling."

"When you felt me calling you, you hitched your horse and walked down a sacred path into your future. The big medicine is yours. You have a clear mind."

"Is this something you know how to do, Megan, to walk into this future?"

"No, I have never walked into the future. I live in this time. When we met five years ago, I had slipped into your time, which is in my past. I would not tell this to everyone, Standing Elk, but I know if I can handle it, so can you."

"How can this be?"

"I don't know, Standing Elk, but it is good that you and I found a way to be connected across time. Look around. Mark's hut was right over there, and this stump you are sitting next to getting sawdust on your deerskin pants is the exact tree where we watched the patterns of the fireflies. It grew for over two hundred years to become a giant, and judging from the fresh sawdust and dry bubbles of sap on the outer rings of the stump, it was cut down in the last few weeks. And look up. The dragonflies that led you here are sailing through the air as they have since long before they came into the dreams of our ancestors." Megan pointed.

Standing Elk looked around at the trees, at the giant stump, at the fence, at the open lawn where the huts and lean-tos stood chockablock against each other when he rode by this very morning, and he looked at Megan for a long time. She looked back smiling and watched his eyes change slowly from confusion to recognition to sparkling mischief.

"You are not older. It is five years since you left, and you have not aged."

"I am five weeks older, Standing Elk, and this is 1781, five years after when we first met."

"But it is not 1781 here with you. More than two centuries have passed, judging by the girth of this stump. Megan, you are the most youthful wise old crone I have ever seen!"

They laughed.

"Can you answer some questions, Megan?"

"Yes, I may be able to do that. Britain and America have been at peace for a long time and are good friends and allies. Neither country has fought a war against the French nor Spanish since long before my grandparents were born. The Pamunkey and Mattaponi peoples still live nearby, and my family is well and happy."

They looked at each other and laughed again.

"Am I stuck with you forever, Megan?"

"Well, we'll be blessed with memories of each other for the rest of our lives. If my experience is any guide, when you walk out that path you will find your horse waiting for you by the fence in June of 1781. I have some questions."

"My family is well. I have three grandchildren now. I was on my way to find Bruce Wallace. We expect he is carrying important news. Mark may try to get through the British pickets to meet him as well. Finally, my horse's name is Powerful Spirit. I named her after you, Megan."

Megan smiled.

"Megan, I will sit and pray about the wonder of this in many Spirit Lodges. My duty is calling me and I must go quickly to find Bruce as soon as he arrives. These are difficult times and we hope the news he carries is good. Can we meet tomorrow for a long talk?"

"I must go home with my family today, so I doubt we will see each other again. Now you know my time is in your future. Tell your people to take heart. They will endure."

"I know you have knowledge, and I am encouraged by your words."

They both stood and Megan hugged him. "Goodbye, Grandfather."

"Goodbye, granddaughter. Please give my thanks to your family."

Megan watched Standing Elk walk out of the clearing along the path. When he was out of sight, she looked up at the dragonflies and closed her eyes again. She listened to the insect drones and chirps, to the sound of Powerful Spirit's hooves fading away on the dirt road, and to the spaces between the sounds.

Day 5-8:   The British Grenadiers March

The drums began crisply as people gathered to watch the drill. "Prrr-ratz, Prrr-ratz, Prrr-rat-tat-tatz." The regimental sergeant major's shouted order was clear above the drums: "Quick, march!" Rank after rank of Redcoats stepped forward in unison marching from the Powder Magazine toward the Governor's Palace. To a man, the regiment displayed practiced discipline, determination, and confidence.

The fifes began the stirring melody of *The British Grenadiers March*. The familiar, stirring tune was written long before the British marched to victory in the Seven Years' War. It was played on parade to impress citizens and inspire young men to enlist. More, it served in battle to support discipline and focus as blocks of infantry advanced under fire, returning fire only when ordered.

Peter stood on a slight rise and scanned the crowd. He spotted his father on the other side of Palace Green. He waved, but John did not respond.

John studied the tight formation. He imagined the ranks marching toward lines of infantry ranged against them. The soldiers would follow the rhythm of the drums and fifes, maintaining formation and pace in the midst of chaos. Volleys of musket and cannon fire would cut down soldiers dead or screaming. As they fell, men in the next rank would step over them and run forward into the empty spots, replaced in their rank by men behind them. Casualties would be high against a well-trained foe, but the British infantry remained disciplined and deadly.

John looked for Bruce Wallace in the crowd as three senior officers in elegant uniforms and powdered wigs stepped onto the small balcony of the Palace to review the infantry as they reached the gates. The one in the centre was General Cornwallis, but John did not recognize the others.

Peter got the impression his father across Palace Green was experiencing the past. He saw his mother wave from near the Palace gates. That left only Megan unaccounted for. He returned his gaze to the Redcoats.

As the first rank neared the Palace gate, the sergeant major shouted, "Regiment, halt!" With one last repeat of the drum pattern, the Redcoats stood at attention in straight ranks and perfect files with no need to dress the lines. They were part of the world's best professional army in 1781.

Lord Cornwallis stepped to the railing. "The long war to subdue the rebellion shall soon end. Your discipline and vigor brings that outcome. On behalf of the King, thank you for your contributions to return these colonies to their rightful place in the British Empire. There have been skirmishes nearby and enemy agents may try to infiltrate to gather intelligence on our numbers, positions, and plans. They seek to spread disaffection among the citizenry. Therefore, for your protection, and to ensure success of our arms, I declare Williamsburg to be under martial law. All residents must secure themselves in their homes by sunset each day until this order is rescinded or be arrested by His Majesty's forces. It will soon rain, so please hasten home to be warm and dry."

There was a ripple of concern through the crowd and among the soldiers, who wondered whether this indicated a serious military threat. Cornwallis sensed the mood. "This temporary measure is for your protection. Our pickets repel attempts to cross our lines. Tell your friends of the precision of British forces you witnessed on parade and advise them not to fear the rebels. Colonel, instruct the sergeant major to put the infantry at ease. I ask the citizens to disperse now. In ten minutes our troops shall escort people remaining on the streets back to their homes."

"We've got to get out of here," thought Peter making his way to the Palace.

At the southern end of Palace Green, John spotted Bruce Wallace in the haze from the British cooking fires. "I heard from Standing Elk that your family had returned," Bruce greeted him. "Over these five years as things you talked about came to pass, I wondered how you knew."

"I studied the situation and made some good guesses. Most of what I told you faded from your memory because it was wrong."

"You are not a good liar, but ach, it's good to see you, John."

"Good to see you too, Bruce."

"You are looking at a tired old spy, John. The brave group you convened in the hedges, and good-hearted souls we recruited along the way, help the Continental Army and militias stay out of trouble. Reverend Walker, the Freemason, has been helpful with information he says comes through the Church and the Lodges. Like you, he has an uncanny knack for making good guesses about what will happen."

John smiled. "And the Reverend once thought there were no grand mysteries in the Masonic Order. How is the campaign going?"

"At moments we made a big impact. I met Captain Patrick Ferguson. You were right about his new breech-loading rifle. At Brandywine Creek, I told him that sniping Continental officers encourages them to shoot ours. That chat saved the lives of Washington and Lafayette. Later that day the Americans were chased back but Ferguson was badly wounded. I assigned myself the task of gathering the rifles for safekeeping."

"Good work, Sir. Where are they being stored so carefully?"

Bruce smiled. "Most of them are safely under the Thousand Acre Swamp in Delaware. I was up all night getting there in a wagon and out in a rowboat throughout the next morning. I worked alone. If someone finds them, I doubt the years under water helped them much."

"Well done, Bruce!"

"Remember Flora McDonald, who helped Bonnie Prince Charlie escape the English over the sea to Skye? She sided with the Crown in North Carolina. Can you imagine? The English imprisoned her after Culloden but she took their side out of anger against the large land holders who kept the frontier people down."

Bruce sighed. "Hugh Mercer fell during Washington's victory at Princeton in '77. He was on the ground wounded. Redcoats demanded his surrender but he kept slashing his sword, so they bayoneted him. As he lay in bed slowly dying of wounds, Mercer swore he swung his sword and the British followed the rules of war to stop him. He died with honor and prevented revenge against British prisoners." He paused at the memory of the friend who saved his life after Culloden.

"I found George Washington by the Hudson last week and urged him to secretly march south. He was not happy when I told him the warship *H.M.S. Savage* sailed up the Potomac, burned plantations, and pressed his manager at Mount Vernon to provide supplies or see his plantation in ruins. Seventeen of Washington's slaves ran off with the British. The economy of the colonies has been devastated. When I compare the well-fed Redcoats around here to our hungry militiamen, I see we are losing this war. Our men return to their farms when their enlistment is up or desert to wander home in hope of finding someone or something there after the Redcoats marched through.

"We heard the French Navy would sail here to turn it around, but if they are coming they are as invisible as elves. I was encouraged when Washington said he hoped to reach Virginia by autumn, but I since learned from New York that General Clinton has committed to sail here with a larger force than Cornwallis has. Together they could finish Lafayette's raids, occupy Richmond permanently, and defeat Washington. The American cause may be lost, John."

John listened and studied Bruce. "It may not be as bad as you think."

"I have not given up but there are so many towns in British and Loyalist hands, the future for independence does not look bright. Tell me what you know, John."

"I told you, none of us know anything for sure."

"Aye, but can you make one of your extraordinary guesses again?"

"Well, I would guess a tough old warrior like you might be paying attention to the work on a deep water port at Yorktown."

"Not a hard guess for a grizzled old fighter," replied Bruce.

"Well, Bruce, wouldn't the victorious army under Cornwallis be better off by the water to greet Clinton and get resupplied or redeployed?"

"They won't leave before defeating Lafayette, whose men harry the British. Cornwallis received orders to build a deepwater port at Yorktown for the British fleet, but work is proceeding very slowly. It might be better for the British, but how would it be convenient for anyone else?"

"How would Yorktown be convenient for anyone else?" John wondered how much to reveal. "The port and fortifications would be within range of ships' guns." He began to hum a tune and softly sang: *"Frère Jacques, frère Jacques, Dormez-vous? Dormez-vous?"*

"I have heard that tune. The French troops sing it over a flagon. Oh! I am slow in my dotage, John. The French army or the French fleet? When?"

"Bruce, I suggest you encourage Cornwallis to move to Yorktown, the sooner the better. So much history happened in Williamsburg before the Virginia capital moved to Richmond, that someday people might visit to imagine what this was like long ago. It would be a shame if the town were destroyed in a bombardment. Speaking of that, can you do me a favor?"

"Certainly, what can I do?"

"Find a reason to be far from Yorktown by the end of summer. Find a task here in Williamsburg such as welcoming General Washington if he should come."

"Understood, John. Thank you."

"Well, Bruce. My family is wandering around somewhere, and I don't want them arrested by the Redcoats because I hummed a French tune to a double agent, do I? Stay alive, Bruce!" John extended his hand.

"I expect I'll live a while longer, especially if I hear soldiers singing that tune." Bruce hugged him. "John why do I feel I shall never see you again?"

"I'm sorry to say it's probably true, Bruce. I will remember you, and I pray you and your family thrive."

"I will pray the same for you. I have a question for you, John. You do not just come from another place; you come from a future time, don't you? How are you able to do that?"

"I've been told I have a vivid imagination."

"If it is your imagination, how can I see you?"

"You must have a vivid imagination, too." John turned to go.

"One more question, John. I promise; the last one."

"All right, Bruce. One more question for *auld lang syne*."

"When you fought those wars in the jungles, deserts, and Asian mountains wherever it was you were, what nation were you fighting for?"

John looked back at Bruce Wallace. How much harm could it do? He needs a little encouragement. "I fought for the United States of America."

"I'll be damned. Thank you, John. I shall get Cornwallis to Yorktown."

John turned and walked purposefully up Palace Green hoping to find his family two centuries later. Bruce watched him disappear into the mist.

When John got close to the Palace, the rest of his family was watching for him. He waved and Peter excitedly waved back.

A Redcoat approached Susan and the kids. "You had best be moving along home quickly. It is safer and drier inside your homes."

John approached and called out in a commanding voice, "Thank you, Corporal, I will personally escort my family safely home."

"Very good, Sir." The corporal moved on.

"It's all in the tone of voice, I guess." Susan shrugged.

"Hi, Dad. How did it go?" asked Megan.

"I found Bruce Wallace and we did what we needed to do. Sorry I'm late. Let's cross the bridge and get on the road before it pours. We can talk on the drive home.

In sight of the bridge, Megan stopped. "What, Pete?"

"I didn't say anything."

"Someone called my name."

Susan listened a moment. "I didn't hear anything. Let's get to the car before the rain."

"Megan!" This time they all heard it.

Through the trees, a man ran toward them. He had run a long way and needed a moment to catch his breath. Megan hugged him. "Mark!"

"I am happy to see you, Megan. When Standing Elk told me you were here, I ran the long way around town to avoid the Redcoats." He paused again for breath. "Mister and Missus Sinclair, Peter, I am glad you came back. For five years, I have wanted to thank you again for what you did to help so many people."

"You're welcome, Mark. From what I hear, you've helped many yourself."

288

"I am part of a team, Mister Sinclair, people you brought together. We have done what we could over the years, but we have not been able to end the fighting."

"How have you been, Mark?"

"Things are miraculous, Megan. I kept in touch with my former master, Anderson, who went to Richmond when the capital moved. Through our Indian friends, we warned of the raids by Benedict Arnold. The warning allowed Governor Jefferson to escape when Richmond was sacked. Anderson hid his iron and was back in business when Arnold left."

"You did a great thing, Mark."

"I have been promised grants of land by General Washington, Governor Jefferson, the Congress, and my former master for my services. I will need many hands to work all those lands. As Bartholomew and Maggie taught me, I will keep no one in bondage and will pay a fair wage. We shall rotate crops and let lands lie fallow to renew them with leaves, ashes, and bone meal. I will give land to native peoples and work with Standing Elk to be the best of neighbors. Much healing will be needed among peoples when this war ends. I pray I live to see the dream come true."

John spoke again. "Mark Smith, Edmond Brown, you're a good man and I'm glad my daughter became your friend. I spoke with Bruce Wallace today and gave him reason to expect the war will not continue much longer. The British will move to Yorktown and prepare a deep-water port there. They will be in a trap and when it snaps shut, most of the fighting will be over. Are you still close to Lafayette?"

"I am."

"Good. When your business is done here, get past the British sentries alive and back to Lafayette. Tell him that Washington and Rochambeau will arrive at the end of summer and, before this year is over, the world will be turned upside down. Will you deliver that message for me?"

"When I tell the Marquis that the message comes directly from John Sinclair, the General who created the Chain of Information, he will take my report seriously."

"Good. We must cover many miles before nightfall. Mark, live a long and happy life. Megan, walk Mark down to the road then run back here. We should leave together."

"Thanks, General Dad."

"Don't take long, Megan. Rain is coming and Redcoats are everywhere."

Megan walked Mark around the bend in the road and took his hand. "I feel embarrassed by public displays of affection, Mark, as my father knows. He sent me with you so I could kiss you goodbye. May I kiss you?"

"You do not need to ask." Mark leaned forward to kiss her lips.

"Goodbye, Mark. I am sad to leave. I'll remember you all my life."

"Megan, must this be goodbye? Tell me how to find you when the war ends. I will have the means to give us a good life together."

"I wish we could. I will never forget that you wanted to be with me. Please live that good life with a wonderful woman. You live in my heart."

"But Megan..."

"It can't possibly work, Mark. I have to go very far with my family now. It's not safe for you or me to be out after dusk and with this rain starting, it's dusk now. Goodbye, dear Mark." She kissed him and ran back along the path. She looked back at the curve and saw him still standing there. She blew him a kiss and he returned the gesture. Then she turned and hurried ahead.

Her parents and Peter were standing by the bridge. They crossed together and reached the car just before a heavy rain began.

Day 5-9.   Remembering the Ancestors

John drove cautiously as the wipers barely kept up with the downpour. The Sinclairs rode in contemplation. After half an hour, when the rain let up a bit, Susan broke the silence. "What an extraordinary visit. I didn't think I'd be able to go back in time again, but I contacted Jane and it felt good to know she is well in 1781. Did you guys find the people you knew?"

"I ran into Bruce Wallace and revealed some of the future to him. Now he's motivated to get Cornwallis to move his army to Yorktown."

"That had an impact, Dad. They ought to put up your statue."

"Megan, you got to say goodbye to Mark. How was the rest of your afternoon?" asked Susan.

"I was sitting quietly by myself when Standing Elk walked into our time. It was amazing. We were watching dragonflies when an Indian chief from 1781 saw an airplane overhead. How did it go for you, Pete?"

"I finally found Annie behind the Powell House. She encouraged Evie to leave for the North with her boys because Samuel Abdul Latif could help them get settled before he sailed to England and then Africa. I encouraged them to take the opportunity and go."

"What happened?"

"They got into the wagon and disappeared. Dilli gave me a painting he made after they tried to find freedom last time." Peter handed the painting to his mother.

"Look at this! We have a small watercolor like this at home!"

"We do?" asked Peter. "Where?"

"It's tucked between the pages of the Bible your dad's father gave him. Grandpa inherited the Bible with the painting from his grandmother after her husband Robert Sinclair died. He wanted it to stay in the Sinclair family. Grandpa told us his ancestor came to Ohio in the 1800s. His family was in Nova Scotia since the Revolution."

"Were they Loyalists?" asked Megan. "If they lived in Nova Scotia they may have been."

"We don't know who they were, Megan. I'll show you the painting. At the top it says 'Freedom Sky' and at the bottom, 'D. Sinclair. Dartmouth, Nova Scotia, September, 1782'. That was one of your ancestors and we don't know anything about him — except that he lived in Nova Scotia and gave this painting to his grandson who was leaving for Ohio, and asked him to pass it on in the family."

Peter closed his eyes and heard the sparkle of Dilli's laughter in the wagon. "I can tell you about him," he said quietly. "His name was Dilli, named after a man whose father came to Virginia from India and who died in battle. Dilli's father was Augustus, a healer who escaped to freedom and died of smallpox near Norfolk on January 2, 1776. His mother was a beautiful slave named Evie, a laundress at the Powell House, who risked running north two generations before the Underground Railroad because she prayed for a better life for her sons. It looks like they made it."

"That's the family you helped, Peter. A grandfather of the man who settled in Ohio and married the German widow was an escaped slave you helped get away to freedom," Megan said. "They took our family name."

"If Evie and Dilli had not gotten to freedom, Dad, Megan, and I would not have been born," Peter realized. "They lived before we did so we carry their name." Everyone was quiet as that knowledge settled in. The windshield wipers counted off the seconds going by.

John had a thought. "We had to go back to colonial times in order for us to be here at all."

Peter nodded. "We followed the path that was there to be walked, Dad. We may never understand how it happened, but I'm grateful it did."

John drove onto the ramp for I-95 North toward Washington.

Megan pulled a notebook from her backpack and began to write. After a few minutes she said, "The history we learned that got me an A on that paper is not as interesting as how we learned it. We lived it. I will write a story instead of a history paper. I don't care if I get college credit or not. Is it all right with you guys if I write about what you did?"

"Good idea. We can tell our stories by the fireplace."

"That will be great, Dad. I can record you and work it into the story."

The rain abated to a light mist. Megan stared out the window at the patterns in the trees as they sped by. She wrote and scratched something out and wrote again. "I've got the beginning for the story that starts on our way to Williamsburg. Do you want to hear it?"

"Sure, Honey."

"All right, here it is:

"To the people of the Virginia Colony in 1775, the forests and fields flanking Interstate 95 might look familiar. The smooth highway from the Potomac to the Tidewater would seem a marvel. The cars hurtling through a misting rain early this Friday morning in May would be beyond their wildest imagining."

Selected Bibliography

Bailyn, Bernard & DeWolfe, Barbara. Voyagers to the West: A Passage in the Peopling of America on the Eve of the Revolution. New York: Knopf, 1986.

Boorstin, Daniel J. The Americans: The Democratic Experience. New York: Random House, 1973.

Butler, Jon. Becoming America: The Revolution before 1776: Cambridge, Mass.: Harvard University Press, 2000.

Catton, Bruce & Catton, William Bruce. The Bold and Magnificent Dream: America's Founding Years, 1492-1815. Garden City, N.Y.: Doubleday, 1978.

Ferris, Robert G. & Morris, Richard E. The Signers of the Declaration of Independence: Arlington, Va.: Interpretive Publications, 1982.

Harms, Robert W. The Diligent: A Voyage through the Worlds of the Slave Trade. New York: Basic Books, 2002.

Hartoonian, Michael H., Van Scotter, Richard D., & White, William E., *The Idea of America: How Values Shaped Our Republic and Hold the Key to Our Future.* Williamsburg, Va.: Colonial Williamsburg Foundation, 2013

Hibbert, Christopher. Redcoats and Rebels: The American Revolution through British Eyes. New York: Norton, 1990.

Hibbert, Christopher. George III: A Personal History. New York: Basic Books, 1998.

Isaac, Rhys. The Transformation of Virginia, 1740-1790. Chapel Hill: Published for the Institute of Early American History and Culture, Williamsburg, VA., by University of North Carolina Press, 1982.

Jensen, Merrill. The Founding of a Nation; a History of the American Revolution, 1763-1776. New York: Oxford University Press, 1968.

Klein, Herbert S. Slavery in the Americas: A Comparative Study of Virginia and Cuba. Chicago, Illinois: University of Chicago Press, 1967.

Maier, Pauline. From Resistance to Revolution; Colonial Radicals and the Development of American Opposition to Britain, 1765-1776. New York: Knopf, 1972.

Olmert, Michael & Coffman, Susanne E. Official Guide to Colonial Williamsburg. Williamsburg, Va.: Colonial Williamsburg Foundation, 1998.

Raphael, Ray. A People's History of the American Revolution: How Common People Shaped the Fight for Independence. New York: New Press, 2001.

Roberts, Allen E. Freemasonry in American History. Richmond, Va.: Macoy Pub. & Masonic Supply, 1985.

Schlesinger, Arthur M. The Almanac of American History. New York: Putnam, 1983.

Selby, John E. A Chronology of Virginia and the War of Independence, 1763-1783. Charlottesville: Published for the Virginia Independence Bicentennial Commission by the University Press of Virginia, 1973.

Sutton, Ann, & Sutton , Myron. Eastern Forests, National Audubon Society Guide. New York: Knopf, 1985.

Tunis, Edwin. Colonial Living. Cleveland: World Pub., 1957.

Wood, Gordon S. The Radicalism of the American Revolution. New York: A.A. Knopf, 1992.

Excerpts from the Proclamation of 1763 of King George III

WHEREAS we have taken into Our Royal Consideration the extensive and valuable Acquisitions in America, secured to our Crown by the late Definitive Treaty of Peace, concluded at Paris the 10th Day of February last; and being desirous that all Our loving Subjects, as well of our Kingdom as of our Colonies in America, may avail themselves with all convenient Speed, of the great Benefits and Advantages which must accrue therefrom to their Commerce, Manufactures, and Navigation, We have thought fit, with the Advice of our Privy Council, to issue this our Royal Proclamation, hereby to publish and declare to all our loving Subjects, that we have, with the Advice of our Said Privy Council, granted our Letters Patent, under our Great Seal of Great Britain, to erect, within the Countries and Islands ceded and confirmed to Us by the said Treaty, Four distinct and separate Governments, styled and called by the names of Quebec, East Florida, West Florida and Grenada...

And Whereas, We are desirous, upon all occasions, to testify our Royal Sense and Approbation of the Conduct and bravery of the Officers and Soldiers of our Armies, and to reward the same, We do hereby command and impower our Governors of our said Three new Colonies, and all other our Governors of our several Provinces on the Continent of North America, to grant without Fee or Reward, to such reduced Officers as have served in North America during the late War, and to such Private Soldiers as have been or shall be disbanded in America, and are actually residing there, and shall personally apply for the same, the following Quantities of Lands, subject, at the Expiration of Ten Years, to the same Quit-Rents as other Lands are subject to in the Province within which they are granted, as also subject to the same Conditions of Cultivation and Improvement; viz.

To every Person having the Rank of a Field Officer – 5,000 Acres.

To every Captain – 3,000 Acres.

To every Subaltern or Staff Officer – 2,000 Acres.

To every Non-Commission Officer – 200 Acres.

To every Private Man – 50 Acres.

And whereas it is just and reasonable, and essential to our Interest, and the Security of our Colonies, that the several Nations or Tribes of Indians with whom We are connected, and who live under our Protection, should not be molested or disturbed in the Possession of such Parts of Our Dominions and Territories as, not having been ceded to or purchased by Us, are reserved to them, or any of them, as their Hunting Grounds — We do therefore, with the Advice of our Privy Council, declare it to be our Royal Will and Pleasure, that no Governor or Commander in Chief in any of our Colonies of Quebec, East Florida, or West Florida, do presume, upon any Pretence whatever, to grant Warrants of Survey, or pass any Patents for Lands beyond the Bounds of their respective Governments, as described in their Commissions: as also that no Governor or Commander in Chief in any of our other Colonies or Plantations in

America do presume for the present, and until our further Pleasure be known, to grant Warrants of Survey, or pass Patents for any Lands beyond the Heads or Sources of any of the Rivers which fall into the Atlantic Ocean from the West and North West, or upon any Lands whatever, which, not having been ceded to or purchased by Us as aforesaid, are reserved to the said Indians, or any of them.

And We do hereby strictly forbid, on Pain of our Displeasure, all our loving Subjects from making any Purchases or Settlements whatever, or taking Possession of any of the Lands above reserved, without our especial leave and Licence for that Purpose first obtained.

And We do further strictly enjoin and require all Persons whatever who have either wilfully or inadvertently seated themselves upon any Lands within the Countries above described or upon any other Lands which, not having been ceded to or purchased by Us, are still reserved to the said Indians as aforesaid, forthwith to remove themselves from such Settlements

And whereas great Frauds and Abuses have been committed in purchasing Lands of the Indians, to the great Prejudice of our Interests, and to the great Dissatisfaction of the said Indians: In order, therefore, to prevent such Irregularities for the future, and to the end that the Indians may be convinced of our Justice and determined Resolution to remove all reasonable Cause of Discontent, We do, with the Advice of our Privy Council strictly enjoin and require, that no private Person do presume to make any purchase from the said Indians of any Lands reserved to the said Indians, within those parts of our Colonies where We have thought proper to allow Settlement: but that, if at any Time any of the Said Indians should be inclined to dispose of the said Lands, the same shall be Purchased only for Us, in our Name, at some public Meeting or Assembly of the said Indians, to be held for that Purpose by the Governor or Commander in Chief of our Colony respectively within which they shall lie...

Given at our Court at St. James's the 7th Day of October 1763, in the Third Year of our Reign.

God Save the King

ushistory.org, Proclamation of 1763, Accessed June 30, 2015 http://www.ushistory.org/declaration/related/proc63.htm Copyright 2015

Excerpts of Letter from George Washington to Wm. Crawford

Mount Vernon, September 21, 1767.

Dear Sir: From a sudden hint of your Brother I wrote to you a few days ago in a hurry, since which having had more time for reflection, I am now set down in order to write more deliberately, and with greater precision, to you on the Subject of my last Letter; desiring that if anything in this shoud be found contradictory to that Letter you will wholly be governd by what I am now going to add.

I then desird the favour of you (as I understood Rights might now be had for the Lands, which have fallen within the Pensylvania Line) to look me out a Tract of about 1500, 2000, or more Acres somewhere in your Neighbourhood meaning only by this that it may be as contiguous to your own Settlemt. as such a body of good Land coud be found and about Jacobs Cabbins or somewhere on those Waters I am told this might be done. It will be easy for you to conceive that Ordinary, or even middling Land woud never answer my purpose or expectation so far from Navigation and under such a load of Expence as those Lands are incumbred with; No: A Tract to please me must be rich (of which no Person can be a better judge than yourself) and if possible to be good and level; Coud such a piece of Land as this be found you woud do me a singular favour in falling upon some method to secure it immediately from the attempts of any other as nothing is more certain than that the Lands cannot remain long ungranted when once it is known that Rights are to be had for them…

The other matter, just now hinted at and which I proposed in my last to join you in attempting to secure some of the most valuable Lands in the King's part which I think may be accomplished after a while notwithstanding the Proclamation that restrains it at present and prohibits the Settling of them at all for I can never look upon that Proclamation in any other light (but this I say between ourselves) than as a temporary expedient to quiet the Minds of the Indians and must fall of course in a few years especially when those Indians are consenting to our Occupying the Lands. Any person therefore who neglects the present oppertunity of hunting out good Lands and in some measure marking and distinguishing them for their own (in order to keep others from settling them) will never regain it, if therefore you will be at the trouble of seeking out the Lands I will take upon me the part of securing them so soon as there is a possibility of doing it and will moreover be at all the Cost and charges of Surveying and Patenting &c. after which you shall have such a reasonable proportion of the whole as we may fix upon at our first meeting as I shall find it absolutely necessary and convenient for the better furthering of the design to let some few of my friends be concernd in the Scheme and who must also partake of the advantages.

By this time it may be easy for you to discover, that my Plan is to secure a good deal of Land, You will consequently come in for a very handsome quantity and as you will obtain it without any Costs or expences I am in hopes you will be encouragd to begin the search in time. I woud choose if it were practicable to get pretty large Tracts together, and it might be desirable to have them as near your Settlement, or Fort Pitt, as we coud get them good; but not to neglect others at a greater distance if fine and bodies of it lye in a place. It may be a Matter worthy of your enquiry to find out how the Maryland back line will run, and what is said about laying of Neale's (I think it is and Company's) Grant. I will enquire particularly concerning the Ohio Companys that one may know what to apprehend from them. For my own part I shoud have no objection to a Grant of Land upon the Ohio a good way below Pittsburg but woud willingly secure some good Tracts nearer hand first.

I would recommend it to you to keep this whole matter a profound Secret, or trust it only with those in whom you can confide and who can assist you in bringing it to bear by their discoveries of Land and this advice proceeds from several very good Reasons and in the first place because I might be censurd for the opinion I have given in respect to the King's Proclamation and then if the Scheme I am now proposing to you was known it might give the alarm to others and by putting them upon a Plan of the same nature (before we coud lay a proper foundation for success ourselves) set the different Interests a clashing and probably in the end overturn the whole all which may be avoided by a Silent management and the [operation] snugly carried on by you under the pretence of hunting other Game which you may I presume effectually do at the same time you are in pursuit of Land which when fully discovered advise me of it and if there appears but a bear possibility of succeeding any time hence I will have the Lands immediately Surveyed to keep others off and leave the rest to time and my own Assiduity to Accomplish.

If this Letter shoud reach your hands before you set out I shoud be glad to have your thoughts fully expressd on the Plan I have proposd, or as soon afterwards as conveniently may be as I am desirous of knowing in time how you approve of the Scheme. I am, &c.

G. Washington

Library of Congress, Letter from George Washington to William Crawford, Accessed June 30, 2015,

http://www.loc.gov/teachers/classroommaterials/presentationsandactivities/presentations/timeline/amrev/britref/crawford.html

The Declaration of Independence
IN CONGRESS, July 4, 1776.
The unanimous Declaration of the thirteen United States of America

When in the Course of human events, it becomes necessary for one people to dissolve the political bands which have connected them with another, and to assume among the powers of the earth, the separate and equal station to which the Laws of Nature and of Nature's God entitle them, a decent respect to the opinions of mankind requires that they should declare the causes which impel them to the separation.

We hold these truths to be self-evident, that all men are created equal, that they are endowed by their Creator with certain unalienable Rights, that among these are Life, Liberty and the pursuit of Happiness.--That to secure these rights, Governments are instituted among Men, deriving their just powers from the consent of the governed, -- That whenever any Form of Government becomes destructive of these ends, it is the Right of the People to alter or to abolish it, and to institute new Government, laying its foundation on such principles and organizing its powers in such form, as to them shall seem most likely to effect their Safety and Happiness. Prudence, indeed, will dictate that Governments long established should not be changed for light and transient causes; and accordingly all experience hath shewn, that mankind are more disposed to suffer, while evils are sufferable, than to right themselves by abolishing the forms to which they are accustomed. But when a long train of abuses and usurpations, pursuing invariably the same Object evinces a design to reduce them under absolute Despotism, it is their right, it is their duty, to throw off such Government, and to provide new Guards for their future security.--Such has been the patient sufferance of these Colonies; and such is now the necessity which constrains them to alter their former Systems of Government. The history of the present King of Great Britain is a history of repeated injuries and usurpations, all having in direct object the establishment of an absolute Tyranny over these States. To prove this, let Facts be submitted to a candid world.

He has refused his Assent to Laws, most wholesome and necessary for the public good.

He has forbidden his Governors to pass Laws of immediate and pressing importance, unless suspended in their operation till his Assent should be obtained; and when so suspended, he has utterly neglected to attend to them.

He has refused to pass other Laws for the accommodation of large districts of people, unless those people would relinquish the right of Representation in the Legislature, a right inestimable to them and formidable to tyrants only.

He has called together legislative bodies at places unusual, uncomfortable, and distant from the depository of their public Records, for the sole purpose of fatiguing them into compliance with his measures.

He has dissolved Representative Houses repeatedly, for opposing with manly firmness his invasions on the rights of the people.

He has refused for a long time, after such dissolutions, to cause others to be elected; whereby the Legislative powers, incapable of Annihilation, have returned to the People at large for their exercise; the State remaining in the mean time exposed to all the dangers of invasion from without, and convulsions within.

He has endeavoured to prevent the population of these States; for that purpose obstructing Laws for Naturalization of Foreigners; refusing to pass others to encourage their migrations hither, and raising the conditions of new Appropriations of Lands.

He has obstructed the Administration of Justice, by refusing his Assent to Laws for establishing Judiciary powers.

He has made Judges dependent on his Will alone, for the tenure of their offices, and the amount and payment of their salaries.

He has erected a multitude of New Offices, and sent hither swarms of Officers to harrass our people, and eat out their substance.

He has kept among us, in times of peace, Standing Armies without the Consent of our legislatures.

He has affected to render the Military independent of and superior to the Civil power.

He has combined with others to subject us to a jurisdiction foreign to our constitution, and unacknowledged by our laws; giving his Assent to their Acts of pretended Legislation:

For Quartering large bodies of armed troops among us:

For protecting them, by a mock Trial, from punishment for any Murders which they should commit on the Inhabitants of these States:

For cutting off our Trade with all parts of the world:

For imposing Taxes on us without our Consent:

For depriving us in many cases, of the benefits of Trial by Jury:

For transporting us beyond Seas to be tried for pretended offences

For abolishing the free System of English Laws in a neighbouring Province, establishing therein an Arbitrary government, and enlarging its Boundaries so as to render it at once an example and fit instrument for introducing the same absolute rule into these Colonies:

For taking away our Charters, abolishing our most valuable Laws, and altering fundamentally the Forms of our Governments:

For suspending our own Legislatures, and declaring themselves invested with power to legislate for us in all cases whatsoever.

He has abdicated Government here, by declaring us out of his Protection and waging War against us.

He has plundered our seas, ravaged our Coasts, burnt our towns, and destroyed the lives of our people.

He is at this time transporting large Armies of foreign Mercenaries to compleat the works of death, desolation and tyranny, already begun with circumstances of Cruelty & perfidy scarcely paralleled in the most barbarous ages, and totally unworthy the Head of a civilized nation.

He has constrained our fellow Citizens taken Captive on the high Seas to bear Arms against their Country, to become the executioners of their friends and Brethren, or to fall themselves by their Hands.

He has excited domestic insurrections amongst us, and has endeavoured to bring on the inhabitants of our frontiers, the merciless Indian Savages, whose known rule of warfare, is an undistinguished destruction of all ages, sexes and conditions.

In every stage of these Oppressions We have Petitioned for Redress in the most humble terms: Our repeated Petitions have been answered only by repeated injury. A Prince whose character is thus marked by every act which may define a Tyrant, is unfit to be the ruler of a free people.

Nor have We been wanting in attentions to our Brittish brethren. We have warned them from time to time of attempts by their legislature to extend an unwarrantable jurisdiction over us. We have reminded them of the circumstances of our emigration and settlement here. We have appealed to their native justice and magnanimity, and we have conjured them by the ties of our common kindred to disavow these usurpations, which would inevitably interrupt our connections and correspondence. They too have been deaf to the voice of justice and of consanguinity. We must, therefore, acquiesce in the necessity, which denounces our Separation, and hold them, as we hold the rest of mankind, Enemies in War, in Peace Friends.

We, therefore, the Representatives of the united States of America, in General Congress, Assembled, appealing to the Supreme Judge of the world for the rectitude of our intentions, do, in the Name, and by Authority of the good People of these Colonies, solemnly publish and declare, That these United Colonies are, and of Right ought to be Free and Independent States; that they are Absolved from all Allegiance to the British Crown, and that all political connection between them and the State of Great Britain, is and ought to be totally dissolved; and that as Free and Independent States, they have full Power to levy War, conclude Peace, contract Alliances, establish Commerce, and to do all other Acts and Things which Independent States may of right do. And for the support of this Declaration, with a firm reliance on the protection of divine Providence, we mutually pledge to each other our Lives, our Fortunes and our sacred Honor.

National archives, Declaration of Independence, Accessed June 30, 2015,
http://www.archives.gov/exhibits/charters/declaration_transcript.html

CPSIA information can be obtained
at www.ICGtesting.com
Printed in the USA
BVOW06s1916240417
482140BV00005B/31/P